DIVID YOURSELVES

MW01137487

by Bill Hiatt

with cover art by Michael Federman

This novel is copyrighted by William A. Hiatt, 2013. All rights are reserved. This work may not be reproduced in whole or in part in any form without written permission from the author.

This is a work of fiction. Any resemblance to real persons, living or dead, is purely coincidental.

The front cover illustration has been copyrighted by and purchased from Michael Federman. Tal's face is derived from a photograph copyrighted by Pavel L Photo and Video and licensed from http://www.shutterstock.com. The back cover illustration is based on a photograph copyrighted by SSokolov and licensed from http://www. shutterstock.com.

DEDICATION

This novel is dedicated to my parents, who have always been there for me.

ACKNOWLEDGMENTS

As John Donne wrote, "No man is an island, entire of itself." My students over the years have provided much of the inspiration for this novel, and my colleagues have made its creation possible, because without them, I would be a very different person now, and probably not one with the desire to write—or teach. They have kept me sane during good times and bad.

PROLOGUE

I wrote this book knowing that not everyone who read it would have read *Living with Your Past Selves*, the first book in the series. Consequently, I tried to provide enough background for readers in that situation. However, if you have not read the first book and would like a synopsis of the events in that book, you can find one in "What Has Gone Before," near the end of this book.

CONTENTS

CHAPTER 1: REUNION WITH AN OLD "FRIEND"

It was just a few days after Thanksgiving, but the memory of the feast I had pretended to enjoy was already fading, and even though winter break was only a couple of weeks away, I couldn't seem to get excited about the holidays or even about time off from school, though I could use it. What with a heavy class schedule, soccer practice, band practice, and combat practice, I was feeling the schedule squeeze most of the time. And then there was visiting Carla, as I did every day after soccer practice. People told me I didn't have to visit every single day, but somehow I couldn't stay away from the gaze of those dead eyes, the void where her mind used to be, a void I almost got lost in every time I tried to probe her.

Yeah, probe her. I could read minds, remember, at least when there was a mind to read. Oh, well, if you're just "tuning in" now, I wasn't just the ordinary teenager my parents, and most of the rest of the world, thought I was. At age twelve, the barrier between my current life and all my past lives came crashing down, flooding me with memories of all those lives. I managed to recover from those revelations, but my life was never the same after that. After all, being a reincarnation of the original Taliesin, King Arthur's bard, was hard enough to absorb all by itself, let alone all of the other lives I had to deal with and the discovery that I could work magic. Oh, and let's not forget that someone who knew who I was started trying to kill me shortly after I turned sixteen. Yeah, I beat the odds over and over again in the last few months. Carla was not so lucky.

You see, in the big battle against my enemy, Ceridwen, Carla got hit with the same spell that had awakened my past lives four years ago. The problem was, she got hit with it twice. That extra shot might have killed her; instead, it left her comatose—and I couldn't shake the feeling that her condition was my fault. I had let unsuspecting "civilian" friends go with me to that confrontation, thinking I knew what was going to happen. Well, seeing the future was never one of my gifts, but I had acted as if I could, and now Carla was paying the price.

She could wake up, of course, but the longer she stayed this way, the less chance there was, and her doctors had the disadvantage of having no idea what they were dealing with. Come to think of it, though, what could they have done even if they had known? I didn't think medical schools covered counter-spells these days.

Actually there were two people in Santa Brígida, our little town, who might have been able to help, in theory. Nurse Florence, a member of the Order of the Ladies of the Lake and currently under cover as our high school's nurse, had originally come to Santa Brígida to watch over me after I was "awakened," when I was still confused and vulnerable. Well, at least more confused and vulnerable than I was now—I hadn't quite gotten over the confusion. Anyway, she knew more than a little magic, particularly healing magic. There was also Vanora, a colleague of hers from Wales who saved me in the big battle by preventing me from saving Carla. (Vanora wasn't exactly on my Christmas card list, but I would have forgiven all if she had come up with a way to cure Carla.) Together they had tried pretty much every trick in both of their books and had failed…over and over and over. Ceridwen had crafted that awakening spell herself, and with her dead, no one else knew how it worked. Perhaps if we had kept Ceridwen alive…but no, she had nearly beaten us, and as much as I wanted Carla to be all right—well, let's be honest, as much as I loved Carla—I couldn't have risked everyone else I ever knew or cared about by gambling that we could have found a way to keep Ceridwen prisoner. For that matter, even if she had survived, I couldn't imagine what would have moved her to divulge the secret of the spell.

"Hey, Tal!" said a high, prepubescent voice right behind me. Without turning around, I knew it was the voice of Gianni, Carla's little brother.

"Gianni, are your parents here?" I asked. The hospital was quite a ways from the Rinaldi house, but there was no sign of Mr. and Mrs. Rinaldi.

"Nah, I took a cab. I wanted to see Carla, and Papa had to work late."

"Your mom let you come here by yourself?"

Gianni was studying the floor tiles intently. "She doesn't know."

"What are you trying to do, kid, give her heart failure? She'll miss you and worry."

Gianni's brown eyes looked up at me. "I'm eleven now—she doesn't need to worry."

Yeah, dude, that line would work better if your voice didn't squeak like that.

"Let me just give her a call and see if I can straighten this out." I whipped out my cell and dialed the number from memory. Needless to say, I had been right; Mrs. Rinaldi was anything but delighted to discover that her son was AWOL. However, the fact that Gianni was with me and that I was bringing him home went a long way toward keeping him from being grounded until he turned forty-five. Even though the Rinaldis hadn't really known me that long, they had been treating me like family ever since Carla's coma, assuming, as pretty much everyone else did, that I was Carla's boyfriend, though in fact we had only just started to move in that direction.

"OK, Gianni, I squared it for you this time, but you can't just take a cab again without getting your parents' permission."

"I'll bet you would have done it at my age if you had to."

Well, he had me there, but I was trying to be less impulsive these days, and I certainly wanted him to be.

He talked to Carla for awhile, telling her what had happened at school over the last couple of days. It was predictably a one-sided conversation, just like all my conversations with Carla. One could always hope, though, that Carla was taking it in, that she was getting closer to consciousness with every word.

God, his hair was exactly the same shade of black that hers was, and his facial features were so reminiscent of hers. Sometimes I found it hard to look at him. It wasn't his fault, though, that his very presence made my mute grief even more intense. In any case, we were connected through Carla, and he already looked at me like a brother. I was responsible for taking his sister away. The least I could do was fill in for her.

Gianni hung on until the nurses pretty much kicked us out. We each gave Carla a peck on the cheek and left. As we walked out the front door, I steered Gianni to the left, toward the lot where my new Prius was parked. My parents had resisted getting me a car before, since Santa Brígida was a relatively small place, and we lived in walking distance from the high school, with downtown only a quick bus trip away. Carla's hospital, however, was west down the 101 in Coast Village, much too far to walk and requiring a tortuously long bus ride. How could they say no? Well, they did say no to red—I was going for the color the Welsh dragon, though naturally they didn't know that—and I ended up with that not-quite black shade, gunmetal. All things considered, it was a reasonable compromise.

As soon as we opened the front door of the hospital, I knew something was wrong. When I had gone in to see Carla, the sky had been clear, yet now all I could see in any direction was fog so thick it blotted out the world beyond the hospital steps. Sure, we were close to the ocean, but I had seen this particular kind of fog too often to believe its occurrence was natural. Indeed, every time I had seen fog this thick in the last few months, it meant that something supernatural—and usually bad—was about to happen.

"Gianni, go back inside for a minute. It's better if I bring the car around." I glanced in his direction, but he was fascinated by the glow of the distant parking-lot lights in the fog and didn't seem to be listening.

"Gianni..." I started again, more emphatically, but before I could get any further, a figure appeared at the bottom of the steps, emerging from the fog so abruptly that I jumped a little, despite myself.

Yeah, I would know her anywhere. Same long, glossy black hair, same flawless white skin, same model perfect features and body. Only the gown was different this time: white samite, instead of the red samite I had last seen her wear, perhaps to make her more inconspicuous in the fog.

Morgan Le Fay!

"Why, Taliesin, what a pleasant surprise! I scarcely expected to run into you again. And who is your young friend?"

"Gianni, get inside!" I barked the order in Welsh, knowing he wouldn't remember afterward what had happened. In response to my magic, he turned quickly toward the door.

"No, Gianni, please stay here!" cooed Morgan, also in Welsh. I could feel the magic behind the words, and so could Gianni, who froze, his hand still in midair, reaching toward the door handle.

I needed to get Gianni away from Morgan, but I didn't want his mind pulled in two different directions by two powerful spell casters. My research prior to the battle against Ceridwen gave me the upper hand with certain kinds of magic, but Morgan was at least as powerful as I with simple mind manipulation, if not more so.

Without hesitation I drew my sword, White Hilt, and flames instantly engulfed its blade. Perhaps if Morgan were distracted enough, she would lose her focus on Gianni, and he would follow my original command.

"I see your manners have not improved since last time. I only want to talk." Morgan's voice conveyed an icy calm, but I noticed she did back away a step.

"You tried to kill me last time," I pointed out, trying to sound reasonable and not betray one freezing instant of the fear that frosted my heart. It was not that I was that afraid of facing Morgan in general. I was afraid of facing her with Gianni only a few steps away and totally vulnerable to any malign magic she might hurl at him.

"Some of my actions last time were…ill-advised. I let Ceridwen talk me into attacking you and your friends. What I did was foolish, and I crave your forgiveness."

Well, an apology from Morgan was certainly a surprise—but it was probably also a trick, a way of lulling me into a false sense of security.

"My forgiveness you can have…if you bind yourself with the most solemn oath never to cross my path again." I made sure to keep White Hilt ready and flaming. Having learned to manipulate that flame, I even made it blaze a little hotter.

"That I cannot do, for the universe often plays tricks on us. Our paths may cross, whether I will them to or not. After all, it was Ceridwen who threw you into my little corner of Annwn, and I truly did not intend to meet you tonight. I am as surprised as you are to find you here. My errand is not connected with you in any way, though as long as you are here, you may be able to help me with it."

I watched the undulating flames reflect in her eyes and thought I could see some uneasiness in those eyes as well. If Morgan had actually been looking for me, she would certainly have prepared a way to counter White Hilt's flame. Perhaps she was telling the truth—at least about the meeting being accidental.

I heard Gianni gasp next to me. While Morgan bantered with me, he had been trying to reconcile the two contradictory magic commands and obviously not succeeding. If neither of us released him, he might continue to struggle until he injured his mind.

"Morgan, release the boy, and I will hear you out." Morgan was doubtless loath to relinquish the advantage of having Gianni's safety to hold over my head, but she could see as well as I that the current situation could easily become a stalemate, and she clearly wanted something—if not my help, then at least my willingness to let her do whatever she had come for. She bowed, I could feel her attempted compulsion on Gianni relax, and he unsteadily propelled himself through the door, finally free to respond to my original instructions.

"Now then," she began as soon as the door closed behind Gianni, "I am in search of my sister. Not long ago I received a prophecy that she would soon re-emerge in the world of men, and now I feel her somewhere nearby. She is close, Taliesin, very close indeed."

I looked at her quizzically. "Morgause? She is dead, surely."

Morgan gave me one of her glacial smiles. "Before this fall, you would have said the same of me, and I the same of you. Yet here we are."

"Well, I did die, as you know, and was reincarnated. And I told you when you were seeking Lancelot, I have no art to find the person in whom a specific soul has reincarnated. So if Morgause is again living in this world, she could be anywhere, for all I know. On the other hand, if she, like you, has found a way to cheat death, I might be able to find her—but so could you, and I suspect far easier than I."

"Actually, it is not Morgause I seek, but my other sister, Alcina." I must have looked even more puzzled, and for a moment I thought Morgan was going to lose her temper with me. Then she regained control of herself and added, "You would remember her as Elaine."

"Elaine! Yes, I remember that Arthur had a half-sister named Elaine, but she left long before the fall of Camelot."

"Yes, she found the atmosphere at Camelot somewhat…stifling, and unlike me, she had no particular scores to settle. She wandered through Europe, searching for ways to enhance her magic, and she found quite a few. She settled on an island, not exactly in Annwn, but certainly in an otherworld of some sort. Unfortunately, that island has been empty for centuries, and it contains no clue of what might have become of her."

"Surely," I began, again trying to sound reasonable, "the likelihood that she randomly ended up in Santa Barbara must be remote, even if she is still alive."

"I feel her," snapped Morgan. "I feel her as I have not felt her in hundreds of years. She is nearby—of that I am certain."

If Elaine, or Alcina, or whatever she was calling herself these days, was nearby, the last thing I wanted was for Morgan to find her. After all, Morgan was quite dangerous enough on her own. Letting her reunite with a sister whose magic might be even more powerful than her own was about as desirable as pounding a nail into my forehead, but how could I stop her, short of killing her? I had certainly killed my share of people in earlier lives, but I wasn't exactly eager to continue that habit in this one. Then there was the fact that Morgan would certainly fight back, and a battle between us could get extremely messy, to say the least.

And Gianni, not to mention Carla, was in the building right behind us. So, at least in theory, was Morgan's sister, but I couldn't take the chance that the possible risk to Elaine would restrain Morgan enough. She seemed rational enough at the moment, but I had seen more than enough over the last few weeks to make me question her sanity.

I needed to play for time, to find a way to slow Morgan down while holding out the possibility that I might help her.

"If Elaine is so close," I began, "and you can sense her presence, why has she not sensed yours? Surely she would have appeared by now and given you a sisterly greeting."

I had just been fishing for some way to keep the conversation going, but as soon as I asked the question, I realized it was a reasonable one, and so did Morgan. Good as she was at concealing her feelings, she was clearly a bit perplexed.

"I have asked myself the same question. Taliesin, she is only a little farther away from me than you are—I know it as surely as I know my own name. She should at least have noticed me. However, I am looking for her, and she is not looking for me, so perhaps—wait, now I know exactly where she is!"

I should have known that Morgan was chatting with me and reaching out for her sister at the same time. I had not gained anything at all by trying to keep the conversation going.

"She is…in the building right behind you," said Morgan with eerie certainty.

Great. The one place I least wanted Morgan to be, and that was the one spot she was determined to go.

"She can't be, Morgan. I just came from in there. Surely I would have noticed a presence as strong as hers."

"Perhaps not," said Morgan, regarding me with interest. "I share a bond of blood with her that you do not. What I feel is that bond calling to me. Her power I do not feel at all. That suggests two possibilities: she is hiding from something, or she has lost her powers. Either way she needs my help." Morgan took a step forward. I let the flame on my sword blaze brighter.

"I am not about to let you into this hospital, whether your sister is inside or not, Morgan."

Her eyes blazed brighter than my sword, but she did not immediately let her anger have free reign.

"My little cherub," she said softly. "A little cherub with his flaming sword, guarding the gates. Why are you so intent on keeping me from helping my own sister? I know you understand the importance of family ties."

That last line could easily be interpreted as a threat, but I decided to ignore it for the moment.

"Because I don't trust you," I said simply, getting White Hilt to flame higher for effect. I figured there was not much point in maintaining a pretense of friendliness at this point. "You did try to kill me and my friends, and you would have been quite content to leave my soul trapped in Ceridwen's cauldron forever. You can't think a simple apology really covers all of that."

"My little cherub—"

"Not so little, Morgan, and with thousands of years of experience, as you will find out if you keep pushing me."

"No, not so little at that," replied Morgan, feigning a thoughtful tone and looking me up and down. "Not so little at all. Perhaps I have been foolish to think mere words would satisfy you. Perhaps mine is the kind of apology that needs to be delivered…in bed."

Seriously?

"Morgan…" I began, then had to pause as she stared into my eyes, plainly trying to enchant me. I could feel seductive energy oozing all around my defenses, probing them, poking at them. Fortunately, for someone like me, all Morgan could do was increase the natural temptation, not actually control my mind. At least, I hoped that was all she could do. I started humming, just to be sure. The original Taliesin's magic worked best with musical accompaniment, and so naturally did mine. Too bad I didn't have an instrument with me…

Morgan apparently took my humming to indicate I was nervous about my defenses and tried to press her advantage. "I know the girl you love cannot be your lover now, perhaps ever. Nonetheless, I would not insult you by asking you to betray that love. I offer you only physical satisfaction. A man like you must have…needs, needs that a woman like me could certainly satisfy. I have had hundreds of years of experience, after all. Come to think of it, so have you. Our coupling would have to be magnificent."

Keeping in mind that in this life I was still a sixteen-year-old guy, I wouldn't pretend her offer, backed up by magic or not, wasn't appealing on some level. Being a teenage guy wasn't easy in the first place; imagine what it was like being a teenage guy who could remember hundreds of years of sexual experiences from previous lives. Let's just say I didn't need to spend any time searching for porn on the Internet. I did have to spend a lot of time reconciling my urge to reenact some of those earlier sexual experiences with my desire to be at least a halfway decent guy by the standards of my current society. Morgan herself complicated the issue still further. She was, after all, a beautiful woman, fashion-model beautiful. Her mistake was in reminding me that she was really older than dirt. I couldn't help thinking of the skeleton she'd be right now without all the magic she had expended to keep herself forever young.

What really reinforced my defenses, though, was the jolt of fear that shot through me when I realized that Morgan knew about Carla. Morgan must have been spying on me, just as Ceridwen used to—and Morgan was definitely not someone you wanted knowing all of your secret vulnerabilities.

I suddenly realized the light from White Hilt was fading. I again urged the flames to a great blaze, gave myself the mental equivalent of a cold shower, and focused all my attention on Morgan again.

"I'm not so easy to get around," I said to her with a certainly I did not completely feel. Morgan, not expecting such an outright rejection, at least not so quickly, let some of her rage show.

"Do you really think you can stop me, Taliesin?" she replied harshly. "You took me by surprise once in Annwn. You will not do so again." With that, Morgan threw herself into the concealing fog faster than should have been possible—had she been a mere human. Unfortunately, she was part faerie and capable of moving faster than I was—not superhero fast, but fast enough to conceal herself in her fog before I could fling the fire from my sword at her in a burst that would have reduced her to ashes. But who was I kidding? Even had I been moving at the same speed, I probably wouldn't have roasted her. I just didn't want to kill, not even someone like her. At least, not until I absolutely had to, a point I might reach any minute now.

After all, Morgan could do more than hide herself in the fog. Like most Celtic sorcerers, she could shape-shift into something tiny like a fly, then get into the hospital through an open window on the third floor before I could stop her. Worse, she could use the weather itself against me. The results would not be instantaneous, but in a surprisingly short period of time, she could fry me with lightning right where I stood and step over my charred corpse on the way to the front door.

I could try to counter such a tactic, but Morgan was stronger than I in a straight battle of magic against magic. True, I had learned how to make magic work on modern technology, which as far as I could tell, no one else had managed, and I had another trick or two up my sleeve, like being able to read and broadcast thoughts in a way that would have astounded the original Taliesin. However, there was no denying that in a contest of raw power, Morgan would beat me.

As if on cue, a chilling wind cut through me. So Morgan was going to try storm over stealth.

I did understand meteorology better than she did—that's how I had beaten her that time in Annwn. But then I had used my fire and my scientific knowledge to counter her storm and ended up creating a hurricane to use against her. I couldn't very well do that this time, and Morgan knew it—I had made it very clear that I valued something, or someone, inside the building. My options were limited by the need to protect that structure. A hurricane born of the clash between her magic and mine could probably not be controlled precisely enough to be safe to use this close to the hospital.

Predictably enough, rain started hitting me in ice-cold drops, and the flames on my sword sputtered a little. That was part of Morgan's goal: put out the sword.

I might already be too late, but I knew I needed to summon help.

"Nurse Florence, I need you...ten minutes ago!" I gave the message every ounce of power I possessed, but that kind of mental communication did weaken with distance, and Nurse Florence, our resident lady of the lake, was probably miles away in Santa Brígida. Still, if I managed to connect, I could send her a message without Morgan even realizing I had summoned help.

"Should I bring backup?" Her response tingled in the back of my mind, faint but unmistakable.

"Any of the guys you can grab fast. Morgan Le Fay is trying to find her sister Elaine—in Carla's hospital. Morgan's raising a storm."

"I'll be there as soon as I can."

I felt the connection fade, but at least now I knew help was coming...eventually. Nurse Florence did have some rather unusual methods of transportation at her disposal. The question was how fast she could get to any of my…well, warriors, for lack of a better term. Since they had to conceal their unusual…situation, just as I did mine, they couldn't always appear right on cue, even in an emergency.

Well, no point fussing about how fast my allies could get here. I needed to focus entirely on countering Morgan's arcane attack. In the short time it had taken me to reach Nurse Florence, the wind had intensified until its howl was like that of a rabid wolf, the rain was practically knocking me off my feet, and my sword was radiating more steam than fire. Just in time, I willed the flames to become stronger, to burn back the rain, to envelope me in a flaming shield. I had to concentrate so hard I was shaking, but for the moment I was protected—unless of course someone tried to walk out the front door of the hospital, in which case I would have another problem.

The powers that be in Annwn were none too pleased that so many people already knew my secret. Nurse Florence they accepted as practically one of their own, and they could have swallowed my "warriors." It was the fact that I wouldn't wipe the memories of the other students who had been with us in the final battle during Samhain that really irked them. The leadership in Annwn was all about keeping humans from learning too much. So, yeah, if anyone saw the display I was currently putting on, I would have to wipe that person's memory of it—but I would have to keep him or her out of Morgan's way first. Too many complications.

I knew it was risky trying to "multi-task" with magic, but I did manage to jam the door behind me, and the sudden temperature drop created by Morgan's storm made it easy for me to frost the nearby windows. The manner in which the entry way of the hospital projected out from the rest of the building would block the view of what I was doing from a lot of those windows, but I wanted to be as careful as I could be.

Even that slight change of focus thinned my fire shield a bit, and as the rain's fury increased, it brought the shield near to collapse. It took every bit of concentration I had to stabilize the situation. I started singing softly in Welsh to amplify my power as much as possible. Even so, I knew I could not hold out indefinitely. I had to hope that the cavalry would arrive—soon.

It also worried me that, with this storm raging, Morgan could very easily slip in through some other point of entry while I was blocking the front door. I thought about trying to locate her in the fog, but I guessed she would be masking her presence as much as she could, forcing me to give more of my focus to finding her than I dared right now. I had to depend on her desire to kill me, or at least render me helpless, to keep her outside as long as I was still breathing and conscious.

The lightning flash almost made me jump, and the thunder was loud enough to rattle some of the nearby hospital windows. That lightning was powerful, and it was close. My fire shield might protect me from the rain, but it probably wouldn't stop the lightning, though I was having a hard time thinking through the science involved. The hiss of steam as the rain hit the fire sounded almost deafening now, but even it wasn't enough to drown out the reverberations of the thunder.

Between the racket and my need to concentrate on maintaining the fire shield, I spared a second to wonder what had happened to Gianni. Even inside the hospital such a sudden and intense storm must have been quite noticeable; probably one of the nurses had spotted him and was now keeping him from coming outside to look for me, but he had to be getting awfully worried by now, and I wasn't sure whether my command to go inside would *keep* him inside—I was working too fast at the time to consider all the contingencies. Well, I didn't want to think too much about that; at least he was safe inside right now, and I was pretty sure someone would keep him inside. That was the most I could hope for at the moment.

I was beginning to feel tired. No, not just tired—more like exhausted. Morgan was hitting me with everything she had, though I did wonder why the lightning, which must be striking nearby, wasn't actually hitting me. I wasn't really trying to deflect it, because doing that would take too much power away from the fire shield, but perhaps countering the lightning was more important. If I concentrated on the lightning, I knew I could keep it from striking really close—I had seen that kind of magical defense before. However, if the fire shield collapsed, as it very likely would, the rain would beat down on me so mercilessly that, at the very least, my concentration would shatter. In this kind of situation, logic suggested retreating inside the building, especially since Morgan believed her sister was inside and couldn't exactly level the place. She could, however, follow me in, and I wanted to keep our fight outside if I possibly could.

"Taliesin, let me in!"

I jumped at the sound of the voice coming from right next to me. It was not the voice I wanted to hear, but it was at least someone who would help. I parted the flames on my left just long enough for Vanora to jump through.

Yeah, that's right—the same person I held responsible for Carla's condition. Not only that, but she was still disguised as Carrie Winn, the identity Ceridwen had assumed while she was stalking me. Carrie Winn was too prominent a citizen to just disappear, so Vanora had shifted into Winn's form long enough to keep us all from getting entangled in a police investigation and to tie up other loose ends. Intellectually I understood the need for such a deception. Emotionally, it was hard for me to look at someone who had been willing to condemn me to eternal suffering, no matter how often I told myself that the person really was dead, and what I was seeing was merely an illusion. It was a damn convincing illusion though. I guess it would have to be to serve its purpose. Still…

Vanora knew I didn't like her, in the shape of Carrie Winn or in her natural form, but she was too business-like to acknowledge my surly glance in her direction.

"Viviane's gathering the others. She asked me to help you hold out until they got here."

I had to hand it to her for being cool in a crisis. Without skipping a beat, she started casting a spell to keep the lightning from hitting us. I had seen her do the same thing on Samhain, and it had worked. Between the two of us, we could certainly hold Morgan until the others arrived.

The situation didn't make me like Vanora any better—but I had to admit, however grudgingly, that she was a worthy adversary for Morgan.

Of course, Morgan would quickly sense that she now had more than one opponent, but I doubted she could up her game enough to destroy both of us. At least, I hoped not. There was perhaps more danger of her trying to outflank us and get into the building, but Morgan was not the type to leave two enemies at large in such close proximity to her. Or was that just more wishful thinking on my part?

"Taliesin, let me in!"

This time I froze rather than jumping. I had expected the others to show up soon, so hearing someone else asking to be let inside the fire shield should not have caused my heart to skip a beat. The problem was that the voice outside was Vanora's, just as it had been a couple of minutes before.

I already knew Morgan was a shape-shifter, so I shouldn't really have been surprised. The problem was, who was the fake Vanora—the woman standing next to me, or the woman outside? If I guessed wrong, things could get really nasty really quickly…

The Vanora already inside with me, however, had known who else was coming, something Morgan, who couldn't read minds, probably wouldn't know. On the other hand, now that I thought about it, Morgan's faerie ancestry gave her advantages beyond the speed I had seen earlier. For one thing, her vision was much better than the human norm. The darkness would not have been much of a problem for her, and as the sorceress who had conjured the fog and storm, she should have been able to see through them pretty easily as well, even though I couldn't. Logically, she should have been able to see Vanora arrive. But in that case, why shift into the image of Vanora? She could have fooled me much more easily by becoming Nurse Florence, whom I would have let in without question. She had to know I would not just passively accept two Vanoras. Why was my life always so complicated?

"That has to be Morgan," observed the Vanora standing next to me, her eyes narrowed in concentration, most of her attention focused on keeping the lightning from hitting us. "Perhaps you should give her a…warm welcome."

I tried to gently probe them both, but typically I didn't have much luck getting into the minds of powerful spell casters, and so I couldn't read much more than their power. Casters such as they consciously or unconsciously created shields to protect their minds from the wide variety of mental attacks an opponent might hurl at them. The ancient Celts hadn't visualized reading minds in the way that I had trained myself to do, but the kind of mental shielding Morgan and Vanora had kept me out pretty effectively anyway. By now maintaining such shields had become almost second-nature to them, so maintaining that defense did not require much effort on their parts unless I attacked their shielding—something I didn't dare do until I knew who was who.

I caused the flames to blaze up on the side from which I had heard the other Vanora's voice come—but slowly enough to give her a chance to dodge out of the way, which she did.

"Taliesin," said the second Vanora, in what was, at the very least, a good imitation of her real Vanora's indignant tone, "what are you doing?"

"Demonstrating I'm not that easily fooled, Morgan," I replied, putting a lot of emphasis on that name. "The real Vanora is already here."

"No, she isn't," insisted the second Vanora loudly. "You must have Morgan inside with you."

Well, she must have been right, because at that moment I felt a very sharp, very cold dagger thrust into my right arm.

CHAPTER 2: REINFORCEMENTS

I had good enough reflexes to pull away from Morgan's dagger before she had the chance to thrust it in very far, but I realized at once it was not the blade I had to fear, but whatever Morgan had coated it with. From my life as the first Taliesin, I well remembered just how much skill Morgan had with every substance from herbal remedies to poisons. I could see something gleaming darkly on the dagger, even beneath my blood. It almost seemed to squirm across the blade, as if Morgan had heightened its poisonous nature with some powerful spell.

In seconds my sword felt as if it had been embedded in about half a ton of lead. I managed to shift it to my left hand, but I could feel the poison flowing chillingly in my veins; it would not be long before my left arm also began to succumb.

Keeping my blade between me and Morgan, I took an unsteady step backward and made a quick opening in the fire shield for the real Vanora to step through—except that there was no one there. Morgan, already shifted back into her normal form, laughed heartily at my obvious confusion.

"You aren't the only one who can find new uses for magic," said Morgan, smiling brightly at me as if we were best buds. "I was doing more or less the magic equivalent of throwing my voice. You were hearing me and even sensing me outside, but really I was inside with you the whole time."

It now seemed I had no alternative to killing Morgan if I wanted to protect Carla and Gianni. The problem was that my mind was becoming just as sluggish as my body. I knew I could theoretically shoot fire from my sword in a concentrated burst and scorch her right where she stood, but using both "fire shield mode" and "laser blast" mode at the same time was a little tricky to do under ideal conditions, let alone now, with my brain quickly losing its focus. Nor could my faltering brain figure out how to drop the fire shield quickly enough to blast Morgan before she could dodge away. I dimly realized that the storm raging around us was shredding the fire shield anyway, but I couldn't get myself to concentrate on countering that damage either. Icy rain was splattering my face now, but I could barely feel it. The same rain hit the sword and raised another steam cloud, but I just stared at it. I could see the sword was sputtering and would soon go out, yet I did nothing.

Suddenly my willpower was melting faster than ice in the Sahara. I also knew I should try to counter the poison, but I could not seem to summon any energy to do that either. My sword slid from my nerveless fingers and clattered on the hospital steps. The flames gave up their futile struggle against the rain as soon as I was no longer wielding the sword, and the pathetic remnant of my fire shield fizzled out. I knew that my life, too, would soon be fizzling out.

The rain and wind hit me hard enough to push me to my knees. In what seemed an instant in my half-dead state, but might have been a little longer, Morgan was standing right above me, looking down and smiling her death-promising smile. The storm eased, but not the fog, which engulfed us and made it hard for me to see even Morgan—unless the poison was now blurring my vision.

"My little cherub, you have dropped your sword," she said in mock-sorrow, picking up White Hilt. It would not flame for her, but she was taking no chances that I might somehow manage to grab it long enough to launch one last fire attack.

I knew she could not read minds as I could, but she could read my fear in my eyes well enough.

"Taliesin, do you really think I mean to kill you? Had that been all I wanted, I could just as easily have struck you with the lightning several minutes ago. You know that as well as I do." I did know that much, even though my thoughts were moving as swiftly as stone. For that matter, Morgan could have plunged her trusty dagger through my heart right then and finished the job. I could not have lifted a finger to stop her.

Then, even stranger than Morgan not killing me, she caught me as I nearly fell forward on my face and laid me out, with what felt like gentleness, face-up on the steps. The steps beneath me were cold and wet, but it was better to lie face-up than face-down.

"The potion on the dagger is not poison. It is just a little liquid enchantment I brewed up to take the fight out of anyone who might try to stop me. You will recover from it in a few hours." Morgan smiled again at the mute question in my eyes. "Maybe I have…what do they call it today? A 'soft spot' for you. Or maybe I think your special skills may yet prove useful to me. You may not be any match for me in battle, Taliesin, but you certainly have mastered some aspects of magic that are still beyond me. Who knows at what point I might need something done that only you can do?"

It was hard to reconcile Morgan's attitude with what I could remember of her from my life as the first Taliesin—or even from my previous encounters with her in this one. When Ceridwen had temporarily trapped us in Morgan's part of Annwn, Morgan had seemed willing enough to put all of us at risk to get what she wanted, and she had nearly killed my friend Shahriyar in the final battle with Ceridwen. For her to change so much meant that she really must have found a use for me. Well, whatever it was, I knew I wasn't going to like it.

"Rest now," said Morgan, leaning over and stroking my hair. "Our paths will cross again. Perhaps then you will be more...cooperative." She leaned over even farther and gave me the very slightest kiss on the cheek. I would have shuddered if I had been able to. Even more frightening, however, was the fact that then she stood up, stepped away from me, and started toward the hospital.

Carla! Gianni!

With a colossal effort, I managed to raise my head enough to see Morgan, standing before the front door of the hospital, arms upraised, her black hair and white samite gown rippling a little in the wind that was all that remained of the earlier storm. She was chanting something in Welsh. Not exactly an invisibility spell, but a spell to keep her from being noticed. Morgan had only recently started exploring the modern human world, but clearly she had seen enough to know that a strikingly beautiful woman striding down the hospital wearing a white gown and carrying a long sword would draw a little unwelcome attention.

Morgan finished the spell and then started to struggle with the hospital door, which I had jammed earlier. Unfortunately, it did not take her long to undo my spell, and then she swept through the door and was gone.

I had to get up, but I could not make my muscles work. Even sitting up proved impossible.

The one thought that comforted me was that Morgan had used enough magic beating me to be pretty worn out herself—but how much magic would she need to hurt someone who got in her way? And what would happen when she found her long-lost sister?

I tried again to sit up. My muscles twitched a bit but still felt like over-cooked spaghetti. I tried to reach out psychically, but my mind moved in slow motion, and I did not get even the slightest echo of a connection with anyone. Even if I had managed some faint contact, that would not have helped Carla or Gianni.

Wait! Was that a whiff of the intensely fresh air from Annwn that I felt against my cheek, or was it just my foggy wits playing tricks on me? No, it was real, because suddenly Nurse Florence was bending over me, her eyes betraying her anxiety over my condition. Behind her I could make out Stan Schoenbaum and Dan Stevens, my two oldest friends, even though Dan and I had gone through a four-year-long period of hostility, now forgotten. Then I saw Carlos Reyes, Shahriyar Sassani, and Gordy Hayes, three newer, but still very close, friends. Collectively, they were my warriors, for lack of a better way of putting it. Each one had met the challenge of Gwynn ap Nudd, the king of the Welsh faeries, and in consequence each one wielded a magic sword, and each was tied to me by a *tynged* (binding spell) set up by Nurse Florence and willingly accepted by them.

Well, Morgan, let's see you beat all five of them! Let's see you out-cast Nurse Florence!

I don't know why, given how grave our situation was at this moment, but my mind wandered into thinking about how the group didn't exactly look like the well-oiled fighting machine it was. The guys looked like the high school students they were. Sure, four of them were long-time athletes, with Stan a much more recent recruit. They were all more or less well-muscled. Well, to be honest, Shar was the "more," practically a body builder, and Stan was the "less," though he had been working out enough to not look quite like the mathlete he had always been. Otherwise, they looked more like the cast of a commercial to get more girls to attend Santa Brígida High School than like elite fighters. None of them were exactly "pretty boys," but Dan did have that kind of smile that could melt a female heart, Carlos was reputed to be the reason so many girls came to water polo games, Shar just needed to flex a couple of times to get girls ready to walk barefoot over broken glass for him, and Gordy seemed to be with a different cheerleader every time I saw him. Even Stan was regarded as cute by many of the girls—sort of the nerd-with-possibilities type who appears so often in movies and ends up proving to be the better guy than the star jock at the end.

And Nurse Florence? What can I say? Natural blond hair (but certainly not someone who fit the "dumb blond" stereotype), face like an angel, body like a *Playboy* model. She didn't look like the fearless battlefield healer she became when the occasion called for it. She looked much more like someone high school males would fantasize about. There I could speak from personal experience...

It was then that I was jolted back to reality when I noticed that Carlos's left sleeve was torn, and the edges of the rip were bloodstained. I blinked, trying to process what I was seeing. Actually, all five were bloodied, though not always with their own blood, or so I hoped.

Well, that explained what had taken them so long. They must have run into trouble of some kind on the way.

Nurse Florence had her hands on my shoulders, letting her mind scan my body. I knew that was what she must be doing, though I couldn't feel her probing as I normally could.

"He'll live," she began, directing her remarks to my anxious friends, "but he has a very nasty spell keeping him all but paralyzed physically and too weak mentally to use magic. It will take me time to break something this strong. The five of you need to go in and stop Morgan from whatever she is trying to do." I wanted to second her suggestion, but I couldn't force words out. "Oh, and try to retrieve Tal's sword if you can," she continued. "Morgan seems to have taken it."

Each one took the time to give me an encouraging pat on the shoulder and then rushed in without a word. I couldn't help but feel proud of how well they worked as a team now. I wanted to go in with them, but Nurse Florence was right—I wasn't going anywhere right now. Well, unless they carried me in, which would be pretty silly in a potential battle.

Nurse Florence spent a little time on the nick on my arm, which she healed fairly quickly. Breaking the spell was much harder, just as she had suspected. As she chanted quietly in Welsh, I kept reassuring myself that the guys had the situation handled, that I did not need to worry.

Shahriyar's sword, Shamshir-e Zomorrodnegar, once wielded by King Solomon and later by the Muslim demon slayer, Amir Arsalan, had among its other distinctions the fact that it made the wielder immune to all hostile magic and that it could cut through and dissipate magical effects. That one blade by itself might well be enough to defeat Morgan, and the fact that Shar, even before his combat training with me, had been pure muscle and very successful in both boxing and mixed martial arts made him a very formidable adversary. Facing a spell casting opponent, in fact, he was more likely to prevail than I was, though I hated to admit that (male ego, you know!)

Then there was Carlos's sword, faerie-forged for him personally. One scratch from his blade, and his opponent would start running out of oxygen as if the enemy were drowning. Dan's sword, also faerie-forged just for him, kept him from bleeding from any wounds he suffered, much as Excalibur's scabbard used to do before it was lost. Gordy's sword, yet another faerie-forged and personalized blade, struck fear into any enemy when it was drawn, though a typical spell caster would be too strong-willed to be overcome by the sword's effect.

Stan's sword, like Shar's but in contrast to all the others, was "pre-owned"— but since the original owner had been King David, Stan couldn't really complain too much. Govannon, the faerie smith, had added to it the ability to make Stan's body as muscular as Shar's—a big bonus at a point when Stan had been more nerdy, and even now, though Stan was working out a lot more, the sword still added visibly to his muscle mass, making him much more effective in combat. Of course, the fact that Stan also had a brilliant mind didn't hurt either. Given the chance, he could out-think most opponents, even a good many of the supernatural ones.

So why was I worrying? Surely the five of them could stop Morgan in her tracks. Yeah, surely. But I still shuddered at the thought. I had underestimated opponents before, and I had the horrible feeling that Morgan had at least one other surprise in reserve.

Suddenly a tremor ran through my whole body. Nurse Florence was trying to break the spell, but it was fighting back with unusual intensity. It felt like a thorn-bush inside of me, with a thorn digging into each cell, as Nurse Florence fought to extract it. I had to clench my teeth to keep from screaming as it writhed within me, tearing into anything it could in an effort to stay put.

Nurse Florence looked into my eyes. "Tal, I'm sorry this hurts so much, but I don't know how else to do this. Morgan evidently spent a lot of time crafting this…thing. It is every bit as determined as she is to get what it wants. It does seem dependent on whatever substance Morgan got into your arm wound, though, and that will dissipate eventually. We could wait until it runs its course…"

I wanted to shout "NO!" I wanted at least to shake my head vigorously. All I could manage was the slightest side-to-side motion, but Nurse Florence knew me too well not to know what I wanted.

"All right, Tal. Hang on. This will take a few more minutes, but those minutes will feel like hours. Since the pain is magical, deadening your normal pain responses won't stop it." With that, Nurse Florence went back to trying to pull the spell out by its roots, and I went back to gritting my teeth.

After what seemed a piercing red eternity, I felt the last of the thing's thorny branches wither away. Despite myself, I gasped audibly, but now at least my muscles started responding again, and I was able to sit up. I glanced over at Nurse Florence, who looked back at me wearily.

"I'm surprised you kept from screaming."

"The one advantage of the paralysis," I replied, trying, but not quite succeeding, to give her a facetious smile. "Am I good to go?"

"Tal, you are going to be weak for a while. After all of that struggling, I don't have enough energy myself to lend very much to you. However, if you take it easy—"

"Yeah, that'll happen," I quipped, attempting to jump to my feet—"attempting" being the operative word. Oh, I managed to get to my feet, but very slowly and very shakily.

"You aren't really combat-ready, and you don't have White Hilt."

"I'm going in anyway," I replied, not quite managing the self-confident tone I wanted but at least not sounding as if I were going to faint at any moment.

Nurse Florence, though pretty worn-out herself, took charge of weaving a concealment charm around us, and then we moved into the hospital, more slowly than I would have liked, but as fast as I was able.

The security guard at the front desk was slouched back in his chair, eyes shut, snoring loudly. Morgan's work no doubt. Somehow he must have noticed her coming in. Perhaps the door opening gave her away. I'd seen that guy before, and I had noticed he seemed very alert for someone whose job was, for the most part, routine.

The good news was that no nurses were running for the exits and screaming in terror. The bad news was that the place was as silent as death, aside from the occasional monitor beep. I wasn't sure whether not being able to hear the guys was good news or bad news. The lack of swords clanging in the distance suggested no ongoing battle—but did that mean the guys hadn't been able to find Morgan or that the battle was already over? If it were the latter, the silence betrayed no hint about who had won.

Both Nurse Florence and I let our minds reach out. Morgan could probably conceal herself from me, especially considering the shape

I was in, but at least I could find the guys, and so I did—in Carla's room…with Morgan.

My heart started beating so hard it felt as if it might rip right out of my chest. I did the best I could to run, but my steps were maddeningly slow and just a little shaky on top of that. Worse, by the time I reached Carla's room, my breath was coming out in ragged gasps.

When Nurse Florence and I arrived, Morgan was on the far side of Carla's bed, and the guys were on the side closest to the door, every muscle tensed, ready to throw themselves at Morgan as soon as they could. The reason they had not already charged her became immediately apparent when I got close enough to realize that she had a solid grip on Gianni, and with her other hand, she was holding her dagger to his throat. He wasn't struggling; in fact, he seemed to be asleep, probably courtesy of Morgan's magic. He must have sneaked back into his sister's room to wait for me, and Morgan had found him there.

The big question now was why Morgan went to Carla's room in the first place. There seemed to be only one answer: she had a definite plan that required my help, and she knew exactly how to get me to cooperate.

Have you ever seen your worst nightmare come to life right in front of you? Well, now I had, in living color—hell, in 3-D.

Whatever Morgan wanted, it had to be evil. Yet how could I refuse her anything when she could kill Gianni with one flick of the wrist. She might be a soulless witch, but she was pretty good with a knife, and there was still that faerie speed to contend with.

"I can probably save Gianni even if she cuts his throat," thought Nurse Florence, knowing that Morgan couldn't hear our thoughts.

"Probably isn't good enough!" I shot back. Anyway, I knew how much energy Nurse Florence had needed to expend on breaking the spell on me. If Morgan seriously hurt Gianni, Nurse Florence would have to struggle with his injury and with the effects of the potion that would get in through his wound. She was good, but even she probably couldn't pull that off, especially when she so desperately needed rest.

"Ah, Taliesin!" said Morgan as if we were chatting about the weather. "I wasn't expecting you so soon, but I have never been so glad to see you. Your playmates don't seem to understand how to negotiate. Perhaps I will do better with you."

"Release Gianni, and we will talk," I said as levelly as I could.

Morgan laughed in that glacial way she had, and everyone in the room, even—or did I just imagine it?—Carla, seemed to cringe.

"I let the boy go once, and you almost immediately refused to help me. In fact, you tried to keep me from my sister. No, the boy stays right where he is until you take the most solemn oath I can contrive to help me."

I knew just as well as Morgan that supernatural oaths—with a little help from an appropriate *tynged*—were binding. I couldn't just pretend to agree and then go back on my word. The situation was much like the medieval stories about selling one's soul to the devil…in more ways than one!

"Give me the word, and I'll take her out," muttered Shar, who was standing right next to me. If he threw "Zom" at her with all his strength, it would cut through any possible magical defense and probably at least wound her, given the cramped space she was in…but she could probably at least nick Gianni before the sword hit her.

"Don't do anything yet!" I replied sternly. I could feel Shar's impatience, but he respected my order. Just to be sure, I gave everyone the same order. I could feel the questioning responses, but I ignored them. The guys wanted to get Morgan, just as I did, but before I had even gotten to the room, they had accepted a stalemate rather than hurt Gianni. The others wouldn't like the order any more than Shar did, but they too would obey it rather than see an innocent little kid die. As for Nurse Florence, I couldn't picture her sacrificing Gianni either. I was especially thankful I was dealing with Nurse Florence rather than Vanora, who unquestionably would have wanted to get rid of Morgan, no matter what the cost.

"All right, Morgan, I'm listening. What exactly is it that you want from me?"

"Send your playmates out in the hall first. My words are for you alone." To underscore the fact that she was not making a request, Morgan moved the knife just a little closer to Gianni's throat.

"Out of the question!" answered Nurse Florence forcefully, before I could say anything. "What keeps you from killing Tal and Gianni if we leave?"

"I was under the impression that Taliesin was able to fight his own battles," said Morgan with obvious disdain for Nurse Florence. "In any case, I could just as easily ask you what keeps me safe if they all stay?

Five swordsmen, each with a magic sword and each within striking distance? What keeps them from killing me?"

"I do!" I replied as strongly as I could manage. "Morgan, these are my men," I continued in terms she could understand. "They will not strike unless I give the order. And I pledge I will not without giving you prior warning that I am ending the negotiations—unless you yourself attack one of us, Gianni included."

"Your guarantee is not entirely reassuring, since you are the one who determines how long it will run…but as a show of good faith, I will accept it, if you will be bound by a *tynged* to that effect."

"I will," I replied. We each raised our right hand, golden sparks crackled between our palms, and I felt the *tynged* grip me. Nurse Florence stared at me, clearly understanding I needed to give Morgan some ground in order to have any hope of saving Gianni but just as clearly not liking the situation.

Wanting to avoid another interruption from Nurse Florence, I continued quickly. "Now, Morgan, I ask again, what do you want from me? I half expected you to have found your sister and been gone by now."

Morgan looked at me, clearly puzzled. "But Taliesin, I thought you had realized I have found my sister. There she is." Morgan gestured toward Carla, who looked especially helpless to me.

Morgan's words hit me like sledge hammers. I thought I had prepared myself for anything she could throw at me. Obviously, I was wrong.

CHAPTER 3: YOU ONLY LIVE ONCE—I WISH!

All of my friends acted as if they were holding their breath, waiting for some response from me…but words failed me. Finally Morgan lost patience with the shocked silence around her.

"Evidently I have over-estimated you, Taliesin. You saw this girl's earlier lives awakened on Samhain, before Ceridwen gave her that second blast that left her in this trance. You knew that at least in one of those earlier lives, she was a sorceress, because you felt her power, and you saw her try to contend with Ceridwen on your behalf. Why is it so hard to believe that she could be Elaine?"

"For one thing, she was speaking Italian, not Welsh."

Morgan shook her head sadly. "I told you when first we encountered each other tonight that my sister had traveled through Europe, looking for ways to increase her magic. She ended up in Italy. Remember, I also told you that she went by a new name, Alcina.

"Alcina is just a character in Ariosto's *Orlando Furioso*!" protested Nurse Florence. "The Order has never found any evidence that she was a real person, much less that she was your sister, Elaine. That's just one way Ariosto linked his subject to the matter of Britain. Surely you don't think we are that gullible."

Morgan looked at Nurse Florence even more contemptuously than before. "I was not speaking to you!" she replied in the most regal tone she could manage. Then, switching her attention back to me, she said, "Most people think that I am just a literary character. Most people think you are just a literary character, Taliesin. Yet here we are, just as real as those who doubt us. After all you have seen, after all you have lived through, how can you deny the possibility that Alcina is real and that she is my sister?"

"Suppose Carla was your sister in a previous life," I replied coldly. "What do you want to do with her? Her condition is incurable. There is nothing you or I can do about that."

"Ah," said Morgan triumphantly, "wrong again! I *can* cure her—with your help. I have been watching you ever since Samhain…from a safe distance, of course. I learned more of you and more of your world, as well as improving my knowledge of your English language, which I had started learning when Ceridwen first approached me. During the whole time I was watching, I was also feeling the pull of my sister's blood, as I told you. I wasn't sure at first that my sister was your Carla, but I had my suspicions. The seer in Annwn who verified that Alcina had returned also told me something else: that you and I could bring her back from this deep sleep in which she is now trapped. For once, Taliesin, we are on the same side."

My first reaction was disbelief, naturally. After all, Morgan was a master manipulator who would not hesitate to shape the truth into what she needed it to be. Already though, there was a nagging "what if?" growing inside of me.

"To cure her we would need to know more about the spell Ceridwen used to awaken those past-life memories in the first place, and that knowledge died with her," I pointed out.

"You know Ceridwen recruited me for an ally. I was eager enough to join her, but even eager as I was, I did not forget my ability to bargain. I obtained Ceridwen's promise of help to find the soul of Lancelot, but I insisted on more than that, and so eager was Ceridwen to ensure her victory over you that she would have given me almost anything. She was more than willing to teach me her new knowledge of magic, including the studies she went through to perfect the awakening spell."

The horrible part was that Morgan could be telling the truth. At first I had thought her magic on Samhain *was* Ceridwen's magic, because it differed so much from the traditional spell-casting she had performed back in the days of King Arthur. Ceridwen must have given her at least some knowledge. If Morgan had gotten the secret of awakening from her, then perhaps Morgan could help Carla.

"You're bluffing!" scoffed Nurse Florence.

"Shall I demonstrate, then?" Morgan raised her left hand, a familiar, sickly red glare dancing from finger to finger.

"No!" I shouted. "We need no demonstration."

"Tal, she could be fooling us," thought Nurse Florence. *"Don't agree to anything."*

"But, what is she can help Carla?"

"Remember that who she wants to help is Alcina. What if she can reverse the effect of the second blast of the awakening spell? You've told me yourself that a strong past-life memory can take over the present-life body if the will of that past self is strong enough. Can Carla withstand Alcina?"

Since the Alcina persona, if that was really who it was, had taken over immediately on Samhain, probably not. On the other hand, Stan had the same experience after being hit with the awakening spell; he had been taken over by an Israelite warrior. I had helped him recover, and in the end I had reinforced Stan's willpower enough to give him control and force his other selves to join with his present self again.

If I played this right, I could save Carla and prevent Morgan from reviving Alcina! I really could.

A few days ago, the idea of making any kind of deal with Morgan would have been unspeakably repugnant, but circumstances were different now. I think Nurse Florence sensed my wavering, but I ignored her mental protests and focused all my attention on Morgan.

"If you have been watching me, you know I want Carla cured, but I have a hard time trusting you. You pretended to run into me by accident tonight, but if you have been watching me as long as you say, you would have known I would come to visit Carla."

"True enough, Taliesin—but you are rather late tonight, aren't you? I expected you to be already gone when I got here."

And so I would have been normally. Gianni's unexpected arrival slowed me down just a little.

"You also pretended not to know exactly where your sister was at first."

"Until I stood right by her bed and held her hand, I could not be absolutely sure that Carla was truly Alcina. The seer gave me no help on that. Alcina could have been someone else. You know how faint any sign of consciousness is in this girl," Morgan said, pointing at Carla again. "Even the call of blood is weak. I had to be very close to be certain. I wasn't trying to lie to you, Taliesin. Nor was I trying to create this awkwardness here." She nodded in the direction of the helpless Gianni. "I had hoped to have a conversation under better circumstances."

"Prove that to me by letting Gianni go," I said in as commanding a tone as I could muster. "I can't take your protests of good intention very seriously when you threaten a young boy."

Morgan's smile was cold enough to freeze even White Hilt's fire. "You ask far more than you are willing to give, Taliesin. Have your men sheathe their swords, and I will give Gianni to you."

"Do it," I said to the guys.

"Tal!" said Shar in alarm. While he held Zom, he was immune to Morgan's magic, but sheathed, the sword did not protect him.

"Morgan, another *tynged* I think. No one in this room will harm anyone else in this room until I declare the negotiation at an end." Since we outnumbered Morgan seven to one, that agreement was favorable enough that she should be willing to take it, and she did. The guys and Nurse Florence nodded agreement, some of them rather sullenly.

For this *tynged* all of us raised our right hands, and again the golden sparks crackled, this time in an eight-pointed star formation. (Only someone who knew magic could set a *tynged*, but anyone could be bound by it.) Once I was sure the *tynged* had taken hold, I gestured for the guys to sheathe their swords, which they did with a notable show of reluctance. Actually, with the *tynged* preventing them from harming Morgan while our talks continued, they could just as well have kept their weapons out, but Morgan wanted them away, so away they went. I did notice that Shar kept his hand on Zom's pommel so that he remained protected. That didn't violate Morgan's demand, so I let it pass. After all, he was the one she nearly killed before.

Looking around to satisfy herself that there was no sign of treachery, Morgan gently let the sleeping Gianni down on the edge of Carla's bed. Stan and Gordy pulled him over to our side of the room, and Nurse Florence got him situated in the room's only chair. I did a quick brush across his mind to make sure that he was only sleeping and not under some more malicious spell. Then I turned again to Morgan.

"Now, Morgan, short of awakening someone's previous lives, how can you prove that you have the knowledge you claim?"

"Well," replied Morgan slyly, "I can hardly just tell you how the spell works. Then any collection of spell casters with the right amount of power would do the job. You wouldn't need me."

"What do you suggest then?" I asked impatiently.

"Let me raise the power again without casting it at anyone," suggested Morgan. "Taliesin, you have felt this spell yourself. You and the water witch over there have both seen it in operation. Surely you can sense enough from such a display to test the truth of my words."

"It's too risky!" pronounced Nurse Florence immediately. This time she spoke aloud instead of just thinking. I couldn't help but be a little irritated at the obvious attempt to force my hand.

"The *tynged* would stop me from actually aiming it at anyone," said Morgan to me, pointedly ignoring Nurse Florence.

"Raise the power!" I said to Morgan, also ignoring Nurse Florence, whose face betrayed more shock than I had ever seen before. I felt more than a twinge of guilt. After all, Nurse Florence had saved my life more than once. Even more compelling, she had risked her life to save mine. Still, Carla's coma was my fault. If I could find a way to cure it, I was going to take that way.

Again Morgan raised her left hand and engulfed it in the unhealthy red glow. Nurse Florence and I reached our minds out, poking gently at the force. Instinctively, my mind recoiled from it at the first touch. Glancing quickly around, I saw that Stan had reflexively backed away, and even Carla seemed to twitch in her bed, though I might have just imagined a reaction on her part. Still, the power Morgan wielded definitely felt the same as Ceridwen's awakening spell.

Fighting my instinctive aversion to that magic, I sent my mind back into its heart, seeking to understand its nature, visualize its workings. When at last I had satisfied myself that this spell did not just feel the same, but *was* the same, I pulled back out again, and, conscious of how rude I had been to Nurse Florence, I waited for her confirmation of what I already knew. Not having been the victim of the spell, she needed to study it longer, but after a few more minutes, even she had to agree.

"It is the same power," she admitted. "But that only proves that Morgan knows how to cast the spell, not that she knows how to undo it."

"Really?" replied Morgan angrily. "Do you really think I would be foolish enough to accept only part of the information about the spell as payment?"

"Based on what Ceridwen said at the time, her agenda only required being able to cast the spell. She had no need to undo it. Perhaps she never created a way to undo it."

Nurse Florence and Morgan glared at each other. Well, I could hardly expect them to be friends, and I kept telling myself Nurse Florence was right to be cautious, even though my heart cried out to stop talking and start curing Carla.

"My 'agenda' is more diverse than hers," replied Morgan finally, again addressing me exclusively. "I pressed her for a way to reverse the spell, and she taught me one."

"Then why not just use it?" I asked. "What made you think you need me?"

Morgan sighed. "I said there was a way to reverse the spell. I didn't say that it was easy or that I could do it alone. You may recall the spell seems to take very little effort to cast, a rather unusual characteristic for a spell of such power. But power must always be paid for somehow. Ceridwen paid for it by making the process needed to reverse it insanely difficult. Observe!"

The reddish glow on Morgan's hand turned green, and, before I could move a muscle, the greenness whipped out, grabbed onto something within Carla, and pulled. The guys drew their weapons, and Nurse Florence raised her hands as if to use magic.

"I'm not hurting her!" Morgan snapped. "I said observe! What do your senses tell you?"

I don't know how much the guys could see, but I could see clearly that the green whip had latched onto a tendril of redness from within Carla and was pulling on it steadily, but with absolutely no effect. Again I sent forth my mind into the force Morgan was using. I tasted its nature, and I knew immediately that it was the opposite of the power in the awakening spell. I studied its workings even more diligently than I had probed the workings of the first spell.

After a few minutes Morgan extinguished the green glow. She looked visibly more drained than she had just a few minutes before that. "As you can see," she said tiredly, "there is a way to pull the second dose of that spell out of her and restore her to consciousness, but I cannot do it by myself."

"How about removing both castings and returning her to normal?" asked Stan. I was surprised at first, but then I realized where he was going with the question. I thought I had patched him up pretty well after his awakening, but clearly there was something about his own earlier lives he wanted to be rid of. I don't know how I missed it earlier. I could see it clearly enough in his eyes now.

In sharp contrast to the way in which Morgan reacted to Nurse Florence's questions, she smiled indulgently at Stan's. "Removing the second casting, difficult as it is, is easier than removing both. The second does not...what is the word? 'Stick' I think...yes, stick quite as hard; it doesn't dig into the soul in quite the same way. Two or three strong casters would probably be enough to remove the second. Removing both would require all the rulers of Annwn to work together, which they haven't done for more than a thousand years, or you would need a smaller number of casters of such great power that their like has never been seen among men, nor even among faeries."

"And we are just supposed to trust you that this is so?" asked

Nurse Florence in her most abrasive tone.

"Once we are all bound by an appropriate *tynged* so that you cannot simply cut me out after I share my knowledge of the spell, you can test it for yourself." Again, Morgan answered Nurse Florence's question, but she directed the answer to me alone.

"*Tynged* or not, you and Tal have fundamentally different goals. You both want Carla out of her coma, but Tal wants the original Carla back at the end, and you want Alcina."

Mentally, I tried to silence Nurse Florence, but she ignored me. I had hoped to play dumb on this point and reinforce the strength of Carla's persona without Morgan realizing what was happening until it was too late. Morgan might know the spell, but I knew how to deal with its aftermath. Now, with the conversation out in the open, I could easily lose the element of surprise. It was a good thing that wasn't the only idea I had in mind...

"Sneer at me as much as you want, Morgan," continued Nurse Florence. "There is no way around that problem, and I suspect you know that perfectly well."

"Taliesin, remember I have been watching you," said Morgan, not that I really needed or wanted to be reminded of that. "I know perfectly well what you want, and I certainly know what I want. I believe it is possible to separate Carla from Alcina and to transfer the essence of Alcina into another vessel. We can both have what we want."

By now Nurse Florence was sputtering with indignation. "You can't be serious. No one can split Carla from Alcina, if they both really are in that body. They are different manifestations of the same soul. Are you claiming to be able to split a soul, Morgan? And even if you could, what would be the consequences? Would they both exist as maimed remnants, each conscious of her incompleteness, yet never able to reach completeness? And by *vessel* I assume you mean *body*. Where do you think you can get one of those? Who will you have to murder to do it?"

Morgan remained silent, but if looks could kill, Nurse Florence would certainly be lying dead on the floor. Finally, Morgan turned back to me. "I would not propose something which I was not confident I could do. It will not be simple or easy. It may take months, perhaps even years, but at the end of the process, you will be reunited with Carla, and I will be reunited with my sister. Consider well what I have said. We will meet again...under more suitable circumstances."

By now I was well enough trained to feel the mystical energy building in the room and knew that Morgan was getting ready to slip into Annwn. Nurse Florence knew it too.

"Tal, declare the negotiations ended now, before she leaves, and we might capture her! She's too dangerous to be allowed to roam around at will!" thought Nurse Florence with almost headache-producing intensity.

Yeah, no question there—it was dangerous to let Morgan roam around. If I declared negotiations at an end, the *tynged* would be released, and Morgan would have to face all seven of us; she wasn't likely to allow such good odds in the future if she could help it. Unfortunately, there was one big problem with attacking her now.

"Carla is between her and us. I can't just turn Carla's hospital room into a battlefield!" Nurse Florence nodded. She might not like giving up such a good chance to stop Morgan, but she knew that I was right.

Morgan smiled with something—triumph, maybe—pointed to her left, and then faded into the swirling mists of Annwn. The portal closed with an almost audible thud as soon as she was through it. Glancing to where she pointed, in the far corner of the room, I saw the gleam of White Hilt. She had left it behind, perhaps as a show of good will to convince me that she was sincere, since she could just as easily have taken it with her.

"We can still follow if we hurry…" began Nurse Florence.

"Remember the trouble we ran into on the way over," prompted Dan.

Suddenly, I recalled again the bloodstains on their clothes. In the light of the hospital room, they looked far worse than they had outside. "Morgan has obviously recruited some allies." Dan continued. Who knows what we might run into on the other side?"

"Besides, we need her cooperation if we are to have any chance of reviving Carla," I said as calmly as I could.

Nurse Florence looked at me as if I had just shot her through the heart. "Tal, you can't be seriously thinking of bargaining with her!"

"I have never been more serious in my life. Morgan is the only living person who understands the spell well enough to help us undo it. I have to make a deal with her."

Nurse Florence was speechless, as were most of the others. Stan looked ready to cry, though whether from shock or from relief that maybe his problem would be solved I couldn't tell. Dan looked totally blank.

Shar and Carlos both looked outraged. Gordy, who had in some ways the most expressive face of any of them, looked like a little kid who had just been told that there is no Santa Claus.

"Tal," he said in obvious disbelief, "what the hell?"

CHAPTER 4: TWO CAN PLAY AT THAT GAME

"Tal, you can't possibly mean you want to work with Morgan!" Nurse Florence had retreated behind her professional, detached face, but she was clearly upset, almost more upset than I had ever seen her.

"I love Carla," I replied simply. "I love her so much it hurts. And I can't stand seeing her this way anymore—especially since it is my fault she's here. So yes, I will work with Morgan. I will work with Satan himself, if that's what it takes."

"Pretty much the same thing," muttered Dan.

"Tal, she tried to kill me before!" Shar nearly shouted at me. "How can you forget that so quickly?"

"Yeah!" seconded Gordy. "I bet she would kill any of us—even Carla—to get whatever the hell she wants."

"How do the rest of you feel? Carlos? Stan?"

"Tal, she was just holding a knife to Gianni's throat," replied Carlos. "That tells me all I need to know. No, you can't work with her."

Stan's response was a little more nuanced. "Well," he began weakly, not at all like his recent self-confident manner, "I think Tal needs to at least figure out how much of what she said is actually true. It can't hurt for him to talk to Morgan again."

No, I hadn't been mistaken earlier. Stan had his own reasons for exploring how to reverse the awakening spell. I would have to figure out what those reasons were—later. Right now I had more urgent concerns. I let the guys and Nurse Florence argue with me for a while, scarcely listening to them anymore. Then, at what I hoped was the right moment, I sent a quick message to Nurse Florence: *"Morgan has Gianni 'wired' and is listening in. Can you disconnect him and make it feel to her as if the connection faded naturally?"* Nurse Florence nodded silently and moved quickly to Gianni. While she worked the guys continued to pound me verbally. Fortunately, it was not too long before Nurse Florence gave me a thumbs up.

"I'm going to set a little barrier to make sure she can't listen in by any other means." It was relatively easy to set up a kind of psychic "white noise" to keep anyone from seeing or hearing us from a distance, at least not without making us very aware of it. In my weakened condition, the spell gave me a headache, but I knew Nurse Florence was pretty drained as well, and she had just had to perform very precise magic to free Gianni of Morgan's surveillance.

"OK, now we can relax. Morgan can't hear us anymore."

"That conversation was for Morgan's benefit?" asked Stan.

"It was indeed. Morgan isn't the only one who can psych out an opponent."

"Morgan could hear us?" asked Gordy suspiciously, looking around the room as if he expected to see Morgan looking down at us from the ceiling.

"Yup. She was hearing us through Gianni, but Nurse Florence has broken that connection. Morgan may be suspicious, but she won't entirely discount the conversation she just heard. At the very least, she will contact me again, I'm guessing at some point when the rest of you aren't around, and I'll find out what I can about her intentions."

"That's clever," said Stan, who still clearly had something else on his mind. "But she's never going to tell you how to counter the awakening spell without binding you with a *tynged* that requires you to help her."

I shrugged. "Well, I won't need her help with the spell after all." I could have just explained, but, perhaps because of how worn-out I was, I couldn't resist being a little theatrical. I raised my left hand and made it glow with sickly red energy.

Nurse Florence's calm professionalism came close to cracking completely at that. "Tal, that kind of magic can corrupt the user. Stop at once!" I did, expecting another tongue-lashing, but when I looked somewhat sheepishly in Nurse Florence's direction, she was staring at me with wonder.

"It was amazing enough that you adapted your magic to work with technology, and you did it in just a few days before Samhain. But learning a spell that complex, just by seeing it once? That should be impossible. How did you do it?" she asked.

"Two spells, actually," I said, trying not to sound as if I was bragging—which I totally was. "Naturally I can do the reversal spell too. As for explaining how I learned them, well, I just…entered each spell, the way druids have entered the forces of nature for millenniums, the way you enter the body of someone you want to heal, the way I can enter a piece of technology. If I can adjust my mind enough to become one with a spell, I can *feel* the magic rather than just seeing; I can feel how it would be to cast it."

"I understand in theory," Nurse Florence replied slowly, "but to do it so fast? Sorcerers spend months, even years learning their magic."

I shrugged again. "When Gwion Bach accidentally drank the potion from the cauldron of knowledge, he learned a great deal of complex magic almost instantly. That potion must have changed him on a very deep level. Then, as you'll recall, the witch Ceridwen managed to swallow him during a shape-shifting contest, and he ended up being reborn as the original Taliesin, another fundamental change. You know I have the skills of all my previous lives. I must also have whatever fundamental change in nature happened to Gwion Bach and to the original Taliesin—who, by the way, did have some training, but more as a way of concealing the true extent of his 'difference' and throwing off his enemies than as a way of actually learning his magic, which he knew he could learn much more quickly."

"How long have you known? Did you get the idea from Taliesin's memories?" Nurse Florence knew we had other pressing matters to attend to, but she let her thirst for knowledge get the better of her anyway.

"I got a suspicion from Taliesin's memories, but as far as I can remember, he never actually tried to learn a spell the way I just did. Of course, for most of the time he was at Camelot, Merlin typically took care of any casting that needed to be done, so there wasn't as much pressure on Taliesin as there has been on me."

Nurse Florence was clearly still amazed, but she quickly switched back into professional mode and threw me off balance. "It's a good thing you insulated the room against eavesdropping. Tal, there are already some pretty powerful people in Annwn who are nervous about you. If anyone outside of our group realized that you could learn new spells just by having them cast in your presence, it would make your critics even more nervous."

"Critics? I solved a big problem for them when I stopped Ceridwen. Why should I have any critics in the first place?"

Suddenly, Nurse Florence was all about getting back on schedule. "That's an important conversation…for another time. I have kept us from being noticed by the hospital staff only with great difficulty. I'm tired, I can feel the spells thinning, and you and the guys need to get back home soon…to say nothing of Gianni." She looked critically around the room. "They need cleaning up first, and Stan's ripped out of his shirt again."

Stan had been trying to wear more loose-fitting clothing for those occasions when he wielded his sword and increased his muscle mass, but occasionally he forgot, as with tonight's shirt, which was hanging down his chest in shreds.

In the old days, when we had been trying to conceal the connections among us from Ceridwen, Nurse Florence had to buy the guys replacement clothing, and we had just tossed the bloody stuff, but now that pretty much any spell caster or other supernatural being around knew who my warriors were, Nurse Florence no longer bothered to minimize the magical residue on them. Instead, she used a spell to draw the blood from their clothing. She couldn't knit synthetic fabrics back together, but I had learned how to do that (with a lot of help from Stan, who could always visualize the underlying science better than I), so I took care of that kind of repair work, and in just a few minutes, everyone was looking more or less normal.

After that it was a simple matter to re-sheathe White Hilt; pick up Gianni, still sound asleep; get out of the hospital; remove all of the don't-notice-me" kind of magic; and arrange transportation.

"It probably isn't safe to go through Annwn to get back to Santa Brígida," I observed, then realized I was probably just stating the excruciatingly obvious. "The Prius only seats four."

Nurse Florence already had her cell phone out. "I could get home by water, but that might be...disconcerting for any passengers, so I'll call a cab for Shar, Gordy, Carlos, and me. You take Stan, Dan, and Gianni." I must have looked worried, because she added, "First, though, I'll call Vanora, and she'll make some security arrangements, both magical and otherwise, for the hospital. Morgan is not getting in again, no matter what."

"Thanks," I said, trying to make sure my sincere gratitude showed, despite my fatigue. "You always handle the logistics so well."

I checked my phone and realized I had three missed calls from Mrs. Rinaldi, so I called back to reassure her that Gianni was indeed on the way. Then I hit the lock button on my Prius remote to see which car in the parking lot beeped—from a distance one gunmetal Prius looked pretty much like another, and in case you haven't noticed, there are a lot of them around these days. Having finally found mine, I got my passengers loaded and took off as fast as I safely could. (I didn't particularly want the supreme irony of having us all survive a potentially fatal encounter with Morgan Le Fay, only to get us all killed on the freeway.)

Fortunately, we made the short trip home without incident. I dropped off Gianni first, got my obligatory hug from Mrs. Rinaldi, which

Stan and Dan both kidded me about, excused myself from staying for what was now a very late dinner, dropped off Dan, and then headed for Stan's place, which was only about three doors from mine.

"Tal, can I ask you something?" Stan asked.

I had a weird moment of déjà vu. Those were exactly the words Stan used before he knew about my unusual "situation," when he first asked me about some of the discrepancies in my life. I shook the feeling off. That time I had been caught by surprise. This time I knew exactly what Stan was going to ask. He was going to start a conversation about why he wanted his awakening spell reversed—at least, that's what I hoped he was going to ask about.

"Ask away," I replied. I didn't really want to start what could be a complicated conversation after the day I had just been through, but if something was bugging Stan, I definitely wanted to know about it.

"Tal, I…what the heck?" He sounded so alarmed that I braked and then glanced in his direction.

The shirt that I had mended was hanging in tatters again.

We were only about two minutes from his house at this point, and there was always the possibility that someone could already have seen us, so I didn't want to spend longer mending the shirt again than I had to.

"Sorry, Stan. I must be more tired than I thought. I'll fix you right up again…unless you want to tell your mom one of your lady friends tried to rip it off of you."

Stan looked surprisingly worried, and his cheeks reddened. "Tal, she'd ground me until I'm fifty-five. I can't…"

"Relax, dude," I said with a chuckle. "I was just kidding! Here, let me fix that for you." I leaned over, humming a little bit to heighten the spell, and pulled the surprisingly stubborn threads back again.

"You need to start wearing more cotton, Stan. These synthetics are giving me more of a headache than usual."

We both breathed a sigh of relief when the job was finally done. "I'm sorry that took so long. I guess I really am tired."

"I guess you're rusty. What's it been, a month since you saved the world? You need to work out more, I guess," replied Stan with a grin.

I chuckled again, but more so Stan wouldn't worry than because I really thought the situation was funny. I had thought—hell, we had all thought—that defeating Ceridwen meant we wouldn't have to constantly watch our backs. We knew Morgan had survived on Samhain, but with Ceridwen gone, we assumed that she would have no further reason to hang out in Santa Brígida. Now we knew she had been here the whole time, spying on me and looking for her long-lost sister. At the very least, now we all had to be extremely careful. Hopefully, Morgan now believed that I was going to cooperate with her, but one careless word from any of us could reveal the truth—with bloody consequences.

I let Stan off, drove to my house, got the car in the garage, and had a very late dinner with my parents. Visiting Carla was still a built-in excuse. Neither one of them ever questioned me, pretty much no matter when I came in. I could tell that Mom in particular still worried about me, but I had gotten to be a very good actor in a very short time, and both of them were convinced I would get over my grief eventually.

I had to admit that this particular night the acting was more of a chore than usual, both because I was worried about Morgan and because I suddenly had at least a glimmer of hope that I might finally be able to bring Carla out of her coma. I would have loved to share that news with them, but I would have been hard-pressed to explain, since they knew nothing about my…unusual nature.

At some point in the last your years, I probably should have told them, but after I finally got out of the hospital after my "unexplained breakdown" (for which read, "the awakening of the memories of all my previous lives,") I had a hard enough time convincing them that I was normal again, without trying to convince them I was normal despite believing I was a reincarnation of the original Taliesin. "Yeah, Dad, I can do magic, but I'm not crazy…really, I'm not." Doesn't sound like the world's best strategy, does it?

I don't want you thinking either one of them was stupid. Actually, they were both pretty sharp. What can I say? A little strategically planned sleep here, a little memory erasure there, a bit of illusion somewhere else, and I could keep them from noticing anything unusual. I didn't like doing that kind of thing, but in the last four years that pattern had become so automatic I didn't really think about it most of the time; I did it almost reflexively.

In my defense I couldn't tell them when they were worried about my sanity, and I had since gotten the hint (from the rulers of Annwn, delivered through Nurse Florence) that I must not tell anybody else about myself. In other words, I couldn't really tell them now, even if I wanted to. For better or worse, I had to settle for a well-crafted lie that at least kept them happy and out of harm's way—I hoped. I couldn't restrain a slight shudder, thinking about how much danger they would be in if Morgan figured out I was trying to play her.

"Tal, are you cold?" asked Mom in a concerned tone. "You're shivering."

"No, I'm fine, Mom," I said, making a mental note to be extra careful for a while. Maybe it was just maternal instinct, but she really did have an uncanny way of sensing when something was wrong. She had seemed to sense danger if I went to Carrie Winn's Halloween party, where I could very well have died, and now…"

I looked at her casually, trying to conceal the fact that I was studying her. She definitely looked better rested than she had in the bad old days of October, and really most of the past four years. She almost looked younger. Her brown hair was still liberally sprinkled with gray, but the absence of the perpetually worried expression helped smooth out some of those wrinkles, and she definitely looked less saggy. However, her blue eyes still betrayed a slight concern as she looked back at me across the table.

I tried to avoid reading people's minds unless in cases of emergency, and I did not break that rule this time, but there was something different about Mom, something I couldn't quite figure out. Then the truth hit me, and I jumped slightly despite myself.

I could feel psychic energy coming from her.

Oh, don't get me wrong; it wasn't much, a mere whisper compared to the shout that my power could create. Still, it was more than the average person would broadcast, and it could pose problems later because it would make her at least marginally more resistant to my mental manipulations.

"Tal, you look as if you've seen a ghost!" said Mom, reacting to my sudden movement.

"No, I just remembered I still have reading to do for English. I'd better get to it. May I be excused?"

Mom was clearly still worried, but Dad intervened at that point. "Sure! Get the homework done. You've had too many late nights recently as it is." Then he shot Mom a leave-the-boy-alone; you're-worrying-about-nothing expression. She nodded vaguely at both of us, suddenly preoccupied. Dad winked at me and smiled. He didn't look as obviously younger as Mom, but he too was clearly better rested. I would have to keep it that way.

I got upstairs quickly and closed the door quietly but firmly. Then, instead of doing English homework, which I had actually squeezed in earlier, right before soccer practice, I planned. Nurse Florence and I had our work cut out for us. We needed protective spells for ourselves, our families, hell, maybe the whole town. I had no illusions about really being able to do a protective spell that covered that wide an area, but it was worth thinking about who or what Morgan might lash out at when she discovered she had been tricked.

After a while, though, I realized I was just covering the same ground over and over again. I undressed and slipped into bed, turned the lights out, and fell asleep puzzling over Stan's shirt. Yeah, I had been tired when I mended it, but still, I had never had one of my spells deteriorate like that before. It did not occur to me until much later to wonder whether the spell I had cast in the hospital room to keep anyone from eavesdropping might have reacted in the same way…

That night I had an unusually vivid dream in which I was naked with Carla in her hospital bed. Yeah, it was one of *those* dreams, so I will spare you the details. In the beginning I was just holding her anyway; she was every bit as comatose as she was in real life. Later, though, she was conscious and extremely eager to take our "relationship," or whatever it was in real life, to the next level. Hell, to take it up several levels.

I knew it was only dream sex, but it felt more real somehow than any of the intimacies I could remember from my previous lives. To say my whole body was on fire sounds trite, but that's the closest I could come to it. We were both on fire, burning as one flame, giving ourselves to each other unreservedly.

Then I realized that the woman in my arms, despite making love to me as if we had both been created for the purpose of making love with each other, was not Carla. She looked like her superficially, but when I looked into her eyes, someone else was looking back.

Alcina.

I woke up hoping I hadn't screamed aloud, because I think I did scream in the dream. I listened, but I didn't hear anything like my parents jumping out of bed to see what was wrong. I looked over at the clock. It was three in the morning, but I knew I wasn't getting any more sleep. I would have liked a shower (yeah, a nice cold one!), but I knew that would wake my parents up. I would have liked to play a little music; I hadn't had much time to practice the harp recently, and playing always relaxed me, but again I could hardly avoid waking up my parents in such a situation, so I steeled myself to wait for morning.

I did get up once to study myself in my bathroom mirror. (You've done it yourself, so don't smirk.) I knew the timing was a little odd, but I was having a hard time getting Alcina out of my mind. Even though that encounter had only been in a dream, it did get me to thinking. Ceridwen had tried to lure me to bed. Carla, though the memory hurt now like trying to crawl through barbed wire, had very much wanted to bed me. Morgan had just tried to lure me to bed. Granted, that last one was probably strategy, though Morgan had complimented my looks when she met me for the first time (in this life) in Annwn on Founders' Day. And Ceridwen's attempted seduction really didn't have anything to do with her overall strategy; if anything, her attempt ended up undermining her whole plan. It got me to ask the question that most popular guys ask at some point: was I really that hot? (Of course, most guys don't have to contend with interest from supernatural beings who have murderous intentions, but I was trying hard not to think about that aspect of my situation.)

I couldn't see anything special about my face. I guessed I had a good smile, but even so it was quite the heart melter Dan's was. My brown hair was pretty much run-of-the-mill it seemed to me, but I did try to keep it decently groomed, which was more than I could say for a lot of the guys at school. As for my body, well, I flexed a little bit and studied myself from different angles. I wasn't as powerfully built as Dan or Gordy, and certainly not as Shar, though I had been working out a lot and had pretty good definition, certainly better even than two months ago. However, girls seemed to like tans, and my skin was pretty pale compared to, well…pretty much any of my friends except Stan. I had always had two settings: pale and burned. I guessed it was the Celtic ancestry. I just never tanned. Dan and Gordy both had nice tans, and Carlos and Shar were both naturally darker. I wasn't insecure enough to think I was ugly, but, at least as far as looks were concerned, it didn't seem to me that I stood out that much.

And yet there was something going on. When I started emerging from my loner phase in late summer and early fall, I had certainly generated interest, even from high-status females like cheerleaders. At first I had deflected that interest because I still secretly loved Eva. (She was my child-hood sweetheart, but now she was Dan's girlfriend—you can see why I was keeping those feelings pretty much to myself!) More recently, every-one understood that I was devoted to Carla, and I didn't even need to deflect. Nonetheless, I didn't have to read minds to know that interest still existed. Don't get me wrong; I had no intention of moving on, no matter what happened to our efforts to revive Carla from her coma, but I wouldn't have been human, and I certainly wouldn't have been a guy, if I hadn't been a little pleased that girls found me desirable. Some day I would take the time to relish that feeling.

Yeah, some day, when I didn't have to worry about Carla's body being seized by Alcina, when I didn't have to worry about Morgan mur-dering my parents in their beds because I had double-crossed her, when I didn't have to worry about some other supernatural menace popping up. The last one was perhaps the hardest one to deal with. We might well beat Morgan, but what was to prevent someone else from coming along and making trouble later? Nothing really. Once word got out that Santa Brígida had a powerful caster just waiting to be awakened, Morgan would not be the only one to see some advantage in awakening that caster.

The only way Carla was ever going to be safe was if I could bring her into the same state of balance I had achieved—with her present self in charge, but with access to all of her previous skills and knowledge. Once Carla became the kind of spell caster Alcina evidently had been, she and I together could certainly deter attacks. Until she reached that point, not so much, but if I could get her out of the coma, I had every confidence I could give her that balance. After all, I had succeeded with Stan, hadn't I?

Well, except that something about his situation was clearly both-ering Stan. I sighed and put talking to him on my mental to-do list. If his situation was not as good as I thought, then I needed to know what the problem was, and soon—both for his sake and for Carla's.

CHAPTER 5: "THEY COME NOT SINGLE SPIES"

I was up slightly before dawn, but I often got up pretty early, so my parents wouldn't be particularly alarmed. I showered, dressed, and had the house under a protective spell, all in record time. Someone like Morgan could probably break through the protection if she really put her mind to it, but at least not without my knowing about it, and the high school was only a few blocks away if trouble started during the day.

After finishing my magic, I put on my happy face and did convincing small talk for Mom and Dad over breakfast. Having gotten at least a little sleep last night, I had no difficulty selling my "everything is fine" image. Mom seemed a little fidgety, though, and was still putting out weak but discernible psychic energy. That was a good reminder to talk to Nurse Florence when I got the chance. I was sure there was some logical explanation for Mom's sudden development of powers, but I would worry until I discovered what the explanation was.

"Is there something…different…about the house?" said Mom, looking directly at me. Logically, I would have expected her to look first to my dad. So did he, apparently, since he answered.

"Nothing I can see, hon. What do you think is different?"

Mom suddenly looked embarrassed. "Well, I don't know really. It just *feels* different."

Oh, no! She can feel the protection spell!

At the power level on which she was functioning, she probably shouldn't be able to feel something environmental like that unless she was actively looking for it. However, at the risk of stating the obvious, magic was not always an exact science.

"I read somewhere that our subconscious is always picking up on little details we aren't consciously aware of, Mom. Who knows what's giving you that feeling? There's nothing to worry about, I'm sure." I put a little magic into the last sentence, just enough I hoped to dull whatever worry was picking away at her, and she seemed to relax, though I sensed she was not entirely convinced.

I excused myself quickly, grabbed my backpack, walked over to Stan's house and then walked the rest of the way to school with him. (Yeah, I could have driven, but school was really close, so I usually just walked, and then stopped by after soccer to pick up the car for the drive to Carla's hospital.)

I automatically checked to make sure Stan was armed. Sure enough, he had remembered his sword, just as I had remembered White Hilt. Naturally, the swords were invisible to others, courtesy of a spell by Nurse Florence. Later I had added a twist that made them invisible to security cameras as well. In a pinch I could even make them go unnoticed by metal detectors, but our school didn't have metal detectors, so I only added that extra touch when needed. Ironically, the very concealments that made our swords less visible to ordinary people made them more conspicuous to spell casters, but that couldn't be helped, and anyway, the swords were quite visible enough on their own to those who knew how to look for them.

I probably shouldn't have worried about an attack this morning. Surely Morgan wouldn't attack without further negotiations. Still, there was something about walking down my artificially lush, pretentiously built and outrageously under-priced street that still gave me the creeps. Now that I knew that Ceridwen had developed the whole town of Santa Brígida for the sole purpose of luring my parents to settle here so that she could more easily launch her plot against me when the time came, the place seemed less like home and more like an elaborate trap where danger lurked in every shadow.

Yeah, I knew how paranoid that sounded, and Ceridwen was dead anyway, but I still couldn't make myself comfortable. I would have moved if I had the choice, but my parents really were happy here; I would have to hit them with pretty major magic to get them to move, and using that kind of force would risk injuring their minds. My being uncomfortable certainly didn't justify that kind of risk. Besides, I wanted to stay close to my warriors now, and I couldn't very well get all of them to move. The new, complicated situation with Morgan made me glad that I had people on whom I could depend.

Speaking of which, at that point I remembered I needed to talk to Stan about whatever was bothering him. I tried asking, but his response confused me. He looked around as if he expected someone else to be listening. That would make sense if we were talking about Carla's situation, which I had no intention of doing in an unprotected place, but I couldn't imagine what he could possibly have to say that would be of interest to Morgan or any other potential threat.

"Tal, there isn't time, really, and anyway, I don't want to risk someone else hearing. Let's wait until later."

He looked so worried, so haunted really, that I wanted to press him, an impulse strengthened by the fact that later would be a lot later, since after school I had soccer practice, and Stan had wrestling practice. Still, I decided I had better let him tell me in his own way, so I reconciled myself to waiting until evening, or at least until after practice.

We arrived at school without incident. The fact that I thought that reminded me of how on edge, how tense I was. I had been caught by surprise so often recently that I couldn't help but keep myself ready for potential combat at all times. Still, being in that state constantly could be pretty wearing, as I was reminded throughout the whole school day.

The day seemed to drag unmercifully. I was not usually a clock watcher, but how I watched those hands that day! (Santa Brígida High School was a fairly new facility and could have used digital clocks, but someone evidently thought a more traditional clock would look more at home in the school's overly ornate Spanish Colonial architecture facade.) Each tick was one step closer to finding out what was bugging Stan, seeing Carla again, putting an end to the Morgan threat once and for all.

Lunch finally came and…nothing. Stan and I practically always had lunch together, and I had been certain he would try to pull me aside for a talk, but he didn't show up at all. I tried his cell number, but the call went straight to voice mail.

"Everything OK, Tal?" asked Dan.

"Yeah. I just expected to see Stan."

Gordy, who very much appreciated Stan's tutoring, was instantly on high alert. "You don't think anything is wrong, do you?" The others snickered a little at Gordy's over-protectiveness.

"The only thing wrong here," said Shar with mock seriousness, "is that this cafeteria never serves Persian food."

"They might if we had more than one Persian student," quipped Carlos. "But if it makes you feel any better, the rumor that they serve Mexican food is greatly exaggerated." They both laughed at their overly bland enchiladas.

"No, seriously," persisted Gordy. "Tal, are you sure everything is OK?" His concern was oddly contagious.

"Let me check. I'll just connect with him and make sure." We could be fairly open in our conversation when we had lunch together be-cause we usually ate at a small table in the corner, and the guys' girlfriends understood that this was "guy" time. Eva, Dan's girlfriend, knew about our… situation, but the others did not, and we needed to keep it that way.

I reached out for Stan's mind and quickly discovered two things: he was very agitated, and he was in Nurse Florence's office. If he was that troubled, why didn't he come to me?

"It's probably nothing, but he's with Nurse Florence. I'll go see what's going on," I said as I pushed my chair back and stood, my appetite fading away.

"I'll come with you," said Gordy eagerly, but I waved him off.

"I can handle whatever this is, Gordy, and if I can't, I'll give you a holler, OK?"

Gordy was clearly not happy, and he seemed about to argue, but, seeing the determined look in my eyes, he sat down reluctantly. If Stan was reluctant to talk to me as it was, bringing Gordy along would only complicate the situation. Not only that, but if I let Gordy tag along, the others might have started to worry, and I would have ended up with all of them following me to Nurse Florence's office.

I could feel Gordy's eyes on me the whole way to the cafeteria exit on the other side of the room. I felt like going back and telling him Stan already had one mother and didn't need another one, but I reminded myself that he did mean well…and I sort of had myself to blame for his over-protectiveness. After all, it was I who had recruited him in the first place, basically as a body guard for Stan before Stan had his own magic sword and considerably more combat training than he had started with. Technically, Gordy no longer had the specific function of protecting Stan, but he had taken the job so seriously he was having a hard time letting go of it.

"Hey!" I heard Shar yell, just as I was about to leave the cafeteria. Turning quickly, I saw Shar on his feet, pointing and yelling, "He stole my…wallet!" The other guys were on their feet as well. I could see the thief, by good chance running straight for the exit I was standing in front of, an odd choice given that the other exit had been much closer to him. Well, his poor strategy would make catching him easy…

Except that the thief was carrying, not Shar's wallet, but Zom, Shar's sword, glinting an unmistakable emerald green.

I had planned on hitting him with a little magic to slow him down, but as long as he carried Zom, he would be immune to anything I could do. Worse, I would be no match for him unarmed, and drawing White Hilt against him would make it visible to everyone. They would see it as a fencing foil rather than the flaming sword it actually was, but it would still be hard to explain its sudden appearance. Come to think of it, the students in the packed cafeteria were reacting with such surprise that they clearly were already seeing Zom, hopefully as a fencing foil rather than the glowing blade it actually was, but the thief was running fast enough to make even a fencing foil in his hand seem threatening.

With everyone's attention focused on the runner, I drew White Hilt, which flamed at once, though its fire would not be useful to me against someone wielding Zom. I realized that might be just as well as I took the fraction of a second left before he reached me to actually look at him.

It was then I realized he was just a kid, barely twelve at most, but more likely eleven. Either that, or he was the shortest, most baby-faced high school student I had ever seen. Even Stan, before he had his last growth spurt, had looked older than this guy. Hell, even Gianni looked older than he looked. He was black haired, relatively dark-skinned and seemed to be an Arab, though he could also have been a Persian, like Shar. He was at least a foot shorter than I was, maybe more, and his clothes seemed to be far too big for him, suggesting perhaps that his wardrobe was improvised at the last minute, perhaps stolen.

I could tell by the awkward way he held the sword that he had never had decent combat training, suggesting he probably wasn't stealing the sword to use, but to sell, and also suggesting I could probably defeat him easily…if I could find a way of having a discreet sword fight in front of most of the student body.

There was one more factor I needed to take into consideration, besides the number of gawkers: in order to steal Zom, the kid would have to have been able to see it, suggesting that there was something supernatural about him. While he was holding Zom, I couldn't scan him to assess what his abilities might be, but I knew I needed to be a little wary of him. Just because he didn't have combat training didn't mean he couldn't perform magical mischief.

The kid looked at me with surprise when he realized that I was barring his way and that I also had a sword. His body language suggested he might try to run back the way he had come, but the guys were only seconds behind him, and Coach Miller, the teacher who had drawn lunch duty today (lucky him!) was not far behind them. That was a stroke of luck, because Coach Miller was, aside from Nurse Florence, the only staff member who knew my secret. He could help us explain this weirdness to the other students.

The guys had all drawn their swords. Our little thief could see he was outnumbered and "out-gunned." What could he possibly do except surrender?

Well, what he actually did was turn quickly and run very fast—at least faerie fast—to his left, away from any possible exit, unless he planned on trying to double back to the exit clear on the other side of the room. If that was his plan, he was never going to make it, fast or not. Shar and the other guys had plenty of friends—big friends—who were not at all happy about one of their buddies getting robbed. They had been too surprised to move at first, but they were in motion now, and there more than enough of them to corner the thief.

My one worry now was that the thief would try to use the sword, which most students would not realize was as dangerous as it was—that fencing-foil illusion did have its drawbacks. Dan, Shar, Gordy and Carlos, probably thinking the same thing, raced after him in an attempt to get between him and the other students.

The thief was clearly panicked but still determined not to be caught. He had noticed that the cafeteria wall was mostly windows, and in one swift motion he raised Zom and crashed it straight into one of the large panes. Fortunately, the glass was shatter-proof, but the sword stroke was more than enough to make it crumble. The thief jumped through the opening and was running toward the fence bordering the campus almost before I realized what had happened. Outside the overcrowded cafeteria, his speed was even more apparent.

Realizing that he would reach the fence in seconds, I headed out the door, bursting into song as soon as I was outside. I might not naturally be as swift as our thief, but a little magic could make me faster. In seconds I could feel myself accelerating. Unfortunately, people close enough to the cafeteria windows would be able to see both the thief's breathtakingly fast escape and my pursuit, but I would have to worry about that later. Losing Zom was not an option!

"Coach! Keep anyone but the guys from following! Keep everybody else in the cafeteria!" I had never tried mental communication with Coach Miller before, but I had no time to wait and see if the message had registered.

Now that I was moving more rapidly, my much longer legs would give me an advantage over the thief—or so I thought. Of course, I had expected he would have to climb the fence, and that was where I planned to catch him. Imagine my surprise when he jumped over the fence! Wow! I sure hoped nobody saw that maneuver.

Clearly, he was no ordinary kid, and I was just beginning to think I wouldn't be able to catch him when I noticed how awkwardly he landed. Probably having to hang onto the sword threw him off balance, but it looked as if he had twisted his left ankle when he hit. Not only that, but he seemed to be bleeding just a little; probably he nicked himself with Zom sometime during his mad dash or jump. In a pinch the blood would be useful for tracking him, though I hoped I could just catch him now and make tracking unnecessary.

I was at the fence now. I could have used air currents to float myself over it, but that was slow. I could have flown over it, which was much faster, but both approaches were pretty conspicuous if anyone was watching. Besides, though the battle on Samhain had demonstrated the advantages of being able to fly, I hadn't practiced flying as much as I should have. With my luck, I'd fly a little too high and get myself tangled, maybe even fried, in the nearby power lines. I could have climbed the fence pretty quickly too, but the thief was already on the move again, despite the obvious pain in his ankle. He was really only hobbling, but it was the fastest hobble I had ever seen, faster than some guys' running pace. No, climbing would be too slow; I had to do something that ran a much higher risk of giving some passerby an eyeful, though it would at least be easier to explain than flying. Instead of climbing, I took White Hilt and sliced right through the fence in one quick stroke; mere chain link never stood a chance against that kind of blade.

I could always repair the fence later, but it was hard to even describe how big a disaster losing Zom would be. Anyway, now the guys had an easy way to follow us.

The kid was still hobbling away at an incredible pace. I recaptured my speed and raced after him, closing the gap with every long stride. No one was going to steal Zom on my watch!

Unfortunately, the thief could hear my running steps and knew that I was getting closer. Abruptly he flickered, then vanished.

Why can't anything ever be easy?

I hadn't felt any big build-up of magical energy, so at least he hadn't jumped into Annwn. He must have become invisible. I kept running in his general direction and squinted, trying to see through his invisibility spell. Normally people like me could see through that kind of spell with a little effort, but this time I saw nothing. Probably Zom's protection against hostile magic was preventing me from piercing his invisibility.

Well, he might be invisible, but he seemed young enough to make mistakes, like maybe forgetting to make himself inaudible.

In this life I have never really gotten comfortable with shape-shifting, but from time to time I did make little adjustments to make my senses stronger, so I enhanced my hearing and listened carefully. Sure enough, I could hear his feet striking the sidewalk, and I followed the sound. He must have realized quickly what I was doing, because suddenly I could no longer hear those steps. I increased my sense of smell and tried to track him from the smell of his sweat, but as far as I could tell, he wasn't sweating, which was more than I could say about myself. Odd!

Then I realized I was smelling something…

Blood! He was still bleeding. Apparently, the cut was worse than I had thought, and naturally exertion would make him bleed faster. I could also follow his blood trail visually. He might be invisible, but the blood droplets on the pavement were not.

If he had realized my situation, he would have headed for a busy street to inhibit my freedom of action more, but instead he followed his natural impulse and ran away from any possible crowd. He must have known Santa Brígida pretty well, because he got away from the school quickly and raced down one of the smaller residential streets. At a time of day when kids were in school, most parents were at work, and the ones who didn't have to be at work were often involved in some social or charitable activity away from home, a lot of these neighborhoods were pretty empty. All I could hear were my own footsteps and the occasional barking dog.

Dogs! Of course.

I might have all the original Taliesin's magic, and even some twists of my own, but that didn't mean I always remembered to use all of it. I reached my mind out for the dogs, of which there were a great many nearby, and I told them what I needed. Their noses, like mine, would pick up his blood, and dogs, like some other animals, were very sensitive to magic. He could be as invisible as he wanted; the dogs would still know where he was, and their barking would help me track him.

I wished I had the guys with me, but I must have outrun them long ago. I sent out as loud a psychic message to them as I could manage, giving them my approximate location and a quick indication of what we were up against. I was just about to make sure that Nurse Florence was in the loop when an enormous German shepherd leaped over the backyard wall of a house about three doors from where I was, bounded halfway across the street, and started barking furiously. Clearly, the dog had sensed the thief and saw him as a threat. That was more than I had asked for, but I would take it. If I was right, that little distraction might be just what I needed to finally catch that kid.

From the German shepherd's movements I could tell the kid was trying to run from it, but the dog, snarling, was going right after him. I was pretty sure he could outrun the dog under ideal conditions, but he had been running a lot on a twisted ankle, losing blood the whole time, and the dog had probably surprised him.

Then the thief became visible for a moment, evidently to try to threaten the dog with Zom. At the sight of the glowing blade, the dog did indeed back off, but it kept snarling at the kid, who looked frightened. I couldn't help but feel a little sorry for him. I know, I know—looks can be deceiving, and the kid could be some kind of shifter who was using that form to play for my sympathies. But what if he really was just a kid? Well, clearly he wasn't just a kid, but what if he was mentally and physically as young as he looked?

"Hey!" I yelled as I closed in. "Drop the sword!" I didn't really expect him to follow that instruction, but at just that moment the dog lunged at him, at which point he fumbled and dropped the sword, which hit the street with a resounding clang. Preoccupied by another lunge from the dog, the kid didn't immediately reach to pick up the sword, and by the time he thought of it, I had used White Hilt to surround the sword in flames. The dog retreated from the blaze, but I didn't need to distract the kid anymore. After all, he couldn't get to the sword, and now I could use magic to subdue him. Case closed!

Except that it wasn't. Without even blinking, the kid thrust his hand into the fire and pulled out Zom, which dispelled the flames as soon as it touched them.

I gasped, but there was no smell of burned flesh, no sign of even the slightest blister on his hand.

Fast and fireproof? What other surprises did he have in store for me? I did not intend to find out.

By now I was almost upon him. He turned and tried to run again, but the combination of his ankle injury and his blood loss was finally slowing him down enough to make escape unrealistic. His facial expression betrayed the fact that he knew it as well…but it made him look all the more like the frightened kid that perhaps he was.

He became invisible again, seemingly a desperation play, since he obviously knew by now that I could still track him. Then I heard the whoosh of a sword swing and jumped out of the way just in time. So, the little scumbag was out for blood! I was awfully tempted to give him some—

Parrying blind was hard, but the kid's lack of skill with the sword compensated. He was swinging wildly with a blade whose weight he was not used to.

"Give it up!" I yelled at him. "You're more likely to hurt yourself than me!" My ears echoed with another clang as Zom and White Hilt collided again with an emerald flash. Every time I parried with White Hilt, part of its fire was extinguished by Zom's anti-magic touch, but that touch didn't break permanent spells, such as those embedded in White Hilt, so I knew the flames would return shortly. Their loss mattered little right now, since the kid was clearly immune to fire anyway.

I could hear running footsteps and knew without looking in that direction that the guys were running down the street toward us.

"You may as well just give me the sword now," I said, trying to sound reasonable, though I was feeling less and less reasonable by the minutes. "My friends are here now. You can't fight all of us."

"I need the sword!" the kid yelled in high-pitched, heavily accented English. He sounded more out of breath than I was. The running did not seem to have been a problem, but the sword fighting was wearing him down fast.

"Why do you need it?" I asked, hoping that if I kept him talking, he would not try to run again.

"Please, please, just let me have it!" he said in a tone so plaintive it was almost heartbreaking. By now the guys had arrived, and, realizing I was fighting an invisible opponent, formed a wide circle around the general area where the kid had to be. I was pretty sure he was done now. If he had any more tricks, he would certainly have used them to get away before my reinforcements arrived.

Abruptly, the kid threw Zom up in the air, a move that caused it to become visible. He was trying to use the sword as a distraction, but we weren't about to fall for that kind of rookie move. Shar grabbed the sword midair, while the rest of us threw ourselves in the general area we knew he had to be. He managed to jump sideways, but the move did him little good, since he landed on his bad ankle, and the jolt of pain caused him to become visible and then nearly fall. In seconds Dan, Gordy, and Carlos were all on top of him—literally.

"Careful, guys—he's just a kid," I said, and they eased up a little. After determining that all the fight had more or less been knocked out of him, they dragged him off the ground. Dan and Gordy held his arms, and both Carlos and Shar stood nearby, waiting to help if they needed to.

"What's your name?" I asked him. I got no answer. He refused to even look up at me.

"Should we get the answer out of him?" asked Shar, who seemed to want me to say "yes."

"He's just a kid," I repeated.

"Yeah, right," said Dan. "A kid who can run at thirty miles per hour or so? What did you clock him at, Tal?"

"That sounds about right," I replied, studying our captive, who continued to stare fixedly at the ground.

"Let's not forget jumping the fence, turning invisible, and oh, yeah—being able to grab a sword he shouldn't even have been able to see," added Dan.

"He's apparently also fireproof," I noted absently, still looking carefully at him.

"Shifter of some kind, if you ask me. No little kid could do all that!" exclaimed Shar.

At that point our captive began sobbing loudly, his whole body shaking. If he was a shifter, he had the little-kid routine down pat.

Aside from being too large for him, his clothing was pretty worn out and certainly dirty, and though it was hard to tell his head down, I thought I had seen dirt on his face as well. Unless our "shifter" was also a master of disguise, I would say he was homeless.

Until that moment, I hadn't realized there were any homeless people in Santa Brígida. He could have just arrived from somewhere else, I supposed, but how did someone with the kind of power he obviously had end up homeless in the first place?

I tried probing his mind, but his defenses were strong, and I didn't want to risk hurting him, so for the time being, I made peace with the idea that we were not going to have all the answers we needed.

"Let's get him back to school," I said after a minute. "Nurse Florence needs to see him. Maybe she'll have some answers."

As we walked, I called up a fog to hide us. There was something vaguely disturbing about the image of two big, athletic guys like Dan and Gordy dragging a crying little kid along between them, and I didn't want anyone to get the wrong idea. I also figured that there would be a big mess at school, and I wanted to see if we could smuggle the kid in without his being seen. This was no ordinary thief we could just turn over to the police, nor ordinary little kid that we could hand over to social services.

By the time we got back, lunch was over—just as well, given the need for secrecy. We came through the hole in the fence I had made earlier. I took a minute to magically mend the break, hoping no one had noticed it. As we entered the building, I cast one of those don't-notice-me spells around us so that we could get to Nurse Florence's office. It was a good thing, too, because she wasn't in her office.

"Nurse Florence, where are you?" I asked mentally.

"Cafeteria!" That figured. She was probably doing damage control there—and she didn't sound at all happy about it.

Gordy looked at his watch. "We're all late for practice," he said grumpily, "and all because of this little jerk!" The kid, who had been quiet for a while, started sobbing again, more quietly than the first time, but Gordy looked even more unhappy as he tried to reconcile his desire to clobber the thief with his desire to protect the little kid. Shar in particular probably wouldn't admit it, but I think we were all feeling sorry for this little guy.

"I'll clear things up with our coaches," I said quietly. "We need to go to the cafeteria for a while."

We moved liked ghosts toward the cafeteria, unnoticed by the few students we passed on the way. When we got to the cafeteria, though, I reinforced the spell keeping us from being noticed. There were at least fifty students still in the cafeteria; two police officers, who were taking statements; Coach Miller, who seemed to be sending students over to talk to the police one at a time; Principal Simmons, who was watching the proceedings nervously; and Nurse Florence, who was "comforting" some of the students. I had no doubt that what she was really doing was rearranging memories before they talked to the police. When she sensed our presence, she looked over and walked carefully in our direction, more as if she were stretching her legs than actually going anywhere specific. Once she reached us, I extended our protective spell to include her.

"What a mess!" she said in a vaguely reproving tone, looking at me. "I couldn't just erase all memories of the 'incident' this time. Too many students involved and too little time, considering how fast Principal Simmons got here and how quickly she called the police. I had to settle for editing out the more colorful details, you know, like about high school students running around with swords, and you and someone else running incredibly fast. Coach Miller stuck around to do traffic control so that the police talked to the students only after I had a chance to make my adjustments. Still, I'm afraid their stories won't all be consistent. Since I can't read thoughts the way you can, all I can do is command the witnesses to forget certain things and hope that their minds execute that command in a reasonable way." She looked at me irritably. "What were you thinking?"

"That I had to keep Zom from being stolen," I said defensively.

Nurse Florence sighed. "Well, I can't fault you for that. The sword is priceless, and the people who lent it to us would not be happy if it…who is that?" she asked with obvious concern. She had finally noticed our prisoner.

"The little thief who stole Zom," replied Shar, as if that were the only identity the kid had.

Nurse Florence's eyes widened a little. Like me, she had some difficulty visualizing the kid as a master criminal.

"You'd better take him to my office—and keep him there, until I get back."

"Oh, don't worry. He's not going anywhere," replied Shar emphatically.

We hurried back to Nurse Florence's office, managing to slip in without being seen. Magic really did have its advantages. Unfortunately, magic couldn't make the time pass any faster. (Actually, it probably could, but I didn't want to risk complicating our situation any further.) Anyway, after what seemed like an eternity—or at least, like an algebra class— Nurse Florence returned, looking even more exhausted than usual.

"How did it go?" I asked, already knowing.

"Not particularly well, but at least the police didn't leave with any suspicion that anything supernatural was happening, and I doubt any news teams are on their way over to cover the story. The police did, however, manage to put together a pretty accurate description of our 'friend' here. Who is he, by the way?"

"He won't say," answered Gordy sullenly. "He won't say anything. He just cries every so often."

"I do not!" snapped the kid, his voice cracking, his eyes fixed defiantly on Gordy. It was the first time he had spoken since we had captured him.

"Is it really necessary for both of you to hold him like that?" asked Nurse Florence. "I don't think there is too much risk of his getting away from us now."

"You might just be surprised," Dan replied. "You've already heard he's fast. He can jump really high as well—"

"And make himself invisible," I added. "He's also immune to fire, or at least very resistant to it. He might be able to do other things."

"I think Dan and Gordy can let go of him anyway," Nurse Florence replied. "There are six of us in here with him in this tiny office. He could be as fast as the wind…he's still not going anywhere." Reluctantly, Dan and Gordy released his arms. He stretched a little but made no move to take advantage of the situation.

"I'm going to take a look at your injuries now, if that's all right," said Nurse Florence in a professional way, though I could feel her maternal instincts kicking in. Probably she was trying to project a maternal image to the kid.

There was an awkward silence, but eventually the kid nodded yes, and Nurse Florence looked at his cut. She didn't ask where his injuries were, so I figured that, even though the kid was resistant to mind probes, he wasn't resistant to her body probes.

"This is deeper than I'd like, but you didn't nick anything major. I'll have the cut healed in no time." The kid cringed away a little bit when she brought out her ointment, but something about her manner evidently reassured him, and he let her apply the greenish paste. (The ointment wasn't, strictly speaking, necessary, but it did make it easier for Nurse Florence to heal the wound.) Then she held her hand a couple of inches away from the wound, closed her eyes to concentrate for a couple of minutes, wiped off the excess ointment, and there was not even the slightest sign of an injury. The kid's eyes widened with surprise, which told me that, as supernatural as he obviously was, he had never seen healing magic before. Perhaps he was the loner he appeared to be.

Then Nurse Florence turned her attention to his ankle.

"Are you sure you need to fix that?" said Shar, quite pointedly.

The kid looked momentarily frightened, and Nurse Florence glared at Shar. "Yes, we have to fix everything." Then, turning back to the kid, she continued, "We aren't going to hurt you. Shar is just upset, rightly so, that you tried to steal his sword. His life may depend on having it some day." Nurse Florence began working on the ankle, continuing to speak in a casual tone as she did so. "Why did you try to steal the sword?" The kid looked down at the floor again and said nothing.

"You need to answer that question sooner or later, young man," said Nurse Florence somewhat more formally. "You understand we can't just let you run around town stealing things, but if we know what you need, we can find you some better way for you to get it." Still no response.

"All right, your ankle is better now, but I'm still waiting for an answer. We can't help you if—"

"Nobody can help me," he said with a sort of dismal finality I had never heard from a little kid before. For a second I was afraid he was going to start crying again, but he managed to hold himself together, at least outwardly.

"If I had the sword," he almost whispered, "then he would have taken me back. I know he would."

"'He' must be this boy's father," thought Nurse Florence.

"The kid was abandoned? Why?" I asked. I knew that kids were sometimes abandoned, but I had never met someone whose parents had just dumped him.

"Try not to act too surprised. I don't want to say this in front of the boy. During my physical examination I figured out where his powers come from. He's half djinn."

I had encountered more than my share of weirdness in the past four years, but generally it was Celtic weirdness, not Arabic weirdness, so it took me a minute to catch up with her.

"Djinn?"

"In the Quran the djinn are described as being created by Allah from smokeless fire, which explains why the boy is so fire resistant. Islamic law forbids sexual relationships between humans and djinn, but there are a few known cases. I dealt with one half djinn back in Wales, so I can recognize the physical signs. I'm guessing the boy's father is the human partner in a human-

djinn relationship and abandoned the boy when it became obvious he wasn't 'normal.'"

"But how…" I started. Then I realized my shock had caused me to speak aloud, and I switched back to mental dialogue. *"How could a parent abandon a child for any reason, let alone something the child has no control over?"*

"People abandon children for many reasons just as arbitrary as that. I've had to deal with a couple of situations in which students were thrown out by their fathers when the fathers discovered they were gay."

I thought about how, just a few weeks ago, my father had feared I was gay. Even at the darkest point of that misunderstanding, I didn't think he had ever been close to throwing me out. I had to give him credit for not giving up on me.

"So what do we need to do, find his djinn mother?"

"I wish it were that simple. Typically the djinn are no more welcoming of half djinn children than the mortal parents are. Honestly, I'm at a loss on this one. The boy apparently thinks that if he performs some great feat, his father will take him back, but I doubt that's a realistic hope. If anything, the boy's showing up with a stolen magic sword will just reinforce the father's feeling that he wants nothing to do with him."

"How long has he been living on the street like this?"

"No way to tell. His accent tells me he wasn't born here but rather in some Arab country, and then he came here later. But since I don't know how old he is now, I can't even speculate. It could have been days, though I'd guess that's too conservative an estimate, based on the way he is behaving. Unfortunately, he could also have been abandoned years ago."

"Years!" I went from shock to outrage. *"What a scumbag his father must be!"*

"My father is not a scumbag!" screamed the kid. I felt stupid, as if we had been spelling words the kid we were talking in front of actually knew how to spell. After all, if he really was half djinn, why couldn't he pick up thoughts so close to him? None of his earlier actions had suggested he could read minds in the way I could, but I had just mentally shouted right next to him.

Nurse Florence also looked non-plussed, and the guys moved as if to restrain the kid. "That will not be necessary!" she snapped. Then, turning to the kid, she adopted a gentler tone. "We're sorry. We don't really know your father, so perhaps we shouldn't judge. Tal is angry that you have had to fend for yourself when someone should have been taking care of you."

"I did OK on my own!" said the kid defensively. "No one needed to take care of me."

"May I ask your name?" said Nurse Florence. "Mine is Viviane. Gentlemen, would you please introduce yourselves to our guest?"

"You mean, to our prisoner?" asked Shar acidly.

"Guest," replied Nurse Florence, calmly but forcefully. One by one, the guys introduced themselves.

"Now it's your turn," said Nurse Florence gently.

"Khalid," replied the kid finally, after a long pause. It was clear we were not going to get a last name, and Nurse Florence knew better than to press for one.

"All right, Khalid. For the time being, I'm going to see if some of my friends in Annwn will look after you—"

Khalid, though clearly afraid of us, was apparently even more afraid of going to Annwn, though I doubted he had any idea what Annwn even was. "No!" he practically screamed, jumping up and looking as if he would make a dash for the room's only door.

Just as Nurse Florence had predicted, however, the room was just too cramped for his speed to make much difference. In seconds Dan and Gordy had his arms again. He struggled desperately, and if his strength had been as great as his speed, he could have given them much more trouble. As it was though, two seventeen-year-old varsity football players had little difficulty subduing one eleven-year-old.

"What's wrong?" asked Nurse Florence, genuinely puzzled.

Khalid said nothing, but his quivering lip spoke volumes.

"Khalid, we really want to help you, but you need to tell us what's wrong," said Nurse Florence, trying her most calming tone.

Khalid looked even more as if he would bolt at the slightest opportunity. "Just…leave me alone!" Khalid finally begged in a half whisper. "I'll…go somewhere else. And I won't try to steal from you again—I promise."

"I'm afraid we can't do that," Nurse Florence explained patiently. "Khalid, we can see you can take care of yourself—" Dan snickered a little but quickly got control of himself. "—but we still can't just leave you all alone. You have noticed the young men with you all carry swords—"

"You bet he noticed," cut in Shar angrily.

"I can do this more easily without interruptions," said Nurse Florence in her do-what-I-say tone. Switching personas again, she looked into Khalid's eyes. "Khalid, they carry swords because there are…bad people nearby, very bad people. One of them tried to kill all of us just a few weeks ago and nearly succeeded. You have seen what these young men can do. If even they were nearly overcome, can't you see that even someone as fast and clever as you are might not survive on his own?"

For the first time, Khalid actually appeared to be really listening. "You mean like that pale, dark haired lady? The really pretty one?"

We all froze. Was he talking about Morgan?

"What lady, Khalid?" I asked in as neutral a tone as I could.

"I've…I've been watching you guys for a while. She is often watching too."

"Today?"

"No, I didn't see her today, but I wasn't really looking."

"What makes you think she's a bad person?"

Khalid shrugged. "I just feel it. She's…cold, somehow. I can feel darkness when she is nearby. Somehow, I know she might be able to see me, even when I'm invisible, so I stay as far away as I can."

I tried to sound more reassuring than I felt. "If she is the one I am thinking of, that was a good thing to do, Khalid. She is definitely one of the bad people we were talking about."

"I don't want to upset our 'guest,'" said Dan, who still had a grip on one of Khalid's arms, "but how do we know he isn't really working with Morgan? Maybe he isn't even a little kid at all."

Khalid, who had seemed marginally calmer while I was talking to him, began looking very wary, again ready to bolt at the first opportunity.

"He's not a shifter, if that's where you're going with that question, Dan," replied Nurse Florence quickly. "I would have picked up some hint of that while I was working on his injuries. As far as his being an ally of Morgan, well…I can't tell. Khalid, I need to ask you to trust me. I know you have natural defenses that prevent people from seeing into your mind. Can you lower those, just for a minute?"

Khalid's eyes filled with horror, as if Nurse Florence had just suggested cutting open his skull to look inside. I could understand the reaction. Most people don't really want somebody else rummaging around in their heads, and Khalid hadn't exactly had a life that would inspire him to trust others. Unfortunately, someone who really was in league with

Morgan would have the same reaction. As much as I sympathized with the kid, we couldn't have him around unless we knew for sure.

"Khalid," I began gently, "if you have been watching us for a while, you know we aren't bad people, right?"

Khalid did give Shar a hard look first—which Shar returned—but then he nodded yes.

"Then you know we wouldn't really do anything to hurt you."

"But you want to see into my mind! That's…wrong!"

"It's the only way we can help you, Khalid. We have to be sure you aren't working with one of the bad people—"

"I'm not bad!" he protested loudly.

"But how do we know that? All we know about you is that you tried to steal one of our swords. Please, Khalid, try to look at this situation from our point of view. We need some way to know you, to know that you aren't out to get us."

Khalid thought about the problem for a moment, then said, "I know someone who could tell you I'm a good person."

"Who's that?" I asked with an indulgent smile.

"Gianni," he replied innocently.

My heart skipped a beat. Yeah, I did want to trust Khalid, I did want to help him. Still, the idea that he had been around Gianni without my knowing gave me the creeps. I made a valiant effort not to let my uneasiness show.

"How do you know Gianni?" I asked. The sentence came out more tonelessly than I wanted. Dan raised an eyebrow, but Khalid seemed oblivious.

"I've been near here since early November. I…I can take care of myself, like I said, but sometimes…it's nice to talk to someone my age. Every few days I stand at the front of the middle school right when school lets out and kind of pretend I'm just coming out of the school myself. Sometimes I say 'Hi' to some of the people coming out, but usually they don't talk to me much."

Considering that Khalid looked like something the proverbial cat dragged in, I wasn't too surprised, especially in a fairly upscale community like Santa Brígida. I was surprised that one of the adults at the school hadn't noticed a homeless kid hanging out near the school, but if he only showed up right as school was getting out, he might have blended well enough that no one noticed from a distance.

"I had seen Gianni with you, though, so when I said 'Hi' to him, I kinda pretended that I knew you, and he talked to me. He even had me come home with him a couple times and gave me cookies."

Khalid's expression hinted at what I would have suspected anyway—that the cookies were about the only food he hadn't had to steal in weeks. The wave of sympathy about to engulf me, however, didn't quite wash away my feeling of uneasiness about his being around Gianni. In that second I wanted to probe his mind—hard, if necessary—to verify his story, and his permission be damned. I wasn't about to take any chances with Gianni's safety.

Nurse Florence, as if reading my mind, put a restraining hand on my arm.

"Khalid, we all know Gianni, but you could have fooled him. You won't be able to fool us if you allow us to see what is in your mind. Otherwise, we'll have to keep you in a place where we know you can't hurt anyone."

Khalid looked at us one by one, as if trying to find a sympathetic face. Mine was now expressionless. Dan, Shar and Carlos were all looking at him suspiciously. Gordy was clearly puzzled. That only left Nurse Florence, and she was the one who had just given him the ultimatum. He looked so trapped that I began to sympathize with him again, but I squashed the impulse. We needed to know the truth, period. Then I realized what I needed to do to get the truth.

"Khalid, how about a trade?" I asked. "You can look inside my mind if we can look inside yours?"

"Is that wise?" asked Carlos quickly. The others looked equally skeptical.

"Personal stuff only, not information about our dealings with Morgan, the extent of my magic, or anything like that. Nurse Florence can monitor to make sure Khalid doesn't go where he shouldn't. Well, Khalid, what do you say?"

I could tell Khalid was still conflicted, but my willingness to do what we were asking him to do had at least cracked his resistance.

"Will it hurt?" he asked quietly after several seconds had passed. "When you go in my mind, will it hurt?"

"As long as you relax and let it happen, not one bit," replied Nurse Florence in her most reassuring tone.

"Can I look in Tal's first?"

"That's the idea," I replied.

"OK," said Khalid, still visibly reluctant.

"Dan and Gordy, I think you can stop holding him," pointed out Nurse Florence. They did, slowly and with noticeable reluctance—and they stood close enough to seize him again at the slightest sign of trouble.

"Take my hand," I said, extending my right hand as if for a handshake. Khalid took it reluctantly. His hand was shaking just a little and felt grimy against my skin. His skin was also pretty rough for someone his age, but I guessed living on the street would do that. Nurse Florence took my left hand so she could keep track of what was happening more easily. As soon as I felt her mental presence, I opened part of my mind to Khalid. There was no immediate response, so I started projecting to him, and after a few seconds I felt him take hold. In only a few more seconds he let my memories engulf him.

Khalid showed the greatest interest in my memories from the time I was little until I was about his age. I could feel him lingering over times I had enjoyed with my parents, as well as various childhood and adolescent milestones: my first kiss, learning to play the guitar, learning to drive. I didn't have to read his mind to know that most of the memories he was reveling in had no parallel in his own life.

Then he brushed against some of my more recent, more difficult memories. For a few seconds he was even with me on Ceridwen's roof when I almost died, but that kind of experience must have been too intense for him, since he almost immediately broke the connection.

"You...you're a hero," he said to me with something akin to wonder, as if I were some kind of superhero who had stepped straight out of a comic book.

I found myself blushing a little. I'd like to think I was hero, at least sometimes, but because I couldn't share what I had done with most people, I seldom got any outside validation for my feelings. "I would have died without Nurse Florence and all of these guys," I replied as modestly as I could. "They are all heroes."

"I thought you were good people," said Khalid. "I just didn't realize how good."

"OK, buddy, now that you know a little more about us, it's time for us to know a little more about you," I said.

Khalid still looked reluctant.

"Why don't you lie down on that cot over there, and we'll get this over with as quickly as we can," suggested Nurse Florence. Khalid, still moving hesitantly, almost as if his ankle was still injured, settled onto the cot.

"All right, Tal, you and I will each take one of Khalid's hands. Dan and Shar, you each take our other hand, and Gordy and Carlos, you each take one of theirs. I want everyone in on this, so there can be no questions later." The guys obediently held hands, having probably figured out that the physical connection would make it easier for Nurse Florence to broadcast to them.

"Are you ready, Khalid?" Nurse Florence asked. The kid nodded once, and Nurse Florence immediately moved gently into his mind, as did I.

I was almost knocked off of my feet by the overwhelming feeling of sadness, not quite despair, but certainly bordering on it. I already knew his life hadn't been a picnic, but that knowledge had not prepared me for plunging into this ink-black abyss.

I caught very brief flickers of a beautiful woman with jet-black hair and eyes like dark stars, but the image was hazy, as if Khalid had not seen her for years. His mother! Khalid had tried to hold on to that memory, but it was relentlessly fading away, vanishing into the surrounding blackness.

The image of his father was clearer but offered little comfort. Oh, I could feel a few happy memories, vague as the image of Khalid's mother and probably dating from the days before she left, but once his mother had left, his father had become increasingly distant and severe, until the day on which his father could no longer deny Khalid's extraordinary nature, and that day Khalid remembered as a red jumble of pain.

At one point his father hit him—my own jaw ached from the bare-knuckled blow—but that pain was nothing compared to his father's departure, a cowardly escape while Khalid had slept, a knife through his heart that made me want to leap out of his mind screaming. I didn't, because I still didn't know for sure whose side he was on. His background was authentic, but someone who hated his life so much could be an ideal candidate for recruitment by someone like Morgan.

Given the potential danger, Nurse Florence and I looked carefully, but all we could find were distant images of Morgan. Khalid seemed to have avoided her, just as he said. Nor was there any evidence of contact with any other hostile person—or thing, for that matter. We saw his talks with Gianni, little bursts of light highlighting the surrounding blackness, and not even a trace of any sinister purpose; much to my relief, Khalid liked Gianni, wanted to be friends with him, and had no ulterior motive.

We saw his fumbling and unsuccessful attempts to talk to other kids, his numerous thefts, his spying on us, which turned out to be more than just sizing up how to get his hands on Zom. Khalid saw our friendship and wished that he could somehow be a part of it. We even experienced his panic-stricken views of today's chase, images that made my own heart pound and my breath come in short, ragged gasps, images that made my own ankle ache redly.

We felt also his dejection when he was caught, his plan to impress his father by showing up with such a valuable artifact disrupted beyond repair. And I knew why he didn't want to go to Annwn, or any other place outside the Santa Barbara area: he wanted his father to be able to find him when his father changed his mind. (I know, I know—Khalid didn't understand how unlikely that scenario was, and perhaps we would need to wean him off of it over time, but I wasn't going to even try today, when he had already been through so much.)

By that point there could be no doubt: Khalid had been, of necessity, a thief after his father had deserted him, but what he was *not* was a threat to any of us, and he could definitely use our help—big time!

After Nurse Florence and I withdrew from Khalid's mind, I glanced around and saw that the guys were just as moved as I had been. How could anyone be unmoved after getting his soul sand blasted like that? Gordy was actually crying, though I was sure he would deny it if I asked. Dan was at least on the verge of tears, and I picked up a flash of intense emotion from him; he was remembering the death of Jimmie, his own little brother. Khalid was two years older than Jimmie had been then, but it was easy to see that something in Khalid's memories had hit Dan right in the little-brother center in his brain. Carlos was less moved but clearly shocked at what Khalid had been through. Shar looked embarrassed for the way he had reacted to Khalid earlier.

"Any questions?" asked Nurse Florence somewhat redundantly, since clearly there were none.

"Khalid," she continued, "I think we all see now why you don't want to go to Annwn; you have friends, or at least acquaintances you want to get to know here. Aside from your father, the only people you feel any kind of connection with are here."

Well, the biggest reason was his father, as I had just been thinking, but I could see why Nurse Florence didn't want to reinforce that idea, and it was true that Khalid had felt some kind of connections with us.

Nurse Florence paused for a moment. "So no Annwn. We have already decided, have we not, that we can't turn him over to the police?" she asked, looking at us.

"Even if we wanted to, I doubt they could hold on to him," I joked.

"Well, social services isn't going to work either. Khalid wouldn't like that kind of situation, and they couldn't hold on to him either. I can only think of one thing we can do in the short term: one of us needs to take him in…until his father or someone else claims him."

I knew Nurse Florence was adding that last part for Khalid's benefit, trying to navigate the treacherous waters of his forlorn hope without deliberately making it stronger. Fortunately the guys recognized the problem and did not challenge her statement. Anyway, we all had to take a minute to absorb what Nurse Florence was saying.

"How would we explain him to our parents…or anyone, for that matter?" asked Carlos. I had been thinking exactly the same thing myself.

"It won't be hard to create a cover story about his being an exchange student of some kind. I can easily use the Order in Wales as the agency involved. My colleagues will be more than happy to join that pretense when I tell them what is happening.

"Wales?" said Gordy. "He doesn't exactly look like he's from Wales."

"There are Arabs even in Wales," replied Nurse Florence with a smile. "They may be less than half a percent of the population, but they do exist, and that's all we need to establish credibility. I can plant memories in Principal Simmons and Principal Carmichael over at the middle school, so they think they have heard of this particular exchange program before. The rest of the details are easy enough. Khalid's luggage was somehow lost at the Santa Barbara airport; Tal and Stan can plant the appropriate flight information so that Khalid appears in the passenger records from LA to Santa Barbara, and they can take care of the earlier part of his route as well, just in case someone checks. We can also invent some problem with the host family. One of the parents has fallen ill, maybe. Anyway, some story that explains why Khalid suddenly has no place to stay. We just need to know which set of parents to sell it to."

As always, Nurse Florence could cook up an expert cover story, but for a moment I was distracted from the discussion by the mention of Stan. Where was Stan? I hadn't seen him since before school started. I knew he had been with Nurse Florence when the robbery occurred. If he hadn't joined us for the chase, which probably wasn't practical, why wasn't he around when we got back?

Nurse Florence paused, and I realized she must have noticed my inattention.

"Sorry! I just realized Stan isn't around."

"Don't worry about him," said Nurse Florence smoothly. "He'll be back shortly; I'm sure. Let's focus on finding Khalid a home."

"I'll take him," said Dan quickly. I knew Dan was volunteering because of the memory of Jimmie, and I wondered whether having Khalid in his house was really a good idea. It might stir up too many memories.

"No, it's better if I take him," said Shar, much to everyone's surprise, including Khalid's.

"Don't look at me like that!" Shar continued. "Now that I know what his story is, I know we can be friends. And that exchange-student story, no offense, Nurse Florence, is a little lame. I can explain him to my parents as someone who needed to flee from the Middle East fast and is temporarily separated from his parents."

"That sounds much more complicated," replied Nurse Florence doubtfully.

"But it works," insisted Shar. "Remember, my parents had to flee Iran after the overthrow of the Shah in 1979. I guarantee they won't ask too many questions if they think Khalid is a refugee. In fact, they'll pretty much roll out the red carpet. We just need to work out a reason his parents aren't with him. Maybe his parents were already out of the country— damn, which country should we use? Well, we can figure out what the most likely trouble spot is in a minute. Anyway, his parents are in…Austria, let's say. It took my parents a while to get out of Europe and into the United States, so they won't question that. Somehow whoever was taking care of Khalid managed to smuggle him out via the U.S. embassy—"

"Why would the U.S. embassy do that?" asked Carlos.

"My parents aren't going to question the details. I don't know— maybe whoever was taking care of Khalid bribed someone at the embassy. After he got out through embassy channels, he ended up here—"

"Because the embassy couldn't figure out how to send him to

Austria to be with his parents?" said Dan skeptically. "That really doesn't make sense. Your parents are intelligent people. They are bound to notice the problem with that part of the story."

"His parents are dead then." When Shar said that, Khalid gasped audibly. "No, Khalid, not for real. We're just working out what we tell people. Anyway, Khalid has relatives in this country, but the State Department hasn't tracked them down yet, so he needs a place to stay. That works, doesn't it?"

"It works if we are trying to write a movie script," I said with a smirk. "It definitely has great possibilities as the opening to a suspense thriller. But as a credible story in real life, it has more holes than Swiss cheese!"

"Well, then, Khalid's parents are in hiding, and Khalid needs to pretend to be someone else, just in case the people after his parents come looking for him. We can pass him off as a cousin. Most Americans can't tell the difference between Persians and Arabs anyway." I felt a little awkward, since, even though I knew Shar well by now, I couldn't really tell the difference either.

"Your parents would let someone in the house who could make all of you a target?" asked Gordy worriedly. I don't think mine would be willing to do that."

"Yes, the 'Khalid is marked for death' story line seems like asking for trouble," said Nurse Florence without hesitation. "Whatever you think, Shar, I think your parents would be hesitant in the situation you describe, if only because it puts you in danger. However, the idea of pretending he is your cousin has merit. It avoids having to create all the background for a non-existent student-exchange program."

"His family sought asylum, and the State Department turned them down, but somehow they got him into the country illegally. We all know that sometimes legitimate asylum requests get turned down. As to how he got smuggled in," said Shar in an almost defiant tone, looking at both Nurse Florence and me, "he'll just say it is too painful for him to talk about it. My parents will buy that, and we won't get stuck trying to work out plausible mechanics for smuggling him in. Tal doesn't even need to fake passenger lists and that kind of thing, because Khalid wouldn't have appeared under his own name anyway in that scenario."

"Your parents would risk breaking the law?" asked Nurse Florence.

"If they believe Khalid is here because his life could be in danger, yes, absolutely. Besides, we have a very large extended family. If my parents want a little 'plausible deniability,' they can always have him use the name of one of my actual cousins, someone we haven't seen in a few years, assuming that if someone from the INS knocked at the door, they could always claim Khalid had fooled them. But they may not even bother with that. Either way, they will take Khalid in with that cover story—I know it in my gut."

Nurse Florence smiled a little, I think despite herself. "You'd really like to have Khalid with you, wouldn't you, Shar?"

"Yeah," said Shar, looking at Khalid. "Now that I know his real story, I want to help...especially after I made such a jerk out of myself to begin with."

Khalid looked profoundly skeptical, even marginally afraid of Shar, and when Shar moved a little closer, Khalid backed away from him. However, Shar hugged him, and I could see Khalid cringe, then gradually relax a little. After all, no one had hugged him in—what did we learn from his memories? God, three years. That bastard of a father had deserted him when he was eight!

Immediately, I realized my emotions were getting out of control and did my best to calm myself. Khalid might not be a fully functional telepath, but he had overheard part of my conversation with Nurse Florence when I became too agitated, so at the very least, he could pick up nearby thoughts with a sufficient emotional charge.

"Well, we appear to have Khalid well taken care of," said Nurse Florence with obvious relief.

"Practice!" said Gordy abruptly. "We're all gonna catch hell for being so late."

"Coach Miller found a way to explain your absence to your other coaches, so don't worry about that," said Nurse Florence. "I would recommend you all go home and get some rest. Your run half-way across town today should be all the exercise you need. Oh, Tal, you'd better go with Shar, just in case his parents need a little psychic nudge."

"They won't," said Shar confidently.

"Nonetheless," said Nurse Florence in her this-is-an-order tone, "you never have a second chance to make a first impression. If you are right, well, no harm done. If you are wrong, you have the backup you need."

"OK," said Shar grudgingly.

"Why don't you and Khalid wait outside for just a minute? I need to talk to Tal."

Shar took Khalid outside, and the other guys, taking the obvious hint, said their goodbyes and shuffled out quickly. I noticed that each one gave Khalid a hug as he left. I thought I even saw the ghost of a smile on Khalid's lips, but I was too far away to be sure. Then the door closed, and I turned my attention back to Nurse Florence. She sat behind her desk and motioned for me to sit in the chair on the other side.

"I'm sure Shar will do a good job with Khalid, but, Tal, I'm curious why you didn't offer to take Khalid in; he seems to have more rapport with you than anyone, especially after you shared your memories with him."

"I wanted to take him in, Nurse Florence; I really did, but there is… a problem with my mom." Nurse Florence leaned forward.

"That sounds ominous," she said, looking concerned.

"It isn't anything life threatening; it's just that I think she's…getting a little magic."

Nurse Florence raised an eyebrow. "How do you know?"

"She's putting out energy, low-level, but still there, and this morning she noticed the protective spell on the house."

Nurse Florence sat straight up in her chair. "She knows about the existence of spells?"

"No, but she could feel something was different. Her reaction was too immediate to be coincidence," I said somewhat defensively, knowing Nurse Florence was about to make exactly that suggestion.

"Well, actually this kind of situation isn't that uncommon in families with one really strong practitioner."

"You mean the skill is hereditary? I thought I got mine from being a reincarnation of Taliesin."

"I believe you did," replied Nurse Florence slowly, clearly thinking through the possibilities. "However, we know you are also a descendant of the original Taliesin. I have never studied the genealogy involved. I just assumed you were descended from Taliesin on your father's side, but it could just as easily be your mother's side, in which case your mother could have some predisposition. The real answer, though, lies in the nature of this world. Have you asked yourself why most spell casters, faerie or even human, tend to prefer Annwn?"

"No," I said with a little grin, "I can't say that has been exactly my most pressing question."

"I'm serious," said Nurse Florence. "Annwn is a friendlier environment for magic. Remember that modern technology works only erratically at best there. Natural law is—hmmm…I'm not sure how best to express it—softer there. There are worlds where natural law is so hard and fast that magic won't work there at all, or so I'm told. Our world is somewhere in the middle. Scientists can identify predictable natural laws, and technology based on those scientific principles will work. Magic will also work, but for most people it takes a lot more effort than it would in Annwn, and some magic effects aren't possible on Earth at all. Also, from what the Order has been able to discover, many people who might have magic if they grew up in Annwn never discover it here at all. Those of us who do somehow discover our magical ability need to visit Annwn to renew ourselves periodically; otherwise, our spell casting tends to get weaker and weaker."

"I have cast spells both here and in Annwn," I objected after a few seconds. "I don't recall it being all that much easier in Annwn."

"That's because you are an exceptional case. Maybe this is another example of the side-effects of gaining knowledge from Ceridwen's cauldron, or of being reborn from Ceridwen's womb, or of some combination of the two. For whatever reason, the magic is so strong in you that it becomes somehow self-fueling, less reliant on the surrounding environment. That's a good thing, especially considering Arawn's ban keeps you out of Annwn most of the time, so you wouldn't be able to renew yourself very easily. But it's a good thing with a few random side-effects, one of which is that the people around you can be affected. You are like a little piece of Annwn yourself. Those you spend large amounts of time with, if they have any kind of magic potential, are more likely to develop magic— especially if you cast on them."

I thought about how many times I had needed to cast a spell on my mom to keep her from finding out my secret or to keep her out of harm's way. I must have looked very downcast, because Nurse Florence immediately switched from giver of wisdom to giver of comfort. "I wouldn't worry too much. It sounds as if your mother is operating at a very low power level, certainly not strong enough to start reading your mind or something like that. She may occasionally have feelings, as she did today, but she will most likely dismiss them, just as she probably did this time. Now, if she discovered that magic existed, that would be a different problem, but if you don't tell her, I don't see how she ever will."

"I'm sure you are probably right," I said slowly. "I just can't help thinking about how Khalid's father turned on him when he discovered the truth."

"I'm not defending him, but Khalid's father does belong to a religious tradition that sees that kind of human-djinn union as an abomination. Faced with evidence that he had participated unknowingly in such a union was just too much for him to handle. Your parents are not in the same situation at all. If they knew the truth about you, they would probably need time to adjust, but they wouldn't stop loving you. So stop worrying! You know, you really worry too much."

"Yeah, I've only had to fend off one magical attack so far this month, and I've only encountered two supernatural beings, but it's OK—only one of them is evil."

"Is there no end to your sarcasm?" asked Nurse Florence, laughing.

"Actually, no. Oh, but I do have one more serious question before I go. What's up with Stan?"

"I think he wants to tell you, but I should prepare you a little I think. Stan is having delusions of some kind."

Now it was my turn to sit lean forward in my chair. "What? And you're just getting around to mentioning this now?"

"It has been a very busy afternoon," replied Nurse Florence, without a hint of defensiveness. "And I'm sure his problem is nothing you can't fix."

"What's his delusion?"

"Well, part of it is delusion, anyway. Part of it is real. The mental healing you did with him in the days after Samhain is starting to come undone. That past personality that was dominating him when he was first awakened is stirring again."

"That can't be!" I objected. "I did a good job on him. Look at me—I integrated myself four years ago under much more difficult circumstances. Why would doing with Stan exactly what I did with myself last only a few weeks? That doesn't make sense."

"The problem," replied Nurse Florence, "is that there are many things we don't know. When you were awakened, you remembered all of your past lives. Stan, as far as we know, only remembered one. Why wouldn't he have remembered them all, just like you did? I don't like guessing blind, but if I had to guess, I would say that the jolt the cauldron of knowledge gave to Gwion Bach all those centuries ago may once again be the answer. You have already discovered you can learn magic much faster, and in much more diverse ways, than anyone I have ever heard of. Suppose your mind can also more easily encompass past-life memories that would overload most people. That could account for your 'integration' being permanent while Stan's was only short-term."

Now I was really worried. "But what does that mean? Am I going to have to repair Stan every few days for the rest of his life?"

"Let's not jump to conclusions. I would say his mind can't handle the past-life memories as well as yours does. That doesn't necessarily mean he can't be strengthened to the point at which he can handle them better. We may just have to take his situation one day at a time."

"Wait a minute. If all of that is real, what's Stan's delusion?"

"He's claiming to be someone he couldn't possibly be."

"Napoleon?" I said with a smirk. "Because as far as I know, he could be, though he is a little taller than I might expect."

"This is not a joke, Tal. Stan thinks he is…I promised I would let him tell you the specifics, but he thinks he is someone who definitely did not believe in reincarnation."

I thought back to my first encounters with Nurse Florence. Usually, by this point in the conversation, I had everything figured out, but this time I was still confused. "Why would that make any difference?"

"Based on the Order's research, it appears that people end up in something like the afterlife they expect. If someone is expecting Heaven or Hell, that's exactly where they end up. If someone is expected Valhalla, or the Elysian Fields, or the Happy Hunting Ground, that's what they get."

"How would the Order possibly know that?"

"The Order can't know for sure," admitted Nurse Florence. "The data is very limited, but what data they have supports the idea. Imagine the afterlife as a building with a lot of different doors. However, each person is conditioned by his or her religion to only see one of those doors, and that is the one he or she goes through."

"So every religion is wrong, and what happens to us after death is totally subjective?"

"I'm not saying that," replied Nurse Florence cautiously. "Maybe one religion is right, but only its adherents perceive reality correctly. Maybe all of them are right, at least in a symbolic sense. Maybe none of them are right. I don't know anyone with all the answers. I just know I don't have all of them." I must have looked incredibly dissatisfied, because I think Nurse Florence had been done, but she continued. "Having magic is not the same thing as understanding the whole universe. We have insight into a small part of it; that's all. We can probe minds, for instance, and find out whether or not John Smith cheated on that geometry test. But, assuming there is a higher power, we can't probe its mind and get all the answers. We are just as much in the dark as anyone else that way."

"But—"

"That's why it's called faith, Tal. Now you've probably kept Shar and Khalid waiting long enough. We'll talk about this some other time."

I didn't much like being dismissed like that, but I could also tell that Nurse Florence had pretty well exhausted herself today. Between memory adjustments, healings, mind-sharings, and concealment spells, she had been working almost non-stop for hours, and she had been through a rough day yesterday as well. So I swallowed my questions and objections, said good-bye, and went out to meet Shar and Khalid.

As I was leaving the nurse's office, I thought about what Shakespeare had written in *Hamlet*: "When sorrows come, they come not single spies, but in battalions." We were playing an extremely dangerous game with Morgan Le Fay, the girl I loved might be an evil sorceress when we finally awakened her from her coma, we now had a homeless half djinn to help out, my mom was developing inconvenient—to say the least—mental abilities, and now Stan was degenerating back to where he had been on Samhain.

Well, that's got to be all our bad luck for this week, anyway.

Of course, as usual, I was wrong.

CHAPTER 6: DANCING WITH THE DEVIL

I was more than a little on edge as I drove to Shar's house. His parents seemed like nice enough people, but we were about to drop a pretty big bombshell on them. It was hard to feel great about that in the first place, and in the background Stan's problem preyed on my mind.

I wonder what it's like to have only one problem at a time to worry about.

I pulled up in front of the Sassani house. Like most of the houses in Santa Brígida, the facade was impressively, almost overwhelmingly, Spanish colonial. When the Sassanis had first moved from Beverly Hills, they had wanted to remodel, but Shar had told me at some point since we'd become friends, that Carrie Winn herself (the original, not Vanora in disguise) had come by one day to talk them out of the idea. The Sassanis took the hint (or Carrie Winn did a little magical manipulation—there was no way to tell which so long after the fact).

Nonetheless, though the exterior still had its pristine, plastic, made-in-Santa Brígida look of which I was thoroughly tired, the interior was another matter entirely. In fact, it looked more as if someone had transported a little piece of Iran to Santa Brígida. Everywhere you looked, you could see vibrantly colored Persian rugs, several different kinds of marble somehow superimposed over the house's original interior, a wide variety of Middle Eastern and European furniture, some statues that would have looked very much at home in a museum, and a spectacular collection of wall murals portraying the major events of the *Shahnameh*, the great Persian epic. The painter had cleverly made the murals resemble the style of illustration in some of the better illuminated manuscripts, so that the effect, at least for a viewer familiar with those manuscripts, was to make one feel as if he had been magically transported into the manuscript.

Khalid's eyes grew big with wonder. Most people would have been at least somewhat amazed by the Sassani's interior decor, but to someone who had been living on the street for three years, the place must have seemed like paradise. The elaborate—and clearly very expensive—decor always made me wonder why Shar's family had settled for Santa Brígida instead of the more elite Montecito, but I had never had the nerve to ask.

"Shar, you're home early," said Mrs. Sassani as she walked into the entry hall. She must have heard Shar unlocking the front door. She was a tall, dark-haired woman, not precisely beautiful, but always immaculately dressed, looking as if she had just stepped out of a formal portrait. Someone meeting her for the first time might find her to be as formal as the portrait, but she had warmed to me quickly once Shar and I became friends, and I hoped she would do the same for Khalid.

"Tal," she continued as soon as she saw me, "how wonderful to see you! Are you joining us for dinner?"

"Thanks, Mrs. Sassani, but I'm afraid I can't tonight."

She hugged me as she always did, then turned to Khalid. "And who is this young man?" She sounded a little worried. Shar and I had gotten his hair combed and cleaned off his face, but it one took one glance for her to see how worn and ill-fitting Khalid's clothes were. I guess we should have made a stop at the mall first.

"Mother, I need to speak to you for a moment." Shar deftly led her out of the room. I couldn't hear their conversation in the next room, but I knew what they were talking about. My mind reached out in their direction, just enough to make sure Mrs. Sassani wasn't having a meltdown. The rest of my attention focused on Khalid; I wanted to keep him busy while the family conference was going on. Just in case there was a problem, I didn't want him overhearing any of the conversation.

I was also painfully conscious that Khalid was used to stealing things and was now surrounded by small, expensive objects. I believed him when he promised us he would be good, but I didn't see any reason to give temptation more opportunity than necessary. What is that old expression? Oh, yeah, it's, "Idle hands do the devil's work."

"Well, what do you think, Khalid? Can you stay here for a while?"

"It's...it's almost the best place I have ever seen," he replied, looking around, taking in every detail.

I knew without asking that the very best place was his home—with his father. I deliberately didn't ask the question that would have started *that* conversation. Instead, I did the best I could to keep the small talk going. Too bad I didn't have a little brother; I would have known better how to talk to him. As it was, I had the feeling that Khalid wasn't really into the conversation, but I did kind of remember what being eleven was like. Then again, I hadn't been living on the street for three years by the time I turned eleven. Maybe the problem was that our experiences were just too different.

If necessary, I had planned to show him the murals and start telling him their stories, but Shar's conversation with his mom was surprisingly short. In less than five minutes she came racing back into the entry hall, and hugged Khalid very sincerely, just as if he really were related in some way.

"Khalid, Shar has told me you'll be saying with us for awhile. I can't tell you how happy I am. It's been a few years since I have had a little one around the house, and I have missed it."

"He's eleven," muttered Shar, knowing Khalid probably didn't think of himself as a "little one," but his mother was running on hospitality auto-pilot and probably didn't even hear him.

"Shar, why don't you take Khalid upstairs and see if any of your older things will fit him for right now? Tomorrow we'll go get him some clothes of his own."

"Mother, his build isn't much like mine when I was that age. What I had isn't going to fit him any better than what he's already got." Khalid was a relatively slender kid, and Shar had been much bulkier even at age eleven, so he was perhaps right. Mrs. Sassani ran an appraising eye up and down Khalid and then nodded in agreement.

"You're right, Shar. Well, we need to make time before dinner to make a quick run to the mall. Khalid at least needs to have clothes that fit him. We can't have people think our relatives are street urchins."

Khalid looked down at the ground, embarrassed. Mrs. Sassani patted him on the shoulder. "Oh, I'm sorry! I'm not being critical. I know you have had a lot to deal with, Khalid. That's over now—for good. But part of making sure you don't get into trouble is making you look as if you could be related to us. That's all I meant. We'll pick up a few things for you this afternoon and then be more thorough tomorrow."

Khalid, not used to adult attention any more, was clearly getting confused, and Mrs. Sassani was empathetic enough to pick up on his feelings. "Don't worry, Khalid. I know boys your age aren't always that comfortable picking out clothes. Shar will come along and help, won't you, Shar?" Khalid's face brightened immediately. Clearly, he had gotten over his initial fear of Shar.

Shar, like most guys, would have walked over broken glass to avoid going shopping with his mom, but he did want to help Khalid, so he manned up and agreed to go.

"Tal, would you like to join us?"

No, I have to go walk through broken glass.

"I'd love to, Mrs. Sassani, but I haven't visited Carla yet." I hated to use her as an excuse, but it was true that I needed to get out there before visiting hours were over.

"Oh, I understand," she said immediately. Everybody, and I mean everybody, seemed to know about my situation with Carla. I suspected that Mrs. Rinaldi was a gossiper, but I couldn't complain too much, since whatever stories were circulating helped boost my image as a mature, responsible, giving young man, and who knew? I might need to trade on that reputation at some future point.

I said my good-byes and hit the freeway as fast as I could. Despite all of the day's surprises, Carla's situation had never been far from my mind. Knowing that Morgan was lurking around somewhere, I couldn't help worrying. I knew Vanora was supposed to have secured the hospital against any kind of incursion, but I wouldn't really be happy until I examined her arrangements myself. Also, I knew Morgan would be contacting me soon, and frankly, I wished she would just get it over with! Trying to deceive her was going to be hard enough to begin with it. Waiting for the opportunity was even worse, but what could I do about that? Not much! That was pretty much the story of my life these days.

Ah, but there was the chance, a pretty good chance actually, that I could heal Carla, and that made all the petty irritations worth it. To talk to her, to hold in my arms—for real, not in some daydream—what would I not risk for a chance like that?

By the time I pulled into the parking lot, my hands were almost shaking with the combination of anxiety and anticipation. The anxiety eased almost at once, though. I was still not ready to forgive Vanora, but I had to admit that she had handled the task of securing the hospital with speed and thoroughness. There were two of her plain-clothes security men in the parking lot, another two at the front entrance, and I had no doubt there were two at every other reasonable entrance.

Just to be sure, I let my mind wander across the hospital and identified not only guards at all the entrances but two guards patrolling each floor, and two guards on the door to Carla's room. To my satisfaction, the guards were also armed—Morgan was fast, but bullets were faster. True, I had gotten magic to work against guns and other modern technology, but as far as I knew, Morgan couldn't do that.

How Vanora had managed to justify this massive security buildup to the hospital administration I had no idea, but then again, they knew Vanora as Carrie Winn, the hospital's chief benefactor, so if she wanted something—well, really almost anything—she would get it.

As I walked across the parking lot, I checked the magical defenses and found them to be even more impressive. Vanora had set three separate protective spells around the hospital, as far as I could tell: one blocked hostile incoming spells, one prevented anyone of evil intent from entering, and one prevented Morgan specifically from entering. The last one seemed redundant, but I wasn't about to complain.

Despite all of that security, I still found myself looking over my shoulder from time to time as I moved through the hospital. Each time I half expected to see Morgan watching me from some dark corner. Of course, each time I was wrong, but my nervousness did not diminish. I guess I was entitled to feel a little nervous, considering it had been only about a day ago that I had fought a losing battle with Morgan in this very place and then had to keep her from slitting Gianni's throat to get what she wanted.

When I reached Carla's room, both guards greeted me almost as if I was their boss.

"Good evening, Mr. Weaver," said one of them, and then both stepped aside to let me enter.

Making it so easy for me to get into the room was doubtless Vanora's doing. I should have been grateful, but part of me could not let go of the fact that it was to some extent Vanora's fault Carla was in such bad shape in the first place.

The actual visit with Carla was as uneventful and painful as always—with one exception. Near the end of the visit, I actually tried the reversal spell. Yeah, I know, risky, maybe even stupid, since Morgan wasn't supposed to know I could do that spell, but I raised a barrier against any unwanted scrutiny before I started, and anyway Morgan shouldn't be able to be here in person or use a spell to spy on us, not with all Vanora's magic security working against her.

The test reinforced my faith that the spell really was the answer, but it also reinforced Morgan's point that no one spell caster could hope to do it alone. Just as in Morgan's demonstration, the green energy surged from me, hooked a reddish strand of the awakening spell, and pulled...but the end result was like a mouse trying to pull an elephant. I sang to enhance the power of the magic, I willed it to work until sweat filmed my body, until I was shaking like a leaf in a tornado, until my head ached. I did feel a slight movement, but that was all I could manage before I had to abandon the effort, exhausted.

Morgan had said three powerful casters working together could reverse the effects of the second casting of the awakening spell. She was visualizing herself, me, and…someone else. I suddenly realized I had no idea whom Morgan intended to use as the third caster, but I did know whom I wanted to use: Nurse Florence, Vanora, and me. I also knew when I wanted to make the attempt: tomorrow. The longer we delayed, the greater the chance that Morgan would discover I knew the spell and could bypass her entirely. And if she realized that, she would move heaven and earth to stop us from succeeding—or, even worse, she might attempt to recruit enough casters to bypass us and make sure Carla became Alcina.

Yeah, I know I sound paranoid. How could Morgan possibly reach Carla at this point? I had just been optimistic about the security arrangements a few minutes ago. Unfortunately, my mind had kept picking at the issue until I remembered the potential loose thread that could unravel the whole defense. The problem lay in having to ward as large an area as the hospital. Magic protections of that kind worked best when they defended a relatively small area. Stretching such spells as far as these had been stretched invariably made them thinner. Don't get me wrong; Vanora was clearly a powerful spell caster, but not powerful enough to completely redefine how magic functioned. Someone like Morgan might be able to find a weakness in such attenuated defenses, or, if she couldn't, she might succeed in bringing some other caster or casters into the picture. Attacking from several directions was the easiest way to pierce a spell that was spread too thin.

Vanora doubtless knew her approach was flawed. Perhaps that was the reason for using three separate protections, and probably she intended to reinforce them every day. Still, if Morgan found allies, she might penetrate the hospital anyway. I had pretty well talked myself into the need to revive Carla as fast as possible.

In the meantime, exhausted as I was, I squeezed one more spell out of myself. I used a protection spell that covered only her room and kept out anyone of evil intent. I could only do so much spell casting before resting, and I knew the protection would be relatively weak, but having set up some additional security made me feel a little better, and I knew I could reinforce it tomorrow, when I would be fresher.

I managed to drive home, but by the time I got there, fatigue had settled on me like a lead fog. I got through dinner on small talk auto pilot; my parents were used to giving me a little latitude by this time and didn't call me on my relative disengagement.

I dragged myself up the stairs, physically and mentally spent, as eager as I had ever been to climb into bed and forget the rest of the world for awhile.

And there, sitting on my bed and staring at me sheepishly, was Stan.

I did a kind of groggy double-take. "Stan? Is that you? Why didn't my parents tell me you were up here?"

"They kind of...don't know," replied Stan. "I just couldn't take the whole getting invited to dinner thing tonight, and I knew that's what would happen if I came over to talk to you, so I just slipped in while your mom was bringing in the groceries this afternoon."

I looked at Stan uncomprehendingly, my brain dragging itself through a conversation that seemed to flow like molasses. "Why...Oh, yeah, Nurse Florence told me you were having trouble with your previous-life memory trying to take over again."

As my dangerously overtired mind finally started focusing on Stan, I realized that though he was trying to keep his voice calm, there was fear in his eyes, more than I had sometimes seen there in combat.

"Don't worry, Stan. I can fix this. Let me just see—"

"Wait! You better know what you are up against first. He doesn't want me to tell you, but I think you should realize who you are dealing with." Stan paused, seemingly struggling for words.

"It's OK, Stan," I said reassuringly. "Whoever you were isn't going to matter to me."

Stan went pale. Suddenly I realized he wasn't just struggling for words—he was fighting his past self, and it was costing him. He put his hand to his throat as if he were having trouble breathing, and his eyes now looked frightened and desperate.

"Stan, just relax! Stop trying to tell." However, Stan didn't seem to be taking my advice. In seconds he fell out of the chair he had been sitting in and hit the floor like a sack of cement. Then he started writhing convulsively.

His past self was not just trying to keep Stan from talking. He was trying to actually take over Stan's body. The situation was far worse than Nurse Florence had realized. I had to do something fast…but just minutes ago I could barely put one foot in front of the other and was running only on adrenaline now. Still, I had to do what I could. If Stan lost control completely, getting him back in control later would be all the harder.

I went down on my knees next to Stan, grabbed one of his hands, and tried to enter his mind. I was greeted by a wave of mental static so intense that it sent a tremor through my whole body. Well rested, I could have cut through the chaos and reached Stan, but in my present condition, it was just as likely that the chaos would spread to me.

I tried to get up and head for my harp; if ever I needed musical reinforcement, now was the time. Unfortunately, at precisely that moment, Stan jumped up awkwardly. Even before I looked into his eyes, I knew that Stan had left the building.

I should have been on my guard at once, but my reflexes were as limp as everything else, and Stan's past self managed to smack me before I got into a decent defensive position. Already a little off balance, I toppled backwards, and the past self advanced on me, sword out. The only saving grace was that he didn't use the Hebrew phrase that caused the sword to increase his muscle mass. Stan had been training and working out, but I was still in better shape than he was.

Of course, that advantage would have meant much more if I hadn't been exhausted…and if I didn't have to use extreme care in a fight to keep from injuring Stan's body, a constraint his past self would probably not feel towards me.

Stan's past self took a swing with his sword that I only barely managed to dodge. No, whoever had control of Stan's body did not seem to have qualms about hurting me or even killing me.

Crap!

Reluctantly I drew White Hilt, hoping its flames would deter whoever had taken over Stan long enough for me to think of a way to get control of the situation again.

Indeed, Stan's past self dodged back a couple of steps, his blade still up, his eyes watching me warily.

"Now," I said as calmly as I could manage, "it is time for introductions." "Stan" looked at me, plainly not understanding. Then I remembered that this particular past life spoke ancient Hebrew, so I repeated the sentence in that same ancient Hebrew.

"What evil have you done to bring me here?" asked Stan's past self, brandishing his sword threateningly.

"Bringing you here was not my doing. Perhaps I can return you where you belong."

Just lose focus on me for a second, and you will be gone as fast as snow in July.

"I don't trust one word you say! You use witchcraft!" he added accusingly.

I had deduced, when working with Stan right after his awakening, that the past self that was giving him trouble was an Israelite warrior. Well, I had been one myself, centuries before I had been the original Taliesin. That life's memories were mere shadows compared to Taliesin's, but if I concentrated hard enough, perhaps I could draw sufficient memory from that earlier self to communicate better with Stan's earlier self—assuming he hadn't gutted me before I could do that.

"What makes you think I use witchcraft?" I asked in my most innocent tone.

"I have seen you cast spells, and now you stand before me with your flaming sword. How can you deny your guilt?"

The problem with that kind of argument was that I could probably not find any way to counter it that would be consistent with his world view. His mind probably saw everything in black-and-white terms, and all I had to offer him were subtle shades of gray.

"And how comes it that I am in a body not my own, hearing the thoughts of someone else?"

Ever try explaining reincarnation to an ancient Israelite? Well, don't bother!

I remembered Stan telling me once that there were Jewish mystical texts, starting with the *Zohar*, that acknowledged reincarnation, but I was sure that the past self I was dealing with came from a time before such mystical speculation had been dreamed of.

"I told you, I am not the one who put you in your current body, but you and I both agree that it isn't yours. I can tell you are a moral man, one who would not steal another's body. Help me to restore the rightful owner."

"He...he is an ally of yours. You have corrupted him!"

Interesting way to look at the situation.

"Even if that were true, the body is still his, not yours."

"You are trying to confuse me, just as you have confused him."

I realized I needed to change direction a little. "Why are you so quick to assume that I am evil? We fought side by side to defeat Ceridwen. You were the one most responsible for smashing her evil altar."

Stan's past self looked troubled. "I was so confused then, and everything was happening so fast. Yes, you and I did fight on the same side then. And this…Stanford…whose heart is open to me, he believes you are good. Yet I see the evidence before my eyes. The Lord has commanded us not to allow a witch to live."

"I know how this must look to you," I said, making a quick, fiery stroke with White Hilt. "But if, as you admit yourself, I fight evil, why could my power not come from the Lord? What of Moses? Did not he perform mighty works through the power of God?"

The more religious among you might cringe at the comparison. No, I didn't really think I was as important in God's plans as Moses. Still, if you believe that God has a plan, why couldn't the original Taliesin have been part of that plan? Why couldn't I have been? It wasn't exactly as if I worshiped Satan or drank the blood of human sacrifices to gain my power or something like that. OK, so the original Taliesin had been a practitioner of the Old Religion, but he was an ally of the Christians at Arthur's court, not the evil forces gathered against them.

Of course, convincing an ancient Israelite that people of different religions working together might be part of God's plan was not going to be an easier sell than reincarnation, so best to gloss over that part with him.

"How can I be sure that your power comes from the Lord?" asked Stan's past self, still eying me with suspicion. At least I had made a little headway with him.

"You and I pray to the same God and follow the same moral code. You know this from Stanford's memories. Have I ever used my powers for anything but good?"

Stan's past self shifted uncomfortably. "Not that Stanford knows, anyway. Yet your ways are strange."

"Many, many years have passed since your time upon the Earth," I pointed out. "I'm sure that much of what you see is strange, but strange and evil are two different things. My customs are far different from yours. That doesn't mean my heart is."

"I should be able to pray to the Lord and receive an answer to this question," said Stan's past self in obvious frustration. "Yet I cannot, for I have sinned so gravely that the Lord will not hear me."

Well, that piqued my curiosity—to say nothing of the fact that knowing who I was dealing with might help me to be more persuasive.

"Surely your sin cannot be as grave as you imagine," I prompted, hoping that perhaps he would reveal what it was.

He stared at me, his mistrust overshadowed by the most massive guilt I had ever seen. "I cannot even bring myself to say what it was. It was too terrible to speak aloud."

Well, he wasn't going to make this easy.

I cursed myself for not paying more attention to any possible clues the first time I had healed Stan. Of course, then my priority had been putting him back together, not investigating his past self, and, though dominant, his past self had not been as strong as he seemed to be now. Then his responses had been more colored by Stan's personality, not purely "non-Stan," as they clearly were now. Hell, now he was so far removed from Stan that he didn't even understand English.

If only I were not so exhausted, I could probably have read the past self's true identity from where I stood, but now I didn't think I could pick up a strong enough signal without being in physical contact, which I did not think Stan's past self would allow.

"Having already broken faith with the Lord so completely, I will not casually ignore His commands. I must find some way to test you." The stranger in Stan's body had gone back to eying me suspiciously.

At last I actually got a lucky break. As he spoke, I looked into his eyes and caught a glimpse of someone I had known almost three thousand years ago. No, it couldn't be…yet every instinct told me that it was.

"David, the Lord forgave you long ago," I said in a fairly neutral tone, though my emotions were profoundly mixed.

David looked stunned.

"David, son of Jesse, we knew each before, long ago." And so we had. Ever since my awakening, I had possessed really specific knowledge of the original Taliesin and all my lives subsequent to that one, but much more vague recall of the lives preceding the first Taliesin. I recalled my interaction with King David as if it were a half-remembered dream. Yet now, with David once again before me, my relationship with David suddenly seemed as if it were yesterday. I wasn't as used to playing my past self from that time period as I was to playing Taliesin, but I needed to make the best effort I could. Everything might depend on it.

"Surely you have not forgotten Heman, the son of Joel, the son of Samuel? I was one of your musicians, and I was a prophet of the Lord as well."

"You lie!" hissed David. "You are nothing like Heman." Once again, he was making menacing moves with his sword.

"And you are nothing like David, as you well know. Yet you are David. I am nothing like Heman, yet I am Heman. Both of us have been reborn long, long after we first knew each other. Neither one of us has ever heard of such a thing, yet here we are. The Lord has the power to do as he wills. It is not our place to question."

"How do I know you speak the truth?"

I could understand David's unwillingness to believe me. Nothing in his world view could prepare him for what I was trying to get him to believe. Having recovered my memories of that life, however, it was easy enough for me to give him the proof he needed. I could remember every single detail of our lives together—and, being roughly the same age and having been thrown together early in life, there were thousands of details I could easily use.

As I tried to undermine his skepticism, I realized what the problem was, why he was so tortured by guilt. When I had first awakened, many of my previous selves were thrown into a state of shock in which they kept reliving their own deaths. The David I was dealing with was not the too-young boy who had been the only one brave enough to face Goliath, nor the somewhat older general who won the hearts of all the Israelites with his unmatched record against the Philistines, and certainly not the much older and wiser king who finally came to be at peace with himself. David was not reliving his relatively untraumatic death over and over; he was reliving the most traumatic events in his life: his adultery with Bathsheba and the subsequent murder of her husband to prevent the adultery from being discovered.

Just as I thought I was getting a handle on the situation, someone knocked on my bedroom door.

"Tal, is everything all right?"

Oh, good, just what I needed—my newly psychic mother joining the party!

David looked around suspiciously, his sword ready.

"Yeah. I was just showing Stan a few fencing moves. I hope we weren't too loud."

"No, I just…oh, it's nothing really. I just had the strangest feeling. I'm sorry I bothered you." I held my breath until I could no longer hear her receding footsteps. It was odd that she didn't say hello to Stan, but I wasn't about to complain about that. I was just happy her "feelings" hadn't become more specific.

The interruption wasn't the catastrophe it might have been, but it did put David in a less communicative mood for a while. I looked nervously at the clock. My parents were so used to Stan hanging out that Mom hadn't even questioned his presence in my room. However, if he were still there at two o'clock in the morning, that might be much harder to explain. Yet all I had accomplished so far was keeping him from disemboweling me with his sword. Well, perhaps a little bit more; he was willing to believe that I *could* somehow be Heman, but he remained unconvinced that I *was*, despite my knowledge of every detail Heman would know.

Part of the problem was that I was really too weak at this point to do much without his cooperation. Well rested, I could have easily just put him to sleep and gone to work reconnecting him with Stan, but as it was, my subtle efforts to get him to sleep or even to calm down were only making him more suspicious. He sensed something was happening, but the magic never quite established a strong enough connection with his mind to actually work. I cursed myself for having expended so much energy on testing the reversal spell earlier, but there was nothing I could do about that now.

Finally I asked, "What can I possibly do to persuade you of the truth of my words?"

David considered. "You cannot. Only the Lord can do that. If what you say is true, the Lord will provide a sign that you speak the truth."

Want me to part the Pacific Ocean for you?

Since David had already accused me of witchcraft, I didn't know what made him think he could tell a divine sign from a fake one, but I wasn't about to question what might be my only chance to fix this problem.

"Nurse Florence? Our Israelite king wants a miracle to convince him I'm not a witch." I knew my message was very weak, and I prayed earnestly that she would hear and respond.

"WHAT?" I heard in a few seconds.

"Yeah, Stan's really David, and he wants a miracle, but I'm just too

tired. We'll be in my backyard. I need you to create a convincing display for him."

"Well, that's a new one. All right; I'll do what I can."

"David, let us go behind my house and pray. In due course the Lord will provide what you seek. We must sheathe our swords first, as is only fitting for an act of worship." David looked profoundly uneasy, but when I sheathed White Hilt, he followed my example.

I led him down the stairs and out the back door as quietly as I could. My parents were preoccupied with a fairly intense conversation and didn't pay any attention. Just as well, since I doubted David was in any mood to pretend to be Stan—nor able to, judging from the way he was acting.

The backyard's lush greenness normally calmed me, but tonight my nerves were so on edge it had little effect. David and I knelt in the grass, he for illumination from the Lord, and I for a timely rescue by Nurse Florence. I knew that traveling in Annwn was a dangerous proposition with Morgan around, but I hoped Nurse Florence would do it safely this time. Traveling here from her apartment by car would take at least half an hour, and who knew how long David's patience would last?

Just as he seemed to be getting fidgety, I felt Nurse Florence's presence nearby.

"Will an illusion only you two can see do? I don't want to alarm the neighbors."

"Whatever. Just do it quickly!"

As soon as she received my reply, I was suddenly blinded by a ray of pure white light lancing down from the sky and piercing the growing darkness. David jumped up and blinked, trying to see what was happening.

"Get up and raise your hands to the sky!" commanded Nurse Florence. I was a little wobbly on my feet by this time from having knelt, but I did the best I could, knowing that David could see me silhouetted against the "heavenly" light.

"'God' is about to speak to David, but I need you to broadcast to me what to say—I don't know Biblical Hebrew."

"OK," I replied, sending her a simple message to broadcast to David. I was afraid giving Nurse Florence too much Hebrew at once would make it more likely she might make a mistake and cause David to doubt that he was really hearing God.

Even knowing what to expect, I almost jumped when the voice of "God" started booming in my ears and, no doubt, David's as well. Nurse Florence had more expertise with special effects than I had realized.

"David!"

"Yes, Lord," replied David in an awestruck tone.

"Taliesin, whom you once knew as Heman, is my loyal servant. Do not doubt what he tells you. Rather, embrace him as a true friend and comrade. Jonathan himself could not have been any more true."

"Lord, it shall be as you have commanded!" declared David loudly. I was thankful our house was so big, and my parents were near the front of it. I don't know what they would have made of David's part of that conversation.

Abruptly, the blinding light vanished. David, visibly shaken, took the "Lord's" command rather literally and gave me a rib-cracking hug.

"Heman, forgive me for doubting you. It is just that everything is so…different from the way it once was."

"Some things have not changed, my king," I replied as formally as I could. "Our friendship and our loyalty to the Lord, for example."

"No, I see now that they have not. What would you have me do?"

"David, you were meant to…watch over Stanford, not to take over his body. You must permit him to take command of it again."

David looked puzzled. "Gladly, but I know not how to do that."

"Lie down on the grass here. I am going to put you to sleep. Do not resist. While you sleep, I will bring back Stanford."

David lay down without a second thought. "It shall be as you have said. Heman, will I still know what is happening once Stanford is back?"

Not if I can help it!

"Yes," I lied. "You will be with him, and with me, till the end of his days."

David smiled, and I caught a glimpse of the younger David, with his infinite hope for the future. "I will watch over him well."

"Farewell, David," I replied, and then I began to sing. I almost started in Welsh, but I switched to Hebrew just in time. Now that David was cooperating, I had him asleep in seconds.

I used to think our backyard was over-landscaped, in the same way that Santa Brígida in general was artificial, but tonight I was thankful for the ornamental pond, from which Nurse Florence suddenly emerged, making a typical lady-of-the-lake style entrance.

"So he really is David?" asked Nurse Florence as soon as she had walked over to where David/Stan was lying in the grass. "King David?"

"I knew King David in an earlier life," I reminded her. "There is no doubt."

"Well, I guess the Order will have to rethink some of its assumptions. What's wrong, Tal?" Even without the ability to read minds as I could, Nurse Florence was getting to be able to read me like a book.

"I don't know," I thought, shuffling my feet nervously, afraid to say too much aloud, even in front of a sleeping David. "I had to lie to David. I told him I was Heman, without explaining that I had been Heman in the past but was really someone else now."

Nurse Florence understood and followed my lead. "A distinction he probably could not have comprehended," she pointed out.

"And then we fooled him into thinking he was talking to God. I think I'm feeling a little guilty about that."

"You called for my help to do that very thing. It was your idea," replied Nurse Florence in mild exasperation.

"I'm not trying to blame you. I know it was my idea. That doesn't mean I can't have second thoughts."

"Yes it does!" she shot back with considerable intensity. "Look, Tal, we are facing some pretty serious problems, not the least of which is keeping Stan from falling apart. You don't have the luxury of self-doubt right now, understand?"

I nodded, but without much conviction.

"Listen, I would rather not have lied to him either," she continued more softly, "but from the message you sent to me, I assume he wasn't going to cooperate unless we manipulated him a little."

"Yeah, that's about the size of it," I admitted. "And I'm exhausted right now, way too weak to overpower him by magic."

Nurse Florence looked puzzled. "The attempt to capture Khalid was that strenuous?"

"That didn't help, but I had a few other...adventures. We'll talk about them later." I knew she would not approve of my efforts to test the reversal spell, so that was one conversation I was not looking forward to, but she didn't press me for further explanation anyway.

"If you are that tired, how are you going to heal Stan? I don't know how to put this kind of fractured persona together the way you do."

"Honestly, events have been moving so fast, I haven't really thought about that problem," I admitted. *"Perhaps I can guide you through the process."*

"Too cumbersome!" thought Nurse Florence immediately. *"I know enough about your approach to know I couldn't execute it well without practice. Let me lend you my strength; that'll get the job done more efficiently."*

"It may not be that much of a struggle now that David is willing, but you're probably correct about strategy. We'll do it your way."

Nurse Florence and I sat down in the grass next to each other. She took my left hand, and I put my right hand on David/Stan's forehead. As soon as we had gotten settled, I could feel the warmth of her strength surging within me, revitalizing me. I relaxed, started to sing, (this time in Welsh), and let my mind flow into Stan's.

Just as I suspected, the David persona had broken almost completely loose from Stan's mind. I could see the jagged edges on each where the connection between them had shattered. I reached out to David, who sensed me and flowed toward Stan in harmony with my thoughts. I reached into Stan and found him almost impossible to return to consciousness, so stunned by David's utter breakaway that at first I could hardly tell he was still there. The sensation was so eerily like probing Carla that for one horrifying second I thought perhaps he was beyond my reach. Then I felt him, dimly at first, then more strongly. I took hold of him and steered him toward David. The two of met, flowed together, and almost joined.

Yeah, almost joined. Those jagged edges should have fit together perfectly, but they did not. It was as if there were little pieces of the old Stan still missing, pieces that would have completed the connection between the two. But if there were such pieces, I couldn't find them, and those jagged edges kept resisting my best efforts to create a seamless reunion.

Could Nurse Florence have been right? Was I so different from other people that only I could manage to keep my mind from shattering, despite the pressure from all of those other lives?

And if she was right, what was to become of Stan?

I forced myself not to think of that. Instead, I visualized both David and Stan surrounded by the warmth of my friendship. I took that friendship, focused it like a laser, and tried melting the edges of each persona to fuse them together.

I struggled for what seemed like hours, but the best I could do, despite burning through most of Nurse Florence's energy, was a temporary fix. Stan would be in charge of his body again, but David was still not fully re-integrated. Enough pressure, and the connections which I had crudely re-welded would snap apart again. Since David was now an ally rather than a wary stranger, the odds were good he would not deliberately rip away from Stan and try to take over the body again, but if something happened to weaken Stan, like a magic attack or even a more mundane problem, David might suddenly end up back in control, or at least in a position to overwhelm Stan with emotions.

When I finally re-emerged in the physical world, Stan was conscious again, Nurse Florence was looking as drained as she was, and I had a hard time getting to my feet.

Stan rose more slowly. "It didn't work, did it?"

"It worked to an extent," I said tiredly. "We have to do more work sometime soon, but for right now, at least you're you again."

"I seem to be," Stan admitted, though his tone still betrayed worry. "I can still feel David, but…something's different. I'm still feeling guilt, but he isn't as intense about it as he was before."

"Perhaps being able to talk to God made him wonder if he had been forgiven after all," I suggested.

Stan raised an eyebrow at that.

"Later, dude," I continued, knowing it wasn't really safe to discuss that subject if David wasn't completely merged with Stan yet. "Right now let's get you home. It must be late."

Nurse Florence glanced down at her watch. "It feels like three in the morning, but it's really only ten at night."

"That's late enough for me!" I said. "Nurse Florence, thanks again. Can I—" I was about to say something like, "walk you to your car?" before I realized how ridiculous that would be.

"No, thank you, I'll…see myself out," replied Nurse Florence with a grin as she stepped toward the pond.

"Well, good night then," I said, matching her grin. *"Could you perhaps manage a burning bush the next time we do this?"*

"It'll be on my to-do list," replied Nurse Florence as she stepped into the pond and then vanished into it. I had seen her do that several times, but I still couldn't quite get used to it, even though the original Taliesin had certainly grown accustomed to it.

"OK, Stan, your mom probably has the bloodhounds out by now," I said, sounding much cheerier than I felt.

"I planned ahead," said Stan quickly. "I told her I might be spending the night. I wasn't sure what was going to happen."

"It's always good to plan ahead. You want to stay over? I'm sure my parents wouldn't mind."

Stan considered for a minute. "You look like you need your sleep. I'd probably better go home."

"OK, but in that case, I should walk you home."

Stan started to protest but then thought better of it. He only lived three doors down, and he was far more capable of taking care of himself than he had been a year ago, so I'm not sure exactly why I insisted on walking him home. Maybe I was being overprotective. On the other hand, Stan had been close to getting killed more than once in the last few weeks, and Morgan Le Fay was on the loose, so perhaps my caution was warranted.

The walk turned out to be uneventful, and I was home before I knew it, and in bed almost before I knew it. In minutes I was so deep in sleep that I might have slept through a major earthquake—or at least until my alarm went off. Sadly, that was not to be.

It started with a dream. In this dream I woke up—you've dreamed of waking up at least once, right? Anyway, when I awoke, I realized someone was in bed with me. Illogically for real life but consistent with many of my recent dreams, I thought it was Carla. Then a chill passed through me and I stiffened. No, not like that—get your minds out of the gutter! I stiffened with fear, because I realized the other person was not Carla, despite the black hair. No, it was Morgan, staring at me by the moonlight that filtered in through my window and smiling invitingly.

My first impulse was to jump out of bed, but I suddenly realized I was naked. Odd—I was sure I had been wearing pajamas when I went to sleep. Oh, yeah, this was a dream. It had to be a dream, because Morgan couldn't physically get into the house. I didn't know she could dream-walk, but that must be what she was doing. I would have to remember to adjust the protection on the house to prevent that kind of thing in the future.

"I have gotten more enthusiastic welcomes," observed Morgan, her smile broadening. "If you try to scramble any further away from me, you'll fall right out of the bed. It's chilly in here; come over, and warm me up."

"Morgan," I replied, striving for the most dignified tone I could manage under the circumstances, "what do you want from me? I'm pretty sure it isn't sex."

"Don't sell yourself short," said Morgan, leering at me as if she had x-ray vision and was looking right through the sheet and blankets. Fortunately, the ancient Celts had not conceived of x-ray vision, and Morgan was not that much of an innovator when it came to magic.

"I know you," I pointed out, "and you may have slept with many men, but never impulsively. You want something, or you wouldn't be here, so you may as well just tell me what it is."

"I want...many things," she replied evasively, slowly but playfully sliding closer to me. I tried to get a little further away, but she was right—too much further, and I would fall out of bed.

"However, the thing I want the most, even a little more than your sweet body, is an agreement about Alcina."

"I'm inclined to agree with Nurse Florence that separating Alcina from Carla would be pretty difficult, since they only have one soul between them," I pointed out. "How would you solve that problem?" At this point I just managed to clamber out of bed, with a sheet around me, before Morgan could reach me.

Morgan hovered on the edge of the bed for a while, pretending to pout over my escape from the bed. Tiring of that in a short time, she continued. "Don't be misled by the water witch's dogma. Did she not also tell you your playmate Stan could not be a reincarnation of King David?"

The fact that Morgan had somehow learned of that conversation was problematic, but I kept my emotions from showing on my face. "That's a little different," I said.

"Is it? There are many people today who believe a soul can be split in two. And didn't you discover two minds within Stan tonight? Don't look so surprised; you forgot to extend your protection to the green space behind your house. Anyway, didn't you?"

"Two minds are a very different situation than two souls. As far as I can tell, when someone's past-life memories are awakened, the human brain, not knowing what to do with the new information, treats each set of memories as if it were a separate mind. Really, there is still only one mind."

"Then David was just an illusion? If you believe that, why was it so hard for you to banish him?"

Well, she had a point there.

"You know that mentally David is just as real as you or I. Can you really think he doesn't have a soul?"

"I'm sure he has a soul. The problem is that it is the same soul Stan has."

Morgan sighed loudly. "What if I were willing to take all the risks. You could bind me with a *tynged* that would require me to leave forever if I was unable to provide Alcina with both a separate body and a separate soul."

I had forgotten about the body part, yet another major problem. "You're that sure you can manage both?" I asked.

Morgan dismissed the question with a wave of her hand. "If I were not sure, I would not be here."

I was sorely tempted to propose an oath right at that moment, but the terms of it would require careful deliberation. Besides, since I knew the reversal spell myself, I didn't need to make an agreement with Morgan to get Carla back; given enough other casters, I could bring Carla back without her, suppressing Alcina in the process. However, the moment Morgan realized that I would not make a deal with her, she would become a major threat to everyone I loved, maybe even to everyone I knew. Again, I needed to at least pretend to be interested.

"I would need time to work out the terms,"

"As would I," Morgan cut in.

"As would we both then. Let us meet again in a week or so—in more business-like circumstances."

"Oh, where is the fun in that?" asked Morgan in mock seriousness. "You were not such a prude when you were Taliesin the bard." With that, she rose from the bed, without anything wrapped around her, presumably to show me what I was missing. Apparently, I was missing a lot... Had I not been in love with poor, comatose Carla, I might almost have succumbed to Morgan's considerable charms.

"I see from the way you grip your sheet that we will not be making love tonight, Taliesin. Never fear, though—that night will come. We will talk again in a week...though I cannot guarantee the more business-like part. With a wave of her arm, Morgan faded into the moonlight and was gone.

I woke up the moment she stopped dream-walking me, badly

tangled up in the sheets, but otherwise unscathed. I glanced over at the clock. Damn! It was only two o'clock in the morning, too early for a cold shower. Too bad—at this point I could really have used one!

CHAPTER 7: TIME IS OF THE ESSENCE

I got up in the morning thinking that at least today couldn't be worse than yesterday. Then I almost slapped myself because whenever I thought something like that, the day found a way to become worse than the previous one.

Breakfast was even stranger than it had been yesterday. Mom talked at some length about dreaming there was an intruder in the house. I could tell Dad was becoming concerned. If I hadn't known the truth myself, I might have been concerned too. She kept prefacing her remarks with, "I'm sure I'm being silly," but she still sounded a little paranoid anyway. I almost dropped my spoon when she started talking about what the intruder in her dreams looked like—and described Morgan almost exactly!

I wanted to reassure her and my dad. Damn it, I wanted to tell them the truth, but I knew I couldn't. The most I could do was hug my mom extra hard on the way out the door. Somehow, that didn't seem like enough.

My walk to school with Stan was no better. He was quiet and obviously nervous.

"Stan? You aren't holding out on me again?"

"Nothing new has happened," he replied too quickly and too defensively.

I made a practice of not trying to read people's minds unless absolutely necessary. Well, if Stan was already having trouble again, I needed to know it, so as we walked along, I infiltrated his mind, subtly probing for information.

His mind was still welded to David's, but the welds already looked less substantial to me than they had last night. I could see the equivalent of hairline cracks on some of them. I couldn't understand why the situation was changing so fast, especially now that David was trying to be cooperative. I strengthened the joining as much as I could without tipping him off that I was rummaging around in his head. Nurse Florence and I would need to reinforce the connection between him and David—and soon.

I looked for a moment at my own mind, but there was no sign of the degradation so obviously present in Stan's. I could only see one mind, my own, without even an echo from any of my past lives. Sure, I had their memories and skills if I concentrated hard enough, but they were no longer separate entities and had not been since I managed to merge them four years ago. The integration was seamless. No other mind reader could ever tell that my mind had once been shattered into hundreds of past selves. If I had mended mine so well, why couldn't I do the same for Stan?

That question continued to nag at me all morning. I stopped by Nurse Florence's office during nutrition, but naturally she couldn't solve the problem either.

"Tal, you can show me Stan's mind, but you're the expert on how to deal with past selves. I wouldn't really know what I was looking at."

"Is there anyone else who might help?" I asked, already knowing the answer.

"I'm afraid this is such a new problem I wouldn't even know where to start."

"Do you think Stan's condition supports Morgan's theory that a soul can be split?"

Well, that got her attention. Switching immediately to mental communication, she said, *"I thought you were just pretending to entertain the possibility to fool Morgan. You aren't telling me Stan has two souls in him, are you?"*

"I can't really see souls, only minds. He has two minds in him, and I know from last night that they won't merge easily. Maybe that means that each mind is connected to a separate soul." Suddenly, I wanted to believe Morgan, at least on that issue. Because if somehow Stan and David had two separate souls, perhaps David's could be extracted from Stan and sent to whatever afterlife awaited David.

"The soul can't be split," asserted Nurse Florence emphatically. *"And if it could, wouldn't it be evil to do it? What possible good could such a thing bring?"*

"Morgan dream-walked me last night and suggested a tynged that would let her try her theory and then force her into exile forever if her experiment failed."

"It's a trick. Tal, you know who we are dealing with better than I. You know the role she played in bringing down Camelot. We both know how she allied with Ceridwen to destroy us all. Tell me you are not actually considering working with her."

"I'm not really. What I want is to revive Carla without Morgan being anywhere close. The only reason I'm having second thoughts is what is

happening to Stan. I can't seem to put him together correctly even with David cooperating. How am I going to be able to heal Carla if Alcina, who probably won't cooperate, is as powerful as Morgan says? And even if I can, we still have Morgan to deal with afterward."

"Agreed. Vanora has an idea about that." It would be hard for me to accept any of Vanora's ideas, and Nurse Florence knew that, but she kept going anyway. *"She believes the safest approach is to take Carla to the Order's headquarters in Wales. There we can attempt the reversal spell with a number of other spell casters to reinforce our attempts. And if you can't heal Carla appropriately right away, she will stay with the Order until you can. Our headquarters is far easier to defend than the hospital is, and it is likely Morgan won't even know Carla is there."*

"What about Carla's family, and the staff at the hospital?"

"Since Carla is in a coma anyway, it would not be hard to substitute an illusion of some kind."

I couldn't really say I liked the idea, but it did have some merit. Right now, all Morgan needed to do was assemble strong enough casters, and she could awaken Carla herself—and make sure Alcina got the upper hand. True, Vanora had warded the hospital and I had warded Carla's room, but Morgan would keep picking away at the defenses once she discovered them, and she would have the luxury of picking away at them full-time if necessary.

"What do we do with Morgan once she realizes she's been deceived?"

"That's still a work in progress," thought Nurse Florence cautiously. *"But that's going to be a problem no matter what we do with Carla— unless we do exactly what Morgan wants."*

I shifted uneasily in my chair. *"How do we get Carla to Wales?"*

"Water portals would be too tricky with someone in Carla's condition. We'd have to use Annwn."

I raised an eyebrow at that.

"I know, I know, that isn't ideal, but Vanora is working on securing Gwynn's permission to use his territory. If we calculate the route correctly, we can travel from Santa Barbara to Wales without ever leaving his territory. You, Vanora and I, plus the guys and a few of Gwynn's warriors should be enough of a force to keep routine menaces away."

I nodded. Gwynn ap Nudd, the king of the Welsh faeries, respected me and the guys and did regular business with Nurse Florence's Order, so he'd probably be willing to give us safe conduct and protection.

Still, the idea of carrying Carla that distance, even through the relatively flexible geography of Annwn, was daunting. Then again, what other options did we have?

"I don't like it, but it may be our best bet. If Vanora gets Gwynn's support, let's go ahead."

"OK," replied Nurse Florence, switching back to voice. "You'd better go, Tal; your next class is starting soon."

My mind wasn't much on school for the rest of the day. I did try to pull myself together for the soccer game, mostly because I would catch hell from Dan, our team captain, if I didn't. Soccer games, since my parents usually came, were also occasions during which I had to at least appear to be happy and untroubled. I had put my parents through too much already; I owed it to them not to create more worries for them if I could possibly help it.

Fortunately, today's opponents, Saint David's Episcopalian High School, weren't exactly strong opponents, so the fact that I was a little off my normal game wasn't even noticeable. Dan was brilliant, as he always was, the team as a whole performed well, and Saint David's never knew what hit them. OK, so I did actually fumble a relatively simple pass to Dan at one point, and he noticed, but he knew what kind of problems I had on my mind. OK, so one of my chip passes almost hit one of the Saint David's players in the head instead of going above it. Even the Saint David's coach said it was obviously accidental. OK, so one of my attempts at interception only ended up shifting the ball to another Saint David's player. OK, so I wasn't likely to be MVP at this rate. OK, so Coach Morton must have been beginning to wonder if putting me on varsity after four years of not playing soccer was really such a smart move after all.

Frankly, as long as I could somehow take care of Carla and Stan, and at some point my newly psychic mother, I couldn't care less what happened on the soccer field. Well, that wasn't quite true. I didn't want to let the other guys down, and on those rare occasions when I didn't have fourteen different things to worry about simultaneously, I actually enjoyed soccer; it reminded me of the old days, when I could just be a normal kid.

I really hadn't paid too much attention to the stands today, but I did look around a little as the game was ending. Predictably, there were my parents, sitting as always with Mr. and Mrs. Rinaldi, and naturally Gianni. It took me a minute to recognize that the other kid sitting next to Gianni was *Khalid*, but not the ragged thief from yesterday. Instead, he was clearly wearing part of his new Sassani wardrobe. Even from a distance, he looked like a commercial for one of the exclusive clothing stores on Rodeo Drive. If Mrs. Sassani wanted to pass him off as Shar's cousin, she was certainly doing a good job.

I remembered that Gianni had already met him, which probably explained why Khalid was sitting with Gianni's family. Then I realized abruptly that Khalid's earlier meeting with Gianni was problematic, since Khalid was pretending to be Shar's just-arrived cousin. However, the two of them were chatting happily, so I had to assume that Khalid must have given Gianni some plausible explanation. Anyway, there was time enough to worry about that little glitch later.

Sitting some distance away from them was Eva O'Reilly, once my girlfriend, but Dan's for the last four years. She was still every bit the strawberry-blond sex goddess she had always been, but I no longer felt a throbbing ache when I looked at her. Ever since I had fallen in love with Carla, my feelings for Eva had dissipated like thin smoke in a high wind. Oh, we were still friends, and she was one of the few people who had been through Samhain with us and therefore knew my secret, but there was no longer any possibility of a romantic entanglement that could jeopardize my ability to work with—and remain friends with—Dan. When she saw me looking in her direction, she gave me a friendly wave, mercifully oblivious to all the turmoil she had caused me just a few weeks ago. I waved back, knowing that at least I didn't need to worry about her any more.

Then I froze. Sitting only a short distance from Eva was a familiar figure in white samite with pale skin and long, lustrous black hair.

Yeah, that's right—Morgan Le Fay herself…and drawing quite a bit of attention, I might add. Morgan was good at many things, but clearly disguising herself as a soccer mom was not one of them. By now I would have thought Morgan would at least dress modern for public appearances like this, but apparently not. Well, at least some of the soccer dads were getting a cheap thrill out of the situation.

She winked and blew a kiss at me. Dan trotted over to me as soon as he noticed her.

"Is that who I think it is?" he asked worriedly.

"I'm afraid that's exactly who you think it is, and the way my luck is running, she's either here to kill someone or to force herself on me in the showers."

Dan raised an eyebrow. "Sounds like there is a story I haven't heard yet, but that can wait. What do you want us to do about it? Did you summon the rest of the guys?"

"She hasn't really done anything yet, and we can't go into combat mode with an audience like this. I'm afraid the next move is going to have to be hers."

At that point most of the other players were heading for the locker room, and Coach Morton was headed my way, no doubt to tell me to get my head in the game. As it turned out, I was right, and the coach distracted me from watching the stands for a minute. When I looked back up, I saw to my horror that Morgan had walked over and introduced herself to the Rinaldis and my parents.

Quickly I adjusted my eyes and ears for greater acuteness. The introductions among the adults would have sounded mundane if I had not known the context, except for Morgan's interesting explanation of her unorthodox style of dress. Morgan presented herself as a recent immigrant from the small European nation of Cymru. Within the group she was talking to, only my parents might have recognized Cymru as the Welsh name for Wales, but they didn't seem to pick up on that. Morgan had a fifth-century Celtic accent that would not be recognizable even to my parents, despite their Welsh ancestry.

Mrs. Rinaldi, who would have tried to make a leper feel welcome if one had shown up at the game, launched into a discourse about how her parents and her husband's parents had all immigrated to the United States, so she knew a little bit about how that situation felt, and she would be happy to show Morgan around any time, maybe go shopping for some American-style dresses—oh, and really, Morgan simply must come over for dinner some time soon.

While Morgan was feigning interest in Mrs. Rinaldi's friendly banter, I glanced over at my mom, who was not looking friendly at all. In fact, she had taken a step or two away from where Morgan was standing. Her expression, if not actually fearful, was profoundly uneasy. My dad hadn't noticed yet, but I was betting Morgan would notice if she looked in that direction, and the last thing I needed was Morgan realizing that my mom was developing some magical ability.

Dan had maneuvered over to the fence separating the stands from the field, ostensibly to talk to Eva, but really to be closer to Morgan if the situation required it. Shar, whom I hadn't noticed earlier, had appeared from somewhere; probably he had come to give Khalid a ride home and spotted Morgan. Of Khalid himself, there was no sign. Since he had been trying to avoid Morgan, he had probably taken off as soon as she moved in his direction.

It would have been harder to play soccer while wearing a sword, so Dan and I had left ours in the locker room, but I now realized that might have been a mistake. Shar was armed, though, and Zom was the most effective weapon against Morgan we had. He had inserted himself into the group Morgan was chatting with and had his hand on his sword, a clear enough signal to Morgan that the group was under his protection, and by extension, under mine. Of course, Morgan knew that. I was sure her presence was a none-too-subtle threat.

I did a quick mental check. Gordy and Stan were still in wrestling practice, and Carlos was still in swim practice. I sent them a quick message that Morgan was in the stands near the soccer field and that they should come as quickly as they could. I also sent a quick SOS to Nurse Florence. Then, not waiting for her response, I went through the gate and up into the stands, nominally to say hello to my parents, but really to find out what Morgan was up to.

Morgan feigned surprise when she saw me approach. "Why, isn't that Taliesin Weaver? I have heard so much about him." My dad looked pleased; my mom, something close to horrified; her maternal instincts, now magically reinforced, were clearly sounding the alarm.

Faking courtesy, I extended a hand and said, "Pleased to meet you, Ms.—?"

She took my hand, playing with my palm in a flirtatious way nobody else could see. "Call me Morgana, Taliesin."

"What brings you here, Morgana?" I asked in my best innocent tone.

"I have family in the area. I came for a visit and thought I should try to experience some of America while I was here."

Dan had tipped off Eva that something was up, and now he was moving in our direction. Eva had taken off, possibly to get help. Without even looking, I could feel Nurse Florence getting closer.

"I have to say," continued Morgan, "that the people here are so friendly, I'll definitely stay until I've really had time to do some catching up with my family." Translation: Until you give me Alcina, or at least agree to try, you'll never have a moment's peace, because I will find ways to threaten everyone you care about.

"*What is she doing here?*" Nurse Florence's thoughts resounded in my head. It was risky to communicate mentally with Morgan so near, since she could conceivably overhear, but I could feel that Nurse Florence was "broadcasting" very narrowly, targeting just me, so I did the same.

"*As near as I can tell, making clear how much I have to lose if I don't do what she wants.*"

"*What do you want to do?*"

"*There isn't much we can do as long as she's surrounded by innocent bystanders. I guess the short answer is get her alone.*"

"Taliesin," said Morgan loudly. "Is your mind wandering? I was just asking what you were going to do this afternoon. I thought perhaps you could give me a tour of the high school. I've never seen an American high school."

"I'm sorry, Morgana, but I'm afraid I can't today. I have…things to do."

"Taliesin visits our daughter, Carla, every day," said Mrs. Rinaldi. "She's in a coma. He comes every day, without fail. He is an angel." Normally I would be embarrassed by Mrs. Rinaldi gushing about me. Today I was too stressed-out to worry about it.

Morgan eyed me appraisingly. "Yes…an angel is exactly what he seems to be." Gianni giggled a little at that, as if he had somehow picked up on her ironic undertone.

"Well, angel," continued Mrs. Rinaldi, "I think Carla would want you to show this nice stranger around and make her feel welcome."

"I'm sure Tal would be more comfortable giving the tour some other time," interjected my mom, much more firmly than she normally would have. I glanced over in her direction and could tell she had realized that Morgan was the source of her uneasiness.

"Actually, another day might be better," I cut in quickly, hoping to distract Morgan from my mom.

"Another day it is then," replied Morgan. "But I will hold you to that."

With the exception of my mom, none of the adults seemed interested in bringing this conversation to an end. That all changed with the sudden arrival of Vanora, playing Carrie Winn as usual. Just like Ceridwen before her, Vanora swept in, and all adult attention focused on her. She chatted for a few minutes with the Rinaldis and my folks, to Morgan's obvious irritation, then introduced herself to Morgan and invited her on a tour of the city! As an exercise in turning the tables, that was pretty neat. Morgan could hardly refuse the invitation, though it would separate her from all the innocent bystanders she wanted to continue toying with.

Since no one in Santa Brígida would have presumed to get between Carrie Winn and what she wanted, the adults quickly said their good-byes and left, with the Rinaldis taking Gianni along, even though he clearly wanted to hang out with me. That left Morgan; Vanora; Nurse Florence, who came up in the stands as soon as everyone else had left; Dan; and Shar. Glancing behind us, I could see Stan, Gordy, and Carlos all hurrying across the field in our direction, Stan and Gordy having stopped to pick up my sword and Dan's.

I had expected that Morgan might try to make a quick exit in the face of such overwhelming potential force, but she stood her ground, eying Vanora and Nurse Florence particularly defiantly.

"Morgan, what is it you want?" asked Nurse Florence. She was trying for an emotionally neutral tone, but I could tell she could barely restrain herself from a much more abrupt rejoinder.

"I have made it quite clear what I want," replied Morgan icily. "What is not clear is what you people want."

"You gone," said Vanora simply. "You have no right being here."

Morgan turned on her, eyes flashing. "And you have no right trying to keep me from my sister! Did you think I wouldn't notice I am now cut off from her? What gives you the right to do that?"

"Just a precaution to keep you from running off with her and trying the reversal spell on your own." Vanora looked back at Morgan unflinchingly.

"I can't," replied Morgan tersely, inviting an obvious question, but not bothering to answer it. By now Stan, Gordy, and Carlos had reached us and handed Dan and me our swords. Morgan seemed unconcerned by the accumulation of armed force all around her.

None of us wanted to give her the satisfaction, but finally Nurse Florence asked, "Why can't you just find enough casters and do the spell yourself?"

"Because, water witch, Ceridwen showed quite a sense of humor in designing that spell. She never thought she would need to use a reversal spell, so to make the original spell as easy as possible to cast, she made the reversal spell as hard as possible. Not only does it require a high power level, as you already know, but it also requires a caster who has been a target of the original spell. So unless Taliesin's playmate over there," she said, indicating Stan with a dismissive gesture, "has suddenly become a caster, or my sister has developed the ability to cast spells while in a trance, Taliesin is the only person who can cast the spell and make it work. Others can lend their power, but Taliesin must be the driving force."

It seemed out of character for Morgan to admit to such an obvious weakness. Perhaps she was lying, trying to catch us off guard. There was really no way to tell. I couldn't read the mind of someone as powerful as Morgan unless she wanted me to.

"So you see, I need Taliesin to get Alcina back, and since only I know the spell involved, he needs me to get Carla back...unless, of course, he doesn't."

That last phrase put me on high alert, as it did Nurse Florence and Vanora. The others didn't understand that Morgan was voicing the suspicion that I had mastered the spell myself and didn't need her. But how could she know? And, if she did know, or at least suspect, what was she doing giving us such an obvious shot at her? What did she think would prevent us from killing her if we didn't need her knowledge of the spell?

"Don't look so shocked, Taliesin," she continued. "Your shield work wasn't all that good that night at the hospital. I couldn't hear or see from where I was, but I could *feel* that very distinctive spell. You must have done it. Somehow, I know not how, you have learned it just from watching me cast it. And you plan to use it without me, to keep my sister from me forever. Don't deny it—the look in your eyes is a complete confession."

The last time we had confronted Morgan, we had to consider the safety of Carla and Gianni. This time there were no innocent bystanders to worry about, and we had more than enough power to capture Morgan before she could do any more harm. I could see Vanora at least pondering the same idea and coming to the same conclusion. One sorceress, even one as powerful as Morgan, wouldn't stand much of a chance against three other casters and five or six warriors (depending on whether you wanted to count me as a warrior also) with magic swords. Surely this was too easy!

Yeah, well, you could have figured that Morgan would not just walk into our midst without a plan of some kind. She had evidently prepared the area to connect quickly with Annwn, and those of us magical enough to have sensed that kind of connection were too busy worrying about Morgan to notice. Because she had prepared in advance, she was able to vanish with a single gesture, not wait to build up enough energy to open a gateway. Nurse Florence and even the usually unflappable Vanora seemed at a loss for what to do next.

"Let's try to follow her!" I shouted. I couldn't move into Annwn by myself because Arawn's ban against me was still in effect, but in theory Nurse Florence or Vanora might be able to pull all of us through and land us near to the spot in Annwn to which Morgan had escaped if we moved fast enough. It was clear, though, that neither shared my enthusiasm for the idea.

"*Tal, we can't do that without knowing what she has on the other side. This whole situation feels like a trap to me,*" replied Nurse Florence.

"*Yes,*" added Vanora. "*Clearly she wants us to follow. At a guess, she wants to lure most of us to our deaths. You she wants to capture, at least if she was telling the truth, because she needs you for the spell.*"

"*And if she is still at large, she can threaten anyone she wants to in an effort to get me to help her,*" I thought angrily. "*We can't leave her free to strike out at whomever she likes.*"

"*I'm not the one who let her live on Samhain,*" thought Vanora quietly. "*Some of your men had the opportunity to kill her and did not take it.*"

"*Enough bickering!*" barked Nurse Florence with surprising vehemence. "*It may not be wise to follow Morgan, but we do need to act quickly to thwart her. Vanora, have you finished negotiating with Gwynn for safe passage and protection through his land?*" Vanora nodded quickly. "*Then our first priority should be getting Carla to Wales. Morgan is evil, maybe even crazy, but she isn't stupid. Once Carla is safely away from us, Morgan will focus her efforts in Wales, and the Order is much better able to defend their headquarters than we are to defend the hospital or any other site.*"

"*Or Morgan will take hostages and force us to get Carla back from Wales,*" I pointed out. "*In fact, if she isn't stupid, that's the most likely thing she'll do.*"

By now the guys were pretty restless. They knew enough about our protocols to know I was probably communicating with Nurse Florence and Vanora mentally, but they were impatient to know what was happening. I gestured to them to wait just a minute.

"*Taliesin, what exactly do you want us to do? Walk into an ambush? Viviane tells me she and your warriors almost didn't make it to the hospital a couple days ago because of just such an ambush—and that was just one of Morgan's contingency plans. I would bet Morgan has an even larger force at her disposal now."*

"Where is she getting these allies? When we met her in Annwn on Founders' Day, she had empty suits of armor fighting for her."

"We can discuss how Morgan handles her recruiting later," thought Vanora in her most grimly final tone. *"Now, do you want us to get Carla out of Morgan's immediate reach, or not?"*

"We need to move Carla," I agreed, still frustrated that we had not tried to capture Morgan right away. *"But if we all head in the same direction, Morgan is going to figure out what we are doing pretty quickly. You ladies will need to provide some magical distortions to keep her from knowing with certainty where we are."*

"Not a problem," replied Vanora.

"Well, this next request might be. Neither I nor the guys will want to leave our families and friends unless we know they are safe. OK, so we can't go after Morgan now. And you can't ward the whole town against her."

"Yes, you know that kind of spell will never stretch that far."

"But your security force is pretty large, and you have them wired for certain kinds of magic, correct?"

Vanora looked stunned for a moment. *"Clever, Taliesin!"* she replied. *"But how did you know that?"*

Because I'm not as stupid as you seem to think I am, I thought to myself. To her I replied, *"Because I have noticed your security men—and the kind of vibes they put out. It wasn't hard to figure out you had created some kind of magical network using them. Remember, you also asked me and Stan quite a few questions that suggested you were contemplating just such a project."*

"Why, yes, the experience with new forms of magic that you and Stanford have worked out was indispensable in fleshing out what I wanted to do. But how is the nature of my security force relevant?"

"That depends entirely on what you have made them capable of doing. I think they could provide protection for the whole town if properly deployed."

Again I had caught Vanora by surprise. *"Well, borrowing one of your ideas, I can see through any of their eyes if I need to. I can channel spells through them also, enabling me to cast from a greater distance than would ordinarily be possible. I also made them somewhat spell resistant, though they couldn't stand against a really powerful magical attack. Naturally, there is also a very specific tynged in place to keep them from betraying us. But Taliesin,"* she continued, shifting to a more patronizing tone, *"I designed my 'network' to be effective over a short distance, so I could more easily ward Carrie Winn's castle or—"*

"Use them as a security detail to protect yourself," I interjected cynically.

"Or you, if the need arose."

I decided to let that claim go by without comment, since until now I couldn't see what threat Vanora would have needed to protect me against.

"But the problem is, their links to me were designed for short distances. I don't think they are strong enough to cover the whole town."

"Oh, I've poked at them a little bit, Vanora, and I think in a pinch they can pick up your signal across the length of this town…and I think you know that."

"I know no such thing—"

"Well, I do!" I cut in, ignoring her protest. *"Their connection with you may not be as strong, but it will be workable, and you'll have a few hours to reinforce it. That's time enough for some formidable magic preparation if you use those hours well."* Vanora was a lot older and more experienced than I was…in this life. However, this was one of those moments when I was perfectly willing to play the I-was-the-original-Taliesin card.

"But I have to prepare for Carla's removal—"

"Nurse Florence can make what arrangements are needed," I replied, without even waiting for her confirmation.

"The 'network' won't function well while I'm in Annwn—" began Vanora, sure that she had a winning argument.

"Which is exactly why you aren't going to Annwn." If I thought I had seen Vanora at her most shocked earlier, I was wrong…but she was certainly at her most shocked now.

"Were you under the impression that you could give me orders?" she sputtered.

I continued as if I had not heard the question. *"Here's the plan. The rest of us make preparations and then proceed to Annwn with Carla. Vanora will deploy her security detail across the town, with at least one group near each of our families and the others distributed as mobile reinforcements. Vanora can shift quickly from one man to another, scanning for Morgan. And if Morgan manages to slip through, whatever target she tries to hit, she'll be facing several armed men, and even she isn't fast enough to dodge bullets."*

"You'll need some of those men…and me…in Annwn, Taliesin," said Vanora in a very forbidding, I-have-spoken kind of tone. *"We cannot afford to lose Carla to Morgan. And we cannot afford to let anything happen to you. You have irreplaceable abilities, as well as a much greater destiny—"*

I didn't know where all the destiny crap was coming from, so I decided to ignore it. *"We won't lose Carla. And I don't think Morgan will manage to kill me, but if she does, she does. Better that than Morgan slaughtering my family while I'm away."* No, I wasn't at all eager to die, but I knew what I was capable of, what the guys were, and what Nurse Florence was—and we had some of Gwynn's men as well, and his safe passage. That seemed more than enough to deal with anything Morgan could throw at us, even if she was smart enough to figure out where we were, yet foolish enough to risk Gwynn's wrath.

Vanora, who I thought was probably used to having her way even before she started being Carrie Winn twenty-four seven, was clearly annoyed by my taking control of the operation. I absolutely, completely, didn't care, as long as she did her job. The truth was I was tired of being ordered around like an unruly teenager. OK, technically I was a teenager, but I also had thousands of years of experience, including the life of the original Taliesin. I, not Vanora, really knew how Morgan's mind worked. I also had a greater understanding of magic than Vanora did. She was a powerful caster; that much I would happily admit. But even to construct her innovative network, she had needed my help. Who was she to dismiss me as a mere boy?

I know what you're thinking: I was still angry with Vanora for what happened to Carla on Samhain. Well, damn right, I was! And I should have been. Vanora's problem as a decision maker was that she was heartless, perfectly willing to treat people like Carla as collateral damage. In her mind, keeping Carla away from Morgan was more important than restoring Carla to health. Preserving me, for reasons I couldn't fathom, was somehow more important than protecting our friends and family from Morgan's impending wrath. The cold logic of a military commander might justify such choices, but I would never accept them.

"If all of my men and I stay here, transporting Carla safely to Wales becomes problematic. Morgan's strength is greater in Annwn than it is here. I will not allow this kind of mistake." Vanora was thinking calmly, but I could sense something very close to anger behind her words.

"Vanora, Tal may be making his argument rather abruptly," thought Nurse Florence, giving me a scolding look, *"but his point is well-taken. You have enough manpower and magic to keep Morgan from working mischief here while the rest of us are in Annwn. Without that kind of protection for their loved ones, I can't see any of the guys wanting to go to Annwn in the first place."*

"And what about tomorrow and the next day?" asked Vanora, in a tone she doubtless thought of as calm but seemed more like cold to me. *"I'll concede that Taliesin's plan might work long enough for you to transport Carla, but a magic network spread out across the whole town is just as unwieldy in the long run as a warding spell spread out the same way. Either it will absorb my whole attention, and possibly yours as well, or it will in time degrade, and Morgan need only orchestrate attacks from multiple directions to accelerate that process."*

"And that is why," I thought with finality, *"right after we make Carla safe, we go after Morgan. We capture her, or, if we cannot, we kill her."* I was proud of myself for not hesitating on the last part. Vanora was right about one thing: leaving Morgan alive on Samhain had been a mistake, one we were paying for now. I had no desire to kill Morgan, or anyone for that matter. But if it kept Carla safe, and my parents, and my friends, then I would do it.

Vanora was thoroughly bent out of shape by this time. Belatedly, though I wasn't sorry for standing up for what I knew was right, I did realize I should have been more diplomatic instead of letting my emotions interfere. In the end, it was Nurse Florence who got Vanora to accept my suggestion/demand. Even then, Vanora made her protest clear, insisting that if the whole Annwn expedition failed, its failure would be on my head. Finally she cleared out, presumably back to Awen to make her preparations. I didn't give her part of the plan another thought. Vanora might be an emotional iceberg, but I could not imagine her blowing her assignment because it had been forced on her. No, once given a task, she would perform it to the best of her ability. Even I had to admit that about her.

Once the plan was (grudgingly) agreed to, I broadcast the details to the guys. They couldn't normally project their own thoughts for us to have a real conversation, as I could have with Nurse Florence or Vanora, but they could at least hear me, and that was enough in this case.

Nurse Florence hurried off to make final arrangements with Gwynn and with the Order. Dan and I changed back into our street

clothes, which seemed more practical for Annwn than our soccer uni-
forms, and then Dan, Stan, and Gordy piled into my Prius and headed
for the hospital. Shar had just gotten a Lexus from his parents, and so he
took Carlos.

In a very short time, we reached the hospital. Shar and I parked,
and then we rushed to the hospital. No point in trying to be mysterious.
If Nurse Florence and Vanora had "jammed" Morgan's ability to track us,
then she wouldn't be able to see us anyway. If Morgan had defeated the
jamming somehow, she would recognize us, and no nonchalant saunter
was going to fool her.

Once in the hospital, I threw a little don't-notice-me spell around
us just in case. I didn't want to explain to hospital personnel why so many
of us were visiting Carla at one time. We reached her room without incident. Vanora's guards saw us, but they stood aside to allow us in without
comment. Then we spent an awkward few minutes fidgeting until Nurse
Florence arrived, and then more time fidgeting while she wheeled in another bed and then created an illusionary double of Carla to put in it.
Under other circumstances, watching Carla's double become more and
more solid and more and more like Carla as Nurse Florence worked would
have been interesting, and actually it did keep the guys enthralled, but I
was anxious to be on our way. This process took longer than I would have
liked, but there was really no way to speed it up. A visual illusion would
have been hard enough, but this one had to hold up to touch, since doctors and nurses would be examining her, to say nothing of family members
holding her hand. Finally Nurse Florence pronounced herself satisfied,
and, examining the fake Carla with only my physical senses, I had to say
that she would stand up pretty well to scrutiny.

Then, with a little help from Stan, I magicked the various moni-
tors Carla was attached to, so that they would continue to give the kind
of readings they had been giving once we disconnected them from Carla
and connected them to the double. Nurse Florence knew how everything
should be hooked up, so that part went quickly, and we were finally ready
to go. Nurse Florence opened a glowing portal to Annwn and stood back
to allow the others to enter. She and I came last, wheeling Carla's bed.

I had first experienced Annwn about fifteen hundred years ago,
Nurse Florence more recently, the guys even more recently, but each new
visit seemed much like the first time for each of us. Despite the mist that
tended to hang over everything, Annwn was somehow always more vivid,

more alive than the "real" world. We passed from the hospital into a brilliant green meadow surrounded by massive oaks that looked as if they had been growing for a thousand years—and could have been, given the nature of the place. Since modern technology much above the level of a match would not work in Annwn, the place's unspoiled quality would have seemed miraculous even without Annwn's innate magic.

Somewhat to my surprise, twenty faerie archers were waiting for us in the meadow. I knew Gwynn had agreed to provide us an escort, but this one was larger than I expected—not that I was complaining! Given their speed, reflexes, and keen vision, faeries could shoot arrows faster and more accurately than pretty much any other group I could think of. Like most faeries, these were tall, slender, blondish, brilliantly blue-eyed, luminously pale-skinned and not easy to categorize by age, since faeries didn't typically show much sign of it, unless they chose to for effect. However, I doubted that Gwynn would send inexperienced fighters with us. These particular faeries were recognizable as men of the *Tyllwth Teg* by their red-and-white tunics, some decorated with a red, white and black design that looked like an abstract portrayal of Gwynn's three hounds, the *Cwn Annwn*.

I would have preferred more practical attire, recalling that the faerie warriors we met last fall had not been so decoratively dressed. This group seemed more ceremonial. Then it occurred to me that their attire would signal to anyone their connection to Gwynn—a visual symbol of his protection of our party.

"I am Sir Arian," announced one of the faeries as he moved in my direction. "As our king has agreed, we are here to escort you to the gateway to the headquarters of the Order of the Ladies of the Lake in Cardiff." I bowed to him, as did Nurse Florence, and the other members of our party followed our lead.

"However," continued Sir Arian, "there is someone here who is not included in Gwynn ap Nudd's protection." I looked around, puzzled, wondering how the usually meticulous Vanora could have failed to include one of our party members. If anything, she would have included more, since she must originally have negotiated places for herself and some of her security men.

"Someone invisible," added Arian in response to my obvious confusion.

Morgan?

No, I knew that no one could have joined us unseen in the hospital, given how well warded it was, at least not without making a considerable magical ruckus. But then who else would want to sneak in as part of our group? I had been so intent on the preparations for moving Carla that I had not been looking intently enough to see an invisible intruder, but I did so now, and a diminutive figure, trying to hide behind Shar, came slowly into focus.

"Khalid?" I looked at him in astonishment. "What are you doing here?" Knowing his invisibility trick was not working anymore, Khalid stepped somewhat reluctantly away from Shar, who was every bit as amazed as I was. Khalid was trying to adopt a tough-guy facade, but he just didn't have the physical presence to pull it off yet. In fact, his lip quivered almost imperceptibly. Wow, you would have thought I was going to hit him or something. Then I thought about how his life had been going recently, and I realized he probably did expect someone to hit him. I needed to be careful about how I handled him.

"Khalid," I said as calmly as I could. "Why *are* you here?"

"Yeah," added Shar. "My mother's gonna be worried sick."

"It's OK," said Khalid quietly. "She thinks I'm with you. Right after you walked out the door, I told her I was going to ask you if I could go with you. And I am with you…I just didn't ask."

"Khalid, you lied to my mother."

"So did you," he said defensively. "You told her you were going to the library. And I bet you don't tell her you wear a magic sword to school every day, either."

"I don't want her to worry," replied Shar. Well, that was certainly a masterpiece of understatement if ever there was one.

"You still haven't answered my question, Khalid," I prodded. "Why did you come? What we have to do is dangerous, and we've trained for this kind of situation. You haven't."

Khalid looked at me apprehensively, as if being told to go back home would be the worst thing that could happen to him. "I could help. I haven't trained in the way you have, but you've seen how fast I am, and I got Shar's sword away from him."

"That wasn't in a combat situation," pointed out Shar, somewhat defensively.

"Tal, we have to get moving," said Nurse Florence firmly.

"Carla's condition is unprecedented enough that I have no idea how extended exposure to Annwn will affect her."

"Is there a problem?" I asked quickly, looking at Carla.

"No, but we've only been here a few minutes. I'm not saying the situation is dangerous, but I don't think we should take chances."

"Agreed. Sorry, Khalid, but you need to go back. Nurse Florence will open a doorway for you back into the hospital."

"No! I want to go with you guys." Unspoken, but clear from his eyes, was that what he really wanted was to be part of the group. After months and months of living on the street, I couldn't really blame him.

"Tal," said Shar, "is he really going to be any safer in Santa Brígida with Morgan skulking around?" Given the security arrangements in place there, I was certain he would be, and so was Shar, but clearly he felt bad for the kid and wanted to be able to take him with us.

Sir Arian had been studying Khalid intently. "He is not just a human boy, is he?"

"Half djinn," replied Nurse Florence.

"Please, sir," said Khalid. "I *can* help. And I promise not to get in the way!" Much to my surprise, the seemingly solemn Sir Arian chuckled a bit.

"The boy has spirit," he noted. "Viviane, do you accept responsibility for him?"

Nurse Florence clearly did not want Khalid under foot, but she didn't see a quick way of getting rid of him, and she did want to get under way. "Sir Arian, I will accept responsibility."

"Then in the name of Gwynn ap Nudd, I extend your safe conduct and your protection to him." Then, less solemnly, he added, "Gwynn told me to expect at least one surprise from your party, Taliesin." I hoped that was a compliment, but the tone Sir Arian used made it a little hard to tell.

Khalid couldn't have been happier. Only his desire to look less boyish restrained him from jumping twenty feet in the air, though I could tell he was contemplating the idea.

It took a little more time to get the logistics straightened out, but finally we began to move forward. Dan, Stan, Gordy, Shar (with Khalid), and Carlos were at the front of the party. Nurse Florence and I were at the back, following Carla's bed, which was now floating safely on a bit of cloud Nurse Florence had commandeered. I hadn't thought much about the differences between Earth and Annwn that she had been mentioning to me in one of our earlier conversations, but there was no denying it was easier to manipulate the physical world in Annwn.

The faerie archers floated somewhat above us, both to have a better view and a clean shot in the event someone—or something—did choose to attack us.

"Well, I guess that explains why there are no horses," I said, looking up.

"Faerie horses have become even more skittish about taking human riders than in the days of the original Taliesin," replied Nurse Florence. "We didn't have time for that. Don't worry, though; we only have a couple of days' walk ahead of us."

"A couple of days?" asked Stan loudly, looking back at us. "But we only have cover stories for this afternoon!"

"A couple of days here, but more like a couple of hours back in Santa Brígida."

"When we met Gwynn in October, the visit didn't take only one twenty-fourth of the time," objected Stan. "It took more or less the same amount of time here as it did there."

"It is hard to explain in scientific or even rational terms," replied Nurse Florence. "The flow of time here is not connected to the flow of time in our world in any logical way. Just take my word for it."

"Nonetheless," I began, "it does seem odd that we picked a location in Annwn two days away from the gateway to the Order's headquarters. Why not emerge right at the gateway?"

"That's one of the Order's security measures. The headquarters maintains a connection to Annwn, and members of the Order who happen to be in the headquarters can use that connection to enter Annwn and return to the headquarters from the same spot. However, travelers, even Order members from outside headquarters, can't enter through the gateway unless they have entered Annwn at least two days distance from it. That makes it harder for a potentially hostile force to pop in unannounced."

"It also makes it hard on those of us who aren't used to hiking," observed Carlos.

"I thought all that swimming made your legs strong," said Gordy.

"Yeah, you'd think, but it doesn't work quite the same muscles that hiking and running do."

Carlos glanced self-consciously in my direction while he was talking, then quickly looked away. He had mentioned to me before that he often ended up feeling like the odd-man-out during our adventures. He had gotten somewhat less sword training than the others, and though he was as athletic as anyone in the party, except for Shar, the skills he had acquired as a water polo player and a swimmer didn't have the same value on the battlefield as Shar's martial arts training or even Dan and Gordy's football background. To me Carlos looked as effective in combat as anyone else, but he clearly didn't see himself that way, and now here was yet another situation in which he felt less capable than the others. I wanted to make him feel better about himself, to affirm his value to all of us, but I knew just telling him wouldn't do the trick. I would have to think of some way to convince him once we had taken care of Carla and dealt with Morgan.

There were occasional other bursts of conversation, but as we walked on, most of our attention went to sightseeing. The Santa Barbara area did have its park space and nearby forests, but they just couldn't compare to the pristine beauty of the forests of Annwn. While we walked, I sang, partly for entertainment, but also to keep my magic at its height, just in case. I also magicked all of us to be a little faster, except Khalid, who naturally didn't need the boost. The speed would also serve a purpose in the unlikely event of attack, but it would also get us to the Order much faster. Sir Arian glanced down, having no doubt felt the power, and smiled approvingly.

For what seemed like several hours we marched through Annwn, enjoying the scenery and gradually becoming somewhat less alert, though probably the faeries remained as vigilant as ever, and Nurse Florence spent most of her time carefully monitoring Carla's condition. As for me, I was diligently daydreaming about what life would be like with Carla restored. To hold her in my arms again, to kiss her again, even to have a conversation with her again, would move me more than all the natural beauty around me.

Then I noticed the chill. The usual mist made the time of day a little more difficult to figure out in Annwn, but I think we had started in Annwn's morning and were now somewhere in late afternoon. However, it was not the sun gliding toward the west that was causing the sudden cold. The breeze had been relatively warm only moments before. No, something was wrong…very wrong.

Just as I was realizing that we had a problem, Sir Arian landed right next to me. "There is a deep fog rolling in from the east," he began solemnly. "It is not a natural fog. My men and I sense dire evil within. I know not who would dare raise such wickedness in an area ruled by Gwynn ap Nudd, but they will come to regret their arrogant folly."

However much *they* might come to regret it later, I was pretty much regretting it now. We were traveling toward the east, and as I glanced in that direction, I could already see the fog swallowing part of the road we were on. Avoiding it seemed impossible, unless we all flew around it, and the guys couldn't do that. I suppose we could have mag-icked them into the air, but steering that many people who really couldn't steer themselves would be problematic, to say the least—even assuming that the fog couldn't follow us, and I was sure my luck wasn't going to be that good.

"What's our next move, Sir Arian?" Before he could answer me, he had to stretch out his arm so that an owl could land on it, and not just any owl; it was larger than I had ever seen, and its eyes were certainly bigger and brighter. Sir Arian whispered to it in what seemed to be owl language, then sent it flying toward the west.

"Owls are Gwynn's sacred birds," he explained. "That one will carry the message of this incursion to Gwynn, who will be here straighta-way with a much larger force. As for our next move—"

Before he could finish, we both saw the enormous night-black raven emerge from the steadily advancing fog and fly with unnatural swift-ness after the owl. At Sir Arian's signal, nineteen fairy arrows pierced its breast—and it just kept on flying. Sharpening my vision, I looked closely at it and could see why the arrows had not stopped it: it was already dead, reanimated by the darkest of dark magics. Sir Arian could see the same thing.

"Aim for the wings!" he shouted to his men. "Alive or dead, it can't fly if its wings are badly enough damaged."

The next round of arrows punctured the wings in several places, and the raven began to falter, but its momentum was still carrying it closer to the owl. I had already drawn White Hilt, so I simply channeled its flame into a bolt aimed at the raven. Unfortunately, a combination of factors, including my comparative lack of experience with ranged weapons and my inability to adjust the focus of my enhanced distance vision quickly enough, caused me to miss.

Another round of faerie arrows sailed through the air, but the raven struck the owl first, digging its claws into it and causing it to lose control of its flight. The owl tried to turn its head enough to counterattack with its beak, but it was unable to twist that far. In a moment the two birds crashed into the top branches of a nearby alder tree and were lost to sight.

The raven's flight had only distracted us for a couple of minutes, but in that time the fog had picked up speed, cutting its distance from us in half. The guys had already drawn their swords, but there was still no visible enemy. One of Sir Arian's men flew off to attempt a rescue of the messenger owl, while the rest landed with our group.

"I cannot accurately gauge the strength of this menace," warned Sir Arian. "In such circumstances, I would counsel retreat."

Much as I wanted to get Carla to the Order's headquarters, retreat seemed the only option for now—except that the fog, which must have been accelerating exponentially, suddenly engulfed us, rendering retreat difficult, if not impossible. Aside from feeling the cold gnawing at my bones, I realized that I had lost all sense of direction. Perhaps that was the fog's effect, or perhaps it was actually shifting us to a different place. That second kind of attack, difficult to pull off in the regular world, was easier in Annwn, and it would be a serious threat in our present circumstances, because if we could be shifted out of Gwynn's territory, he would not be able to protect us. Then there was the problem of finding our way to the Order's headquarters. Getting lost in Annwn would not be easy with someone like Nurse Florence along, but it was not impossible.

"Don't move!" I yelled to the guys; the faeries I felt sure would know how to handle the situation. If anyone got separated from the party at this point, that person could be in grave danger.

Whether we were being moved or just disoriented, the fog effectively disrupted our defenses. It was thick enough that a threat could get very close to us before we could see any sign that anything was wrong. As for the faerie archers, their primary fighting mode was completely eliminated. They all managed to land, stow their bows on their backs, and draw short swords they carried for just this kind of situation, but unquestionably they were at a disadvantage. Nonetheless, they encircled us, determined to fulfill their trust—or die trying. The question was, what exactly was in the fog?

We did not have to wait too long to find out. The fog did not muffle sounds, and so we had no difficulty hearing the clanking of enough armor to suggest that a sizable force was approaching, though from which direction was impossible to say.

A short distance away, I could just make out the emerald gleam of Zom as Shar wielded it to cut through the fog, which, being magical, could not resist the blade. Clever as that idea was, it didn't get him very far, because Zom only affected the part of the fog it actually touched, so even if Shar took his biggest swing, he could only clear the area within a blade's length of himself, and it started to fill in again very quickly.

The sound of armor all around us had become louder and louder, but I still couldn't tell from what direction it was coming. I gave up trying and instead went back to singing, pouring every ounce of power I could into my words, heightening the guys' abilities, speed, and morale for the fight that had to be only a minute or two away at most. Near me I could hear Nurse Florence casting a spell in an effort to lift the fog.

Then I could see sparks all around me as swords clanged against swords. From what I could tell, we faced a small force—at least I hoped it was small—in black armor. The only thing that saved us from disaster in the first round of attacks was that the attackers swung rather slowly. Otherwise they could have gotten close enough to us to wound us almost before we could respond. Even as it was, we were hard-pressed immediately. Our adversaries might be a bit slow, but they were strong, bringing their blades down with enough force to jar out teeth and nearly rip the swords from our grasps. Only Shar and sword-enhanced Stan really had enough muscle to maintain firm grips in the face of that kind of assault, and the faeries couldn't come close. One of them was disarmed almost immediately, and they quickly switched strategies and started dodging more than parrying.

It did not take me long to figure out that our foes weren't human. I managed to hit the closest ones with fire, but the resultant superheating of their armor didn't elicit any response from them at all, not even a whimper, much less a scream. Could they be animated suits of armor such as we had encountered a couple of months ago during our first meeting with Morgan? No, I thought I could smell burning flesh. Come to think of it, though the armor made it difficult to tell, they could be reanimated dead, like the raven earlier. (I tended not to think of them as undead, because that's really a modern term. At King Arthur's court, one was either alive or dead, and that was it.)

It was Shar who first proved my theory. Zom would not break whatever was animating them just by striking their armor, but any flesh wound might just end their unnatural travesty of life, and hacking away at armor with a sword like Zom, it was only so long before Shar could actually wound an opponent, at which point that opponent clattered to the ground, dead again, just as I had suspected.

The rest of us were not doing as well. It did not take me long to realize I needed fire hot enough to melt the armor on one of these dead knights to do their dead flesh enough damage to "kill" it, but it was dangerous to stir up that much of a blaze in such close proximity to either humans or faeries. Not only that, but Sir Arian was shouting at me to be careful and not anger the forest. I did get a couple good shots in, but I needed to find a way to do better than that before we were overwhelmed.

Gordy and Carlos both had faerie swords designed to affect living adversaries, so neither one was much supernatural use against the dead, though physically they could still cut through ordinary armor pretty well, and fortunately the dead had only ordinary armor. Stan was managing a little better, because the strength his sword gave him enabled him to strike his opponents a little harder. Dan, on the other hand, was managing worse. His sword protected him against bleeding from a wound, but these opponents appeared to be striking to hack off limbs, and not bleeding wouldn't help him much if his arms ended up lying on the ground. To avoid being struck, he had to dodge their blows, just like the faeries did. If we got out of this alive, I would have to remember to point that out to him.

Abruptly the fog melted away. I glanced at Nurse Florence, who was shaking from the effort. As it turned out, the effort was well worth it, because the battle turned decisively at that point. The faeries took to the air and started pounding the remaining dead with archery attacks. The dead were confused by airborne enemies, and the faeries were expert at scoring hits in the armor's joints, weakening it and soon causing it to fall apart. They also hit gaps created by the guys' swords, and those faerie arrows seemed to short-circuit the animation of the dead almost as effectively as Zom did. With better vision, it was easier for me to hit the dead with fire where it would do the most damage. Under these conditions, we made short work of the revived corpses sent against us.

Then, tired from all the sword swinging, arrow shooting, and spell casting, we had to face the one who had sent them.

CHAPTER 8: ONE HELL OF A LIP-LOCK

The good news? We still seemed to be on the same road, in the middle of the same forest, facing in the right direction to proceed on our trip to the headquarters of the Order of the Ladies of the Lake. The bad news? Blocking the road was now a chapel that covered the entire pathway and seemed to press unnaturally into the trees on either side of it. I could almost hear those trees screaming in protest. In theory, we could work our way through the forest and come out on the other side of the road, but I sensed that such a strategy was not really possible. If we tried, the chapel would simply relocate to block our new path. There was no way around, only through.

For those of you who are thinking, "OK, then just walk through the chapel," the situation was more complicated than that. Clearly, this was no ordinary chapel. Quite aside from its sudden appearance in Gwynn's kingdom, an intrusion that had Sir Arian and the other faeries fuming, the chapel was not adorned by any cross, and its front facade appeared to be black marble. Though I could not see the other outer walls very well, as far as I could tell, they were all black marble as well. The heavy bronze double entry doors had a disturbingly unbiblical portrayal of an army of skeletons surrounding a knight. Whatever this place was, it was not a Christian house of worship. Nonetheless, I was willing to bet its construction was typical in at least one way: it would have no back door, so there would be no walking through it. The only way to continue our journey would be to pass whatever test the creator of the chapel had in mind. Above the door hung the shields of many knights, presumably those who had earlier tried and failed to pass the test, if the fact that the shields were hanging upside down was any indication.

The dead knights we had faced had not been carrying shields. It did kind of make me wonder...

"Well, what now?" asked Dan. "I notice the door is slightly ajar. Someone seems to want us to come in."

"But should we?" asked Carlos. "Why not just find a path through the forest and walk around?" I explained my thinking about that, with Sir Arian nodding grimly in agreement.

"If you want to reach your destination, someone will have to go in," Sir Arian said unhappily, "but the situation is doubtful at best. I say

we turn back. Gwynn will want to drive this abomination from his kingdom, and then you can proceed in safety."

"We may not have that luxury," I said sadly. "If Morgan Le Fay
is behind this—" I started, only to be interrupted by an audible hiss from
the faeries. "If she is," I continued, "then this whole situation was set up
precisely to get us to turn around. If that's what she wants, I say we can't
give it to her."

"Morgan would not dare such a thing in Gwynn's kingdom," objected Sir Arian.

"Someone has," observed one of the other faeries.

"I'll go in," I said. "If Morgan spoke the truth, she needs me, so
whatever is in there won't kill me."

"Morgan is not the only possibility," said Nurse Florence. "If she
is behind this, why send an army of the dead that could possibly have
injured Carla and defeated her whole purpose?"

"The army gave us a hard time at first, but it was slow, and it was
ill-equipped, at least as far as its armor was concerned" pointed out Dan.
"If the same group had been given faerie armor, it would have been a
different story. If you ask me, that battle was designed to throw us off a
little, not to kill us. Morgan could be behind it."

"Or it could be a preliminary test to determine who is worthy to
enter the chapel, in which case any evil spell caster might be behind it,"
argued Nurse Florence.

"Any insane, evil spell caster who believes he can risk the wrath
of Gwynn ap Nudd," corrected Sir Arian.

"The only way to know is to go inside," I insisted. "From out
here, we can all sense evil, but that's about it."

"If your mind is set on this course," said Sir Arian, making little
attempt to conceal his unhappiness about the idea, "then I will go in."

"I can't ask you to risk yourself, Sir Arian. This is my journey, so
this is my battle."

"This is all of our journey," said Gordy loudly. "We are a team.
Tal, you may be the leader, but you can't shut us out."

"I do not mean to be abrupt," said Sir Arian, in a voice that suggested he really meant to be more than just abrupt. "However, all of you,
Taliesin included, are *guests* here. You are our responsibility." With a wave
of his hand, he indicated the other faeries. "If anyone goes in, it will be I,
and no other." With that, he literally flew at the door, cutting off any

further objection I might have had. However, just before he reached the chapel, the door slammed shut with a resounding clang. Sir Arian smashed into it at full speed and fell to the ground in a heap. Fortunately, Nurse Florence was on hand, and her healing power would work just as well on faeries as on humans. She and some of Sir Arian's men moved him away from the chapel, at which point the door opened a little bit.

"Clearly, it wants someone specific," suggested Stan.

"Or it wants humans, not faeries," added Shar.

"Well, all we have now is trial and error—and I'm going to be the next trial," I said firmly. If I was going to get this done, I needed to do it while Sir Arian was still unconscious.

What I had thought was a simple enough statement unleashed chaos. The faeries stepped in front of me only a little faster than the guys did.

"You will do as Sir Arian directs," said one of the faeries menacingly. Well, at least he was trying to go for menacing, but what was he really going to do? Shoot me with his arrows?

"And what exactly has he directed?" I asked harshly. "He said he was going in. Clearly, he can't. Has he given you orders to block my path? No, he hasn't. So get out of my way!"

"His intent was clear enough," said the faerie, not giving an inch. "You cannot pass."

I found myself feeling a little desperate. I didn't want to hurt anyone, but I knew turning back was probably exactly what Morgan wanted, and I couldn't allow anyone else to risk himself in the chapel. "I think we both know I can pass. The question is whether I have to sweep the road with you first." The faerie still didn't back down, but I made him flinch a little. Doubtless he was aware that faeries might be faster, but humans were stronger—and I could speed myself up if I needed to. He may also have heard about how well I passed Gwynn's test a couple months back.

"Really?" asked Shar. "And are you going to sweep the road with all of us? Because you might have a little harder time getting past me than past one of our faerie friends."

"Enough alpha-male competitiveness for one day!" shouted Nurse Florence from somewhere behind me. "I need you all to stay where you are and be quiet so I can properly heal Sir Arian." Being sensitive to subtext, I knew that was directed more to me than to anyone else. From her point of view, I was the one creating the problem.

So I was all alone. As far as I could tell, the only hope of getting Carla to Wales and safely away from Morgan was for me to enter the chapel, a course of action everyone else was apparently dead-set against. Even Stan, whom I might have expected to stand up for me, had become part of the human wall blocking my path.

I looked over at Carla. Her beautiful face was so impassive that it might have belonged to a statue. Every instinct I had told me that if Morgan managed to capture her, Morgan would find a way to ensure that Alcina, and only Alcina, emerged from that coma. Carla would be as good as dead. And it would be as much my fault as her current condition was— unless I entered the chapel.

Silly as it was, I began scheming about how to take on all of my friends and the whole faerie escort. Obviously, I couldn't take them all on physically, but perhaps there was some application of magic that would do the job, particularly if I could hit them with something that they weren't expecting.

"I'll go in," shouted a high-pitched voice from behind me.

I'm embarrassed to admit it, but I had forgotten all about Khalid. Generally, he had been hanging close to Shar, so I hadn't worried about him, but now he had taken one of his gigantic leaps and landed halfway to the chapel. Shar, caught by surprise and currently functioning at human speed, had no hope of catching him. The faeries might have had a shot, but they too were taken by surprise and didn't react immediately.

"No!" I yelled, accelerating myself as I ran in his direction. Magic only works so fast, though, and I knew I could not reach a high enough speed in time to catch him. My only slim hope was that Shar was right, and the chapel only wanted humans, in which case Khalid's half djinn nature might keep him out.

Khalid took another literal flying leap and landed right in front of the door. Either Shar was wrong, or Khalid's strange trajectory confused the chapel, or the chapel had no idea what a half djinn was and hesitated a second too long. Regardless, Khalid was able to pop through the door, which slammed shut a second later. My heart pounding so hard that I felt as if it might rip out of my chest, I reached the door an agonizing few seconds after and grabbed the right side handle, but the double doors were frozen in place. Either the chapel was still confused, or it admitted only one at a time—or it had really wanted Khalid all along, which seemed unlikely. Regardless, I should have been paying better attention to him.

Whatever else happened now, I had to get him out.

I raised White Hilt and hit the chapel door with all the power I could muster. The first blow barely made any impression, but as I kept hacking away, I could see it getting hotter. However, it was clearly no ordinary material, and it might take a long time to actually melt it or break it.

By this time pretty much everyone except Nurse Florence and Sir Arian had joined us. Shar started striking the door with Zom, trying to break whatever spell held it shut. "Aim for the crack between the two halves of the door," suggested Stan. "That could be where the locking magic is." It was hard to imagine that just a few months ago Stan had been a science geek, without a clue that magic even existed. Now he was fast becoming a magic geek as well, with an understanding of its operation more perceptive than perhaps anyone in our group except for me and Nurse Florence.

Sure enough, when Shar pushed his blade between the double doors, there was a loud creaking, followed by a green flash, and then the doors shuddered open. All of us rushed in, knowing that the locking spell might regenerate quickly.

Even with light pouring in from the open doorway, the interior was gloomy at best, and just as I suspected, in moments the door slammed shut behind us, leaving us in almost total darkness. There was a light near the altar, but its sickly radiance did not help much. The emerald glow of Zom helped, as did the fire of White Hilt, but neither seemed to create as much light as it should normally have done. Despite the limited light, I could see someone moving near the altar, but not Khalid. The shadowy form was taller and seemed to be female, but even that much was hard to tell.

"Khalid? Where are you?" Shar asked loudly. It was the only time I could remember hearing a note of panic in his voice.

"I'm here," Khalid responded, but it sounded as if he were a thousand miles away, and I could not tell from what direction his voice was coming.

"Silence!" commanded the figure near the altar. "Who dares to bring an army into the Chapel Perilous? The test here is for one knight alone. All of you must leave or face a terrible curse."

"In the name of Gwynn ap Nudd, king of this land, I order you to cease your threats, release the boy Khalid, and let us proceed on our way," demanded one of the faeries, presumably Sir Arian's second in command.

The shadowy figure laughed, and the sound echoed in the unnatural darkness. "I recognize not Gwynn ap Nudd nor any other king. I, and I alone, rule here."

I recalled the name, Chapel Perilous, from Taliesin 1's memories. Sir Lancelot had once told him of such a place. This Chapel Perilous was not exactly as Lancelot had described it, but then that was fifteen hundred years ago, give or take. The sorceress in charge might be different—or horrendously more experienced and hence potentially considerably more dangerous.

"Name yourself and your purpose, woman!" I shouted in a manner much like the original Taliesin's, knowing that would work better than my normal teenage manner.

"Who are you to make demands of me?" hissed the stranger.

"I am Taliesin, bard to King Arthur and wielder of White Hilt," I announced, raising the sword and causing it to flame more brightly. "I am also quite capable of burning this whole place to the ground if need be."

She laughed again, even more derisively. "By entering the Chapel Perilous, you have come under its spell. The only way to leave is to complete the test. If you somehow succeed in destroying me or the building, all you will do is trap yourself forever, without hope of leaving."

I doubted that was true, though the sorceress might believe it. More likely it was just a bluff. She was keeping her cool, but the very fact we had all gotten in when the chapel was clearly designed to admit only one at a time must have at least given her pause.

"What is your test?"

"The test is the boy's, for he entered here first," replied the sorceress. "The rest of you must wait your turns—outside."

"Even in this light, our eyes are sharp enough to shoot her down," whispered a nearby faerie.

"We don't know where Khalid is," I whispered back. "You might hit him accidentally." To her, I responded, "I thought you just said we couldn't leave now without passing the test." The thing about some people who minds are still functioning in the Middle Ages is that they often miss that kind of logical flaw. There was a long pause as the sorceress puzzled over the problem.

"You may sit near the back, and if the boy completes the test, it will be offered to each of you in turn."

"I grow weary of these games," I announced. Casually, I let White Hilt's flames eat into the wood of the nearby pew—or at least, that's what I thought I was doing. The fire made very little impact. I knew I could get the pew to burn eventually, but it was very, very heavily reinforced by magic, so it would not be a fast or easy process, and I might well be exhausted by the time I got to her.

"Shar, perhaps White Hilt is not our best option. Please show our hostess what you can do." Shar, who had been waiting to do exactly that, struck the pew right next to him with a mighty blow, and it split right down the middle. No matter how much magic reinforcement it had, to Zom it would just be ordinary wood.

"I took you for knights, but I see you are just vandals!" shouted the sorceress. "You do not deserve to be tested; you only deserve to die." With one wave of her hand, we were surrounded by flames. In fact, there was a floor-to-ceiling wall of them completely encircling us.

Well, at least that was what we were supposed to think. I doubted she could cast such powerful magic so fast, so I assumed the flames were an illusion, despite the fact that I could smell the acrid smoke and feel the heat of the blaze.

"Shar, I think the fire is an illusion!" I yelled.

"I can't see any fire, so yeah, I'm sure it is," he responded, slicing through it. Naturally, the illusion split as the blade passed through it, but magic fire would have done the same thing—and the spell was not being dispelled by Zom's touch; the fire filled in again as soon as the blade was out of it. These signs made it clear the illusion was a strong one. None of us could really risk moving through it except Shar, who would be protected as always by Zom's anti-magic charm.

"Shar, go get her!" I yelled to him, and he was off. Bizarrely, he appeared to catch fire as he passed through the barrier, and I could smell burning flesh as his blazing form trotted down the aisle. Shuddering, I realized that the flames were getting closer to the rest of us, and I was not eager to see how well this particular sorceress could simulate the sensation of burning flesh, so I tried to sing away the illusory flames. There were moments when they seemed paler and cooler, but then they blazed up again. Quickly I switched strategies and tried to sing all of us into such disbelief that the illusion would not be able to reach us. That approach worked better, and it was only a short time before the fire faded away completely.

By this time Shar had the sorceress cornered behind the altar, but I could tell, even from a distance, that they were at an impasse. We all ran as quickly in that direction as we could, with no further illusions to bother us.

"Let him go!" demanded Shar, doubtless referring to Khalid. "Let him go, and we will leave peacefully."

I doubted I could see much better in the magical gloom of the chapel even if I sharpened my eyesight, but when we were upon the sorceress, I thought I could make out Khalid, his back against the wall behind the altar, surrounded by slowly shifting shadows, shaking with sheer terror.

I tried to remember what Lancelot had told the original Taliesin about the Chapel Perilous. All those centuries ago, it had been inhabited by a sorceress named Hellawes, who was, among other things, a master of illusion, very much like our current foe. I wondered if this could possibly be the same woman. Storytellers said she had died soon after Lancelot had escaped her, but no one had really been around to see her death, so who knew what really happened? Either way, the chapel seemed to have been considerably upgraded since Lancelot had visited it. Suppose the original Hellawes had managed to keep herself alive for fifteen hundred years. She could have found many ways to increase her power in that time.

"I will not let him go...and you will not try to free him either," she added, her voice a hoarse whisper that nonetheless carried all the way to the back of the chapel. "You cannot break the spell faster than I can use it to kill him. And if I die, he dies."

"What is it you want?" I asked loudly. Her attention shifted from Shar to me, and I could see her clearly for the first time, despite the darkness.

At first I thought her eyes were green, but then I realized that was merely the reflection of Zom's emerald glow. Their real color was hard to determine, but they were clearly dark and about as soulless as eyes can get. Her features were beautiful but deathly pale and not quite real, as if I were looking at a masterfully carved statue rather than a person. Her hair was the black of raven's wings, as was her dress, and both made excellent camouflage in the murky interior of the chapel.

"What do I want?" she replied disdainfully. "What I *require* is that each of you face my test. Do that, and you may go in peace. Unfortunately, since you have all somehow forced your way into this place where only one should come at a time, we will have a group test."

I could tell the faeries wanted to fill her full of arrows now that they had a clean shot, but I couldn't allow that any more than I could allow Shar to take her head off. Khalid was trapped in some way, and I couldn't take the chance that her death might somehow cause that trap to kill him. Sure, she could have been bluffing; as I thought about the nature of magic, I figured she probably was…but I couldn't be sure.

"The boy was here first, so the boy will decide the fate of all of you."

I was not liking the sound of that.

"If we are all to be judged together, then we should be able to pick which one of us will be tested," I pointed out. "What is the test?"

Hellawes, if that was who she was, considered a minute. "Perhaps you are right. The boy is possibly not who I would want the most, anyway. I think I would prefer you." The tone was vaguely disquieting and more than a little sexual. Great! What was it that made me so attractive to homicidal spell casters?

Somewhere behind me, I heard Gordy mutter something about sexual endurance tests and then snicker. "Not the time!" replied Dan, relatively harshly. Well, at least I wasn't imagining the tone.

"Tal, you can't accept a challenge like that without knowing what it is!" protested Carlos.

"No, you can't," agreed Shar. "Whatever it is, I'll do it." Thinking about it rationally, Shar, who was immune to magic as long as he held Zom and stronger than I was, would be more likely to pass whatever the test was, but my male ego growled just a little at how easily Shar reached that conclusion. After all, the test could relate to spell casting or singing, and then *I* would be a better choice.

"I have decided," announced Hellawes. "I will test Taliesin, or the boy will die." Everyone else protested, creating a considerable amount of noise. I took a step forward.

I'd like to say I was so prepared because of how heroic I was, but at this moment, I wasn't feeling that heroic. I just knew I couldn't have the death of a little kid on my conscience, even one like Khalid that I hadn't known for that long.

I felt restraining hands on my arms—both Stan and Dan had

stepped forward, and I could feel Carlos and Gordy moving in my direction. Only Shar, keeping his blade trained on Hellawes and one eye on Khalid, stayed where he was.

"I am troubled by your lack of faith," I announced, loudly enough for all of them to hear. "Why are you all so certain the test will result in my death?"

"Because there is strong magic here, and you are not familiar with it," replied one of the faeries. Gee, and I thought I was asking a rhetorical question!

"What is the test?" I asked, taking another step forward.

"All you have to do is kiss me."

At that point I remembered what else Lancelot had told me about Hellawes: that she had wanted his love but knew that she could never win it, so instead she tried to trick him into kissing her. Her kiss was deadly, and she had planned to love his corpse. Well, now at least I had a good idea of where all the dead knights came from. Apparently over the past few centuries, Hellawes had mastered reanimating dead bodies. Too bad she didn't know how to do that when Lancelot was around. However, in his day, the test was whether or not the knight would kiss her. Now the test addressed the more obvious question of whether or not the knight could survive that kiss. Not really surprising, considering Hellawes could have spent fifteen centuries thinking about how to close the loopholes.

I looked at her with eyes alert for magic, and sure enough, I could see an ice-blue glow on her lips: the cold of death.

"Only a kiss?" I asked. "No special conditions? No other stipulations?"

"No," said Hellawes. "Just kiss me, and be done."

"Do I have your word that you will not attempt to change the rules now that you have announced them?"

"You do," she replied, not realizing where I was going.

"TRUST ME!" I broadcast to everyone in the room, hoping no one would get in my way. I stepped forward until I stood near the altar, with Hellawes on one side of me and Shar on the other.

"Shar, let's trade swords for good luck!" I said. At that moment, everyone realized what I was doing—including Hellawes, judging by her expression. Unfortunately, she had already committed herself and could not forbid me the use of Zom now. Supernatural beings are funny that way, but it is one of the few predictable things about them. Someone like

Morgan, with a little more exposure to the real world, might be willing to break an oath unsupported by a *tynged*, but Hellawes probably was not, especially considering the power of the chapel was no doubt somehow connected to the test, and if she broke her word, she would probably find herself at our mercy anyway.

I took Zom from Shar, handed him White Hilt, and advanced on Hellawes, who stood her ground. Either she was brave, or she had not thought she would ever face someone immune to magic and had not developed an escape plan. In a minute it would not matter.

"Surely you would not offer me a kiss with your sword drawn?" she protested.

"Why, of course not, my lady," I replied with mock courtesy, sheathing Zom but being careful to keep my hand on its hilt. As long as I maintained contact, it would still protect me.

I was standing in front of Hellawes now, and the deathly cold blue light seemed to be dancing on her lips. I bent over and kissed her.

I've had a couple of kisses that felt pretty powerful, but none of them produced the fireworks this grim lip lock evoked. When our lips met, there was a blue-green flash, after which the blue glow enveloped Hellawes, who screamed like the damned, fell over backward, and more or less dissolved. For a moment there was a skeleton, still smoldering bluely, and then nothing. Apparently Hellawes's deadly lips had to kill someone with each kiss, and since they could not kill me, the power turned back on her.

Khalid came bounding up to me, now free of whatever spell had held him, and gave me a big hug, then bounded over to Shar and did the same. I heard several audible sighs of relief in the background.

"Imagine what would have happened if he had given her tongue!" joked Gordy.

"What is wrong with you today?" asked Dan. "You must have been between girlfriends a little too long."

"And no wonder," Gordy said with another snicker. "It seems our friend Tal goes through girls rather fast; at this rate there won't be any left for us."

"You wouldn't want the kind we just met," I said, grinning, "unless you are really fixated on older women." The guys and I had a hearty laugh over that. The faeries just looked perplexed, as they often did when faced with human humor.

The interior of the chapel was lightening up a bit. The light on the altar had winked out when Hellawes died, but I noticed some exterior light coming from stained-glass windows that had not been visible before, though they didn't add too much actual illumination; the windows portrayed various scenes of hellfire and blood, and most of the light coming through was a dull red. However, we did not have to put up with such sanguinary lighting for long, both because cracks were appearing in the ceiling and because chunks of stained glass were falling out of the windows. Perhaps the chapel had been so altered by the Hellawes's magic over the years that it could not survive without her.

"Let's get those doors open!" I suggested loudly, visions of the roof caving in on us filling my mind. However, before anyone could reach them, they were already sagging open, so we hastily took advantage of our luck and then watched the disintegration of Chapel Perilous from a safe distance away. Not more than five minutes after we were out, the roof did cave in, and shortly thereafter, the last vestiges of the walls collapsed, raising great clouds of dust that the faeries advised us not to breathe in, just in case. Another five minutes, and no trace remained of the building that had blocked the entire road a short time ago.

"As for you, young man," I said, turning to Khalid, who again at first acted as if he expected to be smacked, "that was very brave, and very foolish, for you to go into the Chapel Perilous like that. Don't ever do anything like that again!"

"I won't, Tal. I promise!" He hugged me again. I was sure he meant what he said…until the next opportunity for brave foolishness arose.

"The big boys in the group should perhaps also promise the same thing," observed Nurse Florence, looking straight at me, though this time she passed on the opportunity for the obvious lecture.

"At least everyone survived," said a healed Sir Arian, who clearly had not expected such a good outcome, "and now our way is clear again. However, we lost much time in that misadventure, and the sun is near to setting. Perhaps we should make camp nearby."

"I suggest putting some distance between us and this spot first," replied Nurse Florence. "If this was not an isolated incident, we might be in for at least one more attack. Tal, what do you think? Did anything happen inside that suggested that sorceress was not working alone?"

"No," I said slowly, "but it is hard to imagine that such an unusual event was just coincidence. I don't know what Morgan could have offered that Hellawes might have wanted, but I would be willing to bet Morgan put her up to it."

"And risked killing you?" asked Nurse Florence.

"If Morgan is behind all of this, I think she just intended for Hellawes to hold us here for a while. She may not have realized what a loose cannon Hellawes was. She does make even Morgan seem sane by comparison. Think of all the power she put into a structure that's sole purpose is to trap and kill total strangers."

"Then you think Morgan herself is coming to collect us?"

"It wouldn't surprise me."

"In that case," Sir Arian said, "perhaps it would be better to keep moving. We faeries can see in the dark, as. I think, can some of you as well."

"And I can sing us renewed strength, so we can go longer without sleep or rest," I added.

"Not the best long-term idea, but it might be all right for a day or so, just long enough to get us to Wales," put in Nurse Florence.

"All right then, let's do it," I replied confidently. The sooner we got Carla to safety, the happier I would be.

We were getting back into our original marching order when one of the faeries shouted a warning.

I looked west, and silhouetted against the misty redness of sunset, I could see a gigantic winged shape growing bigger by the second.

"Is that what I think it is?" asked Stan shakily.

"Yup," I replied, my optimism of only a moment before evaporating. "That's a dragon."

CHAPTER 9: ONE DRAGON CAN RUIN YOUR WHOLE DAY

"Can you take us out of Annwn now?" I asked Nurse Florence quickly.

"Unprepared, not fast enough. I have the image of Santa Brígida in my mind for the return trip, but it will take time to build up the necessary power."

"We will delay its advance," announced Sir Arian as he and his men rose into the air. If my perception of the size of the dragon was accurate, they were probably flying to their deaths. Even as the original Taliesin, I had only encountered dragons a couple of times, but I had seen enough to know they were hard to kill and too powerful to fight without special preparation, which we had no time for now.

The faeries rose to about the dragon's eye level, then flew somewhat to the left of us and started shooting arrows at the advancing dragon, who veered in their direction, eyes narrowed to slits to make them harder targets. A dragon's armor was hard enough to make it virtually impenetrable by most weapons, including faerie arrows, but its eyes were vulnerable. Unfortunately, this dragon was clearly smart enough to know that.

I could feel the power building up as Nurse Florence prepared to open a way back to our world.

"Are we just leaving them here?" asked Gordy, raising his head in the general direction of the faeries.

"No choice," said Nurse Florence brusquely. "With luck, they'll be able to fly away once we're gone."

Except that they had allowed the dragon to get too close. I doubted they could all escape now, and I felt the same unease Gordy did...but staying meant putting Carla at risk, putting everyone at risk. The smart move, repugnant as it was, was to get the hell out of Annwn as fast as possible.

The dragon gave an eardrum-shattering roar and unleashed a stream of fire at one of the faeries, who expertly rolled out of the way. The faeries had now surrounded the dragon and were firing at it from all sides, which would buy them some time, but sooner or later the dragon would fly straight at one of the faeries, and that one would be toast.

I looked at Nurse Florence plaintively. She knew what I wanted to do.

"No, Tal, you can't stay behind and help the faeries. It would be suicide. And do I have to remind you that you are the only one, aside from Morgan, with a chance to save Carla?" At that moment a shimmering gateway opened. At almost the same time, the dragon pivoted in midair, unleashed another earth-shaking roar, and dove straight at us.

"Scatter!" I yelled, knowing we could not all possibly get through the gateway before the dragon reached us. In fact, probably no one could have gotten all the way through before a blast of white-hot flame destroyed the gateway. Had it not been a relatively narrow blast, some of us would have lost our lives right there. It occurred to me that dragons usually aimed for maximum destruction. What was restraining this one?

There were limited places to flee at best, but everyone managed to get under the cover of trees on one side of the road or the other. However, the trees would not provide much protection against a full-scale blast of the dragon's fiery breath, and now the dragon could eliminate the entire party rather easily by just blasting each side of the road with a large enough spray of fire, igniting the trees and trapping everyone.

To my surprise, the dragon did not do that. Instead, he circled a couple of times and then landed on the road, effectively blocking it.

The dragon was as huge as he had looked from a distance. I had always been bothered by the artworks that portrayed the victory of Saint George over an unrealistically small dragon, seldom bigger than his horse, but mostly smaller, and on one or two occasions looking about the size of someone's stray dog. If only adult dragons really were that size! This one looked as if it had roughly five times the length of the Chapel Perilous, not exactly a small structure to begin with.

Its body was covered with ruby-red scales, and its eyes were black as tar pits. Each claw was at least as large as a great sword and could no doubt be lethal even against a heavily armored opponent. Its wing were scarlet but otherwise bat-like, and when fully extended would have been wider across than its body was long. Here and there arrows protruded from the spaces between the dragon's scales, but it was clear that these small wounds bothered him little.

Indeed, the fact that he had landed in the first place suggested he did not regard any of us as much of a threat. Nor were we, for that matter. The special effects on our weapons, particularly my fire attack, would be useless, and though our faerie-forged blades would eventually do some damage, creating a wound of any consequence would require the dragon to sit still for a long time, a highly unlikely scenario—unless he wanted to commit suicide. As for magic, dragons were pretty resistant to it most of the time, and though Nurse Florence and I might be able to create some magical defenses, probably none would be powerful enough to block either the dragon's breath or its ponderous claws.

"Hear me!" thundered the dragon. I could hardly have been more shocked if the creature had started tap-dancing in the middle of the road. Yeah, I had known dragons could talk before, but this was the first time that I had ever heard of a dragon bothering to talk to humans. I signaled the faeries to pause in their attack, not that it would have mattered much one way or the other.

"Hear me!" he roared again. "Most of you are none of my concern. I require but two of you, and the rest may go in peace."

"Which two?" I yelled back, my voice sounding like the faintest of echoes compared to the dragon's mighty bellow.

"The one who is called Taliesin Weaver and the one who is called Alcina."

I had no idea how Morgan had managed to recruit a dragon to her cause, but there could be no other explanation for the creature wanting me and Carla, but nobody else.

"For what purpose do you want them?"

"My purposes are my own, and no concern of yours."

Now I realized why the dragon had been so conservative with his fire. He had no idea what Carla or I looked like, though he might know that Carla was unconscious. He could hardly start an indiscriminate blaze without risking both of us. Knowing his inhibitions might give me a little advantage, at least in terms of keeping everyone alive, but the best I could do with that knowledge would be to create an impasse. He obviously couldn't burn the forest in an effort to find us, but we couldn't kill him or get around him.

"Is there anything we can do?" asked Carlos, who was standing right next to me.

"If I think of anything, you will be the first to know," I replied.

Actually, at this point there was only one thing to do. Nurse Florence would doubtless scold me for it later, but this time I was not just being impulsive. Desperate times call for desperate measures. I began chanting in Welsh, summoning up my power as I walked to the border between the road and the forest.

"Here I am, dragon!" I yelled, stepping out into the middle of the road. "Come and get me!" With that, I rose into the air and flew as fast as I could toward the west. I could hear the dragon sputtering with rage, but he could be as outraged as he wanted; it would still take him time to unfurl his wings and pursue me.

I was not really that well practiced with flying, so it felt awkward, and I feared I had less chance of outrunning him than any of the faeries had. The one advantage I possessed was that I knew the dragon would not kill me, so this maneuver would be less risky for me than for anyone else, and, if it worked, it would draw him away from the rest—and at least I didn't have to worry about running into power lines or other modern obstacles in Annwn.

Of course, the dragon could have stayed in the roadway, demanding that Carla be brought to him and perhaps succeeding in getting her. Morgan would have known that capturing Carla would force my hand, but I had to count on Morgan's not bothering to school the dragon in everything she knew about me. Sure enough, though I dared not turn to look, I could *feel* the dragon's presence behind me, I could hear the flap of his great wings. I also heard the sound of arrows whistling at him, but as long as he kept his eyes guarded pretty well, he could safely ignore the archers and concentrate on me.

I could feel the heat of the dragon's fiery breath as he shot a warning blast over my head.

"Land immediately, or die!" the dragon threatened, but I knew better. Even so, I shuddered, because I could tell he was getting closer. Pretty soon he could grab me with one great swing of his claw, and once captured that way, I would be helpless.

I kept coming back to something Sir Arian had said earlier about being careful how I used White Hilt's fire so as not to offend the forest. What would happen, I wondered, if the dragon offended the forest? Even the original Taliesin had not been in Annwn enough to know the answer to that question, but I had a pretty good idea what the answer might be.

Now for the part that Nurse Florence would later be right to scold me about. I spun around to face the dragon, though doing so enabled him to get closer, and then proceeded to fly backward, making myself feel even more awkward.

"Foolish beast!" I taunted. "I lied. The real Taliesin has escaped while you have been chasing me, and he has taken Alcina with him." The dragon's eyes widened in shock and outrage, and at that moment my strategy paid an unexpected dividend: the faerie archers managed to plant arrows in both eyes. The creature was too massive to be blinded that way, but he was in pain, and his pain made his next shot of fire at me clumsy— a good thing, considering he no longer thought he needed to keep me alive.

I rolled over and dove straight at the ground, then changed direction so that the dragon blasted flames into the trees. I managed to repeat this maneuver two or three times; I probably couldn't have gotten away with that, except that the dragon's eye injuries were slowing his ability to aim. By now there was a sizable forest fire below us, and the rising smoke would have choked me if I had not kept going, even had the dragon not been determined to fry me.

Unfortunately, while flying came naturally to faeries, it did not come naturally to me. I had to expend magical energy just to stay in the air, let alone to keep ahead of a frighteningly fast-moving dragon. Already the exertion was making my head throb and my muscles ache. Pretty soon I would need to stop, and then the dragon would have me.

The only thing that kept me going now, aside from primitive survival instinct, was the feeling of power building below us. This forest was alive, and not just in the biological sense true of forests back home. This forest was sentient, and the enormous blaze the dragon had started had, just as Sir Arian suggested, awakened the forest's wrath. I could tell the faeries felt it, too, but the dragon was still oblivious to it. Unfortunately, it was not oblivious to me and was clearly still intent on killing me—and its attacks were getting closer and closer.

I could see flocks of birds rising into the air, and at first I thought they were fleeing the fire, but they continued to climb, forming massive feathered clouds, and I knew this was no ordinary flight response.

Flames sprayed past me, almost close enough to singe my hair, and I zigzagged, trying to pull the dragon closer to the massing flocks without drawing its attention to them. The dragon gave another ear-splitting roar and dove after me, coming closer and closer to the ground in the process. The faeries, who were nothing if not goal oriented, were still on the dragon and still showering it with arrows, forcing it to keep its injured eyes slitted and its field of vision restricted.

Just when I felt my strength would not hold out, the first flock (if such a mixed group of birds could be called a flock) launched its attack, flying at the dragon's left eye, beaks and claws ready to do damage. Granted, no one bird could do that much, but there were dozens of them, and the dragon was forced to close the eye to avoid their attacks. In less than a minute, another group of birds forced a similar closure of the right eye. The dragon was now effectively blind and needed to fly upward to avoid crashing.

Normally, the dragon could have easily outrun the birds, but now, supercharged by the power of the forest, they kept up with the dragon, menacing its eyes each time it tried to open them. Their location meant that they could not be attacked by fire, and they managed to evade the dragon's attempts to swat them away with its claws. Looking carefully, I could see the aura of forest power that surrounded them, as all the trees and animals for hundreds of miles focused their strength into their small, winged brethren.

I must have been more tired than I thought, because for a few seconds I missed the fact that I was surrounded by faeries. I had a hard time figuring out why they had broken off pursuit.

"The forest will take care of the dragon," said Sir Arian, answering my unasked question. "Even such a creature as that will tire eventually, and anywhere it lands, the forest will attack it. There will be much destruction, but the forest will prevail in the end. It always does." I wished for a moment that the forests on Earth were as capable of defending themselves. Perhaps the polluters would think twice then—or perhaps, like the dragon, they would bring about their own destruction.

"As for you," Sir Arian continued, "let us help you back. You did well to lead the beast away from the others, but your strength is spent."

My male ego wanted to protest, but I knew I could never fly back on my own without resting, and we really couldn't afford that time, so I let two of the faeries take my arms, and though I kept up enough magic to float, I let them provide the motion and the steering.

As we flew back, I was astounded at how many miles we had flown—and at the scale of the devastation the dragon had left in its wake. I felt more than a little twinge of guilt as I looked down at what must be several acres of burning forest.

"Do not worry," said Sir Arian. "The forest will heal here much faster than it does in your world. Visit in a few months, and you will hardly be able to tell that there ever was a fire. His assurance made me feel a little better, though I wished I could have thought of another way to get rid of the dragon.

The flight back seemed longer than covering the same distance earlier had, perhaps because the faeries could not carry me as fast as I had been able to fly, at least during the first stages of my mad dash away from the dragon. However, we did eventually reach our party again, though by this time darkness had descended. The guys were surprised by the faint glow around each of the faeries, and though I had seen it before, I was still moved by its unearthly beauty.

Nurse Florence was upon me almost before my feet touched the ground. "Tal, are you all right?"

"Very tired," I replied quietly, "but otherwise unscathed."

"You know you took a terrible chance—"

"Taliesin did what he had to do," interjected Sir Arian. I was so used to having to defend my own—admittedly sometimes impulsive—actions that it was a rare treat to have someone else defend them. "Had the dragon remained here, some of you would almost certainly have died, and at the very least, you would have been trapped here until the dragon's master arrived. Taliesin's decision to lead the dragon away was both necessary and brave. Now there is a chance for all of us to get out of here alive."

"The dragon's master?" asked Dan.

"Yes, dragons have their own domains and do not normally invade the territory of Gwynn or any other ruler in Annwn without very good reason. Someone must be responsible for this incursion."

"A chance to get out alive?" asked Nurse Florence. "Is our situation that dire?"

Surprisingly, Sir Arian chuckled at the question. "We have faced two powerful and deadly menaces in the same afternoon, and our journey is not even half over. You tell me."

"Well, I could take advantage of Annwn's rather flexible geography and gate us home," said Nurse Florence. "I was about to do just that when the dragon struck. Perhaps this route is no longer safe, as Sir Arian is suggesting."

"But if we do that, we have to start all over again," I pointed out, "and we have to worry about Morgan nonstop until we do. I have a different suggestion, if Gwynn will give us his permission."

"If you have a request to make, make it, Taliesin," urged Sir Arian. "Even if you did not have his respect before, you would certainly have it after today."

"Let us ask Gwynn for permission to spend the night in his castle. I doubt even Morgan could attack us there."

"If Morgan Le Fay is responsible for these outrages, she is already in more trouble than you can imagine," said Sir Arian. "For her to attack Gwynn's castle would be inconceivable. And I believe Gwynn would readily extend his hospitality. But how does that serve your ends? His castle lies farther to the east than your goal—much farther, in fact."

"I am proposing a change in goal. I think you are right, Sir Arian: the road ahead is too dangerous. On the other hand, going back to our own world is dangerous as well. I suggest instead that we rest the night in Gwynn's castle, assuming he will have us, and then tomorrow we perform the reversal spell on Carla."

"What? Here?" said Nurse Florence incredulously.

"You yourself reminded me of how much easier it is to perform magic in Annwn than back in our world. Once we have Carla back and have prevented Alcina from taking control, we can go back to our world and deal with Morgan without having to worry about her finding some way to get to Carla first."

"There is wisdom in what Taliesin says," observed Sir Arian approvingly.

"Yes, I must admit the plan is well-thought-out, especially for being spontaneous," conceded Nurse Florence. "There are those in the Order who will be upset by it, but frankly you know more than any living person about how the post-awakening traumas can be handled. Assuming Gwynn can lend us some casters to give us the power to pull off the spell, I don't see any problem with this idea."

Gordy looked a little puzzled at all this. "But if Gwynn's castle is farther away than the gateway to the Order, isn't the trip going to be even more dangerous?"

"Unlike the Order's headquarters, Gwynn's castle doesn't require that we start from two days away," replied Nurse Florence. "The geography of Annwn is hard to explain if you aren't used to it, but basically the distance from one place to another in Annwn is stable. That is, Gwynn's castle will always be the same distance away from where we stand right now. However, Annwn's geography is more…flexible…in relation to our world. From here I could put us back in Santa Brígida or in London equally easily, even though they are thousands of miles apart in our world."

"Wow, so we could go anywhere?" asked Khalid, eyes wide with wonder. There was something amusing about a boy who was half djinn being so easily awestruck, but I had to remember that he had never had any real contact with the otherworldly part of his heritage.

Nurse Florence laughed. "Anywhere I have been, anyway. I have to be able to see the place in my mind to connect this spot in Annwn to the place we want to go. And any place besides Santa Brígida takes more time to set up. I kept the image of Santa Brígida fresh in mind for the return trip; I'd have to visualize a new destination to properly connect it with this spot in Annwn."

"I had best find another owl and send Gwynn a message," said Sir Arian a little nervously. "There is no telling how long this calm will last, but I do not think too long." With that he shot upward and disappeared into the darkness.

"Assuming Gwynn says yes, how do we get to his castle?" I asked.

"Well," replied Nurse Florence, "he has an understanding with our Order that enables any of us to enter Annwn wherever he happens to be, as I had to do when we were asking for weapons for the battle with Ceridwen, but we are supposed to reserve that kind of interruption for occasions when there is no other choice. Once we get his permission, I would rather use more polite means. There is a fixed gateway to his castle at Glastonbury Tor. I can take us there from here, and then we just need to pass through the gateway at the Tor. Let's see, if I am figuring this right, it is about four in the afternoon in Santa Brígida, which makes it about midnight at Glastonbury. That's good. At least we won't appear in the middle of a flock of tourists. My superiors in the Order really would be bent out of shape by that."

"If we can appear in Glastonbury, why can't we appear in Cardiff and end up at your Order, so you won't get into trouble?" asked Shar.

"It's good of you to worry about me," said Nurse Florence with a smile, "but I won't get into trouble if we don't cause a big scene at Glastonbury. Anyway, remember the Order's security arrangements make that impossible. We can't get into the Order through Annwn except by using their fixed gateway, which we have to travel a minimum of two days in Annwn before we can use."

She wrinkled her forehead a little as she considered other possibilities. "The spells involved wouldn't prevent us from going from anywhere in Annwn to other locations in Cardiff, but…uh, it's hard to explain…if we traveled that way, the headquarters simply wouldn't be there, or at least we would never be able to find it." Shar looked puzzled, and even I was having difficulty following the explanation. "The headquarters isn't really in our world; it exists in a little world of its own. It connects to Annwn, and it connects to our world, but both connections are deliberately complicated by all kinds of magical rules. If the headquarters existed only on Earth, such elaborate security would be impossible."

Nurse Florence had made the mistake of explaining the workings of the headquarters in a way that got Stan asking about the physics of the situation, and I immediately tuned out, as I think did almost everybody else, though Khalid listened with rapt attention. Fortunately for the rest of us, Sir Arian returned in just a few minutes with an invitation for all of us to come to Gwynn's castle.

After that Nurse Florence visualized the summit of Glastonbury Tor, and, once she had the area clearly in her mind, it was not long before she was able to open the now-familiar glowing portal, and we passed through it as quickly as we could. The faeries accompanied us, though they appeared more nervous than when they were facing the dragon. At least since the introduction of gunpowder in Europe, faeries and other similar beings had traveled to Earth less and less—a bullet would normally be faster than even the fastest spell caster.

When we emerged, we were standing right next to Saint Michael's tower on the summit of Glastonbury Tor. As much as I knew the logistics would have been more difficult during the day, I wished that I could have seen the view. I could see a few lights, from what I assumed to be Glastonbury itself, to the west of where we stood, but that was about it. Everything from the rolling green expanses nearby to the Black Mountains in Wales was hidden by the night. It was a clear night, and there was enough moonlight for the guys to be impressed by the tower, now missing both doors and roof, but still an impressive mass of stone rising several stories in the air, with some of its upper-level carvings faintly visible. Even at night I would have liked to sightsee just a little, but naturally Nurse Florence wanted to get us to Gwynn's castle as soon as she could—and the faeries seemed to want that even sooner. I wondered if the faint faerie glow would be visible from a distance, and, if someone did see it, would that spawn yet another UFO story? (The Tor had produced its share over the years!)

Suddenly a glow erupted in the center of the tower, more intense than the typical portal to or from Annwn. Nurse Florence and Sir Arian ushered us through as quickly as they could, and we quickly forgot any missed sightseeing opportunities on the other side once we beheld Gwynn's castle.

Stepping out of the gateway from Glastonbury Tor, we found ourselves in front of the barbican, the outer gateway into the castle itself. The gate itself was flanked by two low towers, in which, judging by the arrow slots in the wall and the faint glow that came through them, clandestine faerie archers lurked, waiting for the slightest sign of trouble to open fire. Through the open gate I could see a long bridge flanked on either side by high walls, on the parapets of which more faerie archers walked, equally ready for action.

At Sir Arian's orders, the gate was opened for us, and we were quickly ushered through the barbican, across the fixed bridge, and to the drawbridge, which was already being lowered by the time we got there. As we walked across, I noticed that the water in the moat, which could not have been that deep, had the look of enormous depth to it, as if one who fell into it would sink forever. Once across, we were in a large courtyard, bigger than Camelot's had been—and Camelot had been pretty big by the standards of its day. Upon the massive outer walls were yet more faerie archers. I had lost count by this time, but I knew this was one castle I would never want to mount an attack against.

Toward the back left as we entered was a huge square tower that had to be the keep, the military center of the castle. To the right lay an even larger building, clearly where Gwynn's residence and court lay. Some of you have doubtless seen the ruins of medieval castles, and a few of them give a pretty good idea of how impressive the castle would have been originally. None of the ones I had ever seen, even as the original Taliesin, at which point the castles were still whole and functioning, had even come close to this.

It was not just the size of the place. There was an energy, a life-force, even within the very stones themselves. They were not the grayish, whitish or faintly yellowed stones I had seen in earthly castles, but were more like marble, and, at least in the interior parts of the castle, highly polished, yet I was sure they had a toughness greater than earthly stone. They also had a faint but noticeable silver sheen to them. The glow of the faeries and the sheen of the walls would have been dazzling enough by themselves, but the light from the numerous torches made the courtyard seem almost like midday.

Sir Arian kept prodding us forward, through a massive door and into a great hallway. Corridors frequently branched off to the right and to the left, but Sir Arian told us to move straight ahead, toward what must surely have been the castle's great hall. When we finally arrived, the place certainly lived up to its name. Statues of faerie and human heroes lined the walls. They were some distance away from us, but they had been sculpted so well they seemed to be alive, especially in the flickering torch-light. The walls were hung with multicolored tapestries of equally great artistic merit that portrayed great events in the histories of Earth and of Annwn, and they too seemed almost alive.

In the center of the room, large wooden tables had been set in a partial square, open on the end at which we entered the room, and at those tables sat the faerie elite, the nobles of Gwynn's kingdom, dressed in a variety of outfits that faerie seamstresses must have spent days sewing. I couldn't tell what kind of fabrics were used and doubted that I could find anything like them in our world.

At the center of the table, facing the entry door, was Gwynn ap Nudd himself, dark-faced and every inch as formidable as he had looked the last time I had seen him. Generally, faeries were of a somewhat more slender build, but Gwynn was massive, not literally a giant, but certainly someone you would avoid challenging to a wrestling match.

"Taliesin!" he shouted as soon as he saw me. "You are most welcome here. Step forward, that I may introduce you to my court." I moved much closer to him and bowed.

"This youth is a reincarnation of Taliesin, King Arthur's bard, and a great hero in this lifetime. He it was who spared us the trouble of having to deal with Ceridwen. Just today I am told he defeated an evil sorceress and helped rid our land of a dragon—and not just some pup at that, but a full-sized monster!"

"Your Majesty, I would have been the dragon's dinner but for the help of the men you sent along as escort," I replied, trying to keep from blushing.

"Heroic and modest as well," said Gwynn, laughing deeply, as he always did. "Perhaps you will favor us with a song later."

I was used to performing in this life, but entertaining hormonal teenagers at a school dance was a little different from being asked to perform for the king of the Welsh faeries and his entire court. Still, I nodded my assent. That was the kind of request I could not really refuse, especially under current circumstances.

"And is this the beautiful maiden you have come to save?" asked Gwynn, leaning over to look at Carla, still in her hospital bed.

"Yes, Majesty, this is Carla Rinaldi."

"She labors under a great weight of dark magic, Taliesin. But I am told you know how to rescue her if you have enough power behind your casting. I myself will lend you my strength, and I think with that you will succeed."

I almost fainted at that. Well, not really, but if anything was going to make me faint, that would have been it. Keep in mind that Gwynn had been worshiped as a god by some early Celtic groups. He had been thought of as the king of winter, ruler of the underworld, gatherer of souls, and leader of the wild hunt. Getting his help with the magic was somewhat like looking for AA batteries and finding a nuclear reactor.

"Majesty, I am overwhelmed by your generosity," I said feebly.

When people said that they had no words to express their feelings, I had always kind of chuckled at them, but this was one situation in which I genuinely didn't know how to express my gratitude. Gwynn, perhaps to avoid throwing me off any further, moved on quickly.

"Viviane! It has been long since you have actually been at court. You must be our guest more often in future."

"Thank you, Majesty," said Nurse Florence, with a bow.

"Shahriyar, another true warrior in our midst."

"I try, Majesty," said Shahriyar, also bowing.

Gwynn greeted Dan and Gordy equally warmly, then moved on to Carlos, whom he had not met before. Then he came to Khalid, and his eyes widened. "Well, boy, who might you be?"

Considering that Khalid had been homeless for about three years, his life before had not really prepared him to chat with royalty. However, thanks to Mrs. Sassani, he did look a little like an Abercrombie and Fitch commercial, and he was certainly sharp enough to follow our leads.

"My name is Khalid, Majesty," he said and made a passable bow.

"I might have wondered why Taliesin would include someone so young in his party, but you are more than just human, aren't you?"

"Actually," said Khalid in a very timid voice, "Tal did not include me. I…hid and sneaked through the portal into this wonderful place." Khalid lowered his head and did not meet Gwynn's eyes, perhaps expecting a reprimand of some kind. Instead, Gwynn responded with another one of his belly laughs.

"Taliesin, I think the boy has some of your spirit! May it serve him as well as it has served you. Khalid, you may have sneaked here, but you are as welcome as anyone else."

I had expected Gwynn to ask more questions about Khalid's nature, but again he moved on. Perhaps he had somehow picked up on how uncomfortable Khalid was with that nature.

"Stanford? Bold as ever, I see. But there is something different about you this time."

"Yes, Majesty, in the battle against Ceridwen I was…awakened…much as Tal was four years before."

"I thought so," said Gwynn, leaning over the table and giving it a resounding rap with his knuckles. "There is someone mighty within you, to say the least. Who were you once?"

Now it was Stan's turn to be uncomfortable. "I… was…King David of Israel, Your Majesty."

Gwynn looked inquisitively in Nurse Florence's direction. "Viviane, more than mere coincidence seems to be at work here."

"I have sometimes thought so myself, Your Majesty," replied Nurse Florence, "but there doesn't seem to be any way to know, at least not yet."

"Well, the purpose will be revealed in good time, no doubt," said Gwynn. "In any case, Stanford, welcome to my court!"

Stan, obviously puzzled, bowed and stepped back. By this point he was not the only one who was puzzled. Sure, it was a pretty large coincidence that King David and I had been reunited after all these years, but what was Gwynn implying? That it was fate? That some higher power was manipulating us? I would have to talk with him about this situation when I got the chance.

"And now, visiting heroes, please do us the honor of joining in our feast—"

"Majesty, we cannot," replied Nurse Florence quickly.

Gwynn winked at her and chuckled. "We will waive the usual rules, Viviane. You may all eat and drink without becoming tied to this realm."

At a gesture from Gwynn, an extra table was brought in and set for us with amazing speed. The faerie servants were clearly as fast as the faerie knights. Nurse Florence moved to look after Carla, but a couple of faerie healers appeared at just that moment and promised to take care of her while Nurse Florence ate. We waited for Nurse Florence and Sir Arian to sit, and then the rest of us scrambled in. I ended up with Sir Arian on my left and Stan on my right. In front of us were a variety of silver plates, goblets, and utensils that looked as if someone spent twenty-four hours a day polishing them. I remembered how impressed I was at the pre-home-coming party at Carrie Winn's, but this experience promised to be far, far above that one.

"I…I don't suppose they have anything kosher," mumbled Stan, not wanting to be rude but clearly uncomfortable at the thought of a roasted pig being shoved at him.

"Stanford, you may have whatever you wish," said Sir Arian. "Just think of it, and it will be brought." He spoke loudly enough for Shar and Khalid to also hear, and they both looked relieved, having probably just had the same anxiety as Stan.

"But," said Nurse Florence, glancing at the silver goblets in front of each of us, "no alcohol!" Sir Arian raised an eyebrow. "I know that except for Khalid, they are all adults by the standards of Annwn, but in the society from which they come, they are still below the legal drinking age. I'm the only legal adult in the party, and I am responsible for them."

"Aw, Mom," said Dan jokingly. "I could really go for a beer right about now." It looked as if a faerie servant was actually approaching at that moment with a frosty mug, but one withering glance from Nurse Florence sent the servant back to the kitchen.

"Nobody's ever going to know," said Gordy, somewhat less jokingly. "All the faerie warriors get to drink what they want. Anyway, I just turned eighteen."

"Which is not twenty-one, now is it?" replied Nurse Florence.

"My parents let me have champagne on New Year's Eve," pointed out Carlos.

"And if your parents were here, they could let you have whatever you want, but I…just can't," said Nurse Florence, almost apologetically. "I know this is awkward. I suppose it is the nature of our relationship at school that makes me insist."

"Being the school nurse is just your cover, isn't it?" asked Gordy, still looking for a loophole.

"And to be good at that 'cover,' I have to live it," replied Nurse Florence with an air of finality.

Having figured out that the moment was awkward, Sir Arian started suggesting different kinds of juice. I found it hard not to giggle over the whole situation, though I think Gordy was actually a little irritated.

Once we all got past the beverage-selection impasse and focused on what we wanted to eat, we were served fairly quickly. Nurse Florence had pineapple juice and what looked like the world's largest fruit salad. I think she had been thinking about the meal from a diet standpoint and was a little overwhelmed by the sheer magnitude of the thing—why are women always on diets? Nonetheless, it did look as if someone had been cutting and artistically arranging fruit for hours to produce the salad, and once Nurse Florence got started, she quickly seemed to forget about the whole concept of calories.

Sir Arian had what he told us was roast boar; the idea was not especially appealing, but I had to admit that it looked very tender. I had always been a sucker for Thanksgiving dinner, so I ended up with turkey—you know, the kind that is so well prepared it just melts in your mouth, accompanied by the smoothest gravy ever, sage dressing, buttery mashed potatoes, and cranberry sauce that seemed to have been made from fresh cranberries. Stan got equally well-prepared roast lamb, with mint jelly that he swore was prepared from fresh ingredients. We all knew, of course, that our various selections had to have been magically created, but who cared when they were that good?

Just as we were finishing, I heard Gwynn's booming voice. "Now it is time for Taliesin the bard to sing for us," an announcement that was followed by raucous applause. I had forgotten all about Gwynn's earlier request, and I rose somewhat nervously. Faeries were used to hearing some of the finest singers and musicians in the universe. I *was* good—but was I good enough for this crowd?

By the time I had walked to the center of the room, a group of faerie musicians with a variety of instruments had assembled to accompany me. I couldn't exactly do rock for this audience, so I searched Taliesin 1's memories and performed some of the songs that had been popular at Arthur's court. My magic flowed through the words to keep me in sync with the musicians, who seemed surprised but pleased by how well we coordinated without rehearsal. The audience responded well, and once I loosened up, I actually enjoyed myself. Since Halloween, Carla's illness had left my band on hiatus, so this was really the first public performance I had done in a couple of months. It reminded me of why I had been drawn to music in the first place, even before I had been awakened and actually became a good performer. Well, I shouldn't be overly modest. Perhaps a great performer.

When the performance ended, the faeries applauded enthusiastically, none more so than Gwynn himself. "Taliesin, it has been ages— literally, since I have heard a human musician who could really perform. Your songs have filled me with joy."

"I am happy that I was able to please Your Majesty and the court," I said solemnly, trying not to blush too obviously.

"Now we should retire," suggested Gwynn. "We faeries sometimes do feast all night, but tomorrow, Taliesin, you, I, and Viviane have a great work of magic to perform, and we should be well-rested. I have summoned servants who will show all of you to your quarters and see to your needs."

After we had said our good-nights and turned toward the door, there was indeed a row of faerie servants waiting for us, but something struck me as odd. All of them were incredibly good-looking. Yeah, I know, faeries in general are good-looking by any reasonable human standard, but these seemed to be a cut above the norm, even for faeries. The one who gestured to Nurse Florence was a man, but all the others were women, which seemed like a weird coincidence. It's true that teenage guys sometimes have overactive imaginations, but I did begin to wonder about how broadly the faeries were ready to interpret the phrase, "see to your needs."

Apparently, Nurse Florence had the same misgiving about the arrangements. "I should…uh…make clear the…uh…the customs of our world," she began, uncharacteristically tongue-tied. "While we appreciate your hospitality, there are certain parts of it of which we may not partake."

The faeries looked puzzled. They were not going to make this easy; I could just tell.

"We are not sure of what you speak," said her faerie escort in a low, melodious voice. "We will honor your wishes, but you will need to speak more plainly."

It was time for me to step up and get Nurse Florence off the hook.

"We could be wrong, but both…Viviane and I had the feeling that perhaps your hospitality extended to…certain areas that…we could not really…" Crap! I wasn't able to come out and just say it either, especially considering how embarrassing it would be if we were wrong.

Out of nowhere, Stan came to the rescue. "Nurse Florence has committed herself to a man in our world, and the rest of us also have commitments, as well as being considered too young in our society to engage in…love-making." The faeries nodded, though some of them looked disappointed. On the whole, that was a better reaction from the standpoint of our egos than if they all looked relieved.

"Speak for yourself!" snapped Gordy. "I am *eighteen*, dammit, and if I didn't get to drink, I ought to at least get to…"

"Gordy!" cut in Dan. "Let's not make this more awkward than it already is."

"How can you be too young, when you are warriors already?" asked the faerie servant standing next to Stan. She looked into his eyes with such obvious desire that he turned bright red.

"Damn good question!" said Gordy, far too loudly.

"GORDY!" said Dan in his insistent, I'm-the-team-captain tone.

"All right!" said Gordy sullenly.

There was a little more subdued bickering and questioning, but finally the conversation died a well-deserved death, and the faeries led us to our chambers. The one with me, exceptionally good looking, even better than Nurse Florence—and I don't say that about too many women—asked me if I was sure I did not want to make love.

"As much as I appreciate the offer, the unconscious girl we brought with us is my love, and I intend to remain true to her."

The faerie sighed. "You are as noble as you are brave and handsome. I will respect your wishes." Nonetheless, she did kiss me, and I had to admit that my heart pounded a little faster. Damn! Aside from Carla, this faerie was the first girl who wanted me and wasn't evil—not a combination I seemed to encounter very often.

As if the initial temptation were not enough, the faerie then wanted to undress me. I had to explain that in my society men generally dressed and undressed themselves, except in sexual situations. She nodded, pulled the covers back, and then, much to my surprise, crawled into the bed.

"What are you doing?" I asked. I was going for an authoritative tone, but my voice cracked just a little bit.

"Just warming up the bed for you," she responded innocently. "It has gotten a little cold. I can stay all night to help keep it warm, if you want me to."

Yeah, I'll bet you can!

I summoned up every ounce of willpower I had left and insisted she leave. When I finally got into bed, it smelled of her, and it was a long time before I could get to sleep.

CHAPTER 10: A TWIST OF FATE?

The next morning was interesting, to say the least. Stan looked as if he hadn't really slept. I guessed that his faerie didn't easily take no for an answer either, and it may have taken him quite a while to figure out how to get rid of her. Of course, he might have not had any sleep precisely because he didn't get rid of her, but Stan had more will-power than people gave him credit for, and he seemed more worn-out than guilty. He let me examine him to make sure David was still pretty well submerged, and he seemed to be, though the connections I had forged between them were fraying somewhat. Once I got Carla back to herself, I needed to spend time reinforcing Stan's fragile equilibrium.

As soon as he saw me, Dan looked me in the eye and said, "Don't worry—I didn't betray Eva," as if that was going to be my first thought. Well, perhaps it would have crossed my mind at some point. Apparently he too had a struggle last night, or I doubted he would have brought the subject up at all.

As for the others, Khalid was developing a perpetually amazed expression, but he evidently looked young enough that his faerie had not tried to talk him into having sex. Shar and Carlos were poker-faced, but Gordy seemed much happier than he should have under the circumstances. Of course, being a teenage guy, he could have been trying to create the impression that something happened that didn't. Yeah, I know, it's strange, but it happens more than you can imagine. I could easily have figured out what had happened to each of them last night with a little probing, but I seldom poked around in people's minds unless I had to, so the mystery of whether Gordy did or didn't would have to remain a mystery.

After a brief but incredibly satisfying faerie breakfast, Gwynn led us out into the courtyard, which was now flooded with a misty early morning sunshine. Gwynn had clearly had his sorcerers working since before daybreak, or perhaps even all night, and a large patch of ground was covered with mystical symbols in faintly glowing gold ink. Four points projected from roughly equidistant spots around the circular edge of the design, making me think of compass points. In the center of the design, Carla's bed had been placed, and the two faerie healers stood on either side of the bed, watching Carla intently.

"The pattern on the ground is intended to amplify our magic,"

Gwynn explained. "One of us will stand at each point during the casting. Your men and some of mine will circle us for protection, though we almost certainly won't need it here."

"Isn't there one point too many?" I asked.

Gwynn chuckled a little. "You at one, me at one, Viviane at one, and I have a special guest. Ah, here she comes now."

Gwynn waved in the general direction of the keep. I could see a beautiful female figure, doubtless also a faerie, advancing toward us, but she was not attired like Gwynn's people. Instead, she wore a blue-black cloak upon which stars seemed to gleam. The silver diadem upon her head suggested that she, like Gwynn, was faerie royalty of some kind.

"Taliesin, Viviane, allow me to introduce Mab, queen of some of the Irish faeries."

Nurse Florence and I both bowed, and Mab nodded to us.

"Mab was visiting me on a diplomatic mission, and, hearing of your problem, she asked if she could help."

"Yes, Taliesin," said Mab in a soft voice. "I was moved by your story and by the challenge of this strange new magic. If you will have me, I think I can contribute much to your efforts."

"We are honored by your participation," I said with another bow.

Not being crazy, I was obviously going to accept an offer like that, though I was amazed that, at least this once, I was having decent luck for a change. Taliesin 1 had never met Mab, but even then she had been active among the faeries, and rumors suggested she was indeed very powerful, so much so that she might be considered the equal of Gwynn himself.

Gwynn and Mab stepped aside for a few moments of private conversation, so I took the opportunity to touch base with Nurse Florence. "Did you know Queen Mab was here?"

"No," replied Nurse Florence, "though the Order has been getting lots of bits and pieces of information about political changes in the faerie realms. There are rumors of an attempt by Oberon and Titania to gain the rule of all of Annwn, and other rumors of a bid by Arawn, your old 'friend,' to regain that rule. Gwynn has been seeking support among the Irish faeries, which is no doubt why Mab is here. Keeping in mind that neither of them is married now, there is even a possibility of a marriage alliance." Mab seemed to me somehow a little too delicate for a warrior type like Gwynn, but then human arranged marriages often produced even more unlikely combinations.

"There is something else you should know," added Nurse Florence, looking around to make sure Gwynn and Mab were far enough away not to overhear. "Morgan has become involved in this faerie politics. Right now, as I think you already know, the divided rule of Annwn necessitates agreement among the various rulers in order to take certain actions. Gwynn has been trying to get all the faeries to unite in condemning Morgan, which would make it easier for him to take her prisoner, but Oberon keeps blocking him. When you were the first Taliesin, you probably remember hearing a story to the effect that Oberon was the son of Julius Caesar and Morgan."

"I think I did, but that's impossible, isn't it? Morgan was Arthur's half-sister, born in my own time, but Caesar lived five hundred years earlier. Besides that, how could a half faerie and a mortal produce a full faerie?"

"No one gave that story much credit until recently. However, it does explain Oberon's behavior. Many folk in Annwn really don't want anyone with faerie blood living among humans, and no one wants faeries and other spell casters performing magic or other acts that could come to the attention of mortals. That's why Ceridwen was so unpopular with the rulers of Annwn.

"Well, Morgan became Ceridwen's ally, a choice not likely to endear her to those rulers, and her appearances in the mortal realm, like the storm she stirred up outside the hospital, are making those same rulers profoundly nervous. Oberon, making a play to become sole ruler, is taking a considerable political risk to come to Morgan's defense. However, if she is related to him, his behavior makes sense."

"But unless someone discovered magic that would enable time travel, that story is still impossible," I pointed out.

Nurse Florence gave me a humorless smile. "You, of all people, should realize what the other possibility is."

When she framed the subject like that, it did not take me long to realize what she meant. "Reincarnation?"

"Exactly. We still don't know much about the way it works, and it was thought until recently that faeries did not reincarnate the way humans do, but it now appears that on rare occasions they do. There is evidence that some time during the conquest of Gaul, Caesar slept with a powerful faerie named the Morrigan, who had been worshiped as a goddess of war by the Irish. She had probably been trying to seduce him into giving up his campaign in Celtic territory, but somehow the plan back-fired.

"Anyway, their brief encounter produced a son, who grew up to be Oberon. There is now evidence that Morgan is either a manifestation of the Morrigan, or perhaps just a simple reincarnation. At some point, Morgan has shown Oberon that evidence and convinced him that she is his mother. As to Caesar's background, during his own lifetime he was loudly claiming descent from Venus, and there is also some possibility that Caesar's mother was either a reincarnation of, or at least possessed by, an earlier faerie queen named Brunehaut."

By this point I was feeling dizzy. "So everything we know about ancient history is false?"

"Says the bard from King Arthur's court that most historians to-day doubt even existed. No, everything isn't false, but between the loss of so many records over time and the conscious work of different groups to rewrite history in their own interest—and particularly to get supernatural elements dismissed as myths—some of it definitely is."

Nurse Florence could see I was more than a little frustrated by all of these revelations. "Tal, I'm not telling you this to upset you, but I want you to know what you are up against. Morgan is not a solo act any more than Ceridwen was, as yesterday's events pretty well demonstrate. She couldn't have found Hellawes that easily, and she certainly couldn't have recruited a dragon, without powerful help. If Oberon himself is not re-sponsible, then at the very least his efforts to defend her are encouraging other forces to provide her with more concrete support. The good news is that Morgan has enormously overplayed her hand. If Gwynn can find proof that Morgan is responsible for such serious incursions into his own territory, even Oberon won't be able to defend her. Until then, though, we have to be a little careful. We can protect ourselves against Morgan, but if we—"

"Before we begin," boomed Gwynn, obviously finished with his conversation with Mab, "I have a gift for one of my guests. Khalid, please come forward."

Now that was a twist! The guys had been required to fight to prove their worthiness for faerie swords, but Gwynn was apparently going to present Khalid with something without requiring any kind of test. Well, the kid did have a way of getting people to sympathize with him, and perhaps when they first met, Gwynn had felt some of the hardship

Khalid had gone through. This would not be the only time a faerie had helped a child.

Khalid stepped forward shakily, obviously taken by surprise, but I noticed Shar encouraging him to go forward. As Khalid approached him, Gwynn held up a small silver dagger and a scabbard. "Khalid, it is clear that you have the heart of a warrior. You should also begin to learn the weapons of a warrior. This dagger will be the first of many weapons you will use in your life. Our faerie smith Govannon forged it for you last night as you slept. Like a faerie sword, it will penetrate material an ordinary blade would not, it will not break, and it has one other special property. Khalid, listen carefully to me."

"Yes, Majesty," Khalid whispered, clearly overcome.

"You are the son of a djinn." Khalid lowered his head as if ashamed, but Gwynn continued as if he did not notice. "The djinn have a reputation for granting wishes, but since your parents are not with you right now, the dagger will grant you one. Mind you, its power is not infinite, but it is not insignificant either. At a moment of great need, the dagger can grant you your heart's desire, if that desire is within reason. Be careful, though, for the dagger can only grant one wish in this way. Choose wisely, or you will live forever with regret." Gwynn helped Khalid attach the scabbard to his belt and then handed him the dagger, which flashed brilliantly in the sunlight.

"Thank you, Majesty!" exclaimed Khalid, who then quickly wiped a tear away, embarrassed. Who could blame him for being overcome with emotion? In a couple of days he had gone from living on the streets to being surrounded by people he cared about and conspicuously favored by royalty. Hell, I couldn't adjust to changes that fast. I could hardly expect an eleven-year-old to handle them.

Shar gave Khalid a hug and then made eye contact with Gwynn, who nodded to him. In that moment I realized that Shar must somehow have arranged this gift, which would explain why Gwynn did not first test Khalid; Gwynn had high regard for Shar as a warrior and would probably grant him a reasonable request, though the wish part was surprising...and, as I thought about it, troubling as well. What did an eleven-year-old know about making that kind of life decision? Particularly since Khalid had a very distorted view of his relationship with his father, I could see him using up his wish almost immediately to be reunited with him. But unless the wish also included an attitude adjustment for Dad, it would certainly be wasted. How would I tell Khalid that, though? Would he believe me even if I did?

"Taliesin, explain to us the spell, so that we may begin," requested Gwynn quietly, perhaps aware that I was lost in thought.

I put my thoughts about Khalid aside and gave all my attention to making sure Gwynn, Mab, and Nurse Florence understood what to do. I did more than just tell them, though; I projected the spell into them, so they understood how it felt to cast it as well as I did. Gwynn and Mab both gasped at my ability to do this. I didn't know Mab well enough to be sure how she felt, but I could tell Gwynn was impressed.

"Now that we know what we are doing, we should begin at once," said Gwynn. "This is not quite as easy a working as I at first thought, and it may take time. I will take the north point; Mab, please take the south; Viviane, take the east; Taliesin, take the west." Once we were positioned and ready, Gwynn said, "Taliesin, we will follow your lead."

I sang a little first to make sure my power was at its maximum, then sent the spell flowing greenly over Carla, grabbing a red tendril of the awakening spell and pulling. I could feel Nurse Florence, Gwynn, and Mab joining me, letting their strength flow through me, and it seemed as if I could now do anything. Yet, though I could see the outer layer of redness clutching Carla much more clearly, it was still holding on.

I sang more forcefully, making the spell pull harder. I saw the golden design on the ground intensify to almost blinding brightness, and at last I felt the redness shift, begin to pull loose. Harder, harder I pulled. My head began to ache, my muscles began to tighten, but I kept on. The redness writhed around her, resisting our efforts to remove it, but its grip continued to weaken. The question was, would we give out before it did?

I lost track of how long we had been working. Afterward, Stan told me the struggle went on for at least two hours, with us four casters looking more and more spent as time passed. Finally, though, the redness ripped loose with a silent scream and, deprived of purpose, quickly dissipated. I staggered a little bit and almost lost my balance, but the work was done.

The process had been even harder than Morgan had suggested, but the second casting of the awakening spell had been removed. I still had the considerable task of making sure Alcina did not take over, but at least now there was hope. For the first time since Halloween, I felt my guilt lighten a little. I would make this situation right after all!

Nurse Florence nearly fainted, but Carlos caught her. Mab and Gwynn were still on their feet, but I had never seen faeries look so drained.

"A great working indeed, but we have done it!" Gwynn pronounced, satisfied.

I heard someone moan nearby. Carla! She was coming out of her coma already. I wanted to run to her, but I was too unsteady on my feet and could barely stagger forward. Stan and Shar helped me to reach her bed. Her eyes opened, she looked at me, and she smiled. It was the sweetest smile I had ever seen.

When I finally reached her, I bent over and gave her the most passionate kiss I could in my current state of exhaustion. Then I looked again into her eyes.

Carla was already gone. Alcina was there, much more quickly and strongly than I had anticipated—and here I was, exhausted.

I tried to reach into her with my mind to bring Carla back to the surface, but with a flick of her mind, she broke the connection.

I was so stupid! Of course Alcina would be in control at first, just as David had been with Stan. I should have taken precautions. Now it was too late…

Alcina gazed into my eyes, and I felt a magic like what Carla had unconsciously projected on Halloween, only many, many times stronger. No, not like Carla's, which had simply made an invitation. Alcina's power did not invite; it compelled. I could feel my grip on reality fading. Everything else was receding from me. Only Alcina was real.

"I recognize you," whispered Alcina in Italian, which I now understood. "You were with me before, when I first came back. This other one, Carla, loves you, and I can see why, handsome one. You will be mine. Distract the others long enough for me to get us out of here."

"Tal?" said someone right next to me. I turned and saw a slender teenager with black curly hair. I should know that face, but somehow I did not. He looked as if he might get in the way, though, so I sucker-punched him in the gut as hard as I could.

"Shar!" he shouted as he went down. Someone struck me from behind, knocking me down. I rolled and managed to get back on my feet, facing my attacker. Again, I felt I should recognize the face, but again I did not. I did notice the muscles ripple in his bronzed arms as he brandished a sword with an emerald glow.

I could hear running footsteps all around me, coming closer. I could feel enormous fatigue, though somehow Alcina was inspiring me to overcome it. I could feel power building nearby and knew that if I could just hold out for a few seconds, we could escape from these people, whoever they were.

I drew my sword, which burst into flames, and I struck it with all my might against the emerald sword, but my adversary did not lose his grip, and the flames of my sword died at the point at which they had struck the emerald sword.

"Tal, snap out of this!" yelled my attacker, bringing his sword down on mine with an enormous clang. My weary arms gave out, and I dropped the sword, its flames expired as it left my hand. However, I could feel the portal opening. I managed to throw myself backward in its general direction. I would abandon the sword if I had to, but I must not fail Alcina!

By now we were surrounded by warriors, both faerie and human. I felt Alcina silently calling out to me, and I moved back toward the bed on which she had been lying. I noticed a number of archers had a clear shot at me but were not taking it. Whoever these people were, they must have intended to take me alive—us alive, since they weren't shooting at Alcina either.

"Let me go, or he dies," said Alcina from behind me. "In his present state I can kill him where he stands, so strong is my hold on him."

"Think carefully what you do," yelled a dark-faced warrior nearby. "Taliesin is under my protection. If you harm him, I will hunt you to the ends of the Earth—and beyond."

"Do not think to threaten me," Alcina yelled back. "I knew you long ago, Gwynn. Your power has its limits. Once I am reestablished, you will not touch me."

"Is she bluffing?" I heard the emerald sword wielder ask. A golden-haired woman nearby answered, too low for Alcina to hear, but I heard. "We can't take the chance."

Suddenly the power behind me just blinked out. I turned as quickly as I could, but I knew what I would see. Alcina was gone.

I felt aching sorrow at being separated from her, but at least I had made possible her escape. If I had to die now, at least I would have that satisfaction.

I made a dive for the sword, but I was too weak to move as fast as I should have. The emerald sword wielder kicked me in the side, knocking me away from the sword. I hit my head, and everything dissolved in blackness.

CHAPTER 11: THE LONG WAY BACK

I floated in and out of consciousness, but I did not know for how long. Sometimes the golden-haired woman loomed over me, beautiful, but nothing compared to my Alcina. Sometimes the dark-faced warrior did the same. Sometimes others, people about my age, looking oddly concerned, considering I didn't know them. At least, I didn't think I did, though at times I felt I should know them.

I heard bits of conversation about how strong her hold was. People must have been talking about Alcina. Sometime soon she would try to rescue me, and we would be together again. Of that I was certain.

At some point I noticed my arms and legs were tied to the bed with stout ropes. I tried to fight against them, but I was too weak. My captors must have been drugging me or using some kind of spell. Surely otherwise I would have recovered my strength by now.

I dimly remembered being able to cast spells myself, but I also seemed to be too weak for that. I tried to find my power, but it floated away from me, eluding my grasp every time. I would only need a little, if I tried to escape while no one was around, but I could not seem to get even the slightest flicker of force out of my numb brain.

As time went on, I heard more specific conversations, but still just bits, and I did not understand them. I can remember one voice asking about which of me was under the spell and suggesting trying to bring out the original Taliesin, whatever that meant. Someone else responded that no one except me knew how to do that. I guessed I must have some special skills, but trying to remember just gave me a headache.

Later I heard someone who sounded like a boy asking if he could use the wish in his dagger to free me. Whoever he was talking to answered that the magic would not be strong enough to do that. I was intrigued by that conversation, but I couldn't keep myself awake for the rest of it.

One time I woke up and found the one with black curly hair holding my hand and talking to me.

"What?" I asked groggily, as my eyes came into focus.

"Tal?" he asked expectantly.

"Who are you?" I asked. I knew I should remember, but I just didn't.

Whoever he was, he dropped my hand and crumpled back into his chair. Eventually, though, he did answer me. "Tal, it's Stan. I'm your friend." That was an odd thing to say, because I seemed to remember punching him.

"If you're my friend, will you help me get out of here and get back to Alcina?"

Stan, if that was really his name, looked even more upset. "Tal, you need to stay here until you get well."

"But I'm not getting well," I mumbled. "I always seem to be the same. This is the longest I've stayed conscious in days...at least I think it is."

"See," said Stan, with false brightness, "you are getting better."

I vaguely recalled something about being able to read minds, but I didn't need to read his to tell that he was lying to me. I didn't really care, though, because I could feel myself slipping back into unconsciousness.

Over time I realized I was being held prisoner. Yes, that must be it. I *was* being drugged or enchanted or something, which was why I had so much difficulty just staying awake. At times I struggled against this weakness, but I felt like someone trying to swim up from the very bottom of the ocean without enough air in his lungs. I hardly ever reached the surface before the air ran out, and I passed out again. I never drowned, though, just drifted back to the bottom of the sea again. How was I supposed to live this way?

One day I woke with a cold feeling on my chest. I raised my head enough to see that someone had placed that green glowing sword there. I squinted a little bit as my eyes focused. There were people in the room— lots of them. Immediately I noticed the golden-haired woman and the dark-faced man.

"It's not going to work; I told you that already," said the woman. "Zom can deflect pretty much any spell before the spell hits the wielder, but bringing someone into contact with the sword after a spell is cast only breaks the spell if it is weak or if it is not acting directly on the victim, like an illusion that isn't hooked directly into the victim's brain."

"Touching me with Zom always takes away my artificial muscle, and that's not a weak spell, is it?" asked the curly headed one from somewhere; I couldn't raise my head enough to see him. "And on Halloween it caused shape-shifters to revert to their normal form."

"Those spells are intended to be temporary, not permanent. In that kind of situation Zom can remove the temporary effect, sometimes even if it is a strong one. I think the problem here is that Tal was already compromised by what happened before. Well, that and the fact that Alcina's spell is designed to be permanent, not temporary. You'll remember that Zom can't counter the effects of the awakening spell either, though it did prevent the spell from being cast on its wielder in the first place."

Normally by this time I would be asleep again, but I felt myself becoming more alert, not less so. Perhaps the sword was removing whatever they were using to keep me under. I tried to sit up and didn't quite succeed, but they noticed. I should have waited until they were gone.

"He's awake," said the dark-faced warrior. "Viviane, if you intend to try that new method, you had better do it soon."

"What are you doing to me?" I said weakly. "Let me go!" I pulled a little on the ropes.

"Eva!" called the golden-haired woman. "Come in now, please!"

People near the doorway moved out of the way. I noticed all the guys my age who had come to see me at various times were all there now. Through the doorway came someone else who looked vaguely familiar. She was a very beautiful strawberry blond, with a nicely curved body, but, again, not as lovely as my Alcina. She looked at me very sadly. I jerked ineffectually at the ropes again.

"Are you ready?" asked the golden-haired woman; I guessed Viviane was her name. The one called Eva nodded. "Everyone else join hands. This is going to take all of us." I could see them all joining hands as Eva advanced toward my bed. I tried to pull away, but being tied down, I really didn't have any place to go.

The room began to fill with golden light. It was everywhere, but in particular, it formed an aura around Eva, making her look like an angel. I wasn't fooled, though. This magic would be bad news for me. I could just feel it. I strained against the bonds, but it was no use.

"It's all right," said Eva, bending over me, the golden light now almost unbearably bright. She bent over quickly and kissed me on the lips. I hadn't been expecting that, or I would have tried to twist my head away from her. As soon as her warm lips touched mine, I felt a jolt of powerful magic burning into me, reaching into my heart, into my very soul. I screamed then, screamed until I was out of breath. I could feel things melting, shifting, transforming within me, and I was powerless to stop any of it.

The worst part, though, was the feeling that Alcina was fading, diminishing, vanishing from within me. I fought to hold on to her, I struggled with every ounce of will I had, but she slipped through my fingers as if I were trying to hold on to mist. She was still in my heart, but she was shrinking, she was shriveling…she was gone.

I looked around me as my memories flooded back, feeling colossally stupid. "What…what happened?"

Nurse Florence looked at Gwynn, who nodded, presumably to confirm that I was back in my right mind, and then turned back to me. "My best guess is that Morgan played us. She gave us enough truth that we believed her statement about the power required to lift the second casting of the awakening spell. In fact, it took far more power than we had anticipated, and that is what Morgan was counting on. I think she expected us to try to reverse the spell without her. She figured, correctly as it turned out, that we would so drain ourselves in the process that when Carla's coma ended and Alcina emerged, she would be able to escape from us, which is exactly what happened.

"Assuming the stories about Alcina are true, bewitching men is one of her specialties. She can make them forget everything else if necessary, remembering only a total devotion to her—a fake devotion, but her victims have no way of detecting its falseness."

"But that shouldn't have worked so easily on someone like me," I protested, feeling my cheeks redden. Perhaps I should have had her clear the room, but I knew my friends were staying to make sure I was all right, and I couldn't really blame them for that.

"Normally, no," replied Nurse Florence. "But remember how exhausted you were. Your natural defenses were much weaker than normal. Also, there were…other factors. We'll discuss them later."

Yeah, just what I needed right now—a little hint of mystery to obsess over.

"But what happened after that?" I asked. "I don't remember very clearly."

"We had to keep you from full consciousness," said Gwynn in a tone that came as close to being apologetic as he was ever likely to get. "If we had not, you might have tried to escape and hurt yourself or somebody else in the process."

"Stan!" I said, suddenly remembered what had happened when Alcina first took control and feeling extra guilty about it. "I hit you! Shar, I drew on you! I'm…I'm so sorry."

"Forget it, man," said Shar. "You weren't yourself—literally."

"Yeah, and anyway it was a pretty sissy punch," said Stan with a big grin. "I could have punched harder than that before I started working out."

"Oh, well, I'll be sure to hit harder the next time!" I said with a wink. "Nurse Florence, from what I remember, it must not have been easy to break the spell."

"It wasn't," she agreed. "Alcina hit you with all the power she had, and you became so convinced you loved her that you fought any attempt we made. Even working at only partial capacity, your resistance made reversal more difficult. And then the standard way of breaking that kind of spell is by reminding the victim of the person he really does love. The problem we had was that your current love was for Carla, who wasn't here and wasn't going to be. So we…"

With mounting apprehension, I realized where this conversation was going, but surely Nurse Florence wasn't going to start exploring my former love for Eva right in front of her and Dan.

"So we brought Eva. You used to care about her, you know, when you were twelve," said Dan, looking profoundly uncomfortable.

"Yes, and then Gwynn and Nurse Florence put everybody's will-power together—"

"And everybody's feeling of friendship for you," put in Carlos.

"Yes," continued Eva a little nervously, "and they channeled it all through my kiss. Wow, I've never felt anything quite like that. It was like…" she left the thought unfinished.

Dan was still looking uncomfortable. He must have wondered how a crush he thought ended four years ago could have been powerful enough to break the spell, even with a lot of help. Well, that was one thing he was going to have to keep wondering about!

"We hoped that remembering not only what you used to feel for Eva, but what you felt for all of us, might be enough to break the spell," said Nurse Florence just in time to keep the silence from becoming too awkward. "As it turns out, we were right."

"I guess I'm just lucky I have friends like all of you," I said, meaning every word. "Now, could somebody untie me?" They all laughed at that, since in the excitement it had kind of slipped their minds that I was tied up, even though they were standing right in front of me.

"I think before we do that, there is a certain faerie maiden who would like to pay you a visit," said Gordy with a snicker.

"You should talk, faerie fu—" started Dan, who stopped at a glare from Eva.

"So it looks like everything is pretty much back to normal," said Stan, who stepped over to help untie me.

"What passes for normal with us, anyway," I observed, rubbing my wrist as soon as it was free. "How long have I been like this?"

"About two weeks," said Shar as he reached over to reclaim Zom.

"Two weeks! What...how are we going to explain that to people?" I had visions of our secrets being revealed to the whole town.

"That's just a little over a day back in Santa Brígida," said Nurse Florence in her best calming voice. "And you know me better than to think I wouldn't provide cover for all of you. I got word to Vanora, who concocted some elaborate story about a special opportunity for a few select students to spend 24 hours with a visiting Nobel laureate. The story was so full of holes I could have driven a bus through it, but you know how the adults of Santa Brígida are about Carrie Winn—she speaks, and they accept whatever she says, especially if she suggests that their children are as wonderful as they already know they are. When you come back, you'll get a little applause and go back to your regular routines, with no one any the wiser.

"By the way, Tal, your security plan for Santa Brígida seems to have worked. As far as we can tell, Morgan didn't attempt any kind of attack, even though we've been gone longer than we thought we would be. Vanora's griping about having to keep that system going for so long, but once you get settled in at home, we can talk about what to do next."

"Of course, now Morgan has what she wants," I said ruefully.

"Maybe not," cautioned Nurse Florence, "but we can worry about that later."

Once untied, I discovered that my muscles were very stiff, but a little magic from Nurse Florence brought them much closer to normal. "You may need to do stretching exercises for the next few days, just to be sure," she said, "but I used magic to keep any muscle atrophy from occurring, and after all, it's not like you were out of commission for six months." She frowned a little. "I did the same thing with Carla. If I hadn't, Alcina wouldn't have been able to make such an easy getaway; she would hardly have been able to move at all."

"No one can blame you for that," I said. "You couldn't have known what was going to happen."

By now Nurse Florence and I were alone in the room. I had thanked everybody, they had assured themselves that I really was OK, and now they were preparing to leave. It was a good thing we were alone, because at that moment I began to realize that something was wrong.

I had started to think about Carla. I worried about her, naturally. I still felt guilty about the mess she was in, and I still felt determined to rescue her from Alcina.

What I didn't feel was any romantic love at all. There was a void in my heart where that love used to be, an aching hole that became more and more obvious to me. Nurse Florence could see my growing horror in my eyes.

"Tal, what's wrong?" she asked, looking very concerned.

"What, what has happened to me?" I asked, much more shrilly than I intended. "I…I don't feel anything for Carla anymore."

"Tal, I was going to wait to tell you this until we got back to Santa Brígida, but…well, there is no easy way to say this. Your love for Carla was never real in the first place."

"WHAT?" I didn't mean to shout. Well, maybe I did. In about thirty seconds I had gone from being grateful to Nurse Florence for curing me to angry with her for somehow ripping a piece of my soul out in the process.

"Tal," she said gently, "think back to Samhain. You told me yourself you could feel Carla broadcasting raw power, including mental images of the two of you, uh, having sex."

"Yeah, but that doesn't mean she was able to cast a spell on me. That's ridiculous! She wouldn't even have known how!"

"For shifting that kind of basic emotional response, she could maybe have done it instinctively. You've told me yourself how quickly you developed feelings for her."

"But my mind is strong enough to block that kind of enchantment!" I protested. "You know that. Even with full power, Alcina couldn't have taken me so easily unless I was completely drained. So how was an untrained caster like Carla able to do it? That just doesn't make sense."

Nurse Florence was trying hard to ignore my mounting anger. Her tone remained the same calm, rational tone she always used to deal with people who were not in full emotional control. "You were not exhausted then, but you were distracted…and on some level, I think you wanted it."

"Are you crazy?" She tried to put her hand on my shoulder, but I brushed it away.

"You loved Eva, but you didn't see any way you could ever be with her. Carla was attractive, and obviously, as you might say, 'into you.' You didn't really love her, but you thought your life would be a lot easier if you did. How hard would your mind have fought against something you wanted to happen?"

The hell of it was, she was right. I couldn't admit that yet, though, not even to myself. "If all of this is true, why didn't you do something about it before?"

"At first I wasn't sure. After the battle on Samhain, all of us had magic residue all over us. I was suspicious of how fast your relationship with Carla progressed, but I also thought it might be partly guilt. As the days passed, and I could still feel foreign magic on you, I became more certain, but I made the mistake of thinking maybe you were better off that way. You were right; at least in the short term, your relationship with Eva couldn't go anywhere. With Carla there was a chance, at least there was if we could cure her. If we hadn't been able to, I would have told you the truth and let you choose what to do about it."

"But you didn't give me a choice! You knew this process would make me stop loving Carla, and you did it anyway!"

"You were hardly in a fit state to be asked, Tal. At that point, I doubt you would even have known who Carla was."

I stared at her, the accusation plain in my eyes.

"Yes, Tal, I knew that if our plan worked, your love for Carla would fall in the same way your love for Alcina would. I lied to the others, Tal, to protect the friendship among you, Dan, and Eva. Even amplified, there's no way a crush you had four years ago would have broken the spell. The spell broke because you have feelings for Eva now. Your artificial feelings for Carla masked your real ones for Eva, but they were still there. And thank God they were, or you might have been enthralled by Alcina forever."

And that's when I realized just how far in hell I really was. I had been so focused on losing my feelings for Carla that I hadn't even thought about Eva, but Nurse Florence was right. When I did think about Eva, I thought immediately about making love to her, and not just because she was so beautiful that every straight guy who saw her wanted to do her. No, I could have handled a physical attraction. Damn, if not I would have taken that gorgeous faerie woman up on her offer. No, my feelings were not just physical. I wanted to make love with Eva because I loved her; I loved her every bit as intensely as I had loved her for the last four years. I loved her even knowing that the only way to be with her was to betray Dan, an idea that hadn't been quite so terrible when he was hostile to me, but now that our friendship had been restored, now that we were comrades in arms? No, I could never do that. So where did that leave me? The girl I could have I didn't love at all. The brand of the girl I could never have was seared into my heart, and until that wound healed, I didn't see how I could ever love another.

I could go back to Carla if we ever found her and managed to restore her. I could pretend. I would have liked to think that at some point I could learn to love her, but my heart told me that would never happen. I could lie to myself, I could lie to her—hell, we could even get married in a few years. I might even make her happy, though I feared at some point she would realize the truth: to me our love had been a mirage, and I was stuck in a waterless desert, a wasteland, wandering alone even when I was with her, wandering alone forever.

I shouldn't have taken my agony out on Nurse Florence; after all, she had saved me…again. But I just couldn't bring myself to admit that she had done what she had to do. I yelled at her a little, and she let me. Then I stormed out of the room without another word. I found the guys in the courtyard…and Eva. I managed to get myself into a long conversation with Gwynn so I wouldn't run the risk of talking to Eva. I doubted I could trust myself right now.

After a while, Nurse Florence appeared. It looked as if she might have been crying, but otherwise she had her professional facade clamped on very tightly. She thanked Gwynn for his hospitality, a gesture which started another round of thank-yous. While that ritual was going on, I sought out Khalid.

"Hey, buddy, I heard you offer to use your wish to save me at one point. That was a great thing to do."

"But it didn't do any good!" protested Khalid.

"You didn't know that when you offered. My point is that you were willing to take your shot at happiness and give it to me."

"Tal, I have never been happier than I am right now," said Khalid, looking up into my eyes. I knew he was lying a little; I could still see the shadow of his father in those eyes. However, he wasn't completely lying. We had taken him on a pretty amazing adventure, but we had also made him a part of our group. He might not be with his father, but at least he wasn't alone anymore.

At about that point, I felt Nurse Florence open the portal, and one by one we passed back into the "real" world.

God! What I wouldn't have given right then to just stay with Gwynn.

At least then I would not have had to look at Eva every day.

CHAPTER 12: SOUL-SEARCHING

Nurse Florence as always handled the logistics flawlessly. We came through the portal from Annwn in Awen, Carrie Winn's mansion/castle. The downside of that was getting treated to Vanora's long list of complaints about how the screw-up on our part of the operation was spreading her too thin. The upside was that we could all go home by limo, reinforcing the story about where we had been for the last twenty-four hours.

I would have liked to talk to Stan, but it was getting pretty close to dinner time, and our parents were expecting us home with tales of what we had gotten out of visiting with a Nobel laureate. He could tell I was upset and wanted to talk, and I knew that after two weeks I really needed to make sure the uneasy peace with David was still working out in his head.

"Stan, meet me after dinner!" I thought to him in the moments before we each got packed into a separate limo. He nodded, so I knew he understood.

Once I got home, my proud parents naturally drilled me about my prestigious meeting with a genius, not to mention how I got selected.

"Not that that's much of a mystery," said Dad with an uncharacteristically broad smile. "It's clear that you have made quite an impression on Carrie Winn."

If you only knew...

"Yeah, I guess she thinks pretty well of me."

"Oh, and you're so modest too," added Mom, beaming.

The problem with visiting faerie realms was that going back home required a considerable adjustment. Colors always seemed a little flatter, for example, when compared with the dazzling brightness of Annwn. Whatever I thought of the architectural choices in Santa Brígida—and, let's face it, I didn't think much of them—I had to admit that I lived in a pretty nice house. Yet its Navajo white walls seemed dull when compared to the glowing silver of Gwynn's castle. Even my mom's pot roast, which I had always liked, was semi-tasteless when measured against the culinary delights of a faerie feast. I knew I would adjust in a few days, but right now I understood why so many mortals who had accidentally stumbled into a faerie realm spent the rest of their lives trying to get back there.

When Dad got a phone call and had to leave the table for a few minutes, Mom's manner suddenly changed. She leaned over to me and spoke so quietly that she was almost whispering, "Tal, is something wrong?"

You mean besides the gaping hole where my love for Carla used to be? You mean besides the throbbing wound my love for Eva has caused to burst wide open again?

"No, Mom, nothing at all. I'm a little tired, but otherwise, just fine."

Mom continued to look worried, however, despite my putting on the most reassuring manner I could.

"Tal, this is going to sound crazy, but I have been having the oddest feelings lately."

I was ashamed to admit it, but I had actually forgotten about my mom's newfound psychic powers for a few days. Well, out of the frying pan, into the nuclear reactor.

"What kind of feelings? Just tell me, Mom—I promise I won't think you're crazy."

"Well, while you were gone, I had the oddest dream about you—strange women trying to kiss you, dragons, castles. And Carla was in the dream, too, and the school nurse, and lots of other people. I don't think I have ever had such a complicated dream."

Mom might not quite be the oracle at Delphi, but she had apparently had a relatively accurate dream out what I was doing in Annwn, and considering Annwn was a different plane of existence, she had to be operating on a fairly high power level.

"It sounds like a very imaginative dream to me, but certainly nothing to worry about. Wasn't it kind of fun?" I asked her.

"You'd think, but I'm not describing it very clearly. There was a feeling of danger. Many times I was frightened for your life. I woke up in a cold sweat, with my heart pounding. That's never happened to me before, not even once."

"Everyone has bad dreams, Mom. I'm still not seeing a problem." By now it was getting hard for me to be as reassuring as I needed to be. I knew I couldn't tell her what was really going on, but I couldn't let her think she was going crazy, either. And in a town with two aware reincarnates (Stan and I), and maybe a third if we could get Carla pulled together (or even find her, for that matter), a half djinn, a lady of the lake, and a shape-shifter disguised as the town's most prominent citizen, my mom was going to get constantly bombarded with psychic impressions that didn't match what she knew, or at least thought she knew, about the world. How could anyone not go crazy in that kind of situation?

"I'm sure you're right, dear, but still…what's happening with you and Carla?"

"She's in a coma, Mom. It's the most stable relationship in town."

"You don't need to be sarcastic. Of course, I know she's in a coma. I've visited her in the hospital. But…have your feelings changed? I'd understand if they have. It must be hard wanting to be in a relationship with someone who may never regain consciousness."

"Mom, nothing has changed. I'll tell you if it does, OK?"

"Is David coming over later?"

"Who's David, Mom?"

Mom looked at me in obvious shock, then pulled herself together a little. "Oh, Tal, I meant Stan. I know his name is Stan. I've no idea why I just called him David."

I do.

"It's OK, Mom. I just think you're worrying too much."

"I'm sure you're right, Tal," she said, though clearly she was nothing of the kind.

Dad was still stuck on the phone, so I helped Mom clear the table and wash the dishes. Yeah, we had a dishwasher, but Mom actually liked doing the dishes by hand, and tonight I decided it was better to just let her do what she wanted to do. It'd be therapeutic, maybe.

I thought about using a little magic to calm her nerves, but under existing circumstances I was afraid to, so I settled for a hug. Then I took a little walk in the general direction of Stan's house. Sure enough, he was walking over to see me. Normally, I would have taken him to my house, but with Mom already sensing King David within him, I just couldn't take the chance. Instead we took a walk a couple of blocks over to the nearest park. Really it was a very small woodsy area with some pretty tall oaks around the perimeter, but it was a nice place to go think at times like this, and unless some guy was taking his girlfriend there, Stan and I would probably be all alone.

As luck would have it, we were alone. We sat down on one of the stone benches near the center. (Yeah, you'd think maybe having big hunks of stone in the middle of an area where kids play might not be the best idea, but hey, they looked classy!)

I was shaken to see how much my efforts to weld Stan and David together had decayed while we were in Annwn, and I set to work to reinforce them again.

"David was pretty well convinced that he might be able to break Alcina's spell by praying over you. He really wanted out to give his idea a try, but I was kind of afraid to let him."

"Good instinct," I muttered as I worked. "Eventually, I think I can get the two of you fully integrated, but in the meantime, it might be dangerous to let him out. Even with his cooperation, it wasn't easy to get you securely back in control the last time he emerged. He means well but doesn't really know what he's doing and can't seem to be in proper sync with you without help. Besides, any number of things could go wrong while he's out, especially if he loses connection with you like he did last time."

Finally I had Stan back together, but the whole process had about the feeling of gluing an amputated limb back on. Well, actually my work *was* better than that, but I still didn't feel satisfied with it.

Well, let's see, if I couldn't get Stan properly back together, when his past self was cooperating, how could I get Carla back together when Alcina would probably never cooperate and had the ability to put up much more of a fight than David could? I decided to leave that question, like so many others, for later.

Once Stan was about as fixed as he was going to get that night, he asked me what was wrong. We had been friends for so long that he did not need to be able to actually read my mind to tell what my general mood was. Since I couldn't risk sharing the Carla/Eva situation with anyone else, I shared it with him.

He let me spill my guts for quite a while, and when I was finally done, he said, "I know this isn't much comfort, but you were dealing with the Eva thing before. Maybe once you get used to it again—"

"Yeah, but to be honest, I was miserable then too. I guess I just have to hope...what's that?" I could hear something like a distant whispering. Maybe now some guy was bringing his girl here.

"I don't hear anything...oh, yes, I do!" said Stan quietly.

"Whispering?"

"Yes, but I can't tell whether it is close to us or relatively far away."

"Taliesin," whispered the voice. I look at Stan, who nodded. He had heard my name too.

"Taliesin!" The voice still whispered, but it was becoming more insistent and felt louder, even though its actual volume remained the same. Stan and I began to search, and eventually we discovered that it was coming from one of the oaks. Yeah, never a dull moment in my life!

"I'm here," I announced, feeling pretty silly for talking to a tree.

"Taliesin, you must come to me."

"Who are you? Where are you?"

"I am Morgan, whom your friends have rudely barred from Santa Brígida. You have double-crossed me. I have Alcina despite you, but now you owe me a favor—and I intend to collect."

Odd! I had been sure Morgan needed me only as a way of getting Alcina, but clearly something else was going on. For once, luck was with me, because now perhaps I could find out where Carla was.

"Morgan, you know I'm not just going to do your bidding. What assurance do I have that you won't kill me, or that your sister won't try to bewitch me again?"

"I offered you a *tynged* before. I am prepared to do the same again. Meet me at Goleta Beach tonight at midnight."

"We need to have some *tynged* in place first, just to cover that meeting. We can work out the rest later, during the meeting."

There was a long pause, but then the oak's whispering began again. "Propose the oath."

"Neither of us will harm the other in any way, physical or mental. Neither one of us will cast a spell on the other. Neither one of us will attempt to take the other prisoner. Neither one of us will bring anyone else to the meeting." Stan started to protest, but I motioned for him to be quiet. "The *tynged* runs until the meeting ends, except that each of us will allow the other to depart after the meeting, making no attempt at harm or hindrance."

"I swear to it."

"As do it," I responded. Weaving a proper *tynged* worked better face to face, but almost instantly I felt the spell snap into place, so I knew our efforts had been successful.

"Until midnight, then," whispered the tree. After that the whispering ceased, and I could feel the power in the park dwindle to nothing. Morgan's presence was gone.

"You shouldn't have done that!" protested Stan. "Morgan never does anything that isn't to her advantage. She can't get at you in Santa Brígida, so she's tricking you into leaving it."

"At least we know our security arrangements are still working," I said with a chuckle.

"This isn't funny, Tal. You know you can't trust her."

"Yeah, but I need to take the chance. She obviously wants something more than just getting Alcina back. My only way to find out what she wants is to meet with her. Oh, and Stan…"

"Yes?" he asked, already suspicious.

"You can't come, and you can't tell anyone else. You have to promise me." Stan looked ready to refuse. "You really have to," I insisted. "If anyone else shows up, Morgan will probably take off, which would pretty much defeat the purpose. Promise not to come or tell anyone."

"Oh, all right," said Stan after a long pause. "But you better come back unharmed, Tal. I would never be able to forgive myself if I let something happen to you."

"Nothing will happen. She can't do a thing to me, remember?"

Glancing at my watch, I saw that it was already ten o'clock at night. I walked a still-nervous Stan back home, chuckling a little to myself, because I used to walk him home in the old days to keep bullies from beating him up. *I'd hate to see what would happen to a bully who tried to beat up Stan now!* I thought. It seemed hard to believe the number of changes in our lives between August and December.

I finally pried myself loose from Stan, made some excuses to my parents, climbed in the Prius, and headed for Goleta. Yeah, I was going to get there way before midnight, but that gave me a good opportunity to prepare. I hadn't been to Goleta Beach in a long time, but it was a simple drive from Santa Brígida: south to I-101, west to the 217, west again to the Sandspit exit, and then over to Sandspit and down to the beach. Hell, I could have done it in my sleep. When I got there, I parked as far north, away from the beach, as I could, and I didn't get out right away. Instead, I sung myself into the most highly spell-resistant state I could achieve, I morphed my eyes enough to give me night vision, and I sped myself up so that I could move as fast as Morgan. If Stan were there, he would have asked why I was doing all that if I was so sure the *tynged* would hold. Well, I wasn't taking any chances. I would never have admitted it to him, but Stan was right—Morgan would not be having this meeting unless she thought she could gain something from it. *Tynged* or no *tynged*, I was going to be careful.

When I was ready, I got out of the car and glanced around. I thought I remembered some kind of lighting in the parking lot area after dark, but I wasn't seeing any sign of it now. Budget cuts, probably, and the beach was certainly closed this late, but the darkness did put me a little more on my guard. There was a little moonlight, but the moon was almost entirely covered by clouds, so it was a good thing I had given myself night visions. Looking north, I could see the glow of headlights from the 217, and with my heightened vision, I could make out the much closer row of palm trees on the north end of the beach. Everything looked normal so far.

Then I looked south and remembered just how big the beach was. To my left (east) was Goleta Beach County Park, with more palms and other trees, as well as a pier that started at the shoreline, just south of a seafood restaurant and a few other buildings, and jutted out into the ocean. As I scanned from left to right, I saw the various picnic grounds, volleyball courts, and other stuff like that; the beach was a fairly popular one, so whoever was in charge of it wanted to make it as attractive as possible to tourists and locals alike.

When most people think of beach, they think of sand, but Goleta Beach was sandy only near the water's edge; the rest of it was as grassy as a regular park, with lots of trees, especially, but not exclusively, on the parking lot side. Some of the trees were big enough to hide behind, but I wasn't seeing or feeling anything out of place. If I looked as far to the right as possible, I could just barely make out lights from UCSB, where Stan had the misadventure with a kelpie that nearly cost his his life. No obvious threat from that direction either, nor any sign of Morgan. No, wait—way down toward the pier, I could feel power building up. That had to be Morgan, but what was she doing with that kind of power? What purpose, within the scope of the *tynged*, could it serve?

What would Nurse Florence have advised me to do in this situation? Run like hell, probably. Well, I should get some credit for thinking about doing just that, and I really didn't want to be overly impulsive, but damn, this could be a really good opportunity. I thought about Carla. True, I didn't love her anymore. Apparently, I had never loved her. That didn't mean, though, that I could just leave her to her fate. I had to risk whatever Morgan was planning in order to have a shot at figuring out how to rescue Carla.

I started walking in the general direction of the pier. Then I almost jumped when I heard Morgan's voice coming from the opposite direction.

"Going somewhere? I thought we had a meeting," said Morgan, almost playfully. I hadn't felt her open a portal behind me, probably because I was so focused on the pier. Her pale skin gleamed in the moonlight, and the wind caused her black samite gown to rustle just slightly.

"And so we do. I thought you were over there, Morgan. Someone is using a lot of power."

To my surprise, Morgan seemed thrown somewhat off-balance by that news, as if she had not been expecting it. "I just arrived, but yes, now I feel it too. Your water witches?"

"You know I couldn't bring anyone with me, so if they were here, it would have to be the biggest coincidence in the history of the universe." Morgan looked at me very intensely.

"If it is any one of your allies, it will tell me that you have somehow circumvented the *tynged*, and this meeting will be over."

"I promise you I have nothing to do with whoever else is here, Morgan."

Morgan's eyes narrowed. "If you speak the truth, some third party may be trying to interfere in our affairs. We should investigate."

"I'd suggest just moving our meeting somewhere else. Whoever or whatever is responsible doesn't seem to be moving this way."

Morgan laughed derisively. "And I thought you were brave! Well, if you won't see what is happening, I certainly will." With that she turned and started walking toward the pier.

Damn male ego! I should have left her to look into any third-party activities on her own, but the implication that I was a coward got to me, and I went along. Besides, she was still the only way I could find Carla.

As we approached, the power seemed steady, neither ebbing nor building, just...well, waiting was what it felt like, though what it was waiting for I couldn't say. Using my enhanced sight, I spotted a figure walking out onto the pier, but I could not tell who it was. Like Morgan, the figure was dressed in black and had long, black hair, but beyond that I could not see enough at this distance. I probed at the figure with my mind, but whoever was there was strongly shielded. It was clearly another caster, and probably therefore the source of the power. If so, perhaps her appearance was coincidental. She continued to walk slowly out onto the dock, show-ing no interest in me and Morgan, if she even knew we were here.

Then I realized what was radiating so much power. It was a portal of some kind, but I had never seen one so big. Now that I was aware of it, I could see its faintly glowing outline. It centered on the pier, but it seemed to stretch for several yards in both directions from the pier, both above the water and below it. The woman on the pier was walking toward it, not purposefully, but almost like one hypnotized or possessed. Her steps seemed uncertain, but she never looked down, even though she came close to stumbling. She just kept her eyes straight ahead and took one halting step after another toward the portal. Within a minute she would step through it into whatever lay beyond.

If someone were trying to take her to some otherworld location against her will, then I should try to prevent that. I glanced over at Mor-gan, who seemed interested but not particularly alarmed.

"You were right, Taliesin. It seems whoever is at work tonight is here for someone else, not us." She turned as if to walk away.

"I need to see what's happening, Morgan. If you are no longer interested, just wait here, and I will rejoin you shortly." Without waiting for her response, I bounded in the direction of the pier, yelling to the woman, who did not respond to the sound of my voice at all. There could be little question that she was under someone else's control, and she was only seconds away from being snatched from the face of the earth. I stepped up my pace to faerie speed, and now I was only a few steps behind her.

Whatever lay beyond the portal, it was night there as well, and somewhere at sea, judging by the salt spray I could feel coming through. However, I couldn't see much, even with enhanced vision. On the other side lay a moonless, starless night, but all I could see was darkness. Some-how the surface of the portal filtered away my night vision, leaving me effectively blind. The woman took another zombie-like step, and then I reached her, grabbed her, and spun her around. At my touch, she dis-solved—a simple illusion, but I had fallen for it!

I knew I needed to get off that pier, but surprise caused me to hesitate just a second, and in that second a gigantic tentacle reached through the portal, grabbed me, and pulled me through. Almost the in-stant I felt myself passing into a different world, the portal winked out of existence, trapping me on the other side.

The one advantage to being on the other side of the portal was that I could now see what was going on better, but that advantage mattered little under the circumstances. The tentacle gripped me so tightly I could barely breathe, so tightly that trying to draw White Hilt was out of the question. The tentacle projected out of an ocean that was churning roughly, not so much from wind as from whatever lay beneath—probably a pretty good imitation of a 1950s B-movie giant octopus or squid would be my guess. In fact the ocean was practically bubbling with sea creatures, as if every living thing for several miles had been drawn to this point. I noticed more than a few shark fins and guessed that whoever had brought me here had also summoned all the sea life to make an escape more difficult. Looking further out, I saw the distant outline of an island, probably a pretty large one, though it was hard to tell from here.

"Don't try to sing or spell cast," said an all-too-familiar voice. I managed to twist my neck just enough to see Alcina riding a killer whale in my general direction. The masses of sea life parted to allow her through.

"Alcina, you are destroying your sister. By bringing you to the beach, she has broken the *tynged*. Perhaps if you let me go, there is still a chance that this breach will not fall upon her with its full force."

Alcina threw back her head and laughed. "Lover, you couldn't be more wrong. I haven't set foot on *your* beach at all. Even if had, though, Morgan did not bring me. I was already at this very spot, ready to open a portal at midnight, when Morgan set up the meeting."

Oops! Guess I should have proposed a different location. Goleta Beach did seem like a pretty odd pick, especially for someone unfamiliar with the area.

"Because I was already in this place, Morgan did not *bring* me. The *tynged* did not require her to disclose anyone who might already be at your beach, much less anyone who was in an otherworld that could connect by portal. Nor did the *tynged* require Morgan to tell you the truth once the meeting started, for that matter. And the *tynged* did not cover anything I might do on my own, only what Morgan might do. I could have my little friend crush you right now, and the *tynged* would not hurt a hair on Morgan's head."

Apparently I needed to hire a lawyer the next time I was setting up a *tynged*. Morgan had trapped me in a way I never anticipated.

"Where is Morgan?" I asked, trying to sound as if I didn't really care. "I would have expected her to come gloat."

Alcina smiled at that. "Oh, she will. She thought it best to stay behind for a few minutes and take care of your friends."

"My friends? I brought no one."

"Yes, like Morgan you *brought* no one. Morgan was aware that Stan was listening in. She imagined he would organize a little backup, even if you told him to stay away."

"Alcina, she had better not hurt him or any of my other friends!" I tried to sound threatening, but it was pretty hard to carry off that effect when a gigantic octopus was just a few muscle twitches away from crushing me.

"My, such a shame that the *tynged* doesn't say anything about what Morgan can do to anybody except you. I think she has been waiting for a long time to see if she could create a tidal wave. Now might be as good a time as any to find out for sure!"

I tried to be as poker-faced as I could. I didn't want to let Alcina see how shaken up I was.

"As for us, lover, we have a date on my little island. First, though, I need to get you in the mood. Just look into my eyes, and I will put things back the way they should be."

I had already guessed that eye contact probably helped Alcina work her magic, so I closed my eyes as tightly as I could…only to feel the pressure from the tentacle around me increase painfully.

"Don't make this difficult, Taliesin. Just open your eyes, and in a very short time, you'll be glad you did." Even her voice was seductive, and I could feel her power touching me already, even with my eyes closed. My heightened magical resistance would make it harder for her to control me, but if I remained her prisoner, she would eventually break down that resistance. The tentacle tightened again, and now I could hardly breathe.

"You…won't…get…what…you…want…if…I'm…dead," I managed to gasp. The tentacle relaxed enough to let me breathe, but it was still uncomfortably tight.

"I suppose you have a point, and there will be plenty of time later to make you mine. Perhaps I should get you settled in on my island."

I didn't really want that, either, though it beat being crushed to death. My current position, close to the portal that had just closed, left some hope that Nurse Florence could still find me by following whatever tenuous connection yet remained between this spot in the ocean and Goleta Beach. The more time that passed, though, the more tattered that connection would become. Worse, the further I was moved away from that spot, the less that connection would help, and Alcina's island seemed to be some distance away.

"Give me a chance to catch my breath," I said, hoping she might give me a minute or two, but she knew as well as I did what I really wanted.

"I think we should return to my island at once," she said, and I risked opening my eyes just enough to see the mass of sea creatures begin to move toward that distant island. There were so many of them that they would hinder the progress of the octopus holding me, but only briefly, and then it too would move, far away from any immediate hope of my rescue.

Then I had one of the most abrupt light-bulb moments in my entire life. Suddenly I remembered something Morgan had said to me when I first confronted her outside the hospital. "She settled on an island, not exactly in Annwn, but certainly in an otherworld of some sort." At the time, I hadn't much cared where Alcina's island was. Now it was the most crucial piece of information I had.

The only reason I couldn't open portals to and from Annwn was that Arawn, the former king, had blocked my ability to do so. But if this wasn't Annwn, I could theoretically open a portal out of it back into my own world. The original Taliesin had known how, and so I knew how. The problem was practice. After Gwynn hold told me why my efforts to connect to Annwn were failing, I had had no need to practice that particular kind of magic—and it was complicated kind of magic, especially since I was coming from a place I had never been before. Still, almost anywhere would be better than here at this point. As long as I got back to my own world, even if I didn't succeed in returning to exactly the same spot, I would at least have a chance. True, ending up at the North Pole or the Sahara, or perhaps right in the path of an erupting volcano would be...well, complicated at best. However, being forced back into subjection to Alcina would be far worse.

Unfortunately, the moment I began to summon the power needed to open a portal, which was considerable, Alcina felt it, and the octopus again tightened its grip. Alcina didn't want to kill me, but she would do a lot of damage if necessary to keep me—I was sure of that.

As if to confirm my worst fear, the octopus plunged me deep into the salty water. It brought me up again, almost immediately, and, dripping, shivering, and gasping as I was, my concentration was broken. I would have to start all over again, and Alcina could keep battering me enough to destroy my focus without killing me.

I reached out for the octopus's mind. It was surrounded and utterly controlled by Alcina, just as I expected, and I wasn't foolish enough to try to break that control, an effort that would have been a total waste of energy. Instead, I used a method that would require less focus to work. Lashing out as hard as I could, I sent a lance of pure thought clattering against Alcina's control and the mind beneath it, striking that mind with stunning force and simultaneously throwing Alcina a little off-balance.

All I had won was a temporary respite. The octopus's hold on me loosened, but it would not remain stunned for long, and if for some reason it did, there was plenty of other marine life Alcina could use against me, including a number of sharks. In just seconds, I had to punch through into my world. I felt the power building; I felt the wall between worlds thinning. Alcina was screaming at me, but I resolutely tuned her out. Fish jumped at me, but none of them could really distract me. One of the sharks circled closer, but I didn't think Alcina had quite figured out how to have the shark restrain me without mauling me, so it got close to me but then hesitated.

In that moment of hesitation, I felt something like a click inside my head as my mind made contact with my own world. Right next to me, a portal glowed invitingly. With a little magical help, I struggled free of the octopus's tentacle and threw myself through the portal. Alcina's screams rang in my ears, and I felt her mind striking against mine, seeking a weak spot in my defenses. Before she could find one I was through the portal, which I slammed shut behind me. Unfortunately, I was stiff and bruised from the octopus, and before I could attempt something like flying, I had fallen into the ocean. The one in Alcina's world had been a bit warmer, like the Atlantic; this one was Pacific cold and a much bigger shock to my system, but at least it gave me hope that I was on the right coast.

The water was much rougher, though, than Goleta Beach had been when I left, and the surf was decidedly heavier. Almost immediately I had to roll under a big wave to avoid being slapped down by it, and my night vision, which fortunately was still working, showed me other big waves rising from the ocean. After dodging two more, I knew I had to get out of the ocean, but trying to swim to shore in all this turbulence would be difficult, so I tried gently but quickly flying upward. I still hadn't practiced much, and the combination of my waterlogged condition and the relatively strong winds added to the difficulty, but just moving straight up, out of the water and above the reach of the waves, turned out to be easy enough to execute.

As I started to climb, however, I could sense enormous power building almost right next to me. Alcina was opening another enormous gateway, obviously with the intent of bringing some of her marine army through with her. Unfortunately for her, the bigger the portal, the harder it is to keep stable, so it was easy for me to give it a couple of blasts of raw magic and cause it to collapse. I figured Alcina had to be getting tired by this time, and it would take her a few minutes to try again. That gave me time to establish where I was and plan my next moves.

Free for the moment from both the battering of the sea and Alcina's attacks, it was not hard for me to spot the pier and realize I had made it back to more or less the same spot from which I had left. I must have managed to hook on to the remnants of the connection Alcina had used without even realizing what I was doing.

Then I heard the guys shouting, and looking toward the northwest, I could see a battle in progress. Morgan had taken to the air, a wise move on her part, since she had no way to counter Zom. The guys had gathered around Shar, close enough to touch Zom and be protected from any magical attack, including lightning from the ominous storm clouds above them. That left the battle at an impasse for the moment, but it wasn't hard for me to sense that Morgan was responsible for the agitation of the sea. Zom might protect the guys against magically generated high waves, but a true tidal wave would submerge them and could still drown them at that point with no further magical impetus.

I could also sense Nurse Florence somewhere around, trying to counter Morgan's magic. Since the ladies of the lake worked better with fresh water, Morgan was winning, but slowly. However, I doubted her goal was actually to kill all of them. What she wanted was clearly to keep them busy until the last traces of the portal through which I had been pulled had faded away, making it impossible for Nurse Florence to follow me. It was a good plan—except that Morgan had not counted on my escaping and coming back. Whatever else happened, I needed to get rid of her before Alcina managed to get another portal opened. I did not want to have to deal with both of them at once!

Awkwardly I zigzagged in Morgan's direction, fighting the more and more powerful winds every second. She was still preoccupied with other things, but when I got close enough, I yelled, "The meeting is over. Leave now, or face my wrath!" Unfortunately, the *tynged* allowed her to go in peace once the meeting was over. I drew White Hilt, and its fire cut through the darkness, but the *tynged* clamped down on me mercilessly when I thought about shooting flames at her.

Morgan was surprised, to say the least, but she recovered quickly. "You should have just let Alcina take you," she hissed at me, practically spitting the words. "Now you have brought more pain to yourself and to your friends."

"You'd better get out of here," I cautioned. "The *tynged* won't protect you if you refuse to leave."

Morgan scowled, but she knew I was right. "Don't be so foolish as to think that this is the end, Taliesin."

"What is it you want, Morgan? You have Alcina back. Why not just take her and go?" I know—foolish questions. What likelihood was there that Morgan would reveal her motivations to me?

"If your wits were half as sharp as you think they are, you would already know!" she replied angrily. Then she turned and flew toward the south, out over the ocean, and was gone. I landed near the guys, who rushed in my direction.

"Tal, are you all right?" asked Nurse Florence, who had noticed the seawater dripping from me.

"Better than I look," I replied quickly. "But we need to brace for another battle. Alcina might open a portal somewhere nearby at any minute, and it would not surprise me at all if Morgan doubled back and tried to catch us off guard."

"Maybe we should just leave, then," suggested Nurse Florence. "Let's take advantage of that security net that Vanora is wearing herself out to create."

"I still have no idea what Morgan wants, but if she gives up for the moment and goes away somewhere with Alcina—" I stopped for a second, shocked by thinking of her only as Alcina—"I mean, if she goes somewhere with Carla, we may never get Carla back."

Nurse Florence sighed. "You have a point." She said something else as well, but I was distracted for a moment by the feeling that someone else was nearby, perhaps invisibly. Focusing my attention, I could just make out Khalid, using his usual strategy of trying to hide behind Shar. Damn! That kid just would not stay out of trouble.

"Khalid," I called. "I can see you. You may as well come out." At that point he stepped from behind Shar and dropped his invisibility. They guys were all understandably shocked to see him, and even Nurse Florence, who, like me, could have seen him if she had concentrated, had been too busy countering Morgan to notice.

"Khalid!" snapped Shar. "I told you to stay home! You can't just go running into battle untrained. Just because you have a weapon doesn't mean you can use it effectively." Khalid was doing his almost-tearful I-was-just-trying-to-help expression, and I could hear in Shar's voice that it was working.

"I could help," Khalid protested. "I'm fast, and I'm stealthy. None of you even knew I was with you!"

"Which means if you had gotten into trouble, none of us would have been able to help you," said Shar, somewhat more gently.

"Wait!" I said abruptly. "I sense Alcina." I hadn't felt another large portal opening, so she must have decided to leave Sea World behind and just come herself. Looking around quickly, I could see her walking slowly up the pier toward the beach. "Shar and I will go after her, because we are least likely to be affected by her mind control."

Actually, the *tyngeds* Nurse Florence had arranged with each of the guys might have protected all of them from being controlled by Alcina…except that I had forced Nurse Florence to make several modifications, including one that released any of them from the obligation to protect me if doing so would threaten their own well-being. I didn't want people being forced into suicide missions on my behalf, and after Samhain that kind of scenario had seemed very likely. If someone chose to die for me, that was one thing, but no one should be compelled to do so by magic.

Anyway, since Alcina's compulsion was so strong, someone under a *tynged* to protect me and under orders from Alcina to attack me might very well have his mind ripped apart by the conflicting demands; chances were good that the personal well-being safeguard of the *tynged* would release him at that point and let Alcina have him. Even had I anticipated this situation, I would have insisted on structuring the *tynged* in the same way, but I did wish they could all be protected from being enslaved by

Alcina in some way that wouldn't destroy them. Probably they could be, but there just wasn't time now.

"Nurse Florence," I continued, "do your best to counter whatever magic attacks she throws at us. The rest of you, keep an eye out for Morgan; she could be back any time. And Khalid...stay out of trouble!" Khalid nodded sullenly, and Shar and I were off at a run toward the beach end of the pier.

"She can control sea creatures, so try to stay out of the water!" I thought to Shar as we ran. Hopefully there was no nearby giant octopus for her to summon, and I didn't think the waters were exactly shark infested, but I had been taken by surprise too often in the past to take anything for granted.

I could smell the lightning in the air before it struck. Somewhere nearby, Morgan was milking electricity out of the already-prepared storm clouds. As far as I could sense, the guys all dodged successfully, but without Shar nearby, they were vulnerable.

"Shar, go back!" I shouted. "I'll take care of Alcina." Shar stopped dead in his tracks, clearly skeptical. Given what had happened last time, I couldn't really blame him.

"I'm protected this time, Shar. Just go!"

Reluctantly, he turned back as thunder roared and there was another lightning flash.

"Running to see me, lover?" asked Alcina mockingly as I got closer. "And here I thought you wanted to get away from me."

I let White Hilt flare and then demanded her surrender. She just laughed. "Are you really going to burn this Carla you care so much about? Go ahead, if that is what you really want."

Well, she had me there—I obviously couldn't kill her. However, if she were as tired as I guessed from traveling between worlds and summoning huge armies of sea creatures, I should be able to restrain her.

I was at the end of the pier, and she stood only a few steps down it. I started singing, pouring every ounce of magic I had into the song, willing her into immobility. Given how strong her own will was, an attack on her body made more sense than a direct attack on her mind.

Of course, Alcina had wanted me to get close enough for her to enthrall me with fake love again, and I could feel her seductive energy twisting all around, probing my defenses, eroding them one grain at a time. Yes, I was protected, but only for a little while, though I avoided looking into her eyes, slowing down her magic at least a little bit.

I could feel Alcina trying to push back my attack, resisting the paralysis I was throwing at her. She was weak, not as weak as I had hoped, but probably enough. The strain of both attacking and defending at the same time would wear out a caster twice as fast as doing just one or the other. Both of us were strained by that same burden, but I felt her wearing out just a little faster than I was.

Focused as I needed to be right then, I could only be dimly aware of what was going on to the west, where the guys and Nurse Florence were once again fighting Morgan. From what I could tell, they had reached another impasse, but I could feel more ocean spray hitting me as the waters around the pier became more agitated. It would not be long before Morgan had created some major disaster. I had to overcome Alcina before that happened.

At that moment I realized there was a way to win our magical duel much more quickly. I could cast the awakening spell on her again, knock her back into a coma, and throw myself into the battle against Morgan. We would drive Morgan off, and we would have Alcina—no, Carla—we would have Carla again, and this time when we peeled off the second casting of the awakening spell, we would be ready. Alcina would not be able to take control of the situation the way she did the first time.

The problem was that the results of hitting someone with the second casting of the awakening spell were unpredictable. The fact that Carla had been rendered comatose the first time didn't mean that the effect would be the same this time. The spell could just as easily kill her.

It wasn't that I had started loving Carla again. Those feelings were still gone, perhaps forever…but at the very least, she was a friend, Gianni was still like a little brother to me, and her parents treated me like a member of the family. Anyway, hell, whose life would I be willing to risk? Anyone's? I doubted it.

On the other hand, I remembered how much I hated being enslaved to Alcina—and I wasn't even aware of what was happening at the time. For all I knew, Carla was conscious of every second and screaming silently for help, any help. Would I want to live like that? No, I would choose death for myself rather than being a spectator to the evil someone was creating using my own body. Yeah, I know—it was easy to say something like that when I wasn't actually faced with the choice, but I really thought I would pick death under those circumstances.

It was one thing, though, to make a choice like that for myself; it was a completely different thing to make that choice for someone else.

I stood for a while, keeping up the magic battle, but paralyzed inside, uncertain what to do. Then, in one white-hot instant, those thoughts were stunned away as lightning struck me—literally.

People can be killed or badly injured by being struck by lightning, but Morgan had carefully crafted this lightning so it was only a pale reflection of what lightning usually is. Still, every hair on my body stood straight out, every nerve tingled, my concentration shattered into a thousand tiny pieces, and I fell to my knees. Alcina, freed from having to defend herself against me, attacked me full-force with every ounce of magic she had. In seconds I could feel the defenses I had put up wearing thin, and I was still too stunned to reinforce them. Barring a miracle, Alcina would have me again in a few minutes. The guys, still dodging Morgan's lightning, would be hard-pressed to come to the rescue, even though they were agonizingly close. Nurse Florence was too far away to feel.

I focused what little concentration I had left on resisting Alcina's influence. I probably couldn't buy myself very much time, but even a few seconds more of freedom was better than nothing.

Suddenly a felt a different presence very nearby. Khalid! He had moved fast enough to dodge Morgan's lighting and was rushing at Alcina with speed far greater than her human body could match. By the time she realized he was there, he had drawn his dagger and was poised to thrust it into her breast.

"Don't kill her!" I whispered urgently. I don't know if he heard me, if his aim was terrible, or if Alcina managed to shift out of the way a little, but he stabbed her in the arm instead of in the heart. She shrieked and stumbled backward, but Khalid stayed on her. I felt her power recede and knew she was trying to aim it at Khalid, but I sensed it wasn't working. Alcina had fashioned her control spell around sexual love, and she probably saw Khalid as too young, blunting her ability to cast the spell on him successfully. Either that, or his half djinn nature gave him some protection. He struck again and again, wounding her several times.

From somewhere Morgan was trying to hit Khalid with lightning. He dodged successfully, but that gave Alcina enough of a breathing space for her to run a few paces away and try to open a portal. She almost succeeded, but a combination of fatigue, pain, and blood loss caused her to lose control of the portal, letting it collapse after just a few seconds.

I managed to struggle to my feet and tried to sing in an effort to speed my recovery. The sounds I produced sounded more like croaking than singing, but I did feel myself revive just slightly. A little more, and I could begin to help Khalid.

He was going to need reinforcements of some kind—and soon. Morgan had shifted her focus toward the pier as soon as Khalid had attacked Alcina, and lightning was striking often enough to rattle the windows in the nearby seafood restaurant. I wondered idly if the restaurant was still open. If it was, the patrons seated near the beach-side windows had been getting quite an eyeful, but fortunately the place looked dark—probably closed. I also wondered if enough lightning strikes would set the pier on fire. Since Alcina was still on the pier, I hoped Morgan would avoid that kind of mistake.

Even as I was thinking about Morgan, she appeared overhead, and I could hear the guys behind me as they surged in my direction. Alcina was still having trouble sustaining a portal; perhaps Khalid had wounded her more deeply than I had imagined. There was fresh blood on her gown, lots of it. I shuddered at the implication of that, but either Nurse Florence (if we were lucky) or Morgan (if we were not) could certainly still heal her. I tried to move in her direction but staggered and felt dizzy. Clearly, I was trying to move too soon. Much as I hated the delay, I kept on singing, which made me feel better, but at an agonizingly slow rate.

Again Morgan had no difficulty creating an impasse with the guys, who clustered around Shar and touched Zom to keep from getting zapped. However, she needed more than that. At minimum, she needed to rescue Alcina, but she probably wanted to snag me again as well.

I could feel Nurse Florence reaching out to me, examining my condition, but I knew she needed to be closer to heal me effectively. At almost the same time, I felt Alcina's power engulf me, much weaker than the first time, but still unmistakable. Then that power faded. Looking over at the pier, I saw Alcina stagger again.

While I was watching Alcina, I realized that Morgan had switched tactics. The guys were moving in fast on Khalid's position. Once they arrived, Shar would have him touch Zom, and he too would be immune to Morgan's lightning, so, instead of keeping up that attack, Morgan created a little whirlpool in the air, not really a tornado, but enough to pull Khalid's body up into the air.

Memories of the battle on Samhain flooded back to me. What

Morgan was doing with Khalid looked a lot like what Ceridwen had done with me. Khalid could not fly like a full-fledged djinn, or even like me, now that I had a little practice. Nor could he manipulate the air currents that were holding him the way I had on Samhain. Had I not had that skill, I would have died then. With a shudder, I realized that Khalid might well die tonight. He was helpless, the guys could not reach him from the ground, and I was still too dazed to be of much use. Nurse Florence, who had been chanting to ward off the lightning, was now at my side, but could she heal me fast enough? I tried to point out Khalid's dilemma, but she told me to relax, and then I felt her healing energy sweeping through me.

Morgan was maneuvering herself toward Alcina's position. The guys tried to move forward, but Morgan pointed to Khalid, thrashing about uselessly in the air, and they got the point. No one wanted to lose Carla again, but no one wanted to see Morgan hurt the kid, either.

As Morgan floated in the direction of her nearly fallen sister, she pulled Khalid along with her, and it dawned on me that she would take him hostage in an effort to force me to go with her, if not immediately, then certainly later.

"Don't try to heal me right now," I mumbled as insistently as I could to Nurse Florence. "Stop Morgan somehow! Whatever else happens, we have to keep Carla and Khalid..." My throat felt too raw to continue, but Nurse Florence had gotten the point, and by now she could see that I was not in any immediate danger of dying.

"I'm no match for Morgan, Tal. The bulk of my training has been in healing and defensive magic. Yes, I can counter some of what she does, but that won't be enough to stop her from getting away with at least one of them."

She paused for a moment, looked me in the eye, and said, "There may be one way. Do you trust me?" I nodded. She put her hands on me, and I felt a sudden, tremendous rush of power revitalizing me, energizing me, giving me a shot at stopping Morgan myself. But she was giving me too much strength too fast, exhausting herself, letting herself drop to a dangerous level. I started to resist, but she shot me a strong mental reiteration of the need to trust her and just kept pouring her power, even her very life-force, into me. Only when she was nearly unconscious did she stop, and by then her vital signs seemed so low I actually feared for her life. Could she, the incarnation of cautious decision-making, really have taken such a huge gamble?

She managed to lie down on the grass rather than falling down. "Go!" she whispered, right before her eyes closed.

Talk about dilemmas. She didn't seem as if her heart was going to stop or anything like that, but she was so fragile that leaving her alone seemed like too big a risk. On the other hand, if I didn't do something, she would have risked her life in vain. Reluctantly, I looked around. In the short time Nurse Florence had emptied practically everything except her very soul into me, Morgan had gotten to Alcina on the pier and was probably checking her condition to decide whether or not she needed any emergency healing before Morgan opened a gateway back to Alcina's island or somewhere else far away from us. Khalid was floating right above, still struggling futilely to escape. If I was going to act, I had to do so right away.

I shot diagonally into the air, heading both up and over, toward the pier. As I did so, I grabbed the air around Khalid and pulled Khalid free before Morgan realized I was back in action. I had intended to set him down gently next to the pier, but he was thrashing so much that instead he fell out of the air, hitting Morgan with considerable force and throwing her off balance. Less frightened than I might have expected, he pulled his dagger, but Morgan, nearly as fast as he was, slapped him out of the way. However, in the seconds that defense took her, the guys thundered down the pier, with Shar in the lead, Zom's emerald flash lighting the way. I landed a little further south on the pier, wedging myself between Morgan and Alcina, drawing White Hilt, and shouting, "Surrender!" as White Hilt's flames lit up the night.

Morgan might have been able to fly away before the guys got to her, she might even have been able to simultaneously dodge my fire, but she couldn't possibly grab Alcina with me standing between them. I also saw in her eyes more than a little fear, despite her attempt to mask it. She wasn't as sure as she had been that I wasn't going to incinerate her on the spot. In fact, much to my amazement, she fell to her knees before me.

"I surrender, Taliesin, but as a member of one of the ruling families of Annwn, I invoke the right to have my fate decided by a ruler of Annwn."

"To what ruling family do you claim kinship?" I asked, already suspecting the answer.

"To the family of Oberon, king of all English faeries." Whether she was truly a reincarnation of Oberon's mother or not, I was not in a position to reject her claim out of hand. The original Taliesin had never been in this exact situation, but he knew enough about faerie law for me to understand the firestorm I would set off if I took her fate in my own hands, and Oberon afterward claimed her as family.

"I accept your surrender but not yet your kinship claim," I said in as authoritative a tone as I could manage. "You will be our prisoner until your right to invoke a relationship with Oberon has been settled."

"As long as you fulfill your obligation to investigate my claim before trying to determine my fate yourself, I accept your terms," replied Morgan, already recovering some of her former haughtiness.

Of course, a long faerie legal wrangle was about the last thing I needed, but at least Morgan would be out of circulation for a while. Well, at least she would be if I could figure out the answers to questions like, "Where can we keep her prisoner?" Even more pressing questions needed to be answered first.

"Shar, check on Al…check on Carla; if she's still bleeding, try to stop it. Everybody else, cover Morgan. I need to check on Nurse Florence." The pier was too narrow for all the guys to actually be within striking distance of Morgan. As Shar moved around her to reach Alcina, however, Dan moved into position and held his blade at Morgan's neck. Just in case Morgan somehow got out of range before he could strike, Khalid stood close at hand, holding his dagger. I would have had him step back, but what would really have been the point? The kid would find a way to do what he wanted, regardless of what I said.

I sprinted back to where Nurse Florence lay, unmoving. Even from a distance, I could sense she was still alive, but just barely. It was at this point I wished I had been more insistent about her teaching me to heal. The original Taliesin had been able to do simple things like stopping bleeding, but he had never faced a situation like this. I couldn't very well call the paramedics. I hated to even think it, but there was only one person I could call. I pulled out my cell and called Carrie Winn's private number.

"Yes?" said Vanora groggily, but as always in Carrie Winn's voice.

"It's Tal." I could almost feel her become wide awake, even over the phone. "I'm sorry to bother you, but we have a situation. We captured Morgan and Alcina, but Nurse Florence is just barely alive, and I don't know how to heal her. We're at Goleta Beach, near the pier."

"I'm on my way!" she said very quickly, then hung up on me. I might not like the woman, but she had proved she would do whatever needed to be done. I glanced over at the guys, who seemed to have their part of the situation in hand, and then I focused on keeping Nurse Florence alive. I hadn't mastered the kind of energy transfer she had used to revive me, but I knew how to sing energy into people, so I started singing my heart out, and though she didn't revive noticeably, at least she did not sink any closer to death.

It suddenly occurred to me as I sang that, though I had not studied healing magic in detail, I had certainly experienced and witnessed a great deal of it. Could I perhaps have learned some of it without realizing that was what I was doing? Before I could explore that possibility, however, a portal snapped open nearby, and a clearly exhausted Vanora, in her usual guise as Carrie Winn, stepped through. She must not have been able to locate a body of fresh water nearby, so the only way to get here fast was the Annwn shortcut, much as the Order cautioned against using that route too much.

"Tal, let me see her," she said, all business. I stepped out of the way, and Vanora quickly knelt at Nurse Florence's side to examine her.

"Thankfully, she will live!" Vanora said after a minute. "It will take time for me to get her ready to travel, though. Some of my security men will be here soon to take Morgan and Alcina into custody." She looked up at me. "I'll want to get the details of what happened here, but I need to take care of Viviane first. Good job, though." Then she was focused on the healing, and I knew enough not to try to talk to her anymore, so I walked toward the pier, just to make sure everything was still all right.

Even at first glance, I could see that everything had gone horribly and completely wrong in the few minutes I had sustained Nurse Florence before Vanora arrived. Stan was convulsing on the pier, and Dan had just swung his sword away from Morgan's throat and straight at a distracted Gordy, whose concern for Stan nearly got him killed. He noticed Dan's attack only barely in time to parry Dan's blow, and because Gordy wasn't really well positioned, he staggered backward, in turn knocking Carlos off-balance. Dan advanced relentlessly, swinging like a crazed killer, wielding his blade with a kind of berserk energy that kept both Gordy and Carlos on the defensive, as well as apparently protecting Dan from being struck with fear by Gordy's sword.

Meanwhile, Morgan had taken advantage of the uproar to drive one of her ever-present daggers into Shar, who had just been getting up from where he knelt by Alcina, Zom raised, presumably about to try to disarm Dan. Shar managed to twist, wrenching the dagger out of Morgan's hand and aiming Zom right at her, but her strike had gone deep, and even through his shirt I could tell blood was oozing down his back.

What could have caused all this mayhem? There could only be one answer.

Alcina!

She must have regained consciousness while Shar was checking her for bleeding. Perhaps feigning continued unconsciousness, she might have tried to control him, but, assuming he was retaining skin contact with Zom, she wouldn't have been able to. Realizing she wasn't getting anywhere, she had reached out for Stan, perhaps seeing him as the most vulnerable, but somehow her attempts to control him had gone awry, perhaps because of David's presence within him. I'd need to be closer to be sure. Then she had managed to get some kind of hold on Dan, how strong I couldn't yet tell, but I feared pretty strong from the way he was acting.

In any case, Vanora could not take her attention away from Nurse Florence right now, and her security men were at least a few minutes out. If the situation could be saved at all, I would have to do the saving.

I let White Hilt blaze and floated up onto the pier, as close to Morgan as I could get without getting between her and Shar's blade.

"You have already surrendered, Morgan. Stand down, or I will give no quarter!" Morgan shot up into the air, and I followed, matching her speed in a way she probably didn't anticipate.

"Last chance!" I yelled.

Again Morgan's first response was derisive laughter. "If you had the guts to kill me, you would have done it already!" she shouted back, mockingly.

Trying hard not to think, I let White Hilt's flames engulf her. No, I didn't want to kill her, even now. I just had no choice.

I had braced myself for her agonized screams as the fire bit into her skin. I'm not sure whether I was more shocked or relieved when I heard none. Probing within the flames, I could tell that she had prepared herself for a fire attack in much the same way I had prepared myself for Alcina's mind control. If I could keep up the fire long enough, though, I would eventually eat through her protection, so our duel became a question of which one of us could last longer, much as my earlier duel with

Alcina might have if Morgan and Khalid had not intervened.

I could still hear the clash of faerie steel below, and though I kept most of my attention on Morgan, I risked a quick scan of the area below. Shar seemed to be trying to force Alcina to remove her spells—not a good tactic, since she knew he couldn't really hurt her. Even from up here, I could feel him weakening. Gordy and Carlos were holding Dan at bay, but only just. Stan was still writhing helplessly behind them.

Where was Khalid? From up in the sky, I couldn't tell. I guessed he was trying to maneuver invisibly. If so, I was too far away to be sure. I could only hope he wouldn't get himself hurt in the battle.

Abruptly my attention was pulled back to Morgan. I knew she would try something, but I wasn't expecting the approach I was feeling. Morgan's signature attack had always been electrical storms, so I figured I would be dodging lightning any second. Instead, I felt intense cold coming from the center of my fire, slashing at it, weakening it. I tried making the fire hotter, but the cold almost immediately became more intense, as if in direct response.

In a moment a sword tore through the outer edge of the fire, its blade gleaming icily in the moonlight. I tried to seal the gap, but the sword sliced through the flame, not with its metal, but with the intense cold it generated.

Perhaps from us Morgan had learned the advantage of keeping a surprise weapon in reserve. Perhaps she had just obtained this sword. Either way, I doubted the fact that its power was the exact opposite of White Hilt's was coincidental. Morgan had prepared very well for a battle she knew would happen sooner or later. That said, I wasn't seeing any sign that she could channel the power of her sword in the way I could channel White Hilt's. Clearly, the sword could radiate cold, but at least she could not throw waves of cold at me. Well, she couldn't unless she was saving that for a later surprise.

Glancing north, I thought I could headlights coming down Sandspit. If so, that probably meant the cavalry, in the form of Vanora's security men, was coming to the rescue. They could resolve the still-raging battle on the pier, but they couldn't help much with Morgan. That part of the battle I would have to win on my own.

In the past I had been good about thinking "outside the box," but right now inspiration seemed to have deserted me. All I could think to do was keep the fire at maximum intensity until one of us tired, and if it happened to be me, I would be in big trouble.

I risked another scan of the pier and cringed inwardly at what I could sense. Shar, realizing that threatening Alcina was not working, charged Dan in an effort to disarm him. Normally he could have, but he was still bleeding, and Dan still had a manic, adrenaline-overdrive kind of strength. To my horror, he managed to knock Zom out of Shar's hand. Shar made a clumsy grab for Zom, missed, and then recoiled as Dan stabbed him in the right arm. Zom tumbled into the ocean, and I knew Shar could never follow it in his current condition. I would have thought Gordy and Carlos could have attacked Dan from the other side, but he had them enough off-balance that in the few seconds it took Gordy to make a decent thrust, Dan twisted to face him and successfully parried. Of course, Shar, Gordy, and Carlos were all handicapped by not wanting to hurt Dan. Dan, in his magic-crazed state, seemed to have no such inhibition.

I glanced north again. No more headlights. Straining a little, I could see that the vehicles were not Vanora's security vehicles after all. Most likely a few guys had decided to take their girls parking for some late-night shenanigans.

Where were Vanora's security people? If they didn't arrive soon, Dan might conceivably win the battle on the pier. Perhaps Alcina would escape with him at that point, and we'd be right back in a hostage situation. Considering the shape Dan was in right now, we'd be lucky if that was all that happened.

Morgan still seemed to be hacking away at my fire without trying a direct attack, so I risked letting my mind wander back toward Santa Brígida to see where they were. It took a couple of minutes, but I found them—trapped way back on 101, on the wrong side of a jackknifed truck that effectively blocked all westbound traffic at that point. Brushing across the driver's mind, I discovered he had swerved in an effort to avoid a deer and lost control.

Deer on the 101? Pretty much impossible—unless of course Morgan had conjured something up, an illusion perhaps. I hadn't felt her sending any power in that direction recently, but I could somehow have missed it, or she could have preset some kind of trap in the time right after she had been forced to leave the "meeting." She certainly knew that Vanora's security force was tied up in Santa Brígida, but perhaps she wanted to ensure that if they were redeployed, they would not get in her way. If so, she had succeeded beyond her wildest dreams. It might take hours to get the westbound 101 open again, and even if the highway patrol managed to extricate the vehicles currently on the interstate, that operation would take longer than we had.

Well, desperate times called for desperate measures. I hated to lose Morgan, but I had to take the chance. The most I could hope for with her in the short term was another stand-off, and the way conditions on the ground were, there would be casualties unless I intervened. Knowing she still needed me for something suggested she might follow me if I descended, so I took the chance. Releasing her from the flame, I dropped with almost sound-barrier-breaking speed. She hadn't expected that move and floated in the air, bits of ice drifting from her blade as she watched me fall, her mouth open in surprise, her eyebrows raised.

I was coming down so fast I barely had time to look around, but I could see that Shar was trying to stop the copious flow of blood from his arm and that Gordy and Carlos couldn't seem to do much more than keep Dan from lopping their heads off. Alcina? She still looked unconscious, but if she had enthralled Dan as completely as it seemed, she wouldn't have to stay conscious for his rampage to continue; the spell had a life of its own, as I well knew.

At least no one was dead yet. Bracing myself, I hit the water with almost stunning force and dove until I grabbed Zom, after which I came gasping to the surface and shot back into the air. As I had hoped, Morgan had descended, but much more cautiously. Seeing the emerald flash of Zom in my hands must have given her pause, because she knew it put me out of reach of her magic. However, there was no way I could cover all my scattered friends on the dock, so she would probably decide to threaten them to get me to back off.

Zom felt...alien in my hand. The hilt was oddly cold, and slippery, as if it would slide out of my hand at the slightest provocation. Clearly, it was not my sword; it was Shar's now, and somehow it knew that.

"Sorry," I whispered to it, "but Shar can't do what we need right now. I'm just borrowing you to save him. I swear I will return you when this is over."

What was I thinking? That my only choice was yet another longshot.

White Hilt originally had been just a flaming sword. In the stress of a battle with a *pwca*, a battle I was losing, I had developed the idea of using my mind to redirect the flame, to use it like a shield or like a laser. There was no reason in theory that Zom's energy might not be likewise directed. The sword did block any hostile magic, but not friendly magic; Shar had been able to pass through portals to Annwn while carrying it, for example. Would it block manipulation by its own wielder? I hoped not, but there was only one way to find out.

At first I got no response—the emerald glow seemed dull and would not shift even an inch in response to my prompting. Then I began to feel just the slightest shift as the sword grudgingly accepted me as its wielder, if only temporarily. The emerald glow flared, and I could see Morgan back herself away a little, uncertain what I planned to do but not liking the possibilities.

Just as I was about to get the result I wanted, my attention was drawn to a sudden movement further down the dock. Stan had jumped up, his sword surrounded in a pure white glow I had seen once before, on Samhain, and charged at Dan. Gordy and Carlos, tired and unnerved by having to fight their good friend, willingly let Stan through, though Gordy, ever protective of the person who helped solve his academic problems, clearly had some mixed feelings.

Dan's feelings, however, were not really his own and clearly weren't mixed. He threw himself at Stan with a battle cry and brought his blade crashing down on Stan's. Since Stan's sword endowed him with extra muscle, that kind of tactic could not disarm him easily, so it was no surprise when Dan's blade clanged off harmlessly. It was a surprise when the clash created a white flash that caused Dan to stagger backward, a sudden look of fear in his eyes.

Stan's sword did not normally have that kind of power—well, except once, when Stan had been David. Clearly, David had taken over again.

It would be nice if once, just once, I could get one problem solved before another one popped up!

At least David had shifted the battle in our favor. Dan, who had been holding off two attackers and briefly managed a third as well, fell back in the face of David's onslaught. I turned in Morgan's direction, and, focusing my whole attention on Zom, willed its protective power to become a weapon, to strike out at her in a magic-shredding emerald blast. For one chilling moment I thought Zom would ignore my will, but then it nearly jerked out of my hand, so violent was the emerald spray that streaked from it, that arced out from it like vibrant green lightning, that struck Morgan full in the chest, engulfing her, stripping away the temporary spells as certainly as actually being struck by the blade itself would have. The original Taliesin had seen Morgan many times, and I had seen her more times than I would have liked, but neither of us had ever seen her as utterly surprised as she was in the split second before she plunged into the cold waters of the Pacific.

She would recover quickly, but before that happened, Dan had to be subdued. I looked over just in time to see David knock Dan's sword from his hand.

"David!" I yelled, "Don't kill him!" I forgot to switch to Hebrew, but evidently David still had enough connection with Stan to understand English and even to respond in it.

"I know who he is!" David yelled back. "I know who he is...from Stan. But something is not right."

Dan lunged at him again, but David had only to wave the sword in his general direction, and something in the white glow frightened him enough to make him back off. Even though Dan seemed immune to the fear radiating from Gordy's sword, he was not immune to something about David's sword.

"A powerful evil force has taken hold of him," I yelled back to David. "We must break its power to free him." I aimed Zom right at Dan and willed it to unleash an even more powerful burst of anti-magic than the one with which I had hit Morgan. For a few seconds Dan was greener than the nearby grass, and his facial expression seemed less deranged, far more like his normal self. That momentary normality lasted a few seconds after Zom's burst ended, but then I could see him slipping back into the grip of Alcina's spell.

I should have known from seeing Zom in action before: it always prevented new spells from hitting its wielder, and it could break a weak or temporary spell on someone else, but the most it could do with a strong or permanent spell was disrupt it momentarily. Once Zom was no longer in contact with that spell, the magic came right back, just as Alcina's spell on Dan was coming back. I wondered whether hitting him over and over again would eventually beat the spell. Well, what did I really have to lose? I aimed Zom at Dan again and hit him with everything I had, at the same time reaching out to touch his mind so I could monitor the state of the spell within him. I did not intend to stop until I felt the spell break.

Again Dan's expression normalized quickly, but I could still feel the spell within him, beaten back for now but still biding its time, waiting for the moment when it could surge back over him. I poured so much anti-magic into him his blood must have started to glow emerald, so much that I could feel Zom throbbing in my hand, clearly near the limit of how much power it could produce in such a short time…but the spell remained intact.

I lowered Zom, feeling defeated. At least I had tried. Now we would have to use the same process on Dan that had been used to break the spell on me. The question was, how to restore Dan to normal, not to mention Stan, without spending so long at it that we blew all of our covers? It must be nearly three o'clock on the morning as it was. How could any of us explain our long absences to our parents? We had just played the Carrie Winn card earlier in the week. Would it be ridiculous to use it again so soon?

While I was brooding over that problem, Morgan, who had presumably been hiding on the other side of the pier, popped out of concealment and swung her icy sword straight at Shar. Unarmed and weakened from blood loss, he fell back away from the blade, but not quite fast enough, and Morgan inflicted another flesh wound on the arm, this one aggravated by the extreme cold her sword radiated. Shar, who probably had the highest tolerance for pain of any of us, actually screamed, and, though the cold prevented immediate bleeding, I could see what looked like a very large gash. Shar crumpled up, possibly on the verge of passing out, and Morgan brushed past him and grabbed Alcina in her arms, with the obvious intention of flying away with her. Dan, fearful as he was of David's sword, was making it impossible for David, or for Gordy or Carlos, for that matter, to get around him without hurting him, which none of them wanted to do.

I raised Zom again and tried to open fire, but all I got at first was a flicker. Horrified, I looked down at it. Its emerald glow was dull; I had pushed it too far trying to break the spell on Dan. I could feel it coming back; I could see its glow brightening by the second, but Morgan could be airborne with Alcina in seconds, and all we had risked tonight would have been for nothing.

I conjured up my own flying spell and shot in Morgan's direction like a bullet. Seeing me coming, she held her blade at Shar's throat.

"Let us go, Taliesin. I would hate to kill your valiant friend, but I will do it if I must."

Near the edge of my awareness, I felt Dan take a wound in the arm, but, energized by a fanatical desire to protect Alcina at all costs, he apparently held on to his sword and kept fighting. It was up to me to save Shar and Carla...but how could I do that?

"Drop that sword!" she commanded as I landed on the dock, nicking Shar's throat to underscore the order.

I knew I couldn't drop Zom at this point. At the best, that would allow Morgan and Alcina to escape. At the worst, I was running a little low on magic and magic resistance, and either or both of them might conceivably recapture me or do harm to someone else—and then escape as well.

What was that old saying? It's always darkest before the dawn...but now we seemed on the verge of an endless night. My best option strategically seemed to be to allow her to do her worst with Shar in the hope of healing him afterward. Nurse Florence had suggested she might be able to heal Gianni under similar circumstances.

I reached out with my mind to see how Vanora was doing with Nurse Florence—and the endless night got darker. Not only was Vanora, already wearied from maintaining the security system I had demanded, now pretty much exhausted, but Nurse Florence was not reviving. Had she drained herself too far to come back? Even if she started to revive now, Vanora and Nurse Florence probably wouldn't have enough energy between them to heal a mortal wound.

Morgan drew a little more blood from Shar to make her point. "Decide, Taliesin! Decide now." My only recourse at this point was to let Morgan and Alcina go.

There was, however, yet another abrupt jolt in this roller-coaster night full of them. I suddenly became aware of Khalid nearby. I glanced over to see him raising his dagger above his head. Morgan noticed this move as well and was momentarily distracted, but she did not realize the significance of what was about to happen: Khalid was about to make his wish!

"Save my friends!" I heard him yell in his high-pitched voice, and I almost screamed in frustration. Wishes were notoriously tricky in the first place. One needed to word them very carefully. Khalid's extremely general wish could be interpreted in many different ways by a wish-granting supernatural being, but this situation was even worse, since he was invoking a preset spell on his faerie dagger. Had Gwynn crafted the spell with such complexity that it could even process such a vague request?

The dagger pulsed with rapidly rotating white, black, and red glows, so at least it was trying to respond to Khalid. Then, just when I thought that was all it was going to do, its power struck like lightning in several different directions at once: one bolt hit Morgan, knocking the sword from her hand and throwing her flat on the pier with stunning force; one bolt hit Shar, giving his wounds a multi-colored glow before they vanished; one bolt hit Dan, disarming him, healing his wounds and then lingering over him, as if trying to break the love spell; one bolt hit David, but his sword flashed white, and the bolt faded, seemingly with no effect; one bolt hit Alcina and lingered over her as Dan's had lingered over him; one bolt hit Nurse Florence, filling her with life-giving energy and pulling her back from the very edge of death itself.

Without hesitating I bounded over to Morgan and Alcina, making sure they were both as unconscious as they seemed. Yeah, they were definitely out. I took Morgan's sword and then took a little longer look at Alcina. Khalid's wish still worked away at her, as if trying to suppress the Alcina personality. Unfortunately, all wishes have their limits, and this one could clearly not reverse the awakening spell, though it seemed determined to keep trying. I trotted over to where Dan lay, still also engulfed in tricolored light, but though the wish could heal his body, it was not making a dent in Alcina's spell.

By that point Nurse Florence and Vanora had rejoined us. "Viviane, do you feel well enough to secure the prisoners?" asked Vanora in her most businesslike tone.

Nurse Florence nodded and gave me a little smile. "Taliesin and I will discuss what else needs to be done."

"She was dying five minutes ago!" I protested. "Shouldn't she at least rest for a little while?"

"I'm fine," said Nurse Florence in one of her reassuring tones, "and it looks as if all I have to do is keep them unconscious until Vanora's men get here."

I would have argued further, but Nurse Florence was already walking up the pier toward where Morgan and Alcina lay.

"Well, this operation could have gone better," observed Vanora dryly, "but no one could argue with the outcome. We could not have hoped for more than the capture of both Morgan and Alcina."

"We could have hoped for no one to fall under Alcina's spell," I replied a little coldly. I just didn't like Vanora's clinical attitude in this kind of situation. Vanora did not immediately reply, which gave me a chance to look over at David.

"David, I told you how dangerous it was for you to take over Stan's body like this. Why did you do it?"

"I had no choice," replied David solemnly. "Stan was under the control of that witch. He still is as far as I can tell. If he had remained in command of his limbs, his body would have been used in the fight against us."

Gently, I reached into Stan's mind, and I could see that David was right: Stan's mind was in a frenzy trying to take back control and rescue Alcina. As I moved back to a broader view, however, I was even more dismayed by the ugly gashes where my painstakingly forged connections between David's consciousness and Stan's had once been. Now, except for one tenuous connection that was giving David access to enough of Stan's memories for David to understand English, they were totally separate beings for all practical purposes, even more so than they had been that night in my garden, probably wrenched apart by the conflict between them over whether or not to side with Alcina in the battle.

"All right, David, you did the only thing you could have done, but don't worry—we can break the spell on Stan. Let me just take a look at Dan and see how he's doing." David nodded, still serious, as he always seemed to be.

The guys were watching Dan uneasily. The tricolored light still swirled around him, but it seemed to be getting fainter, as if the wish was exhausting what energy remained to it and would soon vanish completely, its work only partly done. A quick glance in Dan's mind told me he was still in Alcina's grip and would need to be restrained once he regained consciousness.

Khalid was standing nearby, looking at me with big eyes, lips trembling just a little. Shar joined me at that point, and together we walked over to thank the kid for saving all of us. However, before we quite reached him, he started sobbing.

"Khalid, what's wrong?" asked Shar, putting his arm around Khalid. Khalid hung on to him as if letting go would mean his death, maybe both of their deaths.

"I...I...used...my...wish," he stammered between sobs.

"We know that," I said. "You saved at least some of us, maybe all of us tonight. We're all more proud of you than we can say."

Khalid was still hugging Shar hard enough to crack his ribs, but his tear-filled eyes looked in my direction.

"I...would...do...it again. I *had* to do it...but...now...now I'll never be able to...be with my father again."

Crap! I should have seen that coming.

"Khalid, I don't know what kind of wish you were thinking about making," said Shar in a gentle tone I had never heard him use before. "I do know one thing, though: if you want to be with your father, we will find a way to make it happen some day."

I almost tried to cut Shar off, knowing that Khalid's father would probably never accept him and, in any case, was no fit parent for him as far as I was concerned. I just couldn't bring myself to say that in front of a nearly shattered Khalid.

Khalid was looking at Shar with something akin to wonder. "Promise?" he asked incredulously.

"Yes, Khalid, I promise!" replied Shar without hesitation. I cringed inwardly, but there was nothing I could do. Then I cringed again when I felt something very like a *tynged* snap into place around Shar. Neither Shar nor Khalid had the power to create a binding spell, yet somehow one had popped into being as a result of Shar's promise.

I jumped a little when someone tapped me on the shoulder. Turning around, I found myself once again face-to-face with Vanora.

"Taliesin, we need to tie up loose ends here as soon as possible. Maintaining the pretense of normality is quite difficult enough as it is." Vanora was clearly barely standing by this point, but it was still hard for me to deal with her officious tone in a situation like this.

"What exactly are the loose ends in this situation?" I asked irritably.

Vanora sighed. "I should think putting right Stan and Dan needs to be taken care of before we head home. We can't very well just let them go about their normal routines when they are still controlled by Alcina, but we can't exactly explain their sudden disappearances either."

As much as it irked me to admit it, she was right.

"I can take care of Stan," said David.

"David, you could take care of Stan in combat, but you aren't very good at pretending to be him, especially as...separated from him as you are now," I pointed out. "I know this is hard for you to understand, but what we are, what you and Stan are, is not something we can reveal to everyone."

He looked at me, puzzled once again.

"Do you remember what it was like after you had been anointed king, but Saul was still in possession of the office?"

David nodded.

"You had to keep who you were to yourself for years, right?"

David nodded again.

"Well, that's what Stan has to do, for different reasons. That's what we all have to do."

"I have learned some of that from Stan," David conceded, "though I still don't really understand it. I have learned to trust you, though. I will do whatever you ask of me."

"Your help is invaluable to Stan and me," I said respectfully.

"So what is our plan?" prompted Vanora.

"As I recall, we need to remind the victims of this spell of their own true loves in order to break Alcina's hold on them. For Dan that's Eva O'Reilly. For Stan it's..."

Much to my surprise, I suddenly realized that I didn't know who my best friend was in love with, or even if he was in love at all. Since becoming more popular, Stan had dated a few girls, cheerleaders mostly, but I didn't think he loved any of them—he just liked actually being able to ask a pretty girl out and have her say yes. We weren't going to break any spells with feelings like that.

"If he isn't in love right now, that could be a big problem," said Nurse Florence, who had just walked over, presumably after making sure that Morgan and Alcina were not going to regain consciousness until we wanted them to.

"I know. I could try to probe Stan's mind, but it's such a mess right now that I'm not sure I could tell if he actually loves someone or not."

"He loves Natalie Kim," said David and Gordy, almost in unison. Well, David would know from the times his mind and Stan's were linked, but it stung a little that Stan had shared that kind of information with Gordy but not with me—a clear sign I had been too preoccupied lately. I had once suspected he had feelings for her, but I'd never actually asked, I guess thinking he would tell me when he felt ready. Apparently Gordy had asked and found out.

"All right, here is what we need to do," I said, pushing my personal hurt aside for the moment. "Dan's situation is easy. I'm not limited by the Annwn ban anymore."

I didn't really want to take the time to explain, but Vanora and Nurse Florence both looked sufficiently surprised that I knew they were bound to question me. "Alcina kidnapped me to her island, which apparently is in a different otherworld than Annwn, so I can use Alcina's world to travel to Eva's house and back without ever having to pass through Annwn. I've been to Eva's, so that's not a problem. Like Eva, Natalie has been with us in Annwn and during the battle on Samhain, so she knows our secret. That part won't be a problem. What will be a problem is that I doubt she knows Stan loves her. He hasn't ever even asked her out as far as I know."

"I was working on that," said Gordy.

"Tal," said Nurse Florence gently, "that's going to be very awkward, but perhaps we can give her a different reason for her presence being essential to break the spell on Stan."

"Yes, and that's exactly what I would do, but there's another problem. I've never been to Natalie Kim's, so I can't open a portal that gets me there."

"That is a problem," said Vanora. "Anyone here ever been to Natalie's?"

Judging by the head shakes, that was a unanimous no.

"David, do you think you can act sick for a day or two?" I asked. "If Stan's parents think he is sick, and you make a point of acting as if you are asleep or groggy most of the time, you won't have to do anywhere near as much acting to pretend to be Stan, particularly at school, because Stan's mom is bound to keep him home if he is sick."

"Yes, I'm sure I can behave like a sick person."

"We can induce a slight fever," added Vanora. "Not enough to do any damage, obviously, but enough to make the idea of illness more credible."

"Good!" I said. "I'm sure we can get Natalie over to Stan's house tomorrow afternoon after school, distract Stan's mom somehow, and get the spell broken."

Shar cleared his throat awkwardly at that point, reminding me that I was still holding Zom.

"I suppose you will be keeping that, now that you have discovered how much you can do with it," he said. I could hear the reluctance in his voice when he continued. "I would understand if that was what happened."

"Shar, this is your sword," I said with a smile, handing it back, "and it knows it. I would not think of taking it away, though I might occasionally want to borrow it. Just in emergencies, of course!" Shar took Zom back, visibly relieved, and it seemed to glow more brightly now that it was back in the hands of its true wielder.

Since I wasn't sure of the geography of Alcina's world, I flew a little way into the air before opening the portal. I didn't want to end up in the ocean, potential prey to Alcina's aquatic army, and the only land I had seen, her island, I had never actually been on, and so I might not be able to hit it precisely.

While I was getting positioned and building power to open the portal, I couldn't help feeling almost overcome by the night's events. I had finally decided to kill another human being. Not having succeeded didn't make me feel any better about it, even though I could still argue that it might have been necessary. The very fact that we had ultimately captured Morgan without having to kill her made that argument seem hollow.

Then there was the terrible price my friends were paying because Morgan wanted something from me. Nurse Florence had nearly died tonight. My efforts to get Stan and David integrated back into one personality had suffered a major, perhaps irreversible, setback. Dan was a mess, Shar had nearly died from his wounds, and Khalid had given up the thing he wanted most in the whole world. The fact that what he wanted was never really going to happen didn't matter. I didn't even want to think about my increasingly psychic mother and what she might have gone through tonight.

For the first time since I had managed to get my own past selves reintegrated into my personality four years ago, I realized what I really needed to do.

I needed to find a way to forget my past lives, to lose the magic, to lose the combat skill, the musical abilities, everything.

If I were no longer the reincarnated Taliesin, but just plain old

Tal Weaver, the person I was meant to be, then my friends could go back to the lives they were meant to have. Maybe those lives would not always be what they wanted, maybe some of them would not be exceptional…but even ordinary had to be better than what they were going through now.

CHAPTER 13: THE FUTURE CAN DIE, BUT NOT THE PAST

Given how early in the morning it was, it was lucky I could be very precise with my portal. I had been in Eva's bedroom before. (Get your mind out of the gutter—we were twelve, and we were just kissing!)

I stepped through the portal very carefully so I wouldn't make any noise. I couldn't afford to have her parents wake up and find me lurking around.

Judging by Eva's slow and deep breathing, she was still sound asleep. Before I even looked at her, the situation hit me. Aside from a few short conversations and my effort to get Eva to reconcile with Dan a couple of months ago, this was the first time I had been alone with Eva since...oh my God, since we were twelve!

She had come to visit me in the hospital a few times when everybody thought I was insane. Yeah, before I had gotten control of the past-life memories. I was always asleep or drugged into unconsciousness, though, and we never actually had a conversation. After I got out, I had expected Eva and me to get back together, but I had felt awkward about making the first move. She had seen me at my worst, and as much as I tried to play Mr. Self-Confident, I was embarrassed by the way she had seen me at my lowest point.

I had wanted, desperately wanted, for her to approach me, for her to tell me everything was all right, that she loved me, that she would always love me. She never did any of those things. I finally got up my courage to go over to her house, but her parents had the unwelcome mat out for me, and I never even saw her. For all I knew, she wasn't even home.

After that I did about as well as a twelve-year-old could to move on, especially since Eva ended up with Dan pretty quickly. Dan became hostile around that time, for reasons I didn't figure out until much later, and Eva continued to stay away from me at first, though eventually we became friends again. I fantasized about winning her back from Dan some day, but once Dan became first my ally and then my friend again, even that pale hope faded to black.

No wonder I had been such easy prey for Carla's unconscious love spell; no wonder my defenses had been so compromised when Alcina trapped me. After four years of unrequited love like a twisting knife in my guts, I wanted to love someone, wanted it badly. After I was freed from Alcina's spell and discovered that my love for Carla was also nothing more than a spell, I did my best to stay away from Eva…until now.

Well, I would have had to face her some time. I brushed the past away as if I were brushing cobwebs off my face and focused on recruiting Eva to save Dan. I reached gently into her mind without reading anything and prompted her to awaken quietly. I brought her out so smoothly that she half knew what I wanted before she was even fully conscious.

"Tal, should we go right away?" she whispered.

Damn! As usual, I could smell her jasmine perfume. Her strawberry-blond hair almost glowed in the moonlight, and her skin had the look of alabaster.

No, let's make love first.

"Yeah, we'd better. The longer Dan is enchanted, the harder this is going to be."

Crazily, though, my thoughts about making love were not sarcastic. If she weren't in love with Dan, and he with her, I would have rolled into bed with her without thinking twice about it, and Dan could bloody well wait for another hour…or two. How was I going to get through the rest of high school having to face Eva every day? In one respect Morgan was right after all—it would have been easier to just let Alcina take me.

Given the fact that Samhain had made Eva and me comrades in arms, she got out of bed, quite unselfconscious about being in her satiny-looking nightgown that some guys at school would have given their left arm to see her in. Her reaction would have been quite different if she had been able to read my mind. I guess it was fortunate so few people really possessed that ability.

She quickly threw on a fairly heavy looking green robe, I reopened the portal, took her in my arms, and guided her through it. Contrary to what you might think, putting my arms around her was necessary, since we would probably be over water in Alcina's realm, and I would need to fly straight up as soon as we reached that side of the portal.

Just as I thought, I did have to fly up to avoid sinking into the ocean. I felt Eva's soft warmth against me and longed to make that flight last forever—but the others were waiting, and we might have hard work ahead of us. I linked my mind to Goleta Beach again, opened up another portal, and sailed through it.

I set Eva gently down on the grass near the pier and led her over to where Dan was still being held unconscious. By now the shimmering light of Khalid's wish had faded completely.

"Good! You're here," said Vanora. "We had more power at our command when we broke the same spell on Taliesin, but I think Alcina was not able to establish as effective a hold on Dan...because of the distance, and the fact that she wasn't making eye contact." The last part gave me the odd feeling that she was actually sparing me embarrassment for having been so completely and quickly controlled. She was being...almost human.

Since I wasn't really aware of the preparations they had done last time, Vanora and Nurse Florence organized everyone. Basically, Eva would kiss Dan to remind him of his true love. We three casters would blend her love with the friendship of everyone else, amplify it as much as possible, and hit Dan with it. An ordinary love spell wouldn't require that much magic to beat, but Alcina's specially crafted version was about the most powerful one around.

We moved Dan from the dock to the grass so that we could form a ring around him, with Dan and Eva in the center. Vanora and Nurse Florence established the connections among all of our minds, we let our emotions flow, I sang to make our magic more potent, and then we channeled all that raw power into Eva. Without being told, she knew the moment had come for her kiss. She bent over, kissed Dan tenderly on the lips, and her love swept through him like a flash flood, washing away the stagnant muck of Alcina's evil and restoring Dan's mind to normal.

Dan sat up, looking totally embarrassed and stuttering apologies for what he had done under Alcina's influence.

"I've been there, Dan," I said quickly, helping him to his feet. "You couldn't have stopped what you were doing."

"I could have hurt someone, even killed someone," Dan protested.

"But you didn't," replied Carlos. "We're all OK, and now you're OK. Life is too short for guilt trips."

"That sounds like excellent advice," said Nurse Florence.

We heard rumbling, and, looking across the parking lot, we could see Vanora's security force arriving on the scene. Well, better late than never.

"Hey, it's like four-thirty in the morning," said Carlos. "Where are we going to say we were this time? A pajama party at Carrie Winn's place?"

"After Stan called me, I made sure your parents would sleep until morning," replied Nurse Florence. "With any luck, they won't even know you were gone."

"Good job!" I said. "Let me just make sure Dan is all right, and we can be on our way." To my surprise, Dan stiffened, as if in fear of my getting into his mind.

"Dan, you know I'm not going to go poking around unnecessarily. I just want to make sure there are no lingering traces of Alcina's control."

"Wise precaution under the circumstances," agreed Vanora.

Dan seemed to relax a bit. "Of course, Tal, I guess you have to. Let's make it quick, though."

I put my hand on his arm and let myself gently enter his mind. It took me a few minutes to be sure; this was not a job I could afford to rush. Finally, though, I convinced myself that there was no alien force left in his mind. Well, except…

Except there was some kind of darkness, nowhere near the surface, and seemingly unconnected to Alcina's magic. Nurse Florence had mentioned something similar before around the time of the boxing match. Dan had seemed unreasonable then, vengeful against Stan as a result of a little fling Eva had faked when she was angry with Dan. A stressful time, to be sure, but Dan hadn't acted like himself at all. What was it Nurse Florence had said? Something simple, like "There is a darkness in him." At the time she wasn't sure if the darkness was a product of hostile magic or not, but she figured that at the very least an enemy could exploit it.

Once I had gotten Dan, Stan and I all back together as friends, Dan had started acting like his old self, and I had forgotten the whole thing. But tonight he had been fighting to kill, his violent response to Alcina's commands much different from what mine had been. Somehow that darkness within had played a role in making him the berserker who nearly made Gordy and Carlos into hamburger—would have, in fact, but for David's intervention.

When Alcina controlled me, I hadn't known who my friends were and certainly fought some of them, but I never entertained the idea of using deadly force. Hell, I would have if Alcina had directly ordered it, probably, but I was pretty sure Dan was acting without any direct kill orders.

Talk to Nurse Florence about it! Don't try to fix it yourself on impulse.

I knew I should do exactly what part of me was thinking. Besides, I wasn't in the habit of probing around more than necessary in my friends' minds.

Still, if that darkness was the product of some external force operating on Dan, it wouldn't hurt to figure out what it was. The presence of an alien force all that time suggested a currently unknown enemy, someone who had been around as long as Ceridwen had been getting ready to kill me, maybe even before. Didn't that possibility demand some quick investigating? On the other hand, if the darkness was somehow an inherent part of his mind, I could easily withdraw and discuss the problem with him later.

My mind slid toward the darkness, but the thing had a thick skin, and my gentle probe bounced off of it. I couldn't remember seeing anything quite like this in anyone else's mind, but that didn't prove it wasn't natural in Dan's. Again I probed, this time somewhat more forcefully, and again I was repulsed. Either magic was involved, or this part of his mind was something that Dan himself wanted desperately to hide.

Yeah, I know—I should have backed off, but I had the idea that I was probably dealing with hostile magic, and I just couldn't shake the feeling that it would work toward some evil purpose. Perhaps it would even kill Dan. How could I risk my friend's life over squeamishness about probing too deeply? Surely he would understand.

Gently but firmly, I turned all my strength toward piercing the darkness's defenses, and this time they cracked before me.

God! If I had one do-over for my life up to that moment, I would use it to make myself back off before it was too late.

Within the darkness, I saw in searing clarity the memories that Dan was trying to keep under lock and key, memories of four years ago. I saw him convincing Eva to stop visiting me. Yeah, my condition had been bad enough in real life, but here was Dan, luridly exaggerating it, making me seem hopeless, making me seem like someone who would just drag Eva down with me. The memory was so hauntingly real I could even look into Eva's eyes and see her heart breaking as he went on with his malicious fictions.

I also saw scenes of Dan poisoning her parents against me. When I got out much faster than his stories had suggested was possible, he worked on Eva again, convincing her that I was not as well as I seemed, that I was on a pharmacy full of meds just to seem vaguely normal, that I could go over the edge at any time. My changes in interests probably lent just enough color to what Dan was saying to make his stories seem more plausible. Then he added the finishing touch, just for good measure: he said I no longer loved Eva, didn't really remember our relationship in fact, and when Dan had tried to remind me, I had become very upset and had another relapse. "If you really care about him, Eva," I could hear him saying, "you will leave him alone. If he has any hope of becoming more stable, we can't afford to upset him again."

How could Eva have believed all that trash? I had to remind myself that she was twelve at that point, just as I was, and Dan was the sagacious thirteen-year-old—and, next to Stan, my best friend. Yeah, she believed him because of how close to me he was! And all the time he was stabbing me in the back; he was twisting the knife deeper and deeper. Stan was staying in the hospital until someone physically removed him, and Dan, my other best friend, where was he? Stealing my girlfriend, that's where! Using her love for me to make sure she stayed away from me! You would think she would have realized he was lying when she found out the truth about my situation, but that happened four years later, and somehow she didn't make the connection.

Now so many things made sense. When Nurse Florence had dream-walked him while vetting him as a possible ally for me, what she had seen had convinced her that he felt betrayed by me, that when I abandoned common activities like soccer that we used to do together, I was abandoning him. I had no doubt that was what he told himself on days when he couldn't look himself in the mirror. He was somehow twisting the whole thing around in his head, making it my fault, disliking me as a pathetic attempt to cover the cesspool of guilt at the core of his soul. That also explained his outbursts when he thought Stan was stealing Eva. Yeah, everything was as clear as a bloody, bloody auto accident, but not one I was watching. No, it was my guts strewn all over the freeway.

Dan saw the change in my eyes, in my face, even before I said anything. I wasn't looking in a mirror at that moment, so I don't exactly know what friendship dying looks like, but I bet Dan could tell me—if I didn't rip out his tongue first!

"Tal," he said shakily.

"You bastard!" I shouted. "All these years I thought…I didn't understand what had happened. I thought it was about me. And all this time it was you!"

"Tal, what's wrong?" asked Nurse Florence.

My response was to punch Dan as hard as I could in his handsome, all-American-boy face. He reeled backward, and everyone was in motion, either to support him or to grab me.

"What are you doing, man?" asked Gordy. By now he and Shar had my arms, though I was struggling mightily against them.

"What am I doing? You really want to know what's going on? Here, let me show you!"

"Tal, no!" shouted Dan. Despite the volume, there was a note of begging in his voice. I ignored it. I still had the images of Dan's betrayal in my head. It was child's play to blast them into everyone else's minds, together with enough of my hospital experience to reveal how much he had lied and to show that, far from having any insight into my condition or even any excuse for misunderstanding it, he had never set foot in the hospital at all.

The restraining hands dropped away from me. Everyone looked stunned, some even as blank as zombies, but once what I had showed them soaked in, surely they would all turn on Dan. He had tried to isolate me, and now he would be the one who would be isolated. But I wasn't through yet. Oh no, not by a long shot!

"You used the worst thing that ever happened to me, Dan! You exploited it. You profited from it. I want you to know how I was feeling then. Crazy, huh? Full of meds, huh? You have no idea. But you will, my friend, you will!" I raised my left hand, now cloaked in bloody red light. "You will know it exactly."

I could see Dan cringing away, but he could never run fast enough to outrun the awakening spell.

"Tal, you mustn't!" exclaimed Nurse Florence. I could feel Shar a half a second from knocking me down when I dropped my hand.

"No, Dan, I'm not really going to do that to you. Destroying lives is your specialty, not mine."

I could tell Dan wanted to say something, but the human brain can only process so much so fast, and his was clearly overloaded. Well, I couldn't imagine anything he could say that would be worth hearing ever again. However, nobody else jumped in either, leading to an awkward silence of epic proportions.

Vanora recovered first and started barking orders at the security men, who had frozen in the middle of moving Morgan and Alcina into two of the nearby vans. Nurse Florence pulled herself together then, gave me a quick shot of healing, and then went to heal Dan's more extensively damaged face. I could hardly believe that, but I had to remind myself she was a healer and would probably have done the same for Morgan if necessary.

By that point I was beginning to focus on Eva, whose expression was such a mix of guilt, revulsion and longing that it was effectively unreadable. Angry as I was with Dan, I was not so out of control that I would invade her mind. She looked at Dan then, and I could read the condemnation in her eyes, and so could he. He did not even attempt to explain himself, perhaps still tongue-tied. But what could he have said, really?

Then she looked at me. I don't really know what I was expecting, maybe a lingering embrace and roll credits, standard movie happy ending. That was not what I got. I could tell she was feeling guilt for having fallen for Dan's stories and for not realizing, even when she learned more of the truth, that Dan had lied to her. That was all I could tell with certainty. I did not see old love rekindled. I did see a tear slide down her cheek, then another, then another. I think she whispered, "Sorry!" to me, and then she turned away, moving toward the parking lot. I wanted to follow her, but David unexpectedly blocked my path when I tried to move in that direction.

"Taliesin, have you not more than once tried to convince me that I needed to let go of the past and that I needed to forgive myself for what I have done."

"What you did was about three thousand years ago," I muttered.

"To me, it was like yesterday," he said quietly. "And my sin is far, far worse than his. I stole a man's wife. He stole your childhood girlfriend. Then I killed the man. He did not kill you. If God has forgiven me, then surely you can forgive him."

"God can forgive Dan if He will...but I never will!"

David wanted to say something about the importance of following God's example—I bet he was aching to. Yet he did not, probably realizing that his words would be wasted at that point.

Khalid was crying somewhere nearby. Yes, crying and wrapping his arms around Shar's neck.

"What's wrong?" I asked, feeling a hint of my protective emotions toward him reviving.

"I want…I want things to be like they were before, like they were yesterday."

Yeah, kid, you and me both!

I should have said something comforting. He was just a kid, one who had a really rough life, one who deserved better than to get sucked into my drama.

Yeah, I should have, but I didn't. Instead, I said something like, "Yesterday was just a lie. Today is the truth." Khalid wept even more bitterly, and Shar gave me an intensely angry look.

In a short time, the security detail had Morgan and Alcina tucked away somewhere, the mess cleaned up, and space found for anyone who was without wheels, Eva in particular. Our raw emotions, however, could not be so easily swept away.

I became aware that Dan was getting up and moving in my general direction. Would he have the nerve to try to apologize? I looked into his unreadable eyes and could not tell—and I had no intention of plunging into that garbage heap of a mind.

Dan said nothing. Instead he unsheathed his faerie-forged sword, laid it quietly on the grass in front of me, turned quietly and walked away. I guess that was his lame attempt at resigning as one of my warriors…or, more likely, a way to avoid the embarrassment of being thrown out.

Nurse Florence appeared at my side, her professional detachment feeling pretty frayed. "Tal, we have to talk. Guys, I'd say you're all too tired to drive. We can find space for you in one of the vans, and some of the security men will drive your cars home. Let's do that now. We are getting dangerously close to sunrise, and your parents won't stay asleep too long after that."

The guys, except for Shar, who was clearly angry with the way I had handled Khalid, mumbled a good-bye and disappeared so fast I would have thought they had all suddenly acquired magic. The way my view of reality was changing, that scenario almost seemed plausible.

"You should be ashamed of yourself!" snapped Nurse Florence as soon as everyone else was out of earshot.

"What? I should be ashamed? I think you have me confused with Dan," I replied, my voice dripping with sarcasm.

"Shut up, and listen!" Nurse Florence was practically spitting the words at me. I had never seen her quite like this. The surprise was enough to get me to stop talking, at least for a few seconds, and she took immediate advantage of the opportunity.

"Tal, you threatened to use dark magic on someone tonight! Do you know what that means? It means you are half a step from becoming just like Morgan or Ceridwen!"

"I would never really have done that!" I protested.

"You didn't really intend to carry out the threat, but on some level, you wanted to. I could feel the emotions radiating from you."

"You can't read minds as I can, and we both know it, so don't pretend you can for the purposes of lecturing me."

"I don't have to be able to read minds as you do to pick up that intense a burst of raw feeling. But let's pretend you really didn't want to do it. Calling up that kind of power is dangerous: dangerous to the people around you, and dangerous to your very soul."

I knew I shouldn't be angry with someone who had practically died helping me tonight, but I had been through too much in too short a period of time to have patience for this kind of criticism when I knew I was right. "I know what I'm doing, and I have no intention of walking the left-hand path, now or ever."

"Have you ever stopped to consider that Morgan may have thought the same thing in the beginning? You love Eva, and you feel justifiably outraged that Dan kept you from her. Morgan loved Lancelot, but he had an unlawful passion for Guinevere, over which Morgan felt justifiable, if somewhat self-serving, outrage. But Morgan did not consider the consequences for everyone else of trying to bring their illicit passion to light. Nor did she stop at that. Instead, she ended up trying to destroy everyone connected with them, including her own half-brother Arthur, including all of Camelot.

"Lancelot and Guinevere had done wrong, to be sure. So has Dan. Do you see where I am going with this? You can be Morgan and make a justifiable grievance into the first step toward the apocalypse, or you can follow David's suggestion and find a way to forgive Dan or, if not that, at least find a way to move on yourself."

"If you ask me," said Vanora, who had just walked up behind Nurse Florence, "forgiveness is not the issue. Whatever Taliesin and Dan do personally is up to them, but Dan is now a liability as a warrior. He cannot remain part of Taliesin's force any longer."

Without waiting for a response from Nurse Florence, who seemed surprised by her unexpected interference, Vanora turned to me and said, "Taliesin, you, just like your warriors, are too tired to drive home. Ride with me, and I'll have one of my men get your Prius home. Viviane, you do the same. There's room in van two. Let's not have any more disasters tonight."

With manipulative skill worthy of the real Carrie Winn, Vanora deftly separated me from Nurse Florence, who I could tell was not at all happy about that, and I ended up effectively alone with her, at least in the sense that I suspected she would erase the memory of our conversation from any security man within earshot.

"Taliesin, I must say you are surprising me," Vanora said as the van pulled out. I braced myself for another lecture, though her tone actually sounded positive. "You are becoming a real leader." That could have been the first direct compliment that Vanora had ever given me.

"What do you mean?" I asked, half-suspiciously.

"It takes a real leader to do what needs to be done. Dan needed to be gotten rid of, and you did it, quickly and effectively."

"I'd rather not talk about that situation."

"OK, we won't. Let me just say, though, that I think I have been too hard on you in the past. You may sometimes act in ways I wouldn't advise, but you always seem to end up being successful."

Right at that moment I didn't feel successful, but I didn't feel like opening up to Vanora either, so I just nodded in acknowledgment.

"It gives me renewed faith in the prophecy," she continued.

Little as I wanted to talk, I had to ask. "What prophecy?"

Vanora looked puzzled. "Surely you know. You wrote it down yourself...or rather, the original Taliesin did. The poem in *The Tale of Taliesin* when Maelgwn is questioning him."

I almost snorted in disbelief. "That old thing. It isn't any part of Taliesin 1's memories, so he probably didn't write it. A lot of scribes reworked those stories over the years. Anyway, it's silly."

"Never doubt yourself!" said Vanora with sudden intensity. "That poem, whoever wrote it, I believe to be a genuine reflection of your history...and your future. Think, Taliesin, think! Think what it would mean for a being to have been with God at the beginning of the world, to have been the instructor of the universe in some way, and to be with God again at the end. What would that make you?"

It would make me someone sitting next to a crazy person!

"Vanora, there is no evidence any of that is true."

"The poem makes it clear that you were with King David of Israel, and as it turns out, now that Stan's earlier life as David has been revealed, that statement is true."

"Yeah, I couldn't remember the lives before the original Taliesin in very great detail, but I had actually remembered that much before Stan got awakened."

"If that detail is true, why could they not all be true? And don't you think it is a pretty unbelievable coincidence that among all the billions of people Stan could have been in an earlier life, he just happened to be King David? For that matter, what are the odds of Carla being Alcina? And you knew both of them in earlier lives!"

I didn't like Vanora's tone of voice. It was too intense, too fanatical. I didn't much care for the gleam in her eyes either.

"I have wondered about that myself," I admitted, "and Gwynn and Nurse Florence alluded to it while we are in Annwn. But supposing it is not a coincidence, what does it mean?"

"It can only mean one thing," said Vanora, conviction like iron coming through in her voice. "Your mission on Earth is coming to an important point. Maybe not its conclusion, which would imply the end of the world, but at least something pivotal. Old allies are emerging to help you, and old enemies to oppose you. Ceridwen, Morgan, Alcina, King David, even the half djinn child, Khalid, perhaps...in Santa Brígida. Hardly a place one would expect to find any of them, let alone all of them."

"Ceridwen built Santa Brígida to lure my parents here, so she could try to take back the wisdom I accidentally took so long ago as Gwion Bach. You know that as well as I do. She pulled in Morgan as an ally. David and Alcina were awakened—"

"You were about to say by coincidence, weren't you?" asked Vanora triumphantly. "Only you couldn't say it, because you know how ridiculous it is."

I had a hard time believing that God had somehow arranged my life in a different way than He presumably arranged everyone's life, but I did thank Him nonetheless that the van was pulling up in front of my house, giving me the opportunity to escape from Vanora. I thanked her as fast as I could, and luckily the security man driving the Prius pulled in at just that moment, so I grabbed the remote from him, thanked him also, and hurried inside as fast as I could, consistent with being quiet.

I half expected to find my newly psychic mother sitting in the living room, waiting to confront me, but fortunately Nurse Florence's spell had apparently held. By now it was nearly five o'clock in the morning, and I doubted I would get any sleep, but I slipped out of my clothes and into pajamas so Mom wouldn't wonder why I had slept in my clothes. In the few minutes before my alarm went off, though, I lay down and actually did fall asleep, though it was no restful sleep.

I might have expected my exhaustion would plunge me into dreamless sleep, but instead I started having a very vivid dream. I was surrounded by mist thicker than Annwn's, a mist that obscured almost everything. Out of that mist came a figure. I recognized him as Jimmie, Dan's dead brother, but Jimmie had died at age nine, and the figure before me looked as Jimmie would have looked at age sixteen, like Dan, but certainly not identical to him, a little thinner and a little taller—more of a basketball build than a football one. Yet he also sometimes looked oddly like me, as if he were my brother, too. Well, we had been like brothers when he was alive, so my subconscious mind must have been working overtime to make that visual connection. However, that couldn't explain why he sometimes looked like other brother figures: Stan, Gianni, even Khalid. For being an only child, I certainly had enough people who were like brothers to me. Only twenty-four hours ago, Dan would have been on that list too.

"Jimmie!" I shouted, running toward him. He hugged me warmly, but then he pulled back. I could tell he was upset, actually on the verge of tears. "Jimmie, what's wrong?"

"Tal," he said, his faltering voice sounding almost like Khalid's. "I need to ask you to do something for me."

"Anything, Jimmie, just name it." Aside from Jimmie's morphing physical appearance, this could have been a real conversation from when he was alive. I really would have done anything for him in those days or for Stan...or for Dan. Even in the dream, the thought of Dan cut through my heart like a chain saw.

"Tal, you have to forgive Dan."

I took a step back from him, just as shocked as if he had slapped me across the face. "Jimmie, if you are asking me to forgive him, you know what he did."

Jimmie nodded.

"How can I forgive that?"

"It was bad," Jimmie agreed, "very bad. I know it was. But Tal, I need you to be there for him. I need it...because I can't be." His flesh suddenly lost all color, and in the dream, I remembered that he was dead. For a split second I actually wanted to be whatever kind of weird Celtic messiah Vanora thought I was so that I could sing life back into Jimmie, perhaps even erase the years since he had died, make everything different, everything better. Then I sat up in bed, the dream shattered by the alarm ringing in my ears, my whole body shaking.

Yeah, no doubt about it—today was going to be wonderful!

CHAPTER 14: YOU CAN'T TELL THE PLAYERS
WITHOUT A SCORECARD

As had happened so many other times recently, I showered and got dressed mechanically, not really caring much what I put on, just wanting to get through the daily ritual without falling apart. I did glance in the mirror and made some effort to comb my hair, but I couldn't do much about my red eyes and weary-looking face. Well, actually I suppose I could have done something, but who the hell cared what I looked like at this point?

The short answer to that question was my parents, as I should have predicted. Although somewhat distracted by an early morning news report about a UFO sighting late last night on Goleta Beach—oops, I guess the guys who had gone parking had noticed all the flashing lights from our swords and spells—their focus immediately shifted to me as soon as I came into the room.

"Tal, you look as if you haven't slept. Anything wrong?" asked Dad. I could see memories of my near disintegration four years ago hovering right behind his eyes, shadowy now but ready to gain substance at the slightest hint of trouble. I hadn't realized he was still that tense. Well, come to think of it, he hadn't been. I guess I really looked that bad this morning.

"I had a lot of work last night, and after I finally did finish, I guess I was too wound up to sleep much. I'll try to turn in much earlier tonight."

I could see him relax a little, but Mom just looked more worried. I waited for her to start asking if I knew anyone named Vanora, or to tell me about a dream she had about a battle on Goleta Beach, but instead she said nothing—which actually ended up being worse. Even without reading her mind, I could tell she was afraid to say anything, probably because she knew it would sound crazy, and it was then that I realized one undeniable fact: I would have to tell her the truth, certainly not right now, with Dad listening, but some time soon. I could not let her continue to think she was losing her mind, and if the powers that be in Annwn didn't like it, well, tough!

As soon as I thought that, though, I realized I did actually care about what Gwynn thought, not enough to let my mom go insane, but enough to at least give him a heads-up before I told her. I would see Nurse Florence today and ask her to get in touch with Gwynn for me, since the

Order had the convenient privilege of being able to open a portal directly to wherever he was in Annwn.

Once breakfast was over, I said my good-byes quickly, being sure to give Mom the biggest hug I could. Then I was out the door. I didn't have to wait for Stan this morning, since he was currently David and feigning illness at home, so I got to school a little earlier than normal. That didn't really do me much good, since without Stan I didn't really have anyone to talk to.

Let me rephrase: I didn't have anyone to talk to that I actually wanted to talk to at this point. I really wanted to be alone with my thoughts, and there were a lot of people I didn't want to interact with at all. I didn't think Dan would try, but I didn't really know what to say to Gordy or Carlos either. Shar I would have to apologize to over the way I had handled Khalid, so I added that to my to-do list. Eva? Well, I actually did want to talk to her, but I had no idea what to say. If only she had given me a little more of a clue about how she felt last night! Then again, I could hardly expect her to react that quickly to such an epic change in her life. Today? Well, today might be quite different. Did I dare to hope for more? Why not? She had loved me before. Now that she knew the truth, surely…surely she would love me again.

I suppose I was hanging around in the glassed-in foyer near the front entrance of the school hoping that Eva would show up. Given my luck, though, it was only natural that it was Dan who showed up. I didn't usually hang around up front, so he probably didn't expect to see me— and he certainly didn't want to. He looked very much as if he wanted Khalid's ability to become invisible. Lacking that, he did the best he could to pass by as far on the other side of the foyer as he could without actually merging his body with the window glass on the other side. I wanted to shout at him, I wanted to punch him again, but life was complicated enough as it was, and Principal Simmons was standing nearby, so I settled for staring at him with utter contempt.

I should have remembered how delicate the social ecosystem of a high school is. A fairly large number of students had been milling around during our little drama. Little? Who am I kidding? In high school social terms, it rated somewhere in the same range as the sinking of the *Titanic*. I realized that the news would be all over the campus by third period. If that made life more difficult for Dan, good! Though not quite as satisfying as smearing him with honey and tying him to an anthill, it would give me some pleasure for him to be constantly confronted by the consequences of what he had done. However, I did worry a little bit about how the tensions on campus might affect Eva. Well, it was too late for me to worry about—what the hell?

Standing in the doorway was the image of sixteen-year-old Jimmie, looking at me intently, pleadingly, and pointing in the general direction Dan had gone.

Was I finally going insane for real, or was I now being haunted? Either one would be fully consistent with the way my life was going.

"Who's that?" Nurse Florence had come up behind me without my realizing it, a measure of how preoccupied I was. Following her glance, I could see she was looking at Jimmie. Well, if she could see him too, that ruled out crazy and just left haunted. I wondered if Nurse Florence could do exorcisms.

"You may find this hard to swallow, but he's a ghost. The ghost of Dan's brother, to be precise."

"Tal, we need to talk," she thought back.

"Not now!" I replied, more harshly than I intended. *"I'll stop by later."*

Because, after all, a ghost roaming Santa Brígida High School is hardly the top problem either of us have. Hell, it isn't even in the top five! I thought to myself.

I fully expected Nurse Florence to argue with me, but she let me go without another word…or thought.

On the way to my first class, I ran into Gordy, who was wearing a tank top that looked as if it was pretty well bending school rules to the breaking point.

"Really?" I said, tilting my head a little.

He shrugged. "Sun's out, guns out!" he said, grinning a little. As he walked past, he patted me on the shoulder. "It's going to be all right, Tal." Then he was off down the hall.

I, however, stopped dead in my tracks. God, I was so far out of it that I hadn't even realized it was a sunny day. The fog inside of me must have been blocking it out.

I spent the time until lunch only half paying attention in class at best, and I didn't drop by Nurse Florence's during nutrition as she probably expected. Between anticipation over my next meeting with Eva and the ghostly presence of Jimmie, who seemed determined to keep his eye on me until I did what he wanted, it was pretty hard to focus on anything else.

Oh, I almost forgot to mention the whispering, and the odd looks, puzzled yet intrigued. Everyone knew that Dan and I had been good friends, and after the non-scene in the foyer, an increasingly large number of people wondered what had happened, why there was so much tension between the two of us. Well, they were going to have to go on wondering. Much as I would have liked to destroy Dan's reputation by telling everyone what he had done, I kept Eva in mind, and I kept my lips pressed tightly together.

When the clock had finally completed its tortuously slow crawl to lunch, I sought Eva out. She was with some friends, but I caught her eye, and she drifted in my general direction with affected casualness. When she got close enough, I could her face was paler than normal, her eyes red from sleeplessness. She tried to smile at me, but her face was just not quite up to it. With a growing sense of foreboding, I maneuvered her out into the quad, into the artificial mini-forest landscaped into the heart of the school. It being lunch, there were naturally others there, but I cast a don't-notice-us kind of spell, and we became inconspicuous to everyone else. Actually, I put enough force into the spell to make us more like invisible and inaudible. I wasn't taking any chances that this particular conversation would be interrupted.

"Eva," I started unsteadily, "I'm sorry…"

"What are you sorry for, Tal?" she asked emotionlessly, and I suddenly realized I didn't know. I was sorry Dan turned out to be a scumbag, but I shouldn't be the one apologizing for that. What I was really sorry for, the only thing that I could imagine ever being that sorry for, was that I lost four years with Eva, but what was the use of being sorry for that now, and what could I have possibly done about that before now?

"I'm sorry this has been such a difficult time for you," I finally managed, and that was true enough.

Eva smiled at that, but it was not the warm smile I remembered. "You have a gift for understatement, Tal. Really, though, I'm the one who should be sorry."

"Why?" I prompted after about a minute. She turned away from me as if she could not bear to see me anymore, but I could interpret that kind of gesture in many different ways. What I wouldn't give to know what she was thinking, but reading her mind under these circumstances was something I knew would be wrong.

"Even when I was twelve, I should have known better. Tal, even when I found out the truth about you a couple of months ago, it still didn't dawn on me what Dan had done. I just assumed he had misunderstood somehow. At the very least, I should have made more of an effort to see what was going on for myself. I should have done…something. More, anyway."

I took her gently by the shoulders and turned her back in my direction. "Dan had you believing that seeing you might make me worse. Who could blame you for trying to protect me? You have nothing, and I mean nothing, to feel sorry about."

Taking a gamble, I leaned in for a kiss. In that moment I realized just how sunny the day was. In fact, the sunlight was brighter than anything I had seen outside of Annwn in the last four years, and suddenly the plants and trees were a brilliant green, again unlike anything I had seen outside of Annwn. Maybe, just maybe…

No—I lost the gamble. Eva pulled back. Her movement was subtle, gentle even, but I knew what it meant. How could I be so stupid? She must be at least as emotionally raw as I was. I needed to give her a little time to heal. I had just lost a friend; she had lost someone she thought was the love of her life. Still, the world was once again only as bright as normal.

"Tal, there has been so much misunderstanding between us, so much unasked, so much unspoken." Eva did not turn away again, but she was no longer meeting my eyes. "If nothing else, we have to be honest with each other."

"Of course! Eva, there is so much I want to tell you—"

"Wait!" She cut me off forcefully. "There is something I have to tell you first."

"OK, ladies first!" I said, with a little bow. I couldn't help but notice that Eva could still not meet my eyes.

"Tal, I know what you want."

I could hear the sorrow in her voice, see it in her eyes. I didn't need to read her mind to dread what was coming next.

"Eva, I love you!" I burst in, unable to contain myself. I guess I figured that's what girls always complained guys weren't willing to say. Surely if Eva knew how much I cared about her…

"I guessed you did. All this time, you did. What Dan did would not have hurt you so much if you didn't. Even when you got Dan and me back together at the homecoming dance, even then. I was so blind not to see it!"

"Eva, no one could—"

"Please, Tal, please hear me out before this gets any worse."

Worse? What could get worse?

Yeah, I knew what was coming; I totally did. But I had sunk so deep in denial in the last couple of minutes that my heart refused to pay any attention to my mind.

"Eva, say whatever you want to say," I replied slowly.

"Tal, I can't go back to Dan now. Not after what he's done." She could see I wanted to respond, but her look stopped me. "When we were twelve, Tal, I thought I loved you."

Thought?

"Before your…awakening, I guess you would call it, I thought you were the center of my world. I thought we would always be together. I was heartbroken when Dan convinced me that would never happen. Part of me wishes I could go back, back before any of that happened. I want to be twelve again, and with you."

Again I wanted to interrupt, and again her eyes stopped me.

"Tal, I know it isn't fair of me to say this now, especially after all you have been through—"

That cracking sound was the sound of my denial beginning to give way—

"—but I have to say it anyway. Tal, we were twelve! Maybe you were more mature than I was then. What I was feeling couldn't really have been love."

"It was!" I protested despite myself.

Eva smiled, but it was the saddest smile I had ever seen on her face. She reached over and took my hand. I could feel hers shaking in mine. Or was it mine shaking?

"Tal, you couldn't read my mind then. How could you possibly know what I was feeling? If I really loved you, how could I have fallen in love with Dan? Don't look at me like that! I don't still love him…but Tal, I did—I really did. I wish I hadn't! I wish I could look at you now, tell you I always loved you, and let you take me in your arms, help you to get past all the pain. And you know what else?"

God, what else could there be…after that?

"Even if I had really loved you then, even if I hadn't loved Dan most of the last four years, I don't love you right now, this minute. And I can't make myself love you. I can't turn on the emotion, just like flicking on a light switch. Even if the love was real then, I can't just bring it back!"

Yup, that crack wasn't the denial anymore—long gone. That last one was my heart.

"Eva," I said, trying to keep a pleading tone out of my voice, "you've been through a lot. Maybe you should at least sleep on it before—"

"Tal, I haven't been thinking about anything else since yesterday. Another day is not going to change my feelings."

"All right," I said, feeling more than a little desperate. "I get why you can't just jump from Dan to me. But if you did love me once, even just a little, even puppy love"—God, how I hated that term—"then let's start over, as if we had just began dating. If you really don't have feelings for me, well, then you don't. But how can you know if you don't at least try?" I didn't quite get the last part out without a little pleading in my tone, but I had done the best I could.

Again she gave me that sad smile. "Right now I'm so raw emotionally I just can't commit to anything. I would say, 'maybe some day,' but it wouldn't be fair to tie you down like that. I can't ask you to wait for me to get my act together."

"You can ask me anything you want, Eva!" I said, trying to sound loving but not desperate. Then Eva did move in for a kiss, but it was just a peck on the cheek. She might as well have given me the can't-we-just-be-friends? speech. No doubt that was just around the corner.

"Then I'm asking you to live your life, Tal—without me in it. You're beautiful, inside and out. I know you don't realize it now, but you don't need me and all my baggage to be happy. Half the girls on campus would be willing to go out with you."

I was about to scoff, but again Eva stopped me. "How is it that good-looking guys never realize they are good-looking? Since you stopped being a loner, you've been crush material for more girls than you can imagine. You will find someone to love, someone who knows what she wants, who knows she wants you."

"I don't want someone else; I want you—and I don't care if you have enough baggage to fill a damn hotel!"

"I just can't, Tal!" she responded with equal determination. "I want to love you, but right now I just can't. I can't make myself love you."

I took her in my arms somewhat more roughly than I intended and stared straight into her surprised eyes. "I *can* make you love me!"

Until just a few minutes ago, I hadn't really thought about trying to copy Alcina's powerful love spell, but after all, I had learned the awakening and reversal spells just by watching Morgan cast them, and I had seen Alcina working her magic at close range during the battle at Goleta Beach, to say nothing of having the spell cast on me earlier. I suddenly realized that I knew how to lay as powerful a romantic compulsion on someone as Alcina had been able to.

Eva had said at least twice that she wanted to love me. What would be so wrong about helping her to feel what she truly wanted? I let my power flash into her eyes, and I could feel her sorrow fade as her love for me blossomed.

Just in time I realized that, despite my pitiful rationalization, what I was doing was enslaving Eva, just as Alcina had enslaved me. Once she was in the grip of my spell, she would have to love me, no matter what. I could pretend she really loved me, I could live that kind of lie…and as the years passed, I might forget it was a lie. I might also forget who I was, becoming day by day more like Morgan and Alcina. I wanted nothing more than I wanted Eva in my arms, in my bed, in my heart for as long as I lived…but not like this, never like this.

I managed to pull back just before Eva's inner transformation was complete. I had never seen Alcina reverse her spell, but I knew enough about mind control in general to release Eva successfully, leaving her momentarily stunned, but still herself.

"Eva, I'm so sorry!" I said, as realization dawned in her eyes. "I…I will never try that again, I swear. And I will stay away, if that is what you want."

She still looked confused, but at least she was not angry with me. Nonetheless, too ashamed of what I had almost done to continue the conversation, I turned and bolted out of the courtyard as fast as I could move. I went straight to where I should have gone to begin with: the nurse's office.

Nurse Florence let me tell my whole story without interruption. I told most of it gazing at the floor, afraid to look up and see the harsh judgment in her eyes. When I finally finished, I did look up, and to my infinite relief, she looked concerned, but also understanding. I knew she was the right person to come to.

"Tal, I had no idea you knew how to cast Alcina's love spell," she began.

"Neither did I. Apparently my ability to learn spells has now grown to the point that I can pick them up without even consciously trying as long as I am paying enough attention."

"All the more reason to be careful," she continued. "Tal, that spell is dark magic every bit as much as the awakening spell is. It twists reality in ways it is not meant to be twisted—and it twists the caster in the process. Even starting to use it is dangerous. Look inside yourself as you looking inside Dan last night." I looked at her dubiously. "Just do it, please." Despite the "please," I could tell this was not a request, and I complied immediately.

It did not take me long to discover what Nurse Florence knew I would see. I told myself I wasn't seeing it, but there could be no denying it.

I found a darkness inside of me, just like the one inside of Dan.

"One half-cast spell did that?" I asked incredulously.

Nurse Florence shook her head. "We all have that kind of darkness within us, but it isn't usually as visible as what you see inside yourself right now. Tal, your power places all kinds of temptations in front of you. You have been spending months, years even, steering away from them. Last night, when your anger caused you to threaten Dan with the awakening spell, the darkness became stronger. You felt its power when you started casting the love spell on Eva. You came so close to losing yourself, Tal!"

"I know. Once Eva was totally in love with me, I don't know if I would have been able to resist keeping her that way."

Nurse Florence smiled warmly. "Tal, I may not always agree with your decisions in the moment, but you have a good heart, and apparently also a strong one. Nonetheless, as you power increases, and it seems clear now you could become the strongest caster…well, perhaps ever, you will need to be more and more vigilant. The more you can do, the more you will be tempted to do. The original Taliesin's experience is no help here, either. From what you have told me, he wasn't pushed magically anywhere nearly as strongly as you have been."

I nodded solemnly. "Yeah, with Merlin and the original Viviane around, Taliesin seldom had to exert himself too much, and if he could actually have learned new magic as easily as I, he never realized that. Anyway, I know now just how careful I have to be."

"It will help to keep yourself as clear as possible of negative emotions—which brings me to Dan."

I sat straight up in the chair and stared at her open-mouthed. "How can you bring up that bastard right now?"

"That 'bastard' has fought by your side, Tal. He has risked his life for you, just as much as any of the others. I am even more convinced than ever after today's events that you need to forgive him if you want to keep your own darkness at bay."

"I can't," I said, much more loudly than I intended.

"Not even for Eva? Not even for the next person you are tempted to use dark magic on?"

"That's not fair! And he hurt Eva every bit as much as he hurt me!"

"Tal," said Nurse Florence gently. "I'm not defending what he did; it was horrible. But he was twelve. And there's something else…"

"I'm listening," I said grudgingly.

"You remember that when I was vetting him as a possible guardian for you that I dream-walked him." I nodded. "Well, I don't see how I could have missed a betrayal as drastic as the one you discovered. I admit that dream-walking is not as precise or targeted as mind-reading like yours, but still, a guilty secret that big will show up in his dreams in one way or another. I saw him hurt by what he felt was you betraying him after you got out of the hospital, like dropping out of all the things you used to do together, but I didn't see even a hint of his conscious manipulation of Eva to break her away from you."

"What's that supposed to mean?" I asked impatiently.

"Well, it could mean that the memories of his betrayal weren't in his mind then—which could, in turn, mean that they are false memories, implanted later."

"That's ridiculous! You're grasping at straws here."

"Am I? I examined him enough after that incident with Stan and Eva to know that someone else's magic was on him, and you said yourself that his behavior was uncharacteristic that day. We know now that Ceridwen was trying to isolate you, make you easier prey."

"Sure, by getting Stan and Dan at odds and forcing me to choose. She probably figured I would choose Stan and lose everybody else."

"Ceridwen's schemes were often more complex than that, though. Suppose she wanted to make doubly sure you and Dan separated by planting those memories for you to find later. That kind of memory implant often causes behavioral disruptions. That could account for the darkness, which you thought at one time could be the product of hostile magic, and for Dan's occasional over-the-top reactions."

"But Eva has those memories too!" I protested.

"I never have examined her. There was no time that day, and afterward other matters became far more urgent. Ceridwen could have implanted comparable memories in her. Remember that she too was acting strangely that day. I suspected hostile magic, but those changes could have been the after-effects of having false memories implanted within her. Ceridwen was on campus that day; we know that. With enough planning she could have created that whole betrayal scenario and altered their memories enough to make it seem plausible."

"OK," I said grudgingly, still not entirely convinced, "examine them now. I will too. Let's see whether those memories are real or not."

Nurse Florence sighed. "I doubt it will be that simple to tell, and frankly, we have more pressing business, not the least of which is finding some way to restore Stan and Carla. You know what I would like, Tal?" She leaned forward, eying me intensely. "I would like you to forgive Dan or at least find some way to reincorporate him into the group. We can figure out what happened later, but your warriors need to be united behind you in case some new threat emerges, and another feud with Dan is not going to help that."

I was about to respond indignantly when Nurse Florence's glance over my shoulder indicated that we were not alone. Turning quickly, I saw Jimmie's ghost, looking solid as any normal person, though I was willing to bet he had just walked through the wall. He stopped right next to me, looked straight into my eyes, and shook his head sadly.

"Tal, this isn't normal," said Nurse Florence quickly.

I couldn't help laughing a little. "My best friend has turned into King David. My girlfriend has turned into a medieval sorceress. One of my friends has adopted a half djinn as his little brother. Just a few days ago I had to outwit a dragon. It seems to me a ghost should fit right in!"

"Be serious!" she said to me in a tone that indicated she meant business. "Genuine hauntings are comparatively rare in the first place, and the ghost typically can't remain visible for such long periods of time. Nor do ghosts normally look so realistically human. Tal, if I wasn't magically sensitive, I couldn't tell Jimmie was a ghost. This is probably a result of the same process that made your mother psychic. Somehow, Jimmie's proximity to you has gradually increased his power, allowing him to become visible at will."

I tried to take my eyes off Jimmie and failed. "While we are on the subject, shouldn't Jimmie be appearing the age he was when he died, rather than the age he would be now?"

Nurse Florence nodded. "Ghosts that progress just as if they were still living are very, very rare. The Order suspects it means that the ghost has stayed with family and friends ever since he died."

"So Jimmie was never at peace?" I asked worriedly. The look in his eyes should have answered that question for me.

"It isn't uncommon for people to linger a little after death, especially an unexpected one. My guess is that Jimmie was around long enough to see you and Dan drift apart, and that he has stayed with you both in an effort to get you to reconcile."

"Is that true, Jimmie?" I asked him. He nodded and kept staring into my eyes.

The thought that Jimmie had spent the last seven years as a restless spirit made me want to reach out and hug him, comfort him, find some way to send him on his way. The problem was that what he undoubtedly wanted me to do was the one thing I just couldn't. I would have crawled naked over broken glass for him. But forgive Dan for him? How could I?

Then the realization struck me like lightning. "If Jimmie has been with us all along, then he knows whether those memories Dan and Eva have are true or not!"

Nurse Florence looked alarmed. "Tal, you can't put him in the position of betraying his own brother—or you. We may never put him to rest if you force him into that kind of situation."

"It doesn't matter."

Nurse Florence and I both jumped at the sound of Jimmie's voice, which seemed hauntingly like Dan's voice about a year ago.

"Tal, I was with you in the hospital most of that time. I can only be one place at a time. If Dan made Eva stop liking you, I wasn't around to see it."

"You can...talk now?" I asked stupidly.

"Yeah, I couldn't earlier in the day, but now I can."

"Definitely feeding off your connection to Annwn," said Nurse Florence, her "scientific" interest piqued.

"Tal, haven't I been through enough?" Jimmie asked plaintively. "I died at nine, and then I couldn't figure out how to move on. I wanted to, but at first I wanted to stay with you and Dan more. Then, when I finally began to think I could move on, you went to the hospital, and then I had to stay to see what happened. You got better, but then you weren't friends with Dan anymore, and I knew I couldn't move on until you became friends again. But I was so happy when that finally happened that I wanted to stay just a little longer and enjoy it—and then it didn't last! I stayed too long, and now you aren't friends again, and I can't stand it! You don't know Tal; you just don't know. It hurts! It hurts so bad!"

By this point I was trying to hold back my tears. "What hurts, Jimmie?"

"At first I didn't notice it, but the longer I stay, the more I feel it. I keep feeling the accident. You know, the one that killed me."

I couldn't help remembering the pain I'd felt when I was first hit by the awakening of my previous lives. So many of them were dominated by the memory of violent death.

"This must be a side effect of his staying on this plane of existence for so long," said Nurse Florence. "The only way to relieve him is to help him move on."

"Please, please Tal!" said Jimmie. When he was alive, I could never say no to him. Was I really ready to start now?

Reflexively I reached out to hug him. Of course, I couldn't hug a ghost—except that I did. I felt him in my arms. I even felt his warmth, warmth that had faded away seven years ago. Shocked, I pulled away.

"He's not a ghost! He's a shifter!" I had White Hilt out faster than he could move a muscle. Whatever this shifter wanted, it couldn't be good.

"Wait!" yelled Nurse Florence. "He's physical, but that's not a real body."

Jimmie looked at White Hilt's fire, and I could swear I saw tears glistening in his eyes.

"What do you mean?" I kept my eyes fixed on Jimmie, if that was indeed who he was.

"Ghosts can occasionally assume physical form, normally only briefly. Apparently, Jimmie's greater strength is allowing him to stay solid for a longer period."

"Are you sure?" Having been fooled so often by supernatural beings, I was not taking any chances.

"You know how well I can read someone's physical condition. He isn't breathing. His heart isn't beating. He doesn't even have separate organs."

"He felt warm in my arms!"

"And if you held him long enough, you might have thought you felt his heart beating too, but I can guarantee you it would not be a real one."

Slowly I put away White Hilt. Then I hugged him again. After all, if it was Jimmie, I had never been able to say a proper good-bye to him, so I might as well take advantage of the opportunity. Sure enough, I could have sworn he was breathing and that he had a heartbeat. I wasn't as good as Nurse Florence at reading a body, but I gave it a try, and sure enough, on the inside Jimmie was just a...mass—no distinct parts at all. No shifter could turn into that kind of form and live.

"Tal," said Nurse Florence gently, "as far as I know, there is no record of a ghostly manifestation this strong. We are in completely new territory."

"Not for the first time," I quipped, patting Jimmie on the head. Actually, since this Jimmie was taller than I was, the gesture seemed a little silly, but I had a hard time not thinking of him as the nine-year-old he had been when he died.

"Nonetheless, we need to get him taken care of soon. It's possible if he stays solid too long that it will interfere with his effort to pass on properly."

"I can control it," said Jimmie, who reached out and passed his hand right through me to demonstrate.

"Jimmie, we can't take any chances," insisted Nurse Florence. "Tal, you know what you have to do."

Well, that was the problem. I did know what I had to do. I could not have loved Jimmie more if he had been my own brother. A few weeks ago, I would have said I would do anything to save him from pain. Now it turned out that there was one thing I wouldn't—couldn't—do.

I didn't think I could forgive Dan and go back to being friends, not even for Jimmie.

My only hope was to prove Nurse Florence's theory. Hell, if the memories were false, I would owe Dan the biggest apology in the world.

Of course, if they were real memories, if he had actually stabbed me in the back, taken Eva away from me forever…

Then what? Trap Jimmie here forever, in ever-increasing pain?

"Jimmie, let's go find Dan," I said in such a matter-of-fact way that Nurse Florence seemed not to quite believe what she was hearing.

"Tal, you really need to—" she started to say.

"I know what I need to do," I replied quickly. "While I'm doing it, can you make sure someone tracks down Natalie Kim and explains Stan's situation to her? We'll need her later to cure Stan. Oh, and call Vanora and let her know I'll want to visit Alcina later tonight."

"What?" Nurse Florence was practically aghast.

"I've figured out how to get Carla back in control of her own body. Neither Stan nor Carla is going to be completely healed right away, but with time, we'll complete the process. I'm a man on a mission today, and I'm going to damn well get some things crossed off the to-do list!"

Because then there will be time to find out the truth about Dan.

I was already late for soccer practice by this time, but I had the feeling Dan wasn't there anyway. I could have found him easily enough, but I decided to see what other tricks Jimmie might be able to do.

"Jimmie, can you find Dan?"

Jimmie gave me a smile that reminded me of his nine-year-old mischievousness, despite the greater maturity of his current face. "I can find either one of you, and I can find my parents too!" His brow wrinkled in concentration for only a moment. "Dan is at home."

As we walked down the hall, it did not take me long to realize that Jimmie was visible to everyone. I suppose from a girl's perspective, he was a pretty hot-looking guy, but if that had not been enough to attract notice, his resemblance to Dan certainly would be.

"Jimmie, why are you making yourself visible to everyone?" I muttered under my breath.

"I didn't realize I was visible to anyone but you and Nurse Florence." Jimmie looked panicked.

"Don't worry! We'll be out of here soon."

As we walked, I sent a quick mental message to Nurse Florence, asking her to excuse my absence—and Dan's—with Coach Morton. Then I magicked a couple of teachers and a security guard who would have stopped us from leaving the school. Once out in the student parking lot, I got Jimmie into the Prius, and then I drove him to Dan's on autopilot. The less I thought about things, the better.

"Jimmie, are your parents home?"

"No," he said, sounding disappointed.

"It's better that way. I couldn't explain you to them anyway. I can explain you to Dan." Jimmie sighed but didn't argue.

Dan's house was pretty much the same kind of Spanish-colonial-on-steroids monstrosity that I lived in, though, in an effort to avoid a tract-housing feel, no two of them had exactly the same floor plan. Still, pulling up out front gave me the eerie feeling that I was pulling up in front of my own house in some alternate universe.

Not quite as weird, of course, as having a seven-years-dead friend in my passenger seat, but everything was relative.

We moved quickly up the front path, and I knocked loudly on the front door. No answer.

"You're sure he's here?"

"Yeah," said Jimmie, looking puzzled.

Dan, get your butt out here! I thought loudly. He must have heard my knock and probably knew I was the one knocking. If I were him, maybe I wouldn't have been exactly eager to run to the door either. Well, Dan might be a girlfriend-stealing scumbag, but he was no coward—I had seen proof of that often enough on the battlefield. He opened the door in about a minute, his face a deliberate blank.

"Yeah?" he said suspiciously. I stepped aside to give him a good view of Jimmie. Because Jimmie looked so much older now than he had when he died, it took Dan a minute. He immediately saw the resemblance, of course, but it only gradually dawned on him that he was looking at his dead kid brother.

"Jimmie?" Dan said, half-disbelieving. Then he grabbed him in a rib-crushing bear hug. "Tal, you...brought him back to life?"

Oops! It hadn't occurred to me that Dan would reach that conclusion, but I should have known, considering everything else he had seen.

"Dan," I replied softly. I wasn't quite up to being gentle with him, but I suddenly did feel awful that he believed Jimmie was back to stay. "Dan, that is Jimmie, but he's a ghost. Dan let go of Jimmie and stared at him again in disbelief.

"He's solid!" He protested. "I can feel him, Tal!"

"He can assume the appearance and even the feel of a real body at times. Dan, we need to go inside."

Understanding how odd having someone who looked so much like him show up would look to the neighbors—and what they might say to his parents about it—Dan ushered us in and had us sit down in the large living room that's general layout was the same as mine, though Dan's parents clearly liked leather upholstery more than mine did. I explained the mechanics of Jimmie's reappearance and then got straight to the point.

"Jimmie's a restless spirit now. He knows he should move on, but he can't as long as we are in conflict. I have to forgive you for what you did four years ago, and we have to become friends again in order for Jimmie to find peace."

"Why can't he just stay with us, now that he's back? His physical body may not be real, but it looks real enough to pass. We could make up some story that you could magick my parents into believing. He's some distant cousin, recently orphaned, or something like that. He certainly looks related to us, so that part wouldn't take much selling." Dan was talking faster as he went along, his nervous energy barely held in check. "I'm sure my parents would take him in. They miss Jimmie as much as I do, and even though they wouldn't know he was Jimmie, it would still help them."

"Dan…" I started, not quite sure how to approach such a crazy idea. Actually, when I considered what we had all been through, I could see why Dan thought it might work. If the Sassanis could adopt a half djinn, why couldn't his family adopt a ghost?

"Dan, I want to stay," Jimmie cut in. "I want it more than anything, but I know I can't. I hurt sometimes, remembering the accident, and the pain is getting worse. Don't ask me how I know it will keep getting worse until I can't stand it; I just do."

Dan sat silently for a minute, his face twisted by conflicting emotions. He understood that Jimmie would have to go, but he didn't want to understand. Fortunately, Jimmie stepped up and made him understand. Dan might not have accepted the truth if it was just coming from me. When he finally did accept it, he cried a little, though he tried to pretend he wasn't. I understood he was probably just as emotionally raw as I was, though I didn't want to sympathize with him. After all, he didn't create Jimmie's situation, but he did cause the end of our friendship and the breakup with Eva.

After Dan had finally collected himself, he looked me straight in the eye. As he did that, I realized he really hadn't been earlier. "Well, Tal, the ball is in your court. Can you forgive me?"

"Yes," I lied for Jimmie's benefit. "I think I can."

"Dan, listen closely!" I knew he couldn't respond to me, because he couldn't broadcast his thoughts, but I just needed him to hear me. I had to deceive Jimmie, but it would be cruel to lie to Dan and then have him find out the truth later. Angry as I was with him, I didn't want to play with his emotions like that. Then I would be no better than he was.

"Dan, are you paying attention?" He nodded ever so slightly. *"All right. The truth is, I don't know if I can ever forgive you. I do know I can't right now. But if we stay visibly at odds with each other, Jimmie will be trapped here until his pain becomes uncontrollable. For his sake, I'm willing to pretend if you are."*

He nodded slightly again. He didn't look happy, but whatever he had done to me and to Eva, I knew he wouldn't consign Jimmie to hell.

"You'll take back your sword and be my warrior again. We'll hang out. Publicly we'll be close again. Even the other guys have to be convinced for this to work."

I wasn't done, but Dan got off the couch and bear-hugged me, quite a bit harder than seemed to be necessary. "And after Jimmie leaves?" he whispered to me.

I had thought a little bit about that contingency. Perhaps Jimmie would disappear right away, perhaps it would take a while, but inevitably it would happen—that was the whole point. And once it happened, I couldn't blame Dan for wondering what his status would be.

"I can't guarantee I'll ever forgive you, but I won't ask you to leave to group. If we're still not really friends, and we probably won't be, that will just be between us. I'm sorry I didn't handle the situation that way in the first place."

The odd part was that I really was sorry about that. Not so much for Dan—he had a little public humiliation coming after what he put me through—as for everyone else. Eva aside, since I would have had to tell her, by going public in the way I had, I made the guys, who liked both Dan and me, choose between us. I made Khalid feel like his new family was tearing itself apart. I was shocked, but I shouldn't have let my anger get the best of me that way. All my efforts to not act impulsively had gone down the drain, because I still didn't have the self-control. Well, I was going to develop some if I had to die trying.

When Dan finally let go of me, after one last squeeze that felt genuine, he was doing his best to look happy. Hell, maybe he was happy. At least now he could have his position in the school hierarchy back. Knowing he could do something to help Jimmie probably also made him feel better. Hopefully not too much better, though—I wasn't really ready to let him off the hook all that easily.

We both looked at Jimmie, who was grinning broadly. "Are you really friends again?" he asked.

"We still have some things to work out, but yes, we are." Lucky I was such a good liar!

"Yeah, we can work out our differences," agreed Dan. His words sounded a little hollow, but thank God Jimmie didn't pick up on that.

"Wow, this is the happiest I have been in a long time!" He hugged Dan again, then me. "I can't imagine anything better." I, on the other hand, was still imagining Dan smeared with honey and tied to an anthill, so on the whole it was a good thing that Jimmie couldn't read minds.

Well, cross one of those items off the to-do list. I half expected a brilliant white light to burst into the room and Jimmie to wave good-bye as he walked into it, so the nothing that actually happened was kind of an anticlimax. Evidently Jimmie needed to see us being friends for a little while before he was truly ready to let this world go. What Jimmie needed, Jimmie was going to get, and after the experience of feigning friendship with Dan, I could easily become a professional actor.

"We need to fix Stan this afternoon, and then I need to do something over at Awen. Dan, Jimmie, want to come with? We can pick up Dan's sword on the way." Dan looked a little surprised, but he played along, and Jimmie couldn't have been happier. He sat in the back seat and chattered nonstop while Dan and I sat up front.

Nurse Florence had Dan's sword, and I wasn't eager to go back to school, but I couldn't think of a better visual image for Jimmie's benefit than me presenting Dan with his blade again. I threw a little don't-notice-us magic around, because I didn't want to blow whatever excuse Nurse Florence had made to Coach Morton, and with that magical help, we managed to reach her office unseen. Since she had wanted me to forgive Dan anyway, she was almost ecstatic to see us together, but she was also a little concerned that Jimmie was still trailing along behind us.

"I see Jimmie is still here," she said—certainly a masterpiece of stating the obvious, but also a cue for me to explain to her what was going on.

"Dan and I kind of faked a quick reconciliation for his benefit, but I think he needs to see us being friends for a while before he can say good-bye." She nodded, and though I could tell she didn't like the fact that the reconciliation was merely fake, she did not try to continue the conversation.

"I'd like to return Dan's sword to him," I said. Nurse Florence nodded, went into her storage room for a minute, and returned with his familiar blade, which I made a big point of presenting to Dan as if he were receiving it for the first time. He seemed more comfortable with it hanging once again at his side, and Jimmie looked satisfied. So far, so good—our act was working.

"Is Natalie Kim ready?" I asked.

"Shar, Gordy, and Carlos will have her at Stan's right after practice, and I'll come along too, just to make sure we have enough magical oomph to break the spell on Stan."

"Good! Thanks for setting all that up. I'll take care of Stan's mom. I'm going to need to stay after the spell is broken to make sure I can get Stan back in charge of his body. Then I'd appreciate it if you could join me at Awen. I want to do the same for Carla."

"You mentioned that earlier," said Nurse Florence with evident concern. "How exactly do you plan to do it? I'm sure Alcina is not going to cooperate."

"She will once she is irresistibly in love with me," I said, wincing reflexively in anticipation of Nurse Florence's impending tsunami of disapproval. I did not have long to wait.

"Tal, that spell is dark magic. I thought you knew how risky that is, how…evil that is!"

"It would be evil if I used it to make someone fall in love with me for my own purposes." I shuddered for a moment, thinking of what I had almost done to Eva. "Surely the purpose for which the spell is used makes some difference?"

Nurse Florence shook her head. "I know your motives are pure, Tal, but that kind of compulsion is inherently evil."

"Right now we have Alcina restrained," I pointed out. "This is just a different form of restraint."

"What are you guys talking about?" asked Dan. I really didn't want to spend time bringing him up to speed, but I couldn't very well tell him to shut up with Jimmie standing right there.

"During the battle of Goleta Beach, I learned how to cast that super-powerful love spell Alcina uses. We know from the fact that Alcina cast the spell on Stan but somehow missed David that it can be directed at only one personality within a body, so I should be able to use it on Alcina without having it affect Carla."

Dan chuckled. "Carla has the hots for you anyway, as I recall."

Yeah, you bastard! It's too bad my feelings for her were magically induced, or maybe I could actually end up with somebody to love, since you made any kind of relationship with Eva impossible for me.

"Wouldn't making Alcina fall in love with you make her less willing to relinquish control to Carla?" asked Nurse Florence.

"You'd think, but trust me. From my days under that spell, I know. Absence from Alcina was painful, but I would have done anything she ordered. I would have moved to the other side of the universe if I thought it would make her happy. All I need to do is give the order once she is under the spell, and she will have to give up control of the body to Carla forever, no questions asked."

"So it might work out for Carla, but what about you?" asked Nurse Florence. "Tal, think of dark magic as if it were heroin. Shooting up for some reason to save someone else...Well, OK, I can't think of any way that could ever save someone else, but just imagine it could for the sake of argument. You shoot up to save someone else, but the fact that you are saving someone else doesn't make it anything other than what it is: heroin. It is still addictive; it still damages your body. The reason for shooting up, even if it is noble, cannot change that.

"The same is true of dark magic. You can begin with the best motives in the world; they won't matter in the end. The more you use it, the more you will want to use it. Oh, you will find ways to justify that use to yourself. You may not even realize what you are doing, or, if you do, you still won't be able to stop yourself."

"Has anyone ever attempted what I'm talking about doing?" I asked.

"No, but—"

"Then you don't actually know whether this type of usage will have any bad effects at all."

"I told you!" said Nurse Florence in her firmest tone. "Dark magic is inherently evil, inherently corrupting. I will not allow you to sacrifice yourself in this way. Besides, forgetting about your own soul, we need you...and we need you intact, not horribly compromised."

"Need me for what, exactly?" I could feel anger creeping into my tone and tried to keep it out. "Ceridwen is already gone. Morgan is imprisoned and will be turned over to the faeries soon. Once Stan is healed, once Carla is healed, what do you need me for?"

Nurse Florence was about to about to answer, but Jimmie beat her to the punch. "Tal, you're a hero. I've seen you in action. Doesn't the world always need heroes?" I glanced in Jimmie's direction and almost felt like bursting into tears.

God, Jimmie, if I had only been there right before the accident, with the power I have now! Then I could have saved you.

"Let's ask Vanora before we make a final decision," I said slowly. "If I am going to throw away what may be the only way to save Carla, then at least let me be sure that is the right course of action."

"Of course we can talk to Vanora. I'll make arrangements, and we can go over right after we finish with Stan."

"I need to make a quick stop at home first. I need to tell my mother the truth." Hell, might as well get another lecture about why I shouldn't do what I needed to do.

"The leaders of Annwn aren't going to like that," began Nurse Florence cautiously.

"I don't care!" I replied firmly.

"Please let me finish. I was about to say that you probably need to tell her, given her psychic nature. I can make a good case that she will figure out what is happening eventually, whether you tell her or not. I'll square things with Gwynn and the others as soon as I get the chance."

"Thanks," I said, feeling enormous relief. "Oh, one other thing. Is that ice sword of Morgan's prepared?"

"Enchanted to be invisible when sheathed and to appear like fencing equipment if drawn in public, just like all the others. Why? Do you have an idea of who you would like to see wield it?"

"Not permanently, but I'd like Jimmie to carry it today." Jimmie's face lit up. I expected to get a fight on that issue too, but Nurse Florence took one look at Jimmie and apparently decided his having the sword could do no real harm. She got it out of her storage room, sparkling with the tiny ice chips that fell from it; placed it in an extra scabbard; and handed it to him. I in turn handed it to Jimmie and helped him get the scabbard to hang properly. He looked like it was Christmas, which it very nearly was.

"Has he been solid the whole time you have been gone with him?" asked Nurse Florence worriedly.

"I think so. Jimmie?"

"Yeah. It doesn't seem to take me much effort anymore."

Nurse Florence nodded, and I expected her to start sending me mental messages of doom, but if she was worried about Jimmie's continuing solidity, she kept her concerns to herself this time.

Despite the complexity of our plans, the rest of the afternoon proceeded almost without a hitch. I say almost because Natalie Kim was too smart to be fooled by "You can break the spell because you are a good friend of his." I had the feeling Stan was going to have some explaining to do, along the lines of "Why haven't you ever asked me out? Why are you dating all those cheerleaders?" and other similar questions. Nonetheless, Natalie was more than willing to help with Stan's cure.

His father wasn't home from work yet, and it was an easy matter to put his ever-hovering mother to sleep so that we could get the job done. Between true love's kiss and all the magical amplification we could throw into it, that spell never stood a chance, and Stan was restored to us. It was actually much harder to restore the connections between Stan and David.

"Stan," I said near the end of the process, "I've already told David this, but be careful. I'm only just barely able to make viable connections between you and David. If you think of your personalities as if they are physical objects, it is as if the edges are wearing out. I'm sure I could fix that too, with time, but in the short term I don't think I could put you together again after another incident. I told David that no matter what happens to you, even if you are enchanted again, he is not to take over. You get that too, right?"

Stan smiled weakly. "Yes, Mother."

I laughed heartily over that. "Dude, I'm nothing like your mother!"

"If she had the power you do, she couldn't put any more into my healing than you have," he said softly.

In just a few more minutes, Stan was good to go...which is exactly what he wanted to do. Well, he wasn't going to need to do any heavy lifting on this trip, so I said sure. Aside from the usual crew (Stan, Dan,

Gordy, Shar, Carlos, and, of course, Nurse Florence), we had Jimmie, whose presence everyone else adjusted to with remarkable speed, and Khalid, this time invited.

I had already said something to Shar, but I wanted to apologize to Khalid personally for upsetting him after the battle. Thank God little kids are so resilient! He had already forgiven me before I said anything and was all smiles again, happy to be going on a new adventure with me and his other new pals.

I sent everyone else ahead to Awen, so I could talk to my mom without them all waiting outside the house; at this point that might be psychic overload for her, and I wasn't sure how long the conversation would take. I was risking giving Nurse Florence the time to convince Vanora to turn down my plan for dealing with Alcina, but Vanora was pretty stubborn. She was either going to agree with me or not. A few minutes alone with Nurse Florence weren't all that likely to change the outcome.

I had picked a good day, because Dad was working late, so Mom would be alone in the house. I let myself in and found her quickly, not making dinner, as I might have expected, but sitting on the sofa in the living room, crying softly.

"Mom, what's wrong?" I asked, already knowing. She didn't seem able to answer at first, so I took her in my arms and just let her cry. Eventually she calmed down enough to talk to me.

"Tal, I'm…I'm going crazy…very fast. I'm seeing things, hearing things, having strange feelings for no reason. I shouldn't be telling you this, but you'll know pretty soon anyway. Honey, I may have to go away for treatment."

"You won't have to do that, Mom. There's nothing wrong with you!"

She sighed. "Denial isn't good, Tal. I need to face what is happening."

"Let me tell you what is happening." And so I did.

It took an hour and a half, give or take. I told her everything from August on: my unusual nature and how it came about; Ceridwen's attempt to capture my soul, who Nurse Florence was, who Carrie Winn really was—then and now—how my friends fit in…and that just got us to Halloween. Then I had to explain more recent developments: Morgan

Le Fay, Carla turning into Alcina, Stan revealing he was King David, Khalid's unusual family background, fighting sorceresses and dragons in Annwn, Jimmie coming back. I told her all of it, every bit, even Dan's suspected betrayal, even the fact that Eva would probably never love me.

There were times when she seemed ready to have us both admitted to a mental hospital on the family plan, but I used my demonstration of invoking the fire of White Hilt and a few other simple magic routines to convince her. Really, one image is worth a thousand words.

"Are…are you still my son?" she asked finally, overcome by the idea of hundreds of previous lives, all somehow stored within me.

"I will always be your son," I replied, giving her a kiss on the cheek. She held onto me as if I would disappear in a puff of smoke if she did not.

"But this means all the horrible things I thought were just nightmares or hallucinations were real! You have actually been in mortal danger several times in the last few months! Tal, you have to find a way to get out of this!"

Would that it were that easy!

"Mom, I can't just walk away now. I think, though, that the dangerous times are nearly ended."

"Don't take unnecessary chances!" she cautioned in her don't-make-me-ground-you voice. "Tal, if anything ever happened to you, I really would go crazy."

"I've survived fifteen-hundred-year-old witches, armies of the dead, dragons… I'm not expecting to face anything worse than what I have already faced." I grinned reassuringly. "Actually, tonight promises to be a relatively quiet evening…and if all goes well, Carla's family will get her back."

"That would be wonderful!" agreed Mom. "I guess I can't complain when you save someone. Will you be back in time for dinner?" She asked the last question in such a matter-of-fact way that I couldn't help snickering a little.

"Please make appropriate excuses for me to Dad. If my plan works, I'll need to spend time getting Carla healed, and then we need to re-insert her in the hospital so her doctors can discover her miraculous return to consciousness."

"Well, all right…but remember, be careful!"

"Always!" I replied, giving her another kiss and heading out the door.

Right outside stood Eva, waiting for me.

Come by to twist the knife some more?

"Tal, I don't mean to bother you, but I need to talk to you."

Yeah, definitely to twist the knife.

"Eva, now isn't really a good time. Tomorrow would be better."

"Please, I need to say this. Tal, that spell you started to cast on me. It was a love spell, wasn't it?"

"Yeah," I said quietly, "It was, and I'm sorry. I'm sorry I even considered it, let alone started to do it. I hope you can forgive me." I paused for a second, then said, "I know I have lost your love; I don't ever want to lose your friendship." Hopefully, that would preempt a transition into a let's-just-be-friends kind of dialog.

Eva brushed aside my guilt with a wave of her delicate hand. "You've been through so much. How can I hold a grudge over something that small? I wanted to make sure you knew I wasn't blaming you for that."

It was clear she really didn't understand what effect the spell would have had, and I didn't have the heart to explain.

"The guys tell me you have forgiven Dan."

"I'm working on it," I said tightly. "Eva, I really need to go."

"Can I come with you? I'd like to see Carla, particularly if she really is Carla. Don't look so shocked; Gordy told me what was going on. That's how I knew you'd be home. I've visited the illusionary Carla in the hospital a couple of times and didn't suspect a thing."

I'd rather be cut into tiny pieces by a machete while I am still conscious than have you around right now.

"I'm sure Carla would like to have a girlfriend around if I can get her back. Sure, you can come."

"Carla and I weren't that close, but I do feel a connection with her."

Yeah, you could start a support group for women whose lives have been touched by the supernatural.

"Hop in then," I said, opening the passenger door for her. By the time I got in, her jasmine perfume closed around in one all-pervading, sorrow-provoking vapor. Great! Just exactly what I needed.

"You know Dan is going to be there," I said, giving her—and me—an out.

"He's going to be at school, too, but I'm not going to stop going to school. Better we figure out now how to deal with being in the same place."

I pulled away from the curb with a tightness in my chest and knots in my stomach, wondering how Eva and I were going to deal with being in the same place...and why it was that being with me didn't seem to bother her. Had I really meant that little to her?

The drive over to Carrie Winn's mansion/castle seemed tortuously long. Really it was only about half an hour, not bad in surface street traffic in early evening. When we arrived, the staff at the front door quickly ushered us up a few floors and into a conference room that seemed to be one of the few genuinely modern rooms in the whole place. Vanora, her usual Carrie Winn disguise flawless, was sitting with all the others at a large, round wooden table that looked as if it could have come close to seating all the knights of Camelot.

"Welcome to my round table!" she said with surprising cheeriness. Well, I guess somebody had to say it. I made a point of pulling out a chair for Eva and then, once she got settled, sitting as far away from her as possible.

"Nurse Florence tells me you have a plan to restore Carla Rinaldi to us," prompted Vanora.

Yeah, I bet she did.

"Then she has probably also told you I know how to cast an Alcina-style love spell and intend to give her a taste of her own medicine."

"Please explain in detail what you intend to do," said Vanora, her voice relatively neutral. I took several minutes to lay out in detail exactly what I wanted to do and why I thought it would work. When I finally finished, Vanora said, "You have planned this out very carefully, Taliesin. It sounds worth a try to me."

I had never seen Nurse Florence so utterly caught by surprise. "Vanora, you can't be serious. You know the risks as well as I do."

"Taliesin is stronger than you give him credit for, I think."

"I don't want to embarrass Tal by saying this out loud," broadcast Nurse Florence, making sure I could hear her so that she was not saying it behind my back, *"but he only just resisted the temptation to use the spell on Eva. That's a sure sign he cannot afford to use dark magic again."*

"It's true," I admitted, *"but I did stop myself. I believe I can perform the spell one more time without losing control."*

"I believe so as well," replied Vanora.

"I will not allow it!" said Nurse Florence, switching back to speaking and using the strongest tone I had ever heard her use.

Vanora looked at her with noticeable irritation. "It is not your place to allow or not to allow. Alcina is technically my prisoner…and I outrank you in the Order. Well, this time I am pulling rank. I will give Taliesin the chance he wants. If there were more time, perhaps we would study the problem in greater depth, but there isn't time. I just found out today that the Annwn authorities will be here tomorrow to take Morgan into custody—and they intend to take Alcina into custody as well."

"What?" I interrupted. "Carla is human. Faerie law has no hold over her."

"That's just it," replied Vanora slowly. "*Carla* is human. Alcina, like Morgan, is part faerie. Granted that the current body is human, as long as Alcina is in control of it, the authorities intend to treat her as faerie and proceed accordingly. Once they have her, anything might happen. Annwn's politics are so twisted right now that they could both be released, though I think that's unlikely. They could also both be executed, depending on the composition of the tribunal, though I think that's equally unlikely. Oberon probably can't convince enough of the others to let his 'mother' go free, given the fear of what too much interference in mortal affairs can cause, but I'll bet he can convince enough of them not to execute her.

"In any case, I doubt there will be much interest in curing Carla, except maybe on Gwynn's part, and even less in returning her to us if she isn't cured. My guess would be that she and Morgan will both be imprisoned somewhere in Annwn to keep either of them from meddling with Earth again. And so," she said, turning to Nurse Florence, "unless you are willing to trust the girl's fate to a very unfavorably disposed fortune, Taliesin's plan is all we have."

Nurse Florence sagged visibly, obviously feeling defeated. "Tal, are you sure you can handle this?"

"Tal can do it; he's a hero!" announced Jimmie, sounding a bit like the nine-year-old he no longer appeared to be.

"You bet!" said Khalid, sounding every bit like the eleven-year-old he was.

"Very sure!" I replied quickly, before anyone else could join in the embarrassing cheerleading.

"I have seen you succeed against incredible odds before," admitted Nurse Florence. "Since Carla's life could be at stake, I agree we have to chance your approach. We must be very careful, though."

"Both of us will be there to make sure nothing goes wrong," put in Vanora, obviously relieved that Nurse Florence was going along with the plan.

"Perhaps we warriors will be needed," suggested Dan.

Vanora looked at him with unconcealed contempt. "Alcina is helpless, and if she were not, the last thing we would do is place a lot of teenage males within easy reach of her magic," she said as if explaining the situation to a very young child. Given how glad she was to see Dan go, she was probably very angry I had let him back in.

"If Alcina's magic has indeed been neutralized, I would rather have the guys nearby." I said. "If Alcina is unusually resistant to her own spell, I may need to draw upon their strength as well as yours and mine." No, I didn't really want Dan with me, but I was still conscious of the need to make our renewed friendship plausible for Jimmie.

"If you think you will need them, they may come," agreed Vanora somewhat grudgingly. "Everyone else can remain here."

"Who knows how much longer I have before I will pass on?" asked Jimmie loudly. "I want to spend my time with Dan and Tal!"

"It might be dangerous..." Dan started to say.

Jimmie looked at him and grinned. "Dan, what's she going to do, kill me? I'm...already dead."

"If he gets to go, I get to go," insisted Khalid. Vanora rolled her eyes and looked at me.

"We may as well let Khalid go," I said. "Alcina's magic didn't seem to affect him at Goleta Beach; besides, he's going to find a way to sneak down no matter what we do. As for Jimmie, even if Alcina were at full power, there's nothing she could do to him."

"In that case, I should go too," said Eva. "I want to be there for Carla if she comes back, and if my strength was good enough to borrow on Halloween, I would imagine it is still good enough. I can contribute as well as any of the guys."

"I don't think—" started Dan.

"It's not your choice!" snapped Eva.

Awkward silence followed, but only for a few seconds. Then, again pretending to come to Dan's rescue, I suggested that we should go to Alcina's cell as quickly as possible. With some degree of relief, everyone got up quickly and followed Vanora down a long hallway to a large iron door.

"I apologize that there is no elevator, and the dungeon is down several flights," said Vanora as she moved toward the door.

"The dungeon?" asked Carlos.

Vanora rolled her eyes again. "Aside from the conference room and the various offices on this floor, as well as certain modern conveniences elsewhere, Ceridwen carried the medieval-castle metaphor rather far. The architect's plans call the lowest level of Awen a security holding area, but it was made to look very much like a dungeon. From the architect's notes, it appears she explained the design as being intended for a few years down the road, when she planned to start offering tours. She was throwing money at him so fast that I don't think he questioned what he must have seen as harmless eccentricity." One of Vanora's men swung the heavy door open. "Regardless, we have a hike ahead of us, so we had better get started."

The stairs did indeed descend for several stories, and the lighting, provided by fake torches placed in evenly spaced wall sconces, seemed more decorative than useful. Nurse Florence, Vanora and I could all adapt to the situation, and Khalid and Jimmie could both see in the dark, so we made sure the others didn't stumble on the way down.

Finally the stairs came to an end, and we stood before a large, metal-framed door with heavy iron bars.

"The dungeon!" exclaimed Gordy.

One of Vanora's security men opened the door for us, and we moved as quickly as we could into the eerily realistic dungeon, which included stone walls that had been deliberately aged and covered with what I hoped was fake mold, as well as new steel doors painted to look like badly rusted iron.

"How are Morgan and Alcina being kept from casting spells?" asked Carlos.

"Ceridwen must have expected opposition from the Order when she first established herself here," answered Vanora. "Every cell is equipped with chains that will prevent the prisoner from using magic. Ah, here we are." One of her ever-present security men unlocked the door and led us into the semi-dark cell.

"Who's there?" asked Alcina, obviously confused by the numerous shadowy forms crowding around her. The fake torch on the back wall of her cell was particularly unhelpful.

"I'm going to need light for this," I said, knowing I really should be able to look Alcina in the eyes.

"Lover, have you come to rescue me?" she asked, half-mockingly. "Will you be my knight in shining armor?"

Nurse Florence raised her arms and conjured a soft but sufficient light to fill the cell.

The sight of Carla in chains jarred me, but I reminded myself that I was actually seeing Alcina in chains…hopefully not for long, though.

I stepped toward Alcina as she eyed me with interest rather than the suspicion I might have expected. Was she in for a surprise!

My eyes met hers, and I saw her interest turn to horror as she felt the power surge from my eyes to hers. She closed her eyes, and that would slow me a little, but I had already connected, and I could even now sense her feelings changing, softening. I could tell she had already liked me, lusted after me a little, but now the love that she might not be able to feel for anyone on her own was building, spreading to every part of her mind, breaking down her resistance faster than she could rebuild it. Even someone as strong willed as she was could only hold out a few minutes against the power she herself had so painstakingly fashioned. Ah, sweet irony!

"Darling," purred Alcina. "Can we finally be together? I don't know why I didn't realize earlier how much I loved you. Can you ever forgive me?"

"Gladly, Alcina, but I need you to do something for me, something very important."

"Anything!" I was in her mind far enough to know beyond question that she actually meant what she said.

"Give control of the body back to Carla, and do not take it from her no matter what happens."

"Are you sure that is what you want?" asked Alcina sadly.

"Yes, I'm sure. Will you do it for me?"

Alcina nodded. "It will be as you have said." She closed her eyes, and when those eyes opened again, it was Carla looking out of them. Obviously, this was the outcome I had hoped, but I had not expected it to come about so quickly and neatly.

"Tal, you saved me!" she exclaimed, her voice suggesting that she could hardly believe what had happened. "I...I...you have no idea what it was like, being aware of what my body was doing but being unable to control it. Oh, my God! That witch used my body to get to you —"

I took her in my arms as best I could, since the chains had not been removed yet. "You weren't responsible for that or anything else, Carla. If it was anyone's fault, it was my own. I let Morgan fool me in a way that allowed Alcina to escape with your body and put you through so much."

"You couldn't have known what would happen," whispered Carla, giving me an extremely fervid kiss on the lips.

Suddenly I found myself pulling away from Carla, staggering away in fact. My head was spinning.

"Tal, what's wrong? Is it Alcina?" asked Vanora urgently.

"No!" I managed through clenched teeth. "She really is Carla now. I just...I feel ill."

I had been through a lot in the past few years, but aside from the awakening of my past lives, I had never felt as disoriented as this. I couldn't describe exactly what was happening, but I knew something was wrong, subtly but unmistakably.

Then, just as abruptly as I had felt lost, I found myself again. It must have been Carla's kiss. After all, I didn't love her. Only a few feet away was Eva. I could have Carla but didn't want her. I couldn't have Eva but wanted her desperately, wanted her with every ounce of my heart, wanted her beyond reason.

Why torture myself this way when it would be so easy to have her? All I needed was a few minutes alone with her, and she would be mine forever. I could get her to fake a more gradual transition in public, so Nurse Florence and Vanora wouldn't get suspicious. Child's play, when I got to thinking about it.

Once I had solved that problem, I realized I could easily take care of my other unfinished business: Dan. Jimmie would almost certainly be gone soon...and as soon as he was, I would make Dan pay...and pay...and pay. I wouldn't kill him or anything that drastic, but he would know the kind of pain I had felt. It would be so easy to find ways to bring that about. So easy...

God, what was happening to me? How could I even daydream about enslaving Eva? As big a scumbag as Dan was, could I actually sink to his level,—no, to far below his level?

I was myself again, but I might remain so for only a minute. I could already feel some…thing surging back into my mind.

"Dan!" I yelled shrilly. "Take Eva, and get out of here! It isn't safe!" The guys, instantly combat ready, already had their swords out. Even Jimmie had the ice blade out, somewhat awkwardly, and Khalid brandished his dagger.

"What isn't safe, Tal? What's the threat?" demanded Dan.

The dizziness was hitting me again, but I managed another warning, though this one was more like a whisper.

"I am."

CHAPTER 15: LET SLEEPING WIZARDS LIE

Despite all their training, the guys were stunned into virtual immobility by my warning, which they either didn't understand, or didn't want to understand.

"Hold on, Tal! Hold on!" yelled Nurse Florence. "Dan, Eva, do as he says!"

"Get…Carla..out…of the chains, and get me into them!" I managed. Swirling darkness kept trying to engulf my mind. It might succeed again any second. If I was physically restrained and couldn't work magic, at least I wouldn't be a threat to anyone else.

Vanora yelled at her security guard to get the key—evidently no one had seen the need to bring it to the cell—but long before he got back, Khalid managed to pick the lock.

"Those locks are supposed to be impossible to pick," muttered Vanora.

Khalid glanced over at her, and in a totally serious tone replied, "I have mad skills." If I weren't on the verge of sinking into darkness, I would have laughed very hard. It was good to see that Khalid was adjusting so well.

Carlos moved a stunned Carla out of the way. Gordy and Shar helped me sit on the floor, and Nurse Florence clamped the manacles around my wrists. Their cool weight was oddly comforting. Once they were in place, I became aware of Dan and Eva arguing.

"I'm not going anywhere," insisted Eva.

"You are if I have to carry you out of here!" replied Dan, reaching as if to grab her.

"Try it and I'll demonstrate some of the techniques I picked up in my self-defense class." I could tell from her tone that she meant it, and so could Dan. Nonetheless, he was ready to make the attempt, but Nurse Florence stopped him.

"It's all right. You can both stay. Tal isn't a threat now." Then she looked at me. "Tal, hold on. We all have faith in you. Hang on to yourself, and we will figure this out—I promise!"

"How could he be a threat in the first place?" asked Jimmie incredulously. "He's a hero, and he's our friend!"

"Yes, how?" asked Vanora, looking as confused as anyone. "I knew there was a risk, but I was sure he could resist. I have never seen anyone fall to temptation so fast!"

Nurse Florence clearly wanted to say, "I told you so," but instead she settled for a much more classy approach. "He is strong, Vanora, but he's been through so much, had so many unusual experiences. There could be any number of reasons. The important thing now is for us to reinforce his good qualities and help him to fight off his inner darkness."

"I want to help!" Jimmie blurted out. "I'm a ghost; there must be something I can do."

Though I appreciated Jimmie's desire to help, I couldn't imagine what a ghost could do at this point. Fortunately, Nurse Florence had a better imagination right now than I did.

"If Tal lets you in, you can flow into his mind," she said, seemingly thinking out loud as much as talking to Jimmie. "You aren't perfect, Jimmie, but you were a relatively innocent child when you died, and you and Tal have a very real bond. I think you could reinforce his will to resist. No, I know you could. Tal, will you let him in?" I managed a nod. "Jimmie, do you know what to do?"

"I can figure it out," he said quickly. He sheathed his sword, set the scabbard on the floor, and made himself immaterial. He had been solid for so many hours it took him an effort to return to his natural state. Then he became like mist and surrounded me, creating a pulsing, glowing light—a light that could counterbalance my growing darkness.

Having him in my head was a little like being nine again. Aside from the accident, Jimmie had a very happy childhood, and that joy radiated from his soul like sunlight shimmering on water. With him at my side, I felt I could stand against any threat.

Then came the awkward part. *Tal, you and Dan lied to me! You aren't really becoming friends again!*

We may, I replied lamely. *Jimmie, we both want to, for you, but it isn't that simple.*

Make it that simple! demanded Jimmie.

I wondered what would happen if he started having a temper tantrum in my head. Instead, he opened his mind to me, and I saw Dan the way he saw him: larger than life, dependable as a rock, loving unconditionally. I had seen him that way once too. It seemed so long ago now.

Jimmie, right now I need to focus.

Oh, right. We'll talk later.

For the moment, the darkness was being held in check. I no

longer had the sickening feeling that it would overwhelm me.

Nurse Florence and Vanora had organized everyone else for energy sharing, and they stood ready to channel all that energy, including their own, straight at the darkness. They relaxed, however, when they realized that, with Jimmie's considerable help, I was now back in balance…for the moment.

"I think we can get you out of those chains now," said Nurse Florence, bending over me. She unfastened them with surprising ease, and I looked at her quizzically.

"They weren't really latched all the way, Tal. For you to be able to beat this thing, you have to realize that you don't need to be locked up, that you can control the darkness on your own." My jaw dropped. "Well," continued Nurse Florence, "I guess you aren't the only one who ever takes risks."

"But I couldn't have controlled it…without Jimmie, and he won't be here forever."

"You have to keep telling yourself you can control it, Tal. Yes, Jimmie will have to move on, and I think sooner rather than later. But you have taught yourself so much else. You can teach yourself Jimmie's light as well."

She said that with such absolute certainty that I was almost tempted to believe her, but the process seemed too easy somehow. I had gone through so much more than Jimmie! If I had ever had that kind of pure light, I felt it must have faded long ago.

"No Tal, you still have it!" Jimmie thought encouragingly. *"You just don't realize it."*

"His light isn't like a spell I can just duplicate."

"How do you know?" asked Vanora. "You haven't tried."

She had a point, I supposed. I didn't know I could learn spells just by seeing them done, either…until the first time I did it.

"I'm willing to take a shot at it, but we have to have more of a plan than that. I can't risk putting other people in danger. I need to be sure that whatever I am going to do will keep the darkness in check, not just for now…but forever."

"Gwynn would help, I'm sure," said Nurse Florence, "but I am a little reluctant to take your problem to anyone in Annwn, at least right now. Some of the leaders already worry about you. If they learned that you were potentially unstable…"

"Got it," I said. "He's got thousands of faeries in and around his castle, any one of whom might conceivably be a spy. Better not to risk it."

"The Order can study the problem and help you come up with a solution," suggested Vanora.

"But the Order has never dealt with anything like this," countered Nurse Florence. "Their orientation is more the scholarly accumulation of data than prescribing cures for unusual mystic conditions."

"I think they're up to it," replied Vanora somewhat stiffly, "but it is true that it is not what they normally do. The process might take months, and it would be hard to explain Taliesin's frequent absences from home. Still, what else is there?"

"Merlin," I said quietly.

"You know where Merlin is?" asked Stan. "But I thought—"

"No," I corrected, "*I* don't know. The Order does, though, doesn't it?" I looked at Nurse Florence and Vanora. Neither answered immediately, presumably because Merlin was a highly classified subject.

"What makes you think Merlin could help?" asked Vanora evasively.

"You mean aside from the fact he is the only one I know, not counting high-level Annwn faeries, who might know more about magic than I do? Because of his unusual dual nature. His father was a demon, remember. In fact, Merlin told the original Taliesin once that Satan had intended Merlin to be an Antichrist, or at least so his mother told him. She thought she foiled that scheme by having him baptized, but Merlin knew better. The baptism helped, but he told my earlier self often that keeping his demonic side in check required constant self-discipline on his part."

Nurse Florence nodded. "I'm not as expert as you are at interpreting this kind of thing, but looking into you, I can see the darkness. It looks to me much the way the past-life personality looks in Stan and Carla. Aside from being at the other end of the spectrum, it also looks like Jimmie inside of you—a totally separate personality."

I did a quick check myself. "You're right—and that may explain why my case is different from most. When I was first struggling with the chaos in my head following my awakening, Taliesin 1 appeared to me and told me, among other things, that my brain, not knowing what to do with all those memories of past lives, was interpreting each set of memories as a separate personality. What if my brain, having had that kind of experience already, is interpreting the darkness, which would just be temptation in most people, as an entirely separate personality?"

"Or your high power level is endowing the temptation with personality," suggested Vanora. "Either way, it sounds as if it might be worth consulting with Merlin."

"I agree," said Nurse Florence, and then each looked at the other as if both were surprised to find themselves on the same side.

"There is just one problem," continued Vanora.

"Only one?" I said facetiously.

"Yes…but it's a big one. As you guessed, the Order does know where Merlin is, though we aren't supposed to reveal that location. In this case, however, I think the urgent circumstances would justify our doing so."

"That doesn't sound like much of a problem."

"Oh, *that* isn't the problem. Bear with me. I'm sure you recall that it was Nimue, a renegade lady of the lake, who imprisoned Merlin. She used a combination of a confinement spell Merlin created himself and some of her own touches to trap him. No one has ever been able to figure out how to break the spell, and frankly the Order no longer tries, their assumption being that Merlin is probably insane by now and too dangerous to be let out."

"That's actually two problems," I said dejectedly.

"Count them as you wish," said Vanora. "Actually, I believe that healers as accomplished as Viviane and I, aided by your unique insights into mending shattered minds, could probably cure him if he proved to be insane. That still leaves us with the problem of getting him out in the first place."

"Well," said Gordy. "What's the old expression? 'The impossible just takes a little longer.'"

"I don't know," said Shar. "The problem is, Gordy, it sounds as if we don't have much time."

"Where and how is Merlin imprisoned?" I asked. "Let's at least see if the situation provides any clue. Even if people have worked on it for centuries, it can't hurt to have some fresh perspectives."

"We can only have one, I'm afraid—yours!" thought Vanora. *"The Order might understand why I have to tell you about Merlin, but they won't understand my telling a large number of civilians, even if some of them are*

your men."

"*OK, then. Tell me what you can,*" I said reluctantly. I would have like to share the information with everyone, but I knew better than to try to argue Vanora out of her caution, and I was getting little jolts of pain from Jimmie, a potent reminder of how limited our time might be.

"*The physical location tied to the trap is Bryn Myrrdin, to the east and a little to the north of Carmathen, where Merlin was born. He is said to be trapped in a cave there, but the cave is just a portal to Annwn, where the real trap is: an enormous tower of unbreakable glass, utterly without any imperfection through which Merlin could have escaped by shape-shifting.*"

"*When you say 'unbreakable,' what do you mean? What have people used on it in the past?*"

Vanora gave me a laundry list of every destructive force known to humankind.

"*What? No one tried to nuke it yet?*" I thought.

"*You know perfectly well that complex technologies don't work in Annwn,*" replied Vanora. "*But as you can see, pretty much everything except weapons of modern warfare has been tried on the tower.*"

"*I can get magic to work on technology; perhaps I can get technology to work in a magical realm. It might not even take a nuke. For all we know, a machine gun might do the trick. Anything Nimue didn't anticipate could conceivably—*"

"*Don't even think about it,*" thought Vanora so vehemently that the connection between us almost broke. "*That is the very thing some of Annwn's leaders are worried you might try. One of the great protections of Annwn is that technology doesn't work in it, and they are not about to give up that advantage. Even contemplating such a thing might be enough to have one or more of them send assassins after you.*"

"*OK, OK, I won't try that, but let's make a quick trip to Carmathen and at least see where we stand.*"

Making a quick trip with Nurse Florence or Vanora whisking me through Annwn would have been easy enough. It was deciding who else was going to go that made the process hard—and time consuming. Nurse Florence, Vanora, Jimmie—since he was helping to fend off the darkness—and I were a given. Beyond that, consensus broke down almost completely.

Carla wanted to go, even more after someone with loose lips—I suspect Gordy—told her that my love for her had been the product of magic. She desperately wanted to talk to me, so, with Vanora fussing in the background, I gave her the opportunity to talk. Ironically, once she had the chance, she didn't really know what to say. (Having been there myself, I couldn't help but sympathize.) Finally, she worked up to saying what she would never have forgiven herself for not saying.

"Tal, I know that somehow, without meaning to, I made you love me. I'm sorry that happened, but it doesn't change the fact that I do love you—for real—and I have for months. Can we at least date and see what happens?" Carla was beautiful enough to have almost any guy she wanted; why did she have to fixate on me, especially now?

"Carla, I really do like you, and maybe something would happen eventually if we went out, but right now I'm in love with somebody else. Do you really want to be with a guy whose heart is somewhere else?"

"Yes," she said, tearing up a little, "if that guy is you."

Crap!

"How about this? Right now there is something seriously wrong with me. Let's postpone this discussion until I know if someone can fix it. Right now I don't know if I have anything to offer. I may end up under lock and key in some obscure part of Wales, and you'll never even see me again." The last touch of drama, which I intended to be a little tongue-in-cheek, pushed Carla too far, and she started crying, which meant I took her in my arms, which meant Vanora looked nothing short of exasperated—a look that didn't soften when Carla announced that she was going with me.

"You need to rest," insisted Vanora, "and this trip could be dangerous."

"It was dangerous on the roof at Halloween, too," snapped Carla, "so dangerous that I ended up possessed, or whatever, and then in a coma, and then possessed again…only that time you were fine with it. You even brought some of us on to the roof and into that very danger."

"At Sam…Halloween you were already trapped," said Vanora quietly, but with fire in her eyes. "If Taliesin's efforts on the roof had failed, you would all have died anyway. All I did was bring you up so you could help him and have a chance at survival. Here the situation is different. You aren't trapped. You can stay here and be in no danger at all. And that is what you are going to do, like it or not!"

"Really?" asked Carla, eyes flashing. "You're going to have to hold me here by force…and that will make quite a story for the newspapers, won't it? Especially since I'm supposed to be in the hospital!"

"Don't threaten me, young lady!" I could tell Vanora was getting pretty close to exploding. "I can erase your memories of everything since you went into that coma and return you to the hospital with no one being any the wiser. That's exactly what I will do, too, if you don't stay here willingly."

Even before her awakening, Carla had a little magic of her own, and I could feel energy building around her, as I was sure Vanora could as well. Though an untrained Carla would be no match for Vanora, the fact that she had magic might make it harder to do a clean memory erasure on her, especially if the erasure was involuntary.

"The way I see it," began Nurse Florence, "if we can't get Merlin out, or if he is benign when we do, there is no danger. If, on the other hand, Merlin is insane and attacks us, we will need all the help we can get."

"No!" I said forcefully. "I made the mistake of letting people come to Awen on Samhain, people like Carla who shouldn't have been there, and she paid the price. I'm not going to make the same mistake again. I'm with Vanora on this one."

Carla looked at me as if I had rejected her again, but she was not going to be deterred. "Tal, who made you the boss of me? You do not tell me where I can and cannot go. And guess what? I would have come on Halloween, even knowing what was going to happen to me. I would have come to help you. I will come this time to help you." She looked around, daring anyone to contradict her.

"David feels strongly that I should go," said Stan. "He says that is the only way he can watch over you and me properly."

"You have to take Dan. You and he need to spend time together so you can become friends again!" insisted Jimmie.

"If you might have to face a crazy Merlin, then you need me and Zom," observed Shar.

"If you are taking some of your…warriors, then you should take all of us, just in case," insisted Gordy. "What if there are guards to overcome?"

"Merlin has never seen the power in my sword, so he won't be expecting it," put in Carlos. Considering Govannon had given Carlos's sword a custom-made power, he was probably right.

"What if getting to Merlin involves picking locks?" asked Khalid.

"You have to take me." He noticed Vanora was glaring at him and added, "Remember, mad skills."

"I'm going," said Eva quietly. Like Carla, she could conceivably lend us her strength if needed, but she would be a serious distraction to me if I had to worry about her safety.

"Carla and Eva need to stay here," I said firmly. "They are the most vulnerable to attack." Carla looked angrily in my direction, and I could feel magic crackling around her again.

"Tal, earlier I offered Dan a demonstration of my self-defense skills, but perhaps you would like one as well," Eva said with false sweetness.

"Eva, I can't even guarantee you are safe with me, much less with Merlin."

Well, if Carla hadn't figured out from earlier who I was in love with, that statement would certainly make my feelings clear, but I couldn't help that. She was going to find out eventually anyway.

"We are wasting precious time," said Nurse Florence impatiently. "Tal is fine right now, but we don't know for how long. How long Jimmie can function inside Tal is another wild card. We need to move now. Everyone is going, and that's the end of it."

I could tell Vanora was furious, especially since she had made clear earlier that she outranked Nurse Florence, but she apparently thought better of trying to argue further. After all, if there was any wisdom to be had from Merlin, Nurse Florence was right—we had to get it soon. I could feel spasms running through Jimmie every so often, and my own head was starting to ache.

Once we had reached that tenuous agreement, all that remained was for everyone to gather up what they needed, not a hard task, considering that most of the guys were wearing their weapons. I did notice a little argument between Eva and Carla over who should carry the ice sword, an argument resolved by Gordy grabbing it away from both of them. Was this argument the first fruits of Carla finding out it was Eva I loved? Only time would tell.

When we finally bounced into Annwn and out on Bryn Myrrdin (Merlin's Hill), I realized we should have brought warmer clothing. The weather had been relatively mild for December the night we visited Glastonbury Tor, but this night wasn't. The land was blanketed with snow; the wind tore at us like ice fangs, ripping right through our California clothing. Fortunately, Vanora was prepared to do what needed to be done, said the appropriate incantation, and opened the hidden cave in the side of the hill.

"Step through quickly, everyone," she said briskly. "Then walk to the back of the cave. There is a fixed portal there that will take us back into Annwn, right at the spot Merlin's tower is. Once we are there, we shouldn't feel this cold any more." Urged on more by the bleak winter weather than by her words, everyone got into the cave quickly and crowded to the back, after which Nurse Florence sealed the cave, and Vanora opened the portal. In less than a minute, we were back in Annwn, looking at the most incredible structure I had ever seen.

The tower rose from the middle of a relatively thick forest and seemed to reach clear into the clouds, though it was hard to tell against the night sky. A moon larger than Earth's, at least from our viewpoint, was shining full in that sky, and its light made every inch of the tower sparkle as if a million stars had been used to build it.

Knowing the way my life worked, you might have guessed that we couldn't just walk up to the tower, and you would have been right. We had taken only a few steps away from the portal when the vegetation around us began to attack. Nurse Florence and Vanora both seemed surprised as vines tried to immobilize our limbs, thorns tried to tear our flesh, and tree limbs tried to dash out our brains. Apparently the Order's records had not alluded to this particular defense mechanism.

I would have liked to charm the vegetation to stay away from us, but I sensed it was under the grip of too powerful a spell, and in any case, there wasn't really enough time, so I drew White Hilt and started burning through our leafy opponents. Gordy, realizing the ice sword was more effective in this case than the fear one, froze everything he could hit. Shar broke the enchantment on whatever he hit, rendering it immobile. All the other guys just hacked away, but since faerie weapons could cut pretty much whatever they hit, they still made good headway. Even Khalid's faerie dagger did its share of damage.

I didn't have the nerve to point out that Eva's self-defense course wasn't helping her much in this situation, but I'm sure she realized that herself. She and Carla were constantly getting into trouble and having to be rescued, much to the embarrassment of both of them. (And no, I'm not being sexist. If they had decent weapons, they could probably at least have protected themselves, even without training. This wouldn't have been a good place for anyone to be unarmed, even a guy.)

After two hours of hard fighting, we had cut a wide swath through the forest, leading from the portal to the base of the tower. Fortunately, the immediate area around the tower was clear of vegetation, and no wandering vines tried to grab us once we had reached that area. That, at least, was something.

My muscles ached by that time. Jimmie, probably unused to being in someone else's body, was having a hard time holding on, my headache was getting to be about the size of San Francisco, and I could feel the darkness stirring, sensing an opportunity.

Yeah, it was something to be "out of the woods"—until the ground next to the tower turned suddenly into water, and we all dropped into it like rocks.

Clearly, this was not normal water. It shined like water in the moonlight, but it seemed thicker somehow, harder to swim through, yet also easier to sink into: a magical concoction that was simultaneously lighter and heavier than ordinary water.

Since it was hard to swim and cast spells at the same time, and since I wouldn't have known what to do with this arcane muck anyway, magic was not much help in this situation. Some of us might have drowned if not for Carlos. He had said to me recently that he sometimes felt "like a fish out of water" on our adventures, because he wasn't quite as good a swordsman as the others and didn't feel as useful. This time, though, his experience as an aquatic athlete was all that stood between some of us and death.

Shar, probably because of Zom's anti-magic properties, stood on one lone piece of solid land, and he could get the water to pull away from the blade, but the water filled in right after. He was safe, but he was unable to help others. Gordy, Dan, Stan (with his muscle-enhancing sword) and I managed (just barely) to keep ourselves from drowning, but we couldn't have simultaneously rescued someone else. Our two ladies of the lake found themselves powerless against this not-exactly-water, and Eva and Carla were just not strong enough swimmers. Carlos was the only swimmer powerful enough to rescue the ladies and then help the rest of us get to shore. I managed to magick up his stamina, and he fell down exhausted right after, but he had gotten the job done somehow.

Well, we were still alive, but we had no obvious way to approach the tower. Khalid could have jumped over the water, but then what?

Climb up the tower? The surface was too slippery, and anyway climbing the surface would have done no good. I could have flown over, but then what? We needed to be able to stand next to the tower and really examine it. Or did we?

"Vanora, has anyone ever tried hitting the tower with two extremes simultaneously, like very hot and very cold?"

"Not that I know of," replied Vanora.

"Gordy, please give me the ice sword." He handed it over, and I held it in my left hand, with White Hilt in my right. It took me a few minutes to manipulate both swords at the same time, especially with my intensifying headache, but I managed to do it, and then I sprayed the left of the tower with ice, simultaneously engulfing the right in flame. The tower had resisted the two opposite forces individually before, but never both at once—until now.

My best efforts, cold enough to freeze a big lake, hot enough to burn a forest, produced no visible change in the tower. I had been hoping that opposing tendencies to expand or contract, depending on temperature, might have caused cracking, but if so, it was undetectably small. After that I had to take a rest and have Nurse Florence and Vanora reinforce my control. My exertion had almost weakened me enough for the darkness to have another shot at taking over, and Jimmie, still hanging on valiantly, was putting out a much more pale and flickering light than the pure radiance he had started with. If there was an answer here, we needed to find it quickly.

Then it hit me. "Vanora, how about sonic vibrations?"

She froze for a second. "Well, no, I don't think so. There was no real way to weaponize sound that way in earlier times. I suppose spells could have been designed for that, but sorcerers typically went after more obviously destructive forces like fire. People knew the story of Joshua and the trumpets at the battle of Jericho, but everyone assumed that feat was done by the power of God and could not be replicated by men. I doubt it would have occurred to Nimue to defend against that kind of attack."

"Great!" I could see light at the end of the tunnel now. "Vanora, could you and Nurse Florence enclose everyone else in a soundproof bubble. What I want to try could be deafening." I waited until they figured out how to do that, and then I went to work.

I began by singing a song of liberation in Welsh, letting magical power build as I did so. I had to experiment to figure out how to do what

I wanted, but it did not take me too long to figure out how to modulate the sound of my voice, making it progressively louder and higher in pitch. It wasn't long before I was hitting the tower with wave after wave of extremely high-frequency sound far more powerful than anything a human voice could ever produce naturally.

From Taliesin 1's studies of magic I knew that even the most powerful magic could not produce an object that was truly indestructible. The universe always seemed to insist that there be some flaw, however small, in that invulnerability. Since the magic was shaped by the mind using it, Nimue's world view might determine what kind of flaws existed in the tower; if she didn't see something as a threat, she might not have protected against it specifically.

Great…in theory. However, she could have taken the Jericho story to heart and sound-proofed the tower, in which case I was wasting my time. For all I knew, throwing pomegranates at the tower would bring it down. I could spend years testing different methods—except that I didn't have years. More like minutes. I could feel the darkness rising again, and Jimmie was hanging on by his fingernails.

Then, just when I was about to give up, I began to see the tower vibrating, and I knew there was a chance. The chance became a certainty when I could hear a cracking sound, and shortly afterward, cracks became visible, weaving their way across the entire tower. Finally the tower gave way in one highly satisfying crash, making the most enormous pile of glass shards I could imagine. They still sparkled in the moonlight, but they were no longer a prison. Assuming the crash hadn't killed Merlin—yeah, that thought did cross my mind—then he should be free now.

The others, finally able to leave their sound-proof bubble, cheered. We had accomplished the first part of our mission.

Much to my relief, I could see a figure rising from the ruined tower. Who could it be but Merlin?

As the figure flew closer, my relief crashed as completely as the tower.

He was Merlin all right, or at least what little was left of him. His robe was tattered, his hair wildly uncombed, his eyes lit not by insanity but by hellfire. During his fifteen hundred years trapped in the tower, his demonic side had apparently taken over completely.

Yeah, you heard right—we were facing the dark version of perhaps the most powerful wizard who ever lived, and from his facial expression, he was not putting out the welcome mat...unless he intended to make one out of our skin!

CHAPTER 16: DARKNESS IS THE NEW LIGHT

"Prepare to die!" yelled the demonic Merlin in a booming voice as he shot toward me. Yeah, nothing like the direct approach.

My best bet was to reach Shar and get my hands on Zom. A couple good blasts of anti-magic should render even Merlin helpless, at least for a short time. Unfortunately, we hadn't moved into a tight formation as we should have, and I was some distance away from the others. Merlin saw which direction I was running and sprayed the area between me and the group with fire bursts, creating a wall of flame between us that burned so hot I could feel it from yards away.

Having isolated me, he started aiming the fire directly at me. I used White Hilt to surround myself in my own flame and absorb the hostile blasts, but the strategy just barely worked. Just as the water around the tower had been unlike normal water, Merlin's fire was unlike normal fire. It burned hotter, yet it seemed somehow to move more slowly, almost as if it were heavier. If I wasn't careful, the stuff would drip right through my fire shield. Preventing that result required considerable maneuvering, and I was already so tired from shattering the tower, a situation complicated by the darkness within me, which seemed to be doing flip-flops as Merlin got closer. Jimmie? He was still there, his light flickering like a single candle. I guess ghosts could become exhausted in this kind of supernatural struggle, and his strength was pretty close to gone.

In an effort to confuse Merlin, I raised myself to faerie speed and scrambled, not toward the rest of my group, but off to one side. Frankly, I didn't want to risk Merlin trying to fire bomb everyone else before they could get close enough to Shar. Despite his great power, Merlin's speed was that of a normal human, and it did not seem to occur to him to speed himself up, so for a while at least my efforts to dodge him worked, though it was not long before his hot, slow fire was burning in undulating patches all over the place. Somewhere I could feel Vanora and Nurse Florence pooling their resources for some kind of defensive spell, but I doubted they would have much luck against the kind of off-beat, high intensity magic that Merlin could throw at them. Still, I guessed some protection was better than none.

I wondered what was happening to the guys. By now Shar, whom Zom made immune to any magic fire, even Merlin's, should be close, but I saw no sign of him. Then I realized I was hearing the sound of swords biting into wood. Looking in the general direction of the sounds, I could see a little over the wall of fire, just enough to make out waving branches, and I realized that some more distant part of the forest had sneaked up while everyone was watching me and had attacked as soon as Merlin was free.

I was wearing down a little, slowing, and Merlin's fiery attacks were getting closer. Not only that, but the darkness was surging again; Jimmie's presence was now too faint to stop it, though he was still struggling valiantly against it. I needed more of a plan than just taking evasive action, but my head was pounding worse than ever. I also thought the increasingly pervasive smoke was beginning to get to me. I could smell it everywhere, my lungs ached, and my breathing was getting ragged.

Suddenly Khalid was at my side, dagger in hand. "Tal, what can I do?"

"Get back, Khalid! Merlin may not be able to burn you, but he could switch attacks at any moment."

"That's assuming he sees me coming!" he said with a grin, and then he was gone, moving faster than I could right at that moment. He ran fast as lightning across the burning land, then shot straight up in the air, straight at Merlin, dagger glinting in the firelight.

Khalid was faster than Merlin, but Merlin had seen him coming, figured out he was immune to fire, and, with one flash of lightning from his hands, swept Khalid from the sky, sending him tumbling toward the ground at sickening speed. Merlin had not had the time to conjure maximum power; even so, it was clear Khalid was gravely injured—and Merlin could always take another shot.

At that moment I had been on the verge of succumbing to the darkness, but seeing Khalid in trouble, maybe even dying, sent my adrenaline clear off the charts. Without really knowing what I was doing, I shot light into that darkness, much grayer perhaps than what Jimmie had been able to project at his full strength, but enough to check the darkness's relentless advance. At the same time, I flew with bullet-like speed at the falling Khalid, grabbed him in midair, and cannonballed toward the rest of my party. Merlin might follow, but now I had to risk it. I was not the healer Nurse Florence or Vanora was, but I could tell Khalid needed one. I could see the electrical burn on his left side, not looking so bad on the surface but extending, I was sure, much deeper into his tissues. I could feel him shaking in my arms, shaking almost convulsively.

Unfortunately, I could not easily fly, wield White Hilt, and carry Khalid, so at the moment I was unshielded, and Merlin, as I could have readily predicted, was following, shooting fire in all directions.

"Tal, I need to leave for a minute.

I was shocked to hear Jimmie again. I had thought he was too weak to communicate, but now he seemed revived. Well, he was in me; maybe he was getting secondhand adrenaline. Maybe he had been relieved, if only momentarily, of the strain of fighting the darkness.

"Whatever you need, Jimmie," I thought back quickly, then turned my attention to dodging Merlin's fire bolts.

I don't know what I thought Jimmie needed to leave for, but I suddenly realized he was flying…straight at Merlin! I didn't exactly have eyes in the back of my head, and I couldn't see through the eyes of a ghost the same way I could those of a living person, but I could sense enough to realize what was happening.

Jimmie caused Merlin to hesitate, which was odd, considering how little a single ghost could do against Merlin. Then again, Jimmie was taking advantage of the flexibility of his ghostly form and no longer bore even the slightest resemblance either to Jimmie as a child or as a teenager. Instead, borrowing an image from a storybook he had loved when he was six, he was an angel, several stories tall, with a wingspan the greatest of dragons would envy.

"Halt, wizard!" a very un-Jimmie-like voice boomed loudly enough to shake the ground.

Merlin would see through the elaborate display Jimmie was putting on in a matter of seconds, but those seconds proved just enough for me to reach Nurse Florence and Vanora with Khalid. His shaking was subsiding, but, as far as I could tell, only because his heartbeat was faltering. He was just moments away from cardiac arrest when I handed him over. Thank God the guys had chopped most of the attacking trees into kindling, or the ladies of the lake might have been under attack themselves, unable to help.

Shar ran in my direction, realizing Zom was needed against Merlin, and presumably using every ounce of willpower he had not to run over to Khalid's side. The other guys were more than enough to handle the few surviving trees in the area.

By now Merlin had flown straight through the illusionary angel that was Jimmie and was heading straight for us. Shar continued to hold

Zom, but I put my hand on its hilt, and as I had done at Goleta Beach, I shot a brilliant emerald ray of anti-magic straight at Merlin, praying he was not somehow immune. He shouldn't be, of course, but with someone as powerful as Merlin, one could never tell what surprises he might have up his sleeve.

I could have imagined any number of possible outcomes when that blast connected with Merlin, but what actually happened was beyond imagining. The man, who was perhaps the greatest wizard the world had ever seen, exploded in a burst of emerald flame at the touch of Zom's power, and clouds of ashes swirled in all directions from the explosion.

For a second I thought we must have destroyed some mere illusion, but I had seen Zom strike illusions before, and they simply vanished, with no explosion, no flame, no ashes. Morgan Le Fay had been hit with the same kind of blast that Merlin had suffered, and she had merely been stripped of her active spells and unable to cast any more for a short time. For reasons I could not begin to explain, the touch of Zom had been fatal to Merlin, despite his much greater power. Perhaps that was it—his power had tried to resist, and the friction between it and Zom had destroyed Merlin. Whatever had happened, he was gone, even his ashes now dispersed by the winds of Annwn.

"Merlin is dead! We're safe!" shouted Shar. Then he immediately turned his attention to Khalid, over whom Vanora and Nurse Florence were laboring as if their lives, not his, depended upon it.

Yeah, we're safe—from Merlin. But without him, you're not safe from me. He was my only hope for beating the darkness.

At the moment, the darkness remained at bay, but I was sure it would not be long before it began to eat its way through my defenses. Despite that, I helped the rest of the guys finish off the last couple of trees. That would not prevent the more distant parts of the forest from moving in this direction, but for the moment, everyone could focus on Khalid.

Nurse Florence and Vanora were both trying to heal him, with Carla feeding energy to Vanora and Eva doing so with Nurse Florence. However much they might have cramped the style of the guys earlier by needing to be defended, their assumption that their energy might be needed had proved well-founded. At least Khalid had not died, so there was still hope, but I could sense his vital signs were very faint; bringing someone back from that close to death was always difficult at best.

I knew what I had to do. I had already discovered that I seemed to be able to master magic cast in my presence even if I wasn't in much of a position to pay attention, and I could feel deep within me the spell that Nurse Florence had used to dump practically all of her energy into me. Using it might render me, as it had her, dangerously close to death, but I was confident my life-force would be enough to save Khalid, and since my body was basically uninjured, I figured Vanora and Nurse Florence could more easily bring me back than they could Khalid.

Well, that was what I told myself, anyway. Nurse Florence had only been saved that night by the wish from Khalid's dagger, and we were fresh out of wishes. Of course, Nurse Florence had only had Vanora to heal her, and I had both of them, so I might be all right.

Hell, what if I wasn't? Did I care? Maybe this was my fate: to end my life in a noble way, giving it up for Khalid, sparing everyone else un-believable danger when I inevitably succumbed to the darkness that I could only have found my way out of with Merlin's help, help I could now never have. I don't want you to think I was suicidal. I wanted to live every bit as much as the next guy. But live instead of Khalid, who was only in danger because he insisted on throwing himself into all of my ad-ventures? Live and be a threat to my family and friends for the rest of my life?

I hesitated, but only for a moment. Then I took Khalid's hand in my own, and downloaded my life-force into him before anyone could try to argue me out of it. In seconds I had filled him, at the cost of emptying myself. I let go of his hand and fell to the hard ground.

As usual, there was at least one thing I hadn't considered: with my energy gone, I had nothing with which to fight the darkness—and the darkness knew it. It rose up, like a tidal wave that reached clear to the sky and beyond, ready to submerge me, wash me away, forever. All I could do was watch, thinking, "Let it come." In the end, I would have the last laugh. I could feel myself dying. The darkness might take over, but only for a few seconds. Then it would die with me. Surely, that was what was meant to happen all along.

Abruptly, there was another presence within me. Jimmie, still looking like an angel, had re-entered my body, and was hacking away at the darkness with his sword. His light had revived a little from what it was before, but I knew he could not last long now without rest. Surely that display he had used to slow down Merlin must have taken some effort, and I had seen how fast the darkness had drained him of light before.

What would happen if Jimmie were still in my body when I died? Would he have to experience death again? I needed to tell him to get out before I died, but I somehow couldn't communicate with him.

Jimmie, Jimmie! Get out!

No dice! The harder I tried, the more remote from him I seemed.

Then I felt another presence, warm and insistent.

Carla? No, Alcina!

Great! Seeing me dying must have overridden my strict orders to stay submerged. I couldn't seem to communicate with her, either, so I couldn't order her away, but the damage to Carla was probably already done. If the ties I had created between them had been torn apart, as they had been in Stan when David emerged, nobody but me could fix them—and I was still dying.

Alcina apparently specialized in love spells and controlling marine life. I didn't feel much healing power within her, though she was trying to do something, perhaps sustain me until someone with more of a healing touch was free. Despite her, though, I could feel myself still slipping away second by second.

Next I felt Nurse Florence. I wanted to scream, "NO! Finish with Khalid," but I sensed she had. Weary, she was fighting just as hard to save me, but she needed more energy from somewhere. I didn't feel as if I was slipping toward death anymore, but I wasn't move any further away from it, either.

Then I felt Stan…no, David. I felt David praying over me. Damn! I told them both not to do this. Could I put Stan back together after yet another rending of the bonds between him and David? I doubted it.

I had hoped that if I had to die, at least my friends would all be all right. Now it looked as if Carla would be a mess and Stan would be a mess. Hell, a few minutes ago I had been ready to die if I needed to. Now the universe, with its usual bad timing, seemed to be trying to tell me I still needed to live…and there wasn't a damn thing I could do to save myself at this point.

Then I got a real shock: I could feel Dan in my head. I recoiled from him. I suppose I should have been happy for any help, but I still wasn't ready to forgive him, much less to trust him. Fortunately, I realized after just a few seconds that he was not so much in my mind as reaching through it to connect with Jimmie. How he managed that I didn't know, but they were brothers, and Jimmie did seem to know his way around the supernatural, so perhaps Jimmie somehow drew him in. Anyway, he started channeling his energy to Jimmie, whose light grew brighter almost immediately, pushing the darkness back much faster. Jimmie's sword cuts also seemed to wound the darkness more deeply; Dan knew how to handle a sword much better than Jimmie did.

Now I could also feel Vanora doing her part with an almost fanatical determination. I guess she didn't want her predictions about my future greatness to be proved wrong. God, I was at death's door, she was trying to save me, and I still couldn't see her in a positive light. Was I just the biggest jerk ever…or was I picking up on something about her that wasn't quite right?

Now I could feel myself getting a little stronger, but the change was so small that it might just have been my imagination. At the very least, I had stuck my friends with hours of hard labor to rescue me…and who knows when another group of trees or some other menace would attack? With me in my current state, they would be at a disadvantage in a combat situation.

Before I had time to worry about that, however, I got hit by the biggest mystic power surge I had ever felt in my life. It was as if every spell caster in Annwn had simultaneously started pouring energy into Nurse Florence and Vanora. I was filled with blinding light that tore through the darkness as if it were old and rotting cloth. It gave me such a jolt, however, that I sank into unconsciousness before I could figure out what was happening.

CHAPTER 17: ONE "LAST" TWIST

I returned to consciousness gradually. First, I was aware of lying on the ground. Then I started smelling things burning nearby. Merlin's fires must still be blazing. I could sense several people around me, but that jolt of power had given me such a psychic overload that I couldn't read more than their presences, at least for the moment. I opened my eyes and saw it was still night in Annwn. Carla—or was it Alcina?—was bending over me.

"He's awake!" she shouted to everyone else. Then she turned quickly back to me. "Tal, you're going to be all right," she told me gently as she put her hand on my cheek.

Tal? Not Taliesin?

My mind reading was coming back a little, but only in tiny flashes. Still, it seemed to me as if the person looking into my eyes was Carla. How could that have happened? Perhaps it was better not to look a gift horse in the eyes.

"You will not ever do something like that again!" I couldn't move my head much, but I recognized Vanora from the voice and general tone—giving orders, as usual.

"If I have to save Khalid, or anybody else—except maybe Dan— I will." I was going for an authoritative tone, but my voice came out in a whisper, my intended strength lost. The Dan part? Maybe that was a joke, maybe not. I wasn't completely sure myself, though I guessed I would have to save him, if only for Jimmie's sake.

Nurse Florence came and knelt beside me. "When are you going to stop acting on impulse like that?"

"Maybe in my next life," I whispered and grinned a little bit. At least I thought I was grinning. My face felt kind of numb.

"If you are up to it, Tal, you have a visitor." Suddenly I snapped into a higher state of alertness. A visitor in Annwn? Gwynn perhaps? But how would he have found us? I tried to sit up, but the effort was not entirely successful, and I had to lie back down again.

"Yes, I'd like to see the visitor," I managed. "It seems rude not to."

Nurse Florence smiled and stepped aside. Suddenly bending over me was—no, I had to be hallucinating! I had seen Merlin explode, yet here he was, and looking quite sane and perfectly non-demonic. Just the opposite, in fact. He was once again the benevolent, dignified figure that I remembered, every gray hair in place, beard neatly trimmed, robe spotless except for the subtle arcane designs upon it. In his right hand he carried the highly polished wooden staff that I also remembered well. Before the explosion he had not had it.

"I saw you die," I whispered lamely.

Merlin laughed heartily. "Taliesin, surely you don't think you could have defeated me so easily! And I'm hurt you think I would ever let my demonic side take over."

"Then what was…"

"Oh, just a little creation," said Merlin dismissively. "He was intended to be a test for anyone who managed to release me from the tower."

"He almost killed Khalid!" I said, suddenly angry.

"That would be a good reason to avoid taking children on quests," said Merlin, with just a hint of scolding in his voice. "Rather an odd group of companions you have. The warriors make sense, though their armor is certainly strange, and they appear to be rather a young group. I suppose the two ladies of the lake make sense, though, as you might imagine, I wouldn't trust a lady of the lake myself. But a child, a child ghost, two ordinary women? When we were at Camelot together, you understood our duty to protect women." I could see Eva in the distance, clearly annoyed, clearly wanting to say something. Merlin's presence, however, was so overwhelming that she did not.

"They are…more than what they appear," I replied.

"They would have to be a great deal more to justify bringing them here. Be that as it may, I did not come to argue with you, Taliesin; I came to help you."

"We came here hoping you could help. I would be honored to receive your assistance."

Merlin bowed in acknowledgment. "And help I shall. The ladies of the lake have told me of your current life and your…unusual nature. Indeed, I once foresaw how part of this might come to pass." I recalled that Merlin had the gift of prophecy, though he never got quite as much from it as he would have liked.

"You never told me, uh, the original Taliesin."

"The knowledge would have done him no good. He would have forgotten it all before his next reincarnation, and it would have been lost until your awakening in this life—after which it would have done you little good to know that I had foreseen your awakening."

"Merlin, you obviously kept control of your demonic side even through a millennium and a half of imprisonment. I have come to you for advice on how to keep the darkness within me in check."

"Yes," said Merlin, stroking his beard thoughtfully. "Unfortunately, your situation is not the same as mine. When you, or as you would say, the original Taliesin, still known as Gwion Bach, drank those three drops of wisdom from the cauldron of Ceridwen, his mind, and now yours, became different from that of anyone who has ever lived or anyone who ever will live—at least until you finally relinquish that gift to another. My own dual nature is simple compared to what you are. From what I have been told, and from what I can sense, your past- life memories originally functioned as separate personalities within you."

"That is true, but the darkness is not a past-life memory."

"You rush to conclusions as you rush into everything else, young Taliesin. I know the darkness is not a past-life memory. It is the evil inside of you, just as each one of us has a darkness within that is the embodiment of our own evil. My evil requires more self-discipline than usual to master, because of my demonic ancestry. In your case self-discipline alone will not suffice."

"But why?" I said, my voice finally rising above a whisper but sounding far whinier than I intended. "What is it that makes mine so different?"

Merlin gave me an enigmatic smile that I remembered well from his encounters with the original Taliesin. "You know the answer to that question yourself."

Oh, good! Are we going to do riddles next?

"But I don't...wait! You're trying to tell me my brain is treating my evil side like a separate personality, just as it originally treated each set of past-life memories as a separate personality. Nurse Florence and I both sensed that earlier."

"Then you know what you have to do," said Merlin, giving me another smile.

"But I'm not sure the problem is really that simple. If my evil side has really become a separate personality, then shouldn't my regular personality be all good? Yet I don't feel any different!"

"Your 'evil side,' as you call it, didn't really split off and leave the rest of you all good. The reality is more like someone copied all of your evil impulses and gathered them into a separate personality. It is the way your mind dealt with the increased intensity and complexity of those evil impulses. Unfortunately, that leaves the evil both within you *and* outside you at the same time, both ready to subvert you from within and to take you over from without.

"But enough theory! Now it is time for action. The way you brought all of your past memories into your present life personality—it is that same way that you must master your dark side. Once you have done that, you will still need to resist temptation, as all of us do, but at least the darkness won't remain a different being who could conceivably take over your body."

"Are you strong enough to face that process right now, Tal?" asked Nurse Florence. "Should we lend you more energy?"

"I'm actually starting to feel pretty much like my old self. And somebody," I said, looking inquiringly at Merlin, "fed me enough energy earlier to practically fry my nervous system."

"I did help the ladies just a bit with your healing," replied Merlin. "I momentarily lost sight of the fact that I could feed them far more power than they actually needed."

"Full of surprises as always!" I said with a little grin. "Speaking of which, how are you suddenly fluent in modern English? I was expecting a chance to practice my Welsh."

Merlin smiled a little. "Nimue trapped my body and my power within the tower, but I still retained the ability to observe what was going on in the world. Perhaps the fact that the tower was glass had something to do with that, or perhaps Nimue allowed me to see the goings on in Annwn and on Earth on purpose. Either way, I had fifteen hundred years or so with nothing to do but observe, so I learned as much as I could, including many languages. Unfortunately, you don't have fifteen hundred years to solve your current problem, so perhaps you should start now."

"Well, no time like the present!" I said, dreading this encounter but knowing that Merlin was right; this was the only chance I had of taming my dark side.

"Wait!" Merlin raised a restraining hand. "The ghost needs to come out first! Using him as a way to counter the darkness was ingenious, but the way your mind works, there is a good chance that he may get trapped in there, fused with your mind just like your past lives."

"Jimmie!" I said urgently. "Did you hear Merlin? Out now."

Jimmie flew out of me in a mist, then assumed a human-sized version of his angel form, his sword still clutched tightly in his hand. "Tal, are you sure?" he asked.

I could already feel the darkness pulsing within me at the realization that Jimmie was no longer protecting me.

"I'm sure, Jimmie. I'll be all right."

"As for the rest of you," said Merlin, making a sweeping gesture that encompassed the whole party, "you need to stay out as well. Lending Taliesin strength under normal circumstances is still possible, but you would be wise to stay out of his mind right now. That means you, too, King of Israel." I wasn't sure why he singled David out, except that David had started moving toward me.

"When Taliesin was in the hospital, unconscious, Stan held his hand," said David sheepishly. I'm not sure Stan would have wanted him to announce that to the whole world, but there was no sense in worrying about that now.

"You may hold his hand while he works," said Merlin quietly, "but do not under any circumstances try to use your position as the Lord's anointed to ask God to give you the power to help Taliesin."

David looked incensed. "Are you forbidding me to pray?"

"I am forbidding you to attempt what you are thinking, to drive out his dark side as if it were an evil spirit that could be exorcised. It is part of him, David, and if you attempt to deal with it in the wrong way, you could shatter Taliesin's mind."

David nodded reluctantly.

"You may pray," Merlin continued, "but only in a general way, for God to support Taliesin. Do not ask God to empower you to do the job yourself, because you don't understand what you are dealing with well enough."

David nodded again, somewhat heartened, and took my right hand in his as I was preparing to lie back on the ground.

Jimmie, eying the situation suspiciously, jumped into Dan, who then came over and took my left hand. I wanted to pull my hand away, but I knew Jimmie was watching through Dan's eyes, so I let my hand rest in his—but only for Jimmie's sake.

By now everyone was gathering around me. Merlin directed them to sit around me in a circle and hold hands with each other, as well as with Dan and David. He did remind them again, however, that none of them who were able must enter my mind. "This is Taliesin's battle. If anyone else tries to interfere, any victory won will be an incomplete one. What he needs to do can be done only by him alone."

"Merlin, can you protect my friends from further attacks by the forest?" I asked. "I need to know they are safe in order to concentrate."

"You need have no fear," replied Merlin. "The trees look as if you and your friends have made them afraid of attacking again, but should they be foolish enough to try anything, it will be the last thing they try."

"Thank you, Merlin. Now I can focus on what needs to be done." I lay all the way down and closed my eyes.

It had been almost four years since I had integrated the memories of all my past lives into my present persona, but I could still remember how to find another personality inside of me, and the darkness was not exactly being subtle, so visualizing where it was and willing myself there was relatively easy.

I found myself in a dismal place crafted from my dark side's imagination. The sky was like a photographic negative: leprous white, studded with black stars and a black moon that radiated shadow rather than light. Nor did the white sky actually radiate light either. I made myself able to see in the dark, just as I might have done in the real world, and I could discern ruins. Looking closely at them, particularly at the streets signs jutting crookedly from the rubble here and there, I could see I was looking at the remains of Santa Brígida. Clearly, my evil self was imagining what it would be like to level the place.

I wandered through the ruined streets, thinking to find my foe where my house would be in the real Santa Brígida, but the house was reduced to rubble just as thoroughly as everything else around it. Then I realized the futility of looking around. I could wander aimlessly in the wreckage for a long time, trying to find him—or it—based on where I would go, but I was not really looking for me; I was looking for the evil part of me.

I tried to ignore the visuals and focus on my psychic senses. Where was there a large concentration of power? That would be where my evil self was. Sure enough, I found a great, pulsing energy at what would have been the other side of town: at Awen, Carrie Winn's "castle," by far the most expensive residence in town. Where else would evil set up headquarters?

In the real Santa Brígida, I would never have dared to fly all the way across town, even invisibly, but in this imaginary shadow of the place, I had nothing to lose. Unfortunately, the view from the air was just as desolate as from the ground, but traveling was faster, and speed was essential.

When I reached Awen's imaginary duplicate, it was even more magnificent than the real one—or would have been, if it was not shrouded in darkness. I flew to the roof, which on the real Awen had been the scene of the great battle on Samhain.

My evil self, seated on a massive black marble throne, was enveloped in throbbing, reddish power. He looked like me—if I had been chiseled out of shadows, and if my eyes had been carved from rubies soaked in blood and lit on fire. When he saw me, he jumped from the throne and drew his equivalent of White Hilt, a blade wrapped in sickly green flame.

"Surrender to me now," he demanded in a B-movie villain parody of my voice, "and I will not have to break you completely. You can recede into some distant corner of your mind and live in whatever pleasant daydream you choose."

"And what will you be doing while I am daydreaming my life away?" I asked, drawing White Hilt.

"I'll be doing what you aren't man enough to do. I'll be with Eva, for example."

"There's only one way to be with Eva," I pointed out, planning my strategy.

"Using dark magic," he said in mock horror. "Well, what of it? She'll never know the difference, and making love with her will feel the same, regardless of how she gets into the bed. But that's just the beginning."

I gestured in the direction of the almost-obliterated town. "Is it going to take destroying everything?"

At first my dark side looked puzzled. At that moment I realized he must be seeing a different reality than what I was seeing. Perhaps he was seeing what he wanted immediately, and I was seeing where his path would eventually lead. To test that theory, I projected my view straight into his head. He looked shocked, but his shock quickly turned to anger.

"What trick is this?"

"No trick! Just what I am seeing of the world you have made."

My dark side, whom I was just deciding to think of as Dark Me, laughed then, but it was a joyless sound. "You are seeing what you want to see. You want to think I am pure evil, but I'm not. I'm just willing to look after myself, not always be the martyr like you want to. You felt my thoughts as I took control in the dungeon. Was I plotting mass destruction?"

He had a point, actually. His initial plans just involved winning Eva and punishing Dan—and he was going to wait until Jimmie was gone for that second part. So he really wasn't absolutely evil...just more evil than I was.

"Maybe you aren't yet as destructive as the surroundings I am seeing would suggest—but I bet this is where your plans will lead."

"How, exactly? I get the girl I love, and I get other things I deserve...we deserve. We are an epically great musician, Tal. Only a live audience can feel the power of our ability to put magic into the music now, but with our technological know-how, we can figure out how that magic effect can be transmitted even if the music isn't live, and then the whole world will soon be under our spell. We'll be the leaders of the greatest band in history. And that will just be the beginning."

I had to admit I had had a fantasy like that...when I was twelve and first realized what I could do. I was wiser now. Maybe I would end up as a musician...but because of my musical talent, not my magic.

"The rulers of Annwn will never tolerate that kind of widespread, semi-public use of magic," I protested. "They don't want anyone in the mortal world to realize that magic is out there. You know they will shut us...you...down."

Dark Me snorted derisively. "The rulers of Annwn won't dare to interfere if they know what's good for them. We can reduce our need for them by figuring out how to forge magical weapons and such. I'll bet all we have to do is spend some time watching Govannon. Then we won't need them, and if they are daring enough to try to get us in this world, we will have a big surprise for them—the ability to make technology work in Annwn!

"You know we can do it. At the first sign of trouble, I'll send an army into Annwn, and we'll see how well faerie archers fare against machine guns. Then we'll see how well faerie castles stand up to nukes!"

Where he was going to get nuclear weapons I didn't bother to ask. Start controlling the minds of key U.S. military personnel, probably. Not pure evil, huh? Well, maybe not yet, but it was clear he would do whatever he needed to get what he wanted. His desire to be a rock star wasn't innately evil, but what he would do if anyone got in his way certainly was, though he couldn't see that it was.

"Don't you see? That kind of thinking is what brings about all this destruction."

Dark Me stared at me as if I were an idiot. "I wouldn't really destroy Annwn. I wouldn't have to. The fact that I could would be enough."

"Perhaps the fact that you could would be enough to convince the faeries to launch a preemptive strike. Yeah, maybe they would strike first, and that's what wipes out the whole town. Or maybe your plan works, and you nuke them. Maybe creating a nuclear holocaust in Annwn poisons our world. Or maybe you dodge that bullet, and this devastation comes from something else."

"You've made military preparations yourself," pointed out Dark Me. "We have swords. We fight. Sometimes we kill."

"When we have to! All of my preparations have been defensive. What you want to do is invite an attack. That's completely different!"

"What I want to do is have what I deserve, what we deserve. We have a combination of talents no one has ever had in the history of the world. I want to use those talents, just like anyone uses theirs. You, you want to hide them. You want to let the likes of Vanora and Nurse Florence order you around. You want to play by stupid rules that make no sense. No, you know what? It's even worse than that. Rather than developing to your full potential, you want to mope around all the time about problems you could solve with just a little magic. You want to die, in fact. What was that stunt with Khalid about today? And that's just the most recent one. How many times have you thrown yourself right into death's jaws, even when it wasn't even remotely necessary? Well, you may want to die, but I want to live, and I want to be a big success, and I want to have my love at my side!"

His pitch shouldn't have been that convincing, but as he talked, the world around us morphed more and more into the way he saw things. He looked more and more like me with each passing second, and suddenly we were standing on the roof of Awen in bright sunlight, with Santa Brígida restored, even enhanced. Eva was there too, with her arm around his waist, gazing at him adoringly.

"Suicide is a sin," observed Dark Me. "Has it occurred to you that maybe I'm not the evil one—you are! Maybe you see devastation everywhere because you are going to bring it about!"

Now it was not just that Dark Me looked like me. I was beginning to look as he had in the beginning. I could feel shadows taking the place of my flesh.

As a creature drawn from my own mind, Dark Me knew I felt guilty about the consequences of some of my actions and was using that guilt against me. I also knew that if I continued to doubt myself I would be lost. No, I wasn't perfect, but he was far worse—and if I didn't stop him in the next few minutes, I never would.

I raised White Hilt then, and with a considerable effort, I willed my appearance to return to normal. Dark Me raised his sword as well, expecting to meet fire with fire. He was not expecting me to shoot from the blade, not fire, but the most plausible imitation of Jimmie's light that I could produce. I think there was also a touch of the light that shone from any sword that David was holding.

No, I wasn't arrogant enough to think that my ability to learn spells by watching them cast gave me the ability to replicate the light of Jimmie's goodness, and certainly not whatever power God lent to David. This was, however, all happening in the world Dark Me had created inside my head. If I believed what I created could defeat the darkness—and, more to the point, if he believed it—that would be good enough.

The light that sprayed out of my sword was still grayer than Jimmie's light, but I could see horror in Dark Me's eyes. He countered by spraying from his sword, not green flame, but pure darkness. As he did so, he became as he had been when I had first seen him, as did the world around him. He could not maintain his pretense of rightness when defending himself meant drawing power from my basest impulses.

We battled long on that roof. My light met his darkness midway between us, and we each strained to drive our energy forward. Trying to battle the darkness without knowing the way in which it existed in my head, it had seemed much stronger. However, once I realized the true nature of my dark side, and I knew how to deal with it, I could see it really wasn't stronger than I was.

Sadly, it still seemed equally strong, and my gray light was not quite as effective as Jimmie's white in countering the darkness, which was winning, inch by inch. Unless I could believe more in myself, I would eventually lose.

The problem was that part of what Dark Me had said was true. Could I believe in myself when I had caused people pain, when I had sometimes failed?

I thought about my friends. The guys believed in me enough to follow me into deadly peril. Carla had done the same, even knowing I didn't really love her. So had Eva, even with her ambiguous feelings toward me. So had Nurse Florence. So had Khalid, who was really a total stranger. And Jimmie had stuck with me all those years when Dan and I had been hostile, treating me as much like a brother as he had Dan. Could they all be wrong?

What was David's problem when I first met him? Not that God hadn't forgiven him. That he hadn't forgiven himself!

I did my damnedest to put all my mistakes behind me, and the light got a little whiter, but I was still losing ground, though at a little slower pace.

I knew Jimmie wasn't sinless himself, but he'd had a lot fewer years for self-doubt, and he had never had other people depending on him the way I did, so any mistakes he might have made during his nine years had much less potential to load him down with guilt. That must be why he could achieve such a white light with such seemingly little effort.

I thought about trying to reach Jimmie on the outside and linking to him. Then I remembered what Merlin had said. If anyone else helped me, I would not succeed in reintegrating Dark Me into my personality, at least not completely. I had to figure out a way to beat him, but I was running out of options—and the darkness from his sword was advancing relentlessly upon me.

Come to think of it, beating him wouldn't be enough. When I integrated my past selves, I had to get each one to realize the situation and voluntarily join with me. I had needed David's cooperation even to manage an incomplete connection to Stan. I had needed to gain control of Alcina to get Carla back in charge of her body. I had never succeeded in merging or connecting any past life to its current self without some kind of willingness on the part of that past life. How the hell was I supposed to get that kind of cooperation from Dark Me?

What was it he had said earlier? Something like, "You want to think I am pure evil, but I'm not. I'm just willing to look after myself..." If that were really true, then I might be able to make him see "the light," so to speak. I couldn't read his "mind" without opening myself to other kinds of attack, so I had to try to reach him without really knowing whether my appeal would work or not.

I had been able to project what I was seeing to him earlier, so unless he had blocked that kind of connection, I should still be able to communicate with him that way. We were, after all, still aspects of the same person, despite our current separation.

Keeping up the light from my sword as best I could, I hit his mind full blast with how much damage I had suffered under Alcina's spell. He was really already aware of those effects, of course, but he was clearly in denial. Then I simulated, as best I could, how Eva's mind would react to the same spell and blasted him with that.

"It's a lie!" he shrieked, obviously bothered by the reality I was forcing on him. "Eva will never feel pain, never want anything except to love me!"

"There will be damage," I shouted. "I didn't realize how I was being affected until the spell was broken, but the effect occurred, regardless. People don't have to know they have cancer for it to be growing within them."

"It's not like that! You would have suffered nothing if the spell had remained unbroken."

"Slavery always takes its toll, even if one is not aware he or she is being enslaved. You have my memories. You know I speak the truth."

For good measure I worked up as many vivid scenarios as I could about how Dark Me's schemes might hurt other people, like Stan, and hit him with each one, one at a time. Dark Me tried to resist, tried to deny the truth of my "tricks," but I could tell he was weakening. He flashed in and out of looking like me; the world around him shuddered repeatedly back and forth between his optimistic vision and my view of the destruction, and I could swear that the darkness radiating from his sword was now speckled with gray.

Realizing what I was doing, he tried to fire images at me, images designed to strengthen my guilt and shake my confidence, but I had prepared for that kind of counterattack and remained blind to what he was trying to show me.

After what seemed like hours, the energy from his sword fused with the energy from mine instead of working against it, and the combined energy ripped the sword from his hand. By now the world around us was chaos; he was no longer able to maintain any kind of consistency.

He now looked almost exactly like me, and he fell to the ground, sobbing. I closed the distance between us in seconds, and then I hugged him. (I know—you were expecting me to take his head off in one stroke, or something like that. That might have been more satisfying after all the danger he had created, but it would not have solved the problem.)

"You are…lying to me, trying to trick me," he gasped between sobs. "I will not…believe you!"

"You already do," I whispered gently. "If you did not, the world you have created here would still be intact."

"I don't want to die!" he said with surprising force. "I want to live!"

"You will live…within me. That is what you were meant to do in the first place!"

"But—"

"No buts. You remember what it was like with the past selves. So it will be with you. You will be part of me every bit as much as the original Taliesin and all the others are. We can even continue the argument we were having earlier."

Dark Me considered that as he wiped tears off of his cheeks. "I could make a man out of you yet! I could get you to take what is rightfully ours!"

About the time pigs fly…or I use dark magic again, whichever comes first.

"You can try to move me in that direction."

"Well, I guess that's the best I can do for now."

I hugged him again, and for a moment I thought his acquiescence might be a trick, that he would wrestle free, retrieve his sword, and take off my head with one stroke. Instead, he dissolved in my arms—not dissolved into tears again, just dissolved. He was a cloud of tiny particles all around me. I breathed him in, and we were one being again. (None of my past selves had created such a physical image of reunion; it was apparent to me that Dark Me was a little bit of a drama king.)

In moments the shredded remnants of the world he had created had vanished as well, leaving me free to come out of my trance and rejoin everyone else. It took me awhile to find my way back to consciousness, but at last I could feel David and Dan holding my hands, and I opened my eyes.

Merlin was nodding his head, clearly satisfied. "You have done well, young Taliesin."

"I'm still going to have to fight temptation for the rest of my life," I said ruefully.

"As do we all," Merlin replied, letting his inner demon flash for just a second in his eyes to underscore his point.

I got up off the ground, brushed myself off, and thanked my friends. For a few minutes I was engulfed in a storm of handshakes and hugs—mostly hugs, even from the guys. A handshake was the most Dan dared to offer, though. I nodded to him but decided not to start *the* conversation. That would have to wait until later. First things first.

"Merlin, you have already done so much for me, but I could use your help getting Carla and Stan back the way they should be."

Merlin looked a little uneasy, not a common expression for him. "You are the expert in how to deal with past selves, not I."

I had no idea where Merlin might go after we parted, but I very strongly suspected he would not end up living in Santa Brígida. If I had any chance of getting his help, it would have to be now.

"Merlin, please. You must have some idea."

"I always have *some* idea, but whether or not it is the right one is another question. I once thought it was a good idea to trust Nimue, and look where that got me. If you look at Carla, however—and I mean *really* look—I think you will be pleasantly surprised.

I turned to Carla, scanned her, and discovered that she no longer had two separate presences within her. She was all Carla. Well, not quite. As my past selves had become part of me, Alcina had become part of her. If the process had worked for her as it had for me…"

Apparently Carla could see my question in my eyes. "That's right, Tal; I have access to all of Alcina's memories and abilities, including magic. I'm just like you now."

"Which means you will need training," said Nurse Florence. "Even before, you were using a little magic accidentally. As someone working at Alcina's power level, you will have to learn how to control that power."

"And how not to use dark magic," I pointed out. "I learned that lesson the hard way!"

Carla seemed supercharged with enthusiasm. "It's as if I see a whole new world I never knew existed. I can hardly wait to begin my studies. But don't worry, Tal, I'll still have time for the band and…other things." She hugged me, pressing much closer than she needed to, and whispered in my ear, "Like winning you back. I'll always make time for that!"

As Carla let go of me, I noticed Eva looking at us with, I don't know, an expression I had never seen on her face. It almost looked like…regret.

You have got to be kidding me! So now, with Carla already fixating on me again, now you're interested?

I almost had the nerve to pose that question directly, but when Eva saw I was looking at her, she turned away, and my nerve vanished. Well, back to business.

"This is great, but how did it happen? Merlin?"

"If I had to guess," he said with a wink, since, to the best of my knowledge, he had never guessed at anything, "I would say that Alcina's own spell worked on her so well that she would do anything to please you. She knew what you wanted, Carla fully healed, and somehow she figured out a way to do it. Perhaps she used the bond between you to absorb some of your knowledge of how to integrate past selves."

"I spaced out for a few minutes and thought I was dreaming about Alcina and me having a conversation," said Carla. "She took my hand and just vanished. Then I felt her inside of me somewhere, part of me instead of separate from me, and I snapped back to reality again."

"Yeah, that's about how it works if you know how to do it. Merlin, you must be right. But what about Stan?" I did a quick scan and saw with horror just how mangled the potential connections between Stan and David were. "This is beyond my skill to fix."

"It isn't beyond your skill," said Merlin firmly. "It is beyond your power…but that I can help with." He put his hand on my shoulder, and suddenly I felt strong enough to take on an army…or mend a mind seemingly shattered beyond all hope.

I let myself flow into Stan, and I used my borrowed might to heal both Stan and David and then to create links between them, links that could survive friction between them, links that could survive even David emerging full force to take over Stan's body, something that seemed to happen with remarkable frequency no matter how much I warned them.

I tried to take the final step and merge them into one integrated personality, but I couldn't do it, even with the white-hot power of Merlin behind me. Perhaps they had to do it for themselves. At least I had stabilized their situation for the foreseeable future, and given enough time, I might be able to figure out how to solve the problem once and for all. For now it was comforting to get poor, self-sacrificing Stan back in his own body.

"That's what comes of being too self-sacrificing," whispered Dark Me from somewhere in my mind. "Somebody else has to keep rescuing you." I just ignored him.

Before long Nurse Florence and Vanora started making preparations to bring us back. Annwn time did flow more slowly than our own, but we had been in Annwn for hours, and we needed to get back pretty soon to avoid having to make yet another round of explanations. I suddenly realized I wanted to stay with Merlin awhile longer.

"There is so much I could learn from you. Is there any chance…"

"What?" said Merlin with his unnerving laugh. "Move to your charming little town, masquerade as…oh, let's see…the high school's librarian? Dispense wisdom to you under the guise of checking out books? Have tea with the ladies of the lake every afternoon?"

"Well, when you put it like that…"

"Taliesin, it would actually give me pleasure to pass on what I can to you, but I have the strange suspicion that you will find what you need elsewhere."

"Is that a prophecy, Merlin?" Under the circumstances, it was a logical question.

"It is what you would call a 'hunch.' Regardless, Taliesin, I have been trapped in a tower for fifteen hundred years. Many tasks I was meant to do have been left undone. I need to get the universe back into balance. After that, I think it might be time to start my next life. I should have reincarnated long ago. I never intended to use my powers to stay alive for so long."

"Did the tower force you to stay alive?" I asked.

"No, I did that to myself. I could have escaped the tower by dying, but I foresaw I should stay here."

"For what?"

"For this very day, Taliesin. I didn't know exactly what would happen, but I knew someone would eventually come along who would need my help, someone worthy of that help. I made my demonic fake

Merlin to be sure that someone who came along was truly worthy. I figured that anyone who could defeat my double would certainly be worthy."

"Like someone who could break the unbreakable tower even you couldn't break wouldn't be worthy!" I gave as good an imitation of his laugh as I could. Merlin looked momentarily surprised, and then he joined in the laughter.

"That I could have overlooked such an obvious point! Well, everyone makes mistakes!" Interestingly, the original Taliesin had no memory of Merlin ever even coming close to admitting an error. I suppose the old guy had mellowed a bit over the centuries.

I found myself glancing in Eva's direction and watching how the light from Annwn's sunrise was sparkling in her strawberry-blond hair.

"Ah," said Merlin, following my gaze. "That reminds me. Taliesin, I can tell that finding your true love will not be easy, and I can't help you with that, either. The only one who can is she who was born of the foam."

Good! Now we get to the riddles.

I forced myself to look away from Eva, but Merlin was already gone. I guess he was not one for long good-byes.

"Tal! It's time to go." I looked over to see Jimmie, still in his angel form. Evidently, he had taken a liking to that one.

"Jimmie, I meant to thank you for all you did today."

"Thank me by forgiving Dan…for real this time." I suddenly felt a cold breeze.

"I'll work on it, Jimmie. That's all I can promise right now."

"You're just stuck with me for a while longer, then."

"Jimmie, I don't want to cause you more pain."

"It's funny," said Jimmie, with a big smile. "Since being inside you, the pain seems to have gone away, at least for now."

"Well, I'm glad you got something out of it! Anyway, Jimmie, if I hadn't had your light to copy—"

"My light?" said Jimmie, looking confused. "I just reflected what I saw in you."

Now I was confused, but I pretended I wasn't.

"Love the angel form, by the way." I grinned. "That came from that book you had when you were six, didn't it?"

Jimmie looked at me strangely. "Tal, that was your book, but you did show it to me. I always thought the angel looked like you. It just seemed to fit."

I don't know why I hadn't seen it earlier. The face of Jimmie's angel form did look a lot like me. I could hear Dark Me snickering. I ignored him again.

"This makes me look like your conscience," said Jimmie. "And that's who I'll be until you forgive Dan."

With that, Jimmie turned and walked toward the others. There was a danger in Jimmie haunting me, even beyond Jimmie's possible pain, which was bad enough. The danger was that Dan and I would get too used to having him around. Then we would both lose him again. Well, even with that risk, I still couldn't forgive Dan...yet, anyway.

So there were still a few things left on my to-do list. I had to check Nurse Florence's theory that the memories I had found in Dan's mind were false. I had to figure out how I felt about Carla, to say nothing of what to do about it. I had to find a way to merge Stan and David as they should be. I had to help my mom adjust to her new abilities.

And then I had to find a way to do what I should have done in the first place: break the awakening spell and become just plain old Tal Weaver again—no magic, no memories of the long past—just me.

I was damned if I was ever going to use dark magic again. And I was damned if my friends and family were going to keep on suffering because of who I was.

WHAT HAS GONE BEFORE

In the first book, *Living with Your Past Selves*, Taliesin Weaver (who goes by Tal) is just recovering from the sudden rending of the barriers between this life and all of his previous ones, a crisis that nearly destroyed his mind. By age sixteen, he has learned how to handle the flood of memories and even to take advantage of them. For instance, he can speak languages he never learned—at least not in this life. He has also become an expert musician and swordsman, and he can even work magic. He owes many of these traits to the earliest life he can remember clearly: the life of the original Taliesin, chief bard at the court of King Arthur. He also uses the knowledge from this early life to find the sword White Hilt, which, centuries ago, he helped Arthur steal from Annwn, the Celtic Otherworld. Despite his earlier fear, he has come to accept his new abilities and even to be secretly pleased with them—secretly, because he has an overpowering fear about what would happen if anyone should discover the truth about him.

Just when his life seems to be going OK, his best friend, Stanford (Stan) Schoenbaum, figures out Tal's secret. Tal does what he can to confuse the issue, but that very night the *Gwrach y Rhibyn* (the Welsh banshee) appears outside his house and predicts his death. Much more ominously, the very next day Tal discovers that a *pwca* (shape-shifter) has taken Stan's place and managed to steal White Hilt from Tal. Tal defeats the *pwca* with considerable difficulty, but the shock of having to kill "someone"—which he has not yet had to do in this life—nearly incapacitates him.

He is rescued from being discovered in a situation he cannot explain by Dan Stevens, a former friend recently turned enemy. Dan's bizarre and sudden change of heart is explained when an anonymous voice speaks through Dan and explains that the voice is Tal's ally and will help him, as will the sometimes-possessed Dan. However, the voice refuses to identify itself, and Tal is left to ponder what to do next. He ends up going to Stan's house and telling him everything. Though skeptical of the magic, Stan is eventually won over, and now Tal has at least one more ally.

Together Tal and Stan explore what Tal can do, and Tal practices abilities, like shape shifting, that he has not yet tried in his current life. He and Stan also work out physically—Tal because he realizes he needs more stamina, and Stan because he realizes that girls like muscular guys better. Meanwhile, Dan becomes friendly again, even when not possessed, and Tal and Stan start working out with the football team (of which Dan is the captain) in exchange for tutoring. Their social statuses soar, and Tal again begins to think his life might work out. Unfortunately, he is wrong again.

During the Founders' Day celebration in Santa Brígida, their home town, Tal, Stan, Dan, and several other students who are being honored for various achievements, are torn out of their reality and thrust into Annwn. There they encounter Morgan Le Fay, who insists she did not bring them but nevertheless intends to hold them prisoner for her own purposes. Only the timely intervention of the Voice saves Tal and his fellow students and returns them to reality. At that point Carrie Winn, the most powerful citizen in Santa Brígida, reveals that she is the Voice, now communicating directly because the situation is more dangerous than she thought, and so she and Tal must work together more closely.

Life is just getting back to a rocky kind of normality when Dan gets into a big fight with Eva, his current girlfriend and Tal's ex, ironically over what happened on Founder's Day, which Dan can't remember because of his interaction with the Voice. Eva is so angry with Dan that she pretends to seduce Stan and makes sure Dan finds out. Dan tries to beat up Stan, Tal tries to intervene, and his newly healed friendship with Dan is shattered. Eva and Dan are behaving so uncharacteristically that Tal suspects magic.

To complicate the situation further, Nurse Florence, the school nurse, who also suspects magic in the situation, reveals to Tal that she is the Voice. Tal is now faced with the problem of figuring out whether Carrie Winn or Nurse Florence is really the Voice, a puzzle charged with deadly urgency by the fact that whichever one of them is not the Voice must be the enemy who is clearly out to get Tal.

As if circumstances were not already difficult enough, Tal, who is annoyed with Stan's role in the explosion with Dan, is at best noncommittal when Stan turns to Tal for comfort. Later that evening, Tal learns that Stan has run away. With help from both Carrie Winn and Nurse Florence, as well as a reluctant Dan and a contrite Eva, Tal rescues Stan, who is about to be attacked by a kelpie (another kind of shape-shifter) when Tal's search party finally finds him.

Eva tries to tell the truth about what happened between her and

Stan, but Dan refuses to listen. Tal finally agrees to a footballer ritual, in which he has to box with Shahriyar, the best boxer in the school, in order to get Stan forgiven. Tal gets badly beaten on purpose but is able to manipulate the situation to redeem Stan without destroying Dan's position on campus, though Dan is still not reconciled to the situation.

At the pre-homecoming party at Carrie Winn's mansion, Tal becomes convinced that she is the enemy—the worst one imaginable, given her vast fortune, large security force, and position of complete dominance in the community. Tal tells Nurse Florence about Carrie Winn, and Nurse Florence works on ways to strengthen their magical position, while Tal works on the problem of getting his magic to work on modern technology, so that at the inevitable showdown, he can neutralize Winn's security system and the guns of her security men.

To get his magic to interact with technology, Tal needs to visualize scientific concepts the way Stan can. To do that, he needs to be able to read Stan's mind, but modern telepathy is not part of his inherited magic, so he needs to train himself to use magic differently—in just a couple of weeks, when his band is scheduled to perform at Carrie Winn's Halloween party. He is positive that is when she will make whatever move she has been planning.

At the homecoming dance, where his band is also playing, Tal begins to develop telepathic abilities, and he also engineers a reconciliation between Dan and Eva—a bitter victory, because secretly he wants her for himself, but he knows he can never have her honorably, and he needs to heal the breach with Dan, which he finally manages to do.

Prior to Halloween, Tal also masters techniques to get his magic to work on technology, and Nurse Florence recruits other student allies. With the help of Gywnn ap Nudd, the king of the Welsh faeries, she also obtains more magic swords from Govannon, the faerie smith. Gywnn agrees to Nurse Florence's request in part because Tal and his friends prove their worth to him and partly because he fears the power Carrie Winn is gaining, power that may eventually threaten the security of Annwn itself. (Nurse Florence is in a position to broker this kind of deal because she is a lady of the lake.) Dan and Stan both end up with unique swords, as do new allies Shahriyar, Gordy, and Carlos.

When Halloween arrives, Tal and Nurse Florence discover that their plans are based on completely wrong assumptions. They had believed that Carrie Winn would have to attack stealthily to avoid creating a scene in front of all her guests and staff. Instead, they discover the guests are an illusion, the regular staff has the night off, and Winn's security men are all shifters. Tal and his allies fight the shifters and win the battle, but they can still lose the war, and they discover that the civilians (other students like Eva and Tal's band members) are trapped in the house, leaving Tal no way to retreat—the only possible way to save everyone is to beat Carrie Winn.

Exhausted, he and his allies head to the roof, where Winn is hiding. They think she will be as exhausted as they are. Wrong again, they discover she has the aid of Morgan Le Fay, who was supplying much of the magic early on, leaving Carrie Winn fresh to continue the fight. Even worse, Carrie Winn reveals herself as Ceridwen, a witch with an ancient grudge against Taliesin. Ceridwen has researched magic for hundreds of years and is the one who caused Tal to remember his past lives in the first place. Nothing but his grisly death and the imprisonment of his soul in her cauldron will satisfy her. In the final battle, Tal and his friends prevail, but at a cost. Stan comes face to face with his own previous lives. Carla Rinaldi, the first girl since Eva for whom Tal has feelings, take a double dose of the past-lives spell and ends up comatose. Vanora, a Welsh colleague of Nurse Florence's, takes Carrie Winn's place after Winn's defeat and death, but Tal doesn't want to·deal with Vanora because he blames her for Carla's condition—though not quite as much as he blames himself.

Tal helps Stan through his past-life memory crisis, but he can do nothing for Carla, though he visits her in the hospital every day. He pretends for his family and friends that he is coping. At the end of the book, Tal is superficially more popular and successful than ever, but inwardly he is miserable.

At least he no longer has an enemy to worry about. Or so he thinks...

THE ADVENTURE ISN'T OVER…

If you liked this novel, you might also like the other volumes in the Spell Weaver series, also available from Amazon. Follow the links below to check them out.

Echoes from My Past Lives, a short prequel that tells the story of Tal's original transformation.
http://viewbook.at/B00BZIROVE

Living with Your Past Selves, the novel that started that Spell Weaver phenomenon, tells the story of Tal's struggles against Ceridwen during the days immediately preceding the action in *Divided against Yourselves. Living with Your Past Selves* has received the following awards and recognitions to date:

- Literary Classics International Book Awards, 2013: Gold Medal, Best First Novel
- Literary Classics International Book Awards, 2013: Silver Medal, Best Young Adult Fantasy
- Pinnacle Book Awards, Summer, 2013: Best Book, Young Adult
- Best Indie Book Awards, 2013: Semifinalist, Fantasy
- Foreword Reviews Book of the Year Awards, 2012: Finalist, Fantasy
- Amazon Breakthrough Novel Awards, 2012: Quarterfinalist, Science Fiction/Fantasy/Horror
- Readers' Favorite: Five Star Book
- Indie Reader: Approved Book

http://viewbook.at/B00987M4CI

Of course, there will also be other books in this series, so visit the author from time to time for the latest information on new projects. See "About the Author" for contact information.

If you bought this book relatively early in its life cycle (before January 1, 2014), maybe the release party is still going on (or hasn't even started yet—I can't really set the date and start inviting people until the book actually goes live). Check out https://www.facebook.com/events/1423325781220258/ for some fun and a chance to win prizes.

ABOUT THE AUTHOR

Bill Hiatt has been teaching English at Beverly Hills High School since 1981. Although teaching has been and remains his first love, he has also been drawn to creative writing of various sorts. From high school on, he wrote short stories, a little poetry, and an earlier novel, finished in 1982. In September, 2012 *Living with Your Past Selves* became his first published work. In March, 2013 *Echoes from My Past Lives*, the prequel to *LWYPS*, was published, and you are now reading *Divided against Yourselves*, his third published work…but certainly not his last!

Bill's ancestors came from a wide variety of European backgrounds, with Celtic groups (Irish, Scottish, Breton, and, as you might guess from this novel, Welsh) being the most well represented. His ancestors settled in America long ago, though, some of them as early as the colonial period. He is a third generation Californian who grew up and still currently lives in Culver City, California.

If you would like more information about Bill, this novel, and/or his other writing projects, you can visit him at http://billhiatt.com/, at his author page on Facebook (http://www.facebook.com/#!/pages/Bill-Hiatt/431724706902040/), and on Twitter (https://twitter.com/BillHiatt2).

42867541R00174

Made in the USA
Middletown, DE
23 April 2017